"Haven't you ever felt like there has to be *more*?
Like there's more out there somewhere, just beyond
your grasp, if you could only get to it . . ."

ALSO BY PATRICK NESS

The Knife of Never Letting Go

The Ask and the Answer

Monsters of Men

A Monster Calls

MORE THAN THIS

PATRICK NESS

CANDLEWICK PRESS

"Borrowing Time" written by Aimee Mann, published by Aimee Mann, sub-published by Fintage Publishing B.V. All Rights Reserved

First U.S. paperback edition 2014

Library of Congress Catalog Card Number 2013943065
ISBN 978-0-7636-6258-5 (hardcover)
ISBN 978-0-7636-7620-9 (paperback)

BVG 19 18 17 16
10 9 8 7 6

Printed in Berryville, VA, U.S.A.

This book was typeset in Sabon and Futura.

Candlewick Press
99 Dover Street
Somerville, Massachusetts 02144

visit us at www.candlewick.com

For Phil Rodak

You ask a question in the mirror.
Alas, no answer could be clearer.

– Aimee Mann

Here is the boy, drowning.

In these last moments, it's not the water that's finally done for him; it's the cold. It has bled all the energy from his body and contracted his muscles into a painful uselessness, no matter how much he fights to keep himself above the surface. He is strong, and young, nearly seventeen, but the wintry waves keep coming, each one seemingly larger than the last. They spin him round, topple him over, force him deeper down and down. Even when he can catch his breath in the few terrified seconds he manages to push his face into the air, he is shaking so badly he can barely get half a lungful before he's under again. It isn't enough, grows less each time, and he feels a terrible yearning in his chest as he aches, fruitlessly, for more.

He is in full panic now. He knows he's drifted just slightly too far from shore to make it back, the icy tide pulling him out farther and farther with every wave, pushing him toward the rocks that make this bit of coast so treacherous. He also knows there is no one who'll notice he's gone in time, no one who'll raise the alarm before the water defeats him. He won't be saved by chance, either. There are no beachcombers or tourists to dive in from the shoreline to save him, not this time of year, not in these freezing temperatures.

It is too late for him.

He will die.

And he will die alone.

The sudden, gasping horror of knowing this makes him panic even more. He tries again to break the surface, not daring to think that it might be his last time, not daring to think much at all. He forces his legs to kick, forces his arms to heave himself upward, to at least get his body the right way round, to try and grasp another breath just inches away –

But the current is too strong. It allows him tantalizingly near the surface but spins him upside down before he can get there, dragging him closer to the rocks.

The waves toy with him as he tries again.

And fails.

Then, without warning, the game the sea seems to have been playing, the cruel game of keeping him just alive enough to think he might make it, that game seems to be over.

The current surges, slamming him into the killingly hard rocks. His right shoulder blade snaps in two so loudly he can hear the *crack,* even underwater, even in this rush of tide. The mindless intensity of the pain is so great that he calls out, his mouth instantly filling with freezing, briny seawater. He coughs against it, but only drags more into his lungs. He curves into the pain of his shoulder, blinded by it, paralyzed by its intensity. He is unable to even try and swim now, unable to brace himself as the waves turn him over once more.

Please, is all he thinks. Just the one word, echoing through his head.

Please.

The current grips him a final time. It rears back as if to throw him, and it dashes him headfirst into the rocks. He slams into them with the full, furious weight of an angry ocean behind him. He is unable to even raise his hands to try and soften the blow.

The impact is just behind his left ear. It fractures his skull, splintering it into his brain, the force of it also crushing his third and fourth vertebrae, severing both his cerebral artery and his spinal cord, an injury from which there is no return, no recovery. No chance.

He dies.

PART 1

1

The first moments after the boy's death pass for him in a confused and weighty blur. He is dimly aware of pain, but mostly of a tremendous *fatigue,* as if he has been covered in layer upon layer of impossibly heavy blankets. He struggles against them, blindly, his thrashing increasing as he panics (again) at the invisible ropes that seem to bind him.

His mind isn't clear. It races and throbs like the worst kind of fever, and he is unaware of even thinking. It's more some kind of wild, dying instinct, a terror of what's to come, a terror of what's happened.

A terror of his death.

As if he can still struggle against it, still outrun it.

He even has a distant sensation of momentum, his body continuing its fight against the waves even though that fight has already been lost. He feels a sudden rushing, a surge of terror hurtling him forward, forward, forward, but he must be free of his body somehow because his shoulder no longer hurts as he struggles blindly through the dark, unable to feel anything, it seems, except a terrified urgency to *move*–

And then there is a coolness on his face. Almost as of a breeze, though such a thing seems impossible for so many reasons. It's this coolness that causes his consciousness—His soul? His spirit? Who's to say?—to pause in its fevered spin.

For an instant, he is still.

There's a change in the murk before his eyes. A lightness. A lightness he can enter, somehow, and he can feel himself leaning toward it, his body—so weak, so nearly incapable beneath him—reaching for the growing light.

He falls. Falls onto solidity. The coolness rises from it, and he allows himself to sink into it, let it envelop him.

He is still. He gives up his struggle. He lets oblivion overtake him.

Oblivion is purgatorial and gray. He is passably conscious, not asleep but not quite awake either, as if disconnected from everything, unable to move or think or receive input, able only to exist.

An impossible amount of time passes, a day, a year, maybe even an eternity, there is no way he can know. Finally, in the distance, the light begins to slowly, almost imperceptibly change. A grayness emerges, then a lighter grayness, and he starts to come back to himself.

His first thought, more vaguely sensed than actually articulated, is that it feels as though he's pressed against a cement block. He's dimly aware of how cool it is under him, how solid it feels, like he's clinging to it lest he fly off into space. He hovers around the thought for an indeterminate amount of time, letting it clarify, letting it connect to his body, to other thoughts –

The word *morgue* suddenly flashes somewhere deep inside him – for where else are you laid out on cool, solid blocks – and in rising horror, he opens his eyes, unaware they were even closed. He tries to call out that they must not bury him, they must not cut him open, that there's been a terrible, terrible mistake. But his throat rebels against the formation of words, as if it hasn't been used for years, and he's coughing and sitting up in terror, his eyes muddled and foggy, like he's looking at the world from behind many thick layers of dirty glass.

He blinks repeatedly, trying to see. The vague shapes around him slowly fall into place. He sees that he is not on the cold slab of a morgue –

He is –

He is –

Where is he?

Confused, he squints painfully into what now seems to be rising daylight. He looks around, trying to take it in, trying to see it, make sense of it all.

He seems to be lying on a concrete path that runs through the front yard of a house, stretching from the sidewalk to a front door behind him.

The house is not his own.

And there's more wrong than just that.

• • •

He breathes for a moment, heavily, almost panting, his mind groggy, his vision slowly becoming a little clearer. He feels himself shaking from the chill and pulls his arms around himself, sensing a dampness covering his –

Not *his* clothes.

He looks down at them, his physical reaction slower than the thought that ordered it. He squints again, trying to see them clearly. They don't seem to really be clothes at all, just strips of white cloth that barely fit the name *trousers* or *shirt*, stuck closely around him more like bandages than things to wear. And all along one side, they're wet with –

He stops.

They're not wet with seawater, not with the soaking, briny cold of the ocean he was just –

(drowning in)

And only half of him is wet anyway. The other half, the half that was against the ground, is cool, but quite dry.

He looks around, more confused than ever. Because he can only be wet with *dew*. The sun is low in the sky, and it seems as if it must be morning. Underneath him, he can even make out a dry outline of where he was lying.

As if he had lain there all night.

But that can't be. He remembers the brutal, winter coldness of the water, the dark freezing gray of the sky overhead that would never have let him survive a night out in it –

But that isn't this sky. He lifts his face to it. This sky isn't even winter. The chill is merely the chill of morning, of possibly a warm day to come, of possibly a *summer* day. Nothing at all like the bitter wind of the beach. Nothing at all like when he–

When he died.

He takes another moment to breathe, to just do that, if he can. There is only quiet around him, only the sounds he himself is making.

He turns slowly to look at the house again. It resolves itself more and more as his eyes get used to the light, used–it almost seems–to seeing again.

And then, through the fog and confusion, he feels a soft tremor in his blanketed mind.

A brush, a hint, a featherweight of–

Of–

Is it familiarity?

2

He tries to rise, and the feeling vanishes. Rising is difficult, surprisingly so, and he fails. He feels terrifyingly weak, his muscles resisting even the simple command to stand. Just the effort to sit fully upright leaves him winded, and he has to stop for a moment, panting again.

He reaches out to grab a sturdy-looking plant by the side of the path to try to rise once more –

And pulls his hand back immediately when short spikes prick his fingers.

It's not a regular plant at all. It's a weed, grown staggeringly tall. The flower beds that line the path to the door of the house have all grown extraordinarily wild, much higher than the low stone dividing walls on either side. The shrubberies among them look like they're almost living creatures reaching out to him, poised to do him harm if he moves too close. Other weeds, *enormous* weeds, three, four, even six feet high, have blazed through every inch of dirt and every possible crack in the pavement, one of them crushed underneath him where he lay.

He tries again to rise, finally making it up, though he sways dangerously for a moment. His head is overweighted with grogginess and he's still shivering. The white bandages around him are in no way warm, nor are they even–he notices with alarm–covering him properly as clothing. His legs and torso are wrapped tightly, his arms, too, and most of the width of his back. Bafflingly, though, the entire area from his belly button to the middle of his thighs is naked to the world, front and back, his most private parts unthinkably out in the morning sun. He frantically tries to pull down the too-scanty fabric to cover himself, but it sticks tightly to his skin.

He covers himself with his hand and looks around to see if anyone has seen him.

But there is no one. No one at all.

Is this a dream? he thinks, the words coming to him slowly, thickly, as if from a great distance. *The last dream before death?*

Every yard is as overgrown as this one. Some that had lawns are now sprouting fields of grass shoulder-high. The pavement in the road is cracked, too, with more weeds almost obscenely tall growing right out of the middle, a few approaching the status of *trees*.

There are cars parked along the road, but they're covered in thick layers of dust and dirt, blinding every window. And nearly every one has sunk under four deflated tires.

Nothing is moving. There are no cars coming down the road, and from the look of the weeds, no car has driven down here in an impossibly long time. The road to his left carries on until it meets a much wider street, one that looks like it should be a busy, bustling main road. There are no cars driving there either, and he can see a gigantic hole has opened up across it, forty or fifty feet wide. Out of which a whole glade of weeds seems to be growing.

He listens. He can't hear a single motor anywhere. Not on this street or the next. He waits for a long moment. Then a long moment more. He looks down the other end of the road on his right, and through the gap between two apartment buildings, he can see some raised train tracks and feels himself listening for the trains that might run on them.

But there are no trains.

And no people.

If it's the morning that it seems to be, people should be coming out of their houses, getting in their cars, driving to work. Or if not, then walking their dogs, delivering the mail, heading off to school.

The streets should be full. Front doors should be opening and closing.

But there is no one. No cars, no trains, no people.

And this street, now that he can see more of it as his eyes and mind begin to clear a little more, even the geography of it looks strange. These houses are crammed together, all stuck in a line, with no garages or big front yards and only the narrowest of alleys between every fourth or fifth house. Nothing like his own street back home. In fact, this doesn't look like an American street at all. It looks almost—

It looks almost *English*.

· · ·

The word clangs around his head. It feels important, like it's desperately trying to latch on to something, but his mind is so foggy, so shocked and confused, it only heightens his anxiety.

It's a word that's wrong. That's *very* wrong.

He wavers a little and has to catch his balance on one of the sturdier-looking bushes. He feels a strong urge to go inside, to find something to cover himself with, and this house, this house –

He frowns at it.

What is it about this house?

Surprising himself, without even feeling as if he's decided to, he takes an unsteady step toward it, nearly falling. He still struggles to articulate his thoughts. He cannot say why he's walking toward the house, why it might be anything other than an instinct to get inside, to get out of this weird deserted world, but he's also aware that all of this, whatever it is, feels so much like a dream that only dream logic can possibly apply.

He doesn't know why, but the house draws him.

So he goes.

He reaches the front steps, steps over a crack running along the lowest one, and stops before the door. He waits there a moment, not quite knowing what to do next, not quite sure how it will open, or what he will do if it's locked, but he reaches for it—

It swings open at his lightest touch.

A long hallway is the first thing he sees. The sun is really shining now, filling the clear blue sky behind him—so warm that it *must* be some kind of summer, so warm he can already feel it burning his exposed skin, too pale, too fair to be under such harsh light—but even in this brightness, the hallway almost disappears in darkness halfway down. He can only just see the staircase at the end, leading up to the floors above. Before the stairs, on the left, is the doorway that leads into the main house.

There are no lights on inside, and no sound.

He looks around again. There's still no drone of machinery or engines from anywhere, but he notices for the first time that there's no buzz of insects either, no calls of birds, not even any wind through the foliage.

Nothing but the sound of his own breathing.

He just stands there for a moment. He feels hideously unwell, and so weak, so *tired,* he could almost lay down on this doorstep right here and sleep forever, just forever, and never wake up—

He steps inside the house instead. Hands on either wall to keep himself steady, he moves slowly forward, every second thinking he's going to be stopped, that he's going to hear a voice demanding to know what he's doing trespassing in a strange house. As he stumbles into the shadows, though, his eyes not adjusting to the change in light as fast as they should, he can feel dust under his feet so thick it seems inconceivable that anyone has been here in a long, long time.

It gets darker the farther in he goes, and this seems wrong somehow, the blast of the sun through the open door not illuminating anything, just making the shadows heavier and more threatening to his bleary eyes. He fumbles on, seeing less and less, reaching the bottom of the stairs but turning from them, still hearing nothing, no sounds of habitation, no sound of anything at all except himself.

Alone.

He pauses before the doorway to the living room, feeling a fresh thrust of fear. Anything could be there in the darkness, anything could be silently waiting for him, but he forces himself to look in, letting his eyes get used to the light.

When they do, he sees.

Caught in a few beams of dusty sunlight from the closed blinds at the front, he sees a simple, plain living room, merging into an open dining area on his right, leading to a doorway through to the kitchen at the back of the house.

There is furniture here, like any normal room, except it's all covered in dust so thick it's like an extra cloth draped over everything. The boy, exhausted still, tries to make the shapes match up to words in his head.

His eyes adjust to the light more, the room becoming more of itself, taking shape, revealing details—

Revealing the horse screaming from above the mantelpiece.

A crazed eye, a tongue like a spike, trapped inside a burning world, looking at him from behind a picture frame.

Looking right at him.

The boy cries out at the sight of it because all at once he knows, *knows* beyond a shadow of a doubt, the realization coming like a tidal wave.

He knows where he is.

3

He runs as fast as his exhausted feet will take him, staggering back down the hall, stirring up clouds of dust, heading toward the sunshine like—

(like a drowning man reaching for air—)

He can vaguely hear himself calling out in distress, still wordless, still unformed.

But he knows.

He knows, he knows, he knows.

He stumbles down the front steps, barely able to stay upright, and then not even barely. He falls to his knees and can't find the strength to rise again, as if the sudden rush of knowledge is a weight on his back.

He looks to the house in panic, thinking that something, some*one* must be coming after him, must be in pursuit—

But there's nothing.

There's still no sound. Not of machines or people or animals or insects or anything at all. There's nothing but a quiet so deep he can hear his heart beating in his chest.

My heart, he thinks. And the words come clearly,

cutting through the fog in his mind.

His heart.

His dead heart. His drowned heart.

He begins to shake, as the terrible knowledge of what he saw, the terrible knowledge of what it *means*, starts to overtake him.

This is the house where he used to live.

The house from all those years ago. The house in *England*. The house his mother swore she never wanted to see again. The house they moved across an ocean and a continent to get away from.

But that's impossible. He hasn't seen this house, this *country*, in years. Not since primary school.

Not since–

Not since his brother got out of the hospital.

Not since the very worst thing that ever happened.

No, he thinks.

Oh, please, no.

He knows where he is now. He knows why it would be this place, knows why he would wake up here, after–

After he died.

This is hell.

A hell built exactly for him.

A hell where he would be alone.

Forever.

He's died, and woken up in his own, personal hell.

He vomits.

He falls forward onto his hands, spitting up the contents of his stomach into the bushes on the side of the path. His eyes water from the effort of it, but he can still see that all he's throwing up is a weird, clear gel that tastes vaguely of sugar. It keeps coming until he exhausts himself, and since his eyes are already watering, it seems only a very short step to weeping. He begins to cry, slumping back down to the concrete face-first.

It feels, for a time, like drowning all over again, the yearning for breath, the struggle against something larger than himself that only wants to take him down with it, and there's no fighting it, nothing that can be done to stop it, as it swallows him up and he disappears. Lying on the path, he gives himself over to it, in the same way that the waves kept demanding that he give himself to them –

(though he did fight the waves, up until the very end, he *did*)

And then the exhaustion that's threatened him since he first opened his eyes overtakes him, and he falls into unconsciousness.

Falls away and away and away –

4

"How long are we going to sit here?" Monica asked from the backseat. "I'm fucking freezing."

"Does your girlfriend ever shut up, Harold?" Gudmund teased, looking into the rearview mirror.

"Don't call me Harold," H said, his voice low.

Monica slapped him on the shoulder. "That *was* the part of the sentence you didn't like?"

"You're the one who wanted to come along," H said.

"And what a blast it's turned out to be," Monica said. "Parked outside Callen Fletcher's house waiting for his parents to go to bed so we can steal his Baby Jesus. You sure know how to treat a girl, Harold."

The backseat lit up as Monica started furiously tapping the screen of her phone.

"Turn that off!" Gudmund said, reaching back from the driver's seat to cover it with his hand. "They'll see the light."

Monica snatched it out of his grasp. "Please, we're miles away." She went back to tapping.

Gudmund shook his head and frowned at H in the rear-view mirror. It was weird. They all liked H. They all liked Monica. But it turned out nobody much liked H and

Monica together. Not even, it seemed, H and Monica.

"What are we going to do with it, anyway?" Monica said, still tapping. "I mean, Baby Jesus? Really? Isn't that just a little blasphemous?"

Gudmund pointed out through the windshield. "Isn't that?"

They looked out to the vast Christmas scene that blanketed the Fletchers' front yard like an invasion force. Word was that Mrs. Fletcher was angling not just for Half-market's local paper, but an actual TV news crew over from Portland, maybe even Seattle.

The display started with Santa and all his reindeer in bright fiberglass, lit up from the inside and strung from a tree near the Fletcher house out to their roof so it looked like the over-burdened sleigh was coming in for a landing. Things got worse from there. Lights sprang from every conceivable crevice and outcropping on the house to every tree branch and telephone pole within reach. Ten-foot-tall candy canes made a forest through which mechanical elves waved onlookers slowly into eternity. Off to one side, there was a live, twenty-foot Christmas tree decked out like a cathedral next to a lawn full of prancing Christmas-related animals (including, inexplicably, a rhinoceros in a Santa cap).

In pride of place was a Nativity that made it look as if God had been born in Las Vegas: Mary and Joseph, complete with manger, hay, lowing cattle, bowing shepherds, and rejoicing angels who looked like they'd stopped mid–dance routine.

Right in the center, surrounded by them all, was the spotlit, golden-haloed infant, lifting his hands beatifically

23

toward the peace of all mankind. It was rumored he was carved from imported Venetian marble. This would turn out to be tragically false.

"Well, he's small enough to be portable, is your Baby Jesus," H explained to Monica, who wasn't really listening.

"Easy to grab in one swoop," Gudmund said. "Easier than that rhinoceros anyway. What the hell's up with that?"

"And then you bury him waist deep in someone else's lawn," H continued, raising his hands like the Baby Jesus statue as if he were sticking halfway out of the ground.

"And voilà," Gudmund finished, smiling. "A Christmas miracle."

Monica rolled her eyes. "Can't we just do meth like everybody else?"

The whole car laughed. Yep, everyone was going to be a lot happier when she and H broke up and it could all be normal again.

"It's almost eleven," Monica said, reading her phone. "I thought you said—"

Before she could finish, they were plunged into darkness as the entire Fletcher display shut off in obedience to the county-ordered curfew the neighbors had gone to court to obtain. Even from where they were parked down the gravel road from the house, they could hear shouts of disappointment from the last of the chain of cars that had spent the evening driving leisurely by.

(Callen Fletcher, a tall, awkward boy, spent the time from Thanksgiving to New Year desperately trying not to be noticed in any way at school. He was usually unsuccessful.)

"All right, then," Gudmund said, rubbing his hands together. "We just wait for the cars to clear, and then we make our move."

"This is theft, you know," Monica said. "They're bonkers over that display, and if Baby Jesus suddenly goes missing–"

"They'll go apeshit," H laughed.

"They'll press charges," Monica said.

"We're not going to take him far," Gudmund said, and then he added, mischievously, "I thought Summer Blaydon's house could use a holy visitation."

Monica looked shocked for a moment, then seemingly couldn't stop herself from grinning back. "We'll have to be careful that we don't interrupt some late-night cheerleading practice or something."

"I thought you said it was theft," Gudmund said.

"I did," Monica shrugged, still grinning. "I didn't say I minded."

"Hey!" H snapped at her. "You gonna flirt with him all night or what?"

"Everyone shut up anyway," Gudmund said, turning back. "It's almost time."

There was a silence then, as they waited. The only sound was the squeak of H rubbing his sleeve on the window to clear it of condensation. Gudmund's leg bounced up and down in anticipation. The cars thinned out to nothing on the road, and still the silence ruled as they held their breath without knowing they were doing it.

At last, the street was empty. The Fletchers' porch light clicked off.

25

Gudmund let out a long exhalation and turned to the backseat with a serious look. H nodded back to him. "Let's do it," he said.

"I'm coming, too," Monica said, putting her phone away.

"Never thought you wouldn't," Gudmund said, smiling.

He turned to the person sitting in the passenger's seat.

"You ready, Seth?" he asked.

5

Seth opens his eyes.

He's still lying on the concrete path, curled up into him-self, feeling cramped and stiff against the hard surface. For a moment, he doesn't move.

Seth, he thinks. *Seth is my name.*

It seems a surprise, as if he'd forgotten it until the dream or the memory or whatever the hell it was that just happened. It had been so clear it's almost painful to recall it. And the sudden rush of information that comes with it is painful, too. Not just his name. No, not just that.

He had been *right there,* so much more vividly than any memory or dream would have been. He had actually been there, *with* them. With H and Monica. With Gudmund, who had a car so always drove. His friends. On the night they stole the Baby Jesus out of Callen Fletcher's front yard.

Not two months ago.

Seth, he thinks again. The name slips from his brain strangely, like sand held in an open palm. *I am Seth Wearing.*

I was Seth Wearing.

He takes a deep breath, and his nostrils fill with a gag-making smell from where he was sick in the bushes. He sits up. The sun is higher in the sky. He's been out for a while, but it doesn't feel like noon yet.

If there *is* a noon in this place. If time means anything here.

His head is pounding badly, and even in the confusion of memories laying heavily on him, he becomes aware of a powerful new feeling, one he realizes he's felt all along but can now put a description to, a word, now that things are clearing, now that he knows his own name.

Thirst. He's thirsty. More thirsty than he can ever remember. So much so it drives him almost immediately to his feet. Once more, he's shaky as he stands, but he steadies himself and manages to stay upright. He realizes it's what had driven him into the house before, an unnameable, undeniable urge.

Now that it's named, it feels even more undeniable.

He looks again at the strange, silent, empty neighborhood around him, with its layers of dust and mud. The familiarity that had hinted itself before is much firmer, much clearer now.

His street, yes, where he'd lived when he was small, a street that had been his home. To the left it led up to the High Street with all its shops, and he can remember now, too, the commuter trains off to the right. More, he can remember counting them. On those early mornings, just before they moved from this little English suburb all the way across the world to the freezing coast of the Pacific Northwest, when he used to lie awake, unsleeping, counting trains, as if that would help.

His younger brother's bed empty across the room.

He winces at the memory of that summer and pushes it away.

Because it's summer *now,* isn't it?

He turns to the house again.

His old house.

Unmistakably, his old house.

It looks weather-beaten and untended, the paint peeling away from the window frames, the walls stained from leaky gutters, just like every other house on this street. At some point, the chimney has partially collapsed onto the roof, a small rubble of bricks and dust scattered down the slope to the edge, as if no one ever noticed it falling.

Which maybe no one has.

How? he thinks, struggling to organize coherent thoughts against his thirst. *How can this possibly be?*

The need for water is almost like a living creature inside him now. He's never felt anything like it before, his tongue fat and dry in his mouth, his lips cracked and chapped, bleeding as he tries to lick them damp.

The house looms there, as if waiting for him. He doesn't want to go back inside, not even a little bit, but there is nothing else to do. He must drink. He *must*. The front door is still open from where he ran out before, panicked. He remembers the shock of what awaited him above the mantelpiece, like a punch to the gut, telling him just exactly what hell he'd woken up to–

But he also remembers the dining area leading on from the sitting room, and the kitchen beyond that.

The kitchen.

With its taps.

$\bullet \quad \bullet \quad \bullet$

He moves slowly to the doorway again, coming up the three front steps, now recognizing the crack in the bottom one, a crack never quite serious enough to get fixed.

He looks into his house and the memories keep coming. The long hallway, still shrouded in shadow, is one he crossed countless times as a young boy, tumbling down stairs he can now just barely see in the deepness of the house. He remembers that they lead up to the bedrooms on the floor above and continue up farther still, to the attic.

The attic that used to be his old bedroom. The one he shared with Owen. The one he shared with Owen before—

He stops the thought again. The thirst is nearly bending him double.

He must drink.

Seth must drink.

He thinks his name again. *Seth. I am Seth.*

And I will speak.

"Hello?" he says, and the word is sharply painful, the thirst turning his throat into a desert. "Hello?" he tries again, a bit louder. "Is anyone there?"

There's no answer. And still no sound, nothing but his breathing to let him know he hasn't gone deaf.

He stands at the doorway, not moving yet. It's harder this time to go in, much harder, his fear a palpable thing, fear of what else he might find inside, fear of why he's here, of what it means.

Of what it *will* mean. Forever and ever.

But the thirst is palpable, too, and he forces himself over the threshold, stirring up the dust again. His bandages are no longer anything approaching white, and his skin is streaked with dark stains. He heads deeper inside, stopping just before the bottom of the stairs. He tries the light switch there, but it flips on and off pointlessly, no lights coming on anywhere. He turns from the stairs, not willing to brave the darkness of them just yet, not even really wanting to look at them, just gathering his courage before entering the living room.

He takes a deep, dry breath, coughing again at the dust.

And steps through the doorway.

6

It is as he left it. Scattered rays of sunlight are the only illumination, since the light switches don't work in this room either. A room filled, he now fully realizes, with the furniture of his childhood.

There are the stained red settees, one big, one small, that his father wasn't going to replace until the boys got old enough not to mess them up anymore.

Settees that got left behind in England when they moved to America, left behind in *this* house.

But here is a coffee table that didn't get left behind, a coffee table that should be thousands and thousands of miles from here.

I don't understand, he thinks. *I don't understand.*

He sees a vase of his mother's that made the trip. He sees an ugly end table that didn't. And there, above the mantelpiece –

He feels the same stabbing in his gut despite knowing what to expect.

It's the painting made by his uncle, the painting that came to America, too, with some of this furniture. It's of a shrieking, wrongly proportioned horse with terror in its eyes and that awful spike for its tongue. His uncle had patterned it after Picasso's *Guernica,* surrounding the horse with broken skies and broken, bombed-out bodies.

Seth had long since been told about the real *Guernica* by his father, long since understood the story behind it, but even though his uncle's version was the palest of pale imitations, it was the first painting Seth had ever properly seen, the first real painting his then-five-year-old mind had tried to figure out. For that reason, it loomed larger for him than any classic ever would.

It is something out of a nightmare, something horrible and hysterical, something unable to listen to reason or understand mercy.

And it is a painting he last saw *yesterday,* if yesterday still means anything. If time passed at all in hell. Whatever the answer, it was a painting he saw on his way out of his own house on the other side of the world, the last thing his eyes had glanced over as he shut his front door.

His actual front door. Not this. Not this nightmare version out of a past he'd prefer not to remember.

He watches the painting as long as he can bear, long enough to try and turn it into just a painting, nothing more than that, but he can feel his heart thudding as he looks away from it, his eyes avoiding a dining-room table he also recognizes, and the bookcases full of books, some of whose titles he's read in another country than this. He shuffles as quickly as his weak body will carry him into the kitchen, keeping his thoughts only on his thirst. He heads straight to the sink, almost whimpering with anticipated relief.

When he turns on the taps and nothing happens, he lets out an involuntary cry of despair. He tries them again. One won't move at all, and the other just spins in his hand, producing nothing, no matter how often he twists it.

He can feel a weeping rising in him again, his eyes burning at how salty the tears are in his dehydrated body. He feels so weak, so unsteady that he has to lean forward and put his forehead against the counter, feeling its dusty coolness on his brow and hoping he won't faint.

Of course this is what hell would be like, he thinks. *Of course it is. To always be thirsty but have nothing to drink. Of course.*

It's probably punishment for the Baby Jesus thing. Monica had even said so. He feels a rueful flutter in his stomach, remembering that night again, remembering his friends, how relaxed and easy everything usually was, how they liked that he was the quiet one, how it hadn't mattered that the differences in English and American curriculum meant that he was nearly a year younger than them all despite being in the same grade, how they–but especially Gudmund–included him in everything as only friends could. Even the theft of a deity.

They'd stolen it, almost shamefully easily, their stifled laughter the only real threat to getting caught. They'd lifted the infant out of the manger, surprised at its lightness, and carried it, barely able to contain their hysteria, back to Gudmund's car. They'd been so nervous in the getaway that a light had come on in the Fletcher house as they peeled down the road.

But they'd done it. And then they'd driven out to the head

cheerleader's house as planned, shushing each other vigorously as they snuck Baby Jesus out of the backseat into the middle of the night.

Where H dropped him.

It turned out that Baby Jesus wasn't, in fact, made from Venetian marble, but from some kind of cheap ceramic that broke with astonishing thoroughness when it came into swift contact with the pavement. There had been a hushed, horrified silence as they stood over the bits and pieces.

"We are *so* going to hell," Monica had finally said, and it sure hadn't sounded like she was joking.

Seth hears a sound in his chest and realizes with surprise that it's laughter. He opens his mouth and it comes out in a horrible, painful honk, but he can't stop it. He laughs and laughs some more, no matter how light-headed it makes him, no matter how he still can't quite stand up from the countertop.

Yes. Hell. That'd be about right.

But before he starts to cry again, a feeling that has threatened behind every second of his laughter, he realizes he's been hearing another sound this whole time. A creaking and groaning, like a baying cow lost somewhere in the house.

He looks up.

The groaning is from the pipes. Dirty, rust-colored water is starting to dribble from the kitchen tap.

Seth practically leaps forward in his desperate rush to drink and drink and drink.

7

The water tastes awful, unbelievably so, like metal and mud, but he can't stop himself. He gulps it down as it comes, faster through the tap now. After ten or twelve swallows, he feels a churning in his stomach, leans back, and throws up all the water he just drank into the sink in great, rust-colored cataracts.

He pants heavily for a minute.

Then he sees that the water is running a little clearer, though still not exactly drinkable looking. He waits for as long as he can bear, letting it clear some more, then he drinks again, more slowly, this time taking breaks to breathe and wait.

He keeps the water down. Feels the coolness of it spreading out from his stomach. It feels good, and he notices again how warm it is in this place, but especially in this house. The air is stuffy and oppressive, tasting of the dust that covers everything. His arms are filthy with it just from leaning against the counter.

He begins to feel slightly better, slightly stronger. He drinks again, and then again, until the roaring thirst is finally satisfied. When he stands up fully this time, he does so without feeling dizzy.

The sun through the back window is bright and clear. He

looks around the kitchen. It's definitely his old one, which his mother never stopped complaining about being too small, even after they moved to America, where kitchens tended to be big enough to seat a family of elephants around the breakfast nook. Then again, in his mother's eyes, *everything* in England compared unfavorably to America, and why shouldn't it?

After what England had done to them.

He hasn't thought about it, *really* thought about it, for years. There was no reason to. Why dwell on your worst memory? Not if life had moved on, in a brand-new place, so many new things to learn, so many new people to meet.

And though it had been terrible, his brother had survived, hadn't he? There had been problems, of course, as they watched to see how bad any neurological damage might be as he grew, but his brother had lived and was usually a charming, functional, happy little kid, despite any difficulties.

Though there had been that unthinkable period when they all thought the worst, when they all looked at Seth and while saying over and over that they didn't blame him, still seemed to think –

He pushes it out of his mind, swallowing away the ache in his throat. He looks out toward the darkened sitting room and wonders what he's supposed to *do* here.

Is there a goal? Something to solve?

Or is he just supposed to stay here forever?

Is that what hell is? Trapped forever, alone, in your worst memory?

It makes a kind of sense.

The bandages don't, though, smudged with dark, dusty stains but stuck fast to his body in an arrangement that covers all the wrong parts. And for that matter, the water – now running almost clear – doesn't make sense either. Why satisfy his thirst if this is a punishment?

He still can't hear anything. No machinery, no human voices, no vehicles, nothing. Just the running of the water, the sound of which is so comforting, he can't quite bring himself to turn it off.

He's surprised to feel his stomach rumbling. Emptied twice of all its contents, he realizes that it's hungry, and rather than give in to the fear that this causes – because what do you eat in hell? – he almost automatically opens the nearest cabinet.

The shelves are filled with plates and cups, less dusty because shut away, but still with an air of abandonment. The cabinet next to it has better glasses and the good china, which he recognizes, most but not all of it surviving the shipment to America. He moves quickly on, and in the next cabinet, there is finally food. Bags of desiccated pasta, molding boxes of rice that crumble under his touch, a jar of sugar that's hardened into a single lump that resists the poking of his fingers. Further searching reveals cans of food, some of which are rusted over, others bulging alarmingly, but a few that look okay. He takes out one of chicken noodle soup.

He recognizes the brand. It's one that he and Owen used to be unable to get enough of, used to ask their mother to buy over and over again –

He stops. The memory is a dangerous one. He can feel himself teetering again, an abyss of confusion and despair looking right back up at him, threatening to swallow him if he so much as glances at it.

That can be for later, he tells himself. *You're hungry. Everything else can wait.*

Even thinking it, he doesn't believe it, but he forces himself to read the can again. "Soup," he says, his voice still little more than a croak but better now, after the water. "Soup," he says again, more strongly.

He starts opening drawers. He finds a can opener – rusty and stiff, but usable – in the first one and lets out a small "Ha!" of triumph.

It takes him seventeen tries to get the first cut into the top of the can.

"Goddammit!" he shouts, though his throat isn't quite up to shouting yet and he has to cough it away.

But at last there's an opening, one he can work with. His hands are aching from the simple act of twisting a can opener, and there's a terrible moment when he thinks he's going to be too weak and tired to get any further. But the frustration drives him on and eventually, agonizingly so, there's enough of an opening to drink out of.

He tips the can back into his mouth. The soup has gelatinized and tastes heavily of iron, but it also tastes of chicken noodle, a flavor he's suddenly so grateful for that he starts laughing as he's slurping down the noodles.

Then he also senses that he's crying a bit more, too.

He finishes the can and sets it down with a firm thud.

Stop this, he thinks. *Pull yourself together. What do you need to do here? What's the next thing to do?* He stands a little straighter. *What would Gudmund do?*

And then, for the first time in this place, Seth smiles, small and fleeting, but a smile.

"Gudmund would have a piss," he croaks.

Because that is indeed what he needs to do next.

8

He turns back toward the dark, dusty sitting room.

No. Not yet. He can't face that quite yet. *Definitely* can't face stumbling up the darkened stairs to the bathroom at the top of the first landing.

He turns to the door to the backyard–back *garden,* he remembers, that's what the English call it, what his parents always called it. It takes him a few frustrating minutes to get the lock unstuck, but then he steps out into the sunshine again, across the deck his father had built one summer.

The fences of the neighbors on either side seem amazingly close after all the space his family had ended up with in their American house. The lawn itself is now a forest of wheaty-looking stalks and weeds nearly as high as Seth's head, even as he stands on the low deck. At the back fence, Seth can only just see the top of the old concrete bomb shelter, standing there in its brave arch since World War II. His mother had turned it into a potter's shed, which she never used all that much, and it quickly became a place to store old bikes and broken furniture.

The embankment beyond the back fence rises up to a gnarled wall of barbed wire. He can't see any farther than that because of how the land angles down behind it.

But Seth doesn't think this would be hell if the prison weren't still there.

He averts his eyes and steps to the edge of the deck. He leans forward a bit and waits to pee out into the tall grass.

And waits.

And waits.

And grunts with the effort.

And waits a bit more.

Until at last, with a heartfelt cry of relief, he sends a poisonously dark yellow stream into the yard.

And almost immediately calls out in pain. It's like peeing acid, and he looks down at himself in distress.

Then he looks closer.

There are small cuts, small abrasions and marks all across the skin of his groin and hips. He finds a stray piece of white tape tangled in his thickest body hair and a larger one farther down his exposed thigh.

With a wince, he finishes urinating, and starts examining his body more closely in the sunlight. There are numerous cuts and scrapes in the crooks of both his arms, and a line of them up the side of either buttock. He starts pulling at the bandages around his torso, trying to see underneath them. The adhesive is strong, but it finally gives. There's a strange metallic foil on the inside of each bandage, and it comes away in a sticky mess, tearing off a few chest hairs he never thought much of anyway. The same is true for the bandages on his arms and legs. He works and works at them, leaving behind painful bald spots and finding more abrasions and cuts.

He keeps at it until he completely rids himself of them, coiling them there on the deck, dirty from the dust but the metallic bits catching the sunlight and reflecting it back at him sharply, almost aggressively. There's no writing on them that he can find, and the metallic part is like nothing he's ever seen before in America *or* England.

He steps away from them. There is something alien in the way they look. Something wrong. Something invasive.

Seth crosses his arms tightly against himself, and he shudders, though the sun is beating down clear and hot. He is completely naked now, and that's the next thing that has to be remedied. He feels unbelievably vulnerable like this, more so than the literal fact of it. There is threat here, somewhere, he's suddenly sure of it. He glances back to the fence and the prison he knows lies hidden beyond, but this place is more wrong than even all that's obvious. There's an unreality under all the dust, all the weeds. Ground that seems solid but that might give way any moment.

He keeps shivering under the heat of the sun, under a clear blue sky without a single airplane in it. All at once the energy he spent on eating and drinking catches up with him, exhaustion settling over him like a heavy blanket. He feels so weak, so unbelievably, physically weak.

His arms still crossed, he turns back to his house.

It sits there, waiting for him, a memory asking to be reentered.

9

I'll have to see, Seth tapped onto the screen of his phone. *U know how my mum is.*

It's mOm, U homo, Gudmund wrote back. *And what's her problem now?*

B in History.

Ur mom gets upset about GRADES?!?! What f-ing century does she live in?

Not this one & only girls text this much, U homo.

Seth smiled to himself as his phone immediately vibrated with an incoming call. "I said I'd have to see," he whispered into it.

"What's the matter with her?" Gudmund said. "Doesn't she trust me?"

"Nope."

"Ah, well, she's smarter than I thought."

"She's smarter than everyone thinks. That's why she's always so pissed off. Says she's lived here eight years and everyone still talks to her in a loud, slow voice, like she's a foreigner."

"She is a foreigner."

"She's English. Same language."

"Not really. Why are you talking so quiet?"

"They don't know I'm awake yet."

Seth took a moment to listen from his bed. He could hear his mother stomping around, probably trying to find Owen's clarinet. Owen, meanwhile, was in the next bedroom over, playing a computer game that involved lots of dramatic guitar solos. And every once in a while there was a banging from the kitchen downstairs, where his father was ten months into a three-month DIY project. Typical Saturday morning stuff, so, no, thank you, he'd stay here as long as no one remembered he—

"SETH!" he heard shouted from down the hall.

"Gotta go," he said into the phone.

"You have to come, Sethy," Gudmund insisted. "How many times do I need to say it? My parents are out of town. It's like a commandment to party. And we're not going to get many more chances. Senior year, dude, and then we're out of here."

"I'll do what I can," Seth said hurriedly as his mother's feet came pounding toward his door. "I'll call you back." He hung up as she flung the door open. "Jesus," he said, "knock much?"

"You have no secrets from me," she answered, but with a forced half-smile, and he could tell she was trying to apologize, in her bizarrely hostile way.

"You have no idea what secrets I have," he said.

"I don't doubt that for a second. Get up. We have to go."

"Why do I have to come?"

"Have you seen Owen's clarinet?"

45

"He'll be fine for an hour–"

"Have you seen it?"

"Are you even listening to me?"

"Are you listening to me? Where's Owen's goddamn clarinet?"

"I don't goddamn know! I'm not his goddamn butler!"

"Watch your mouth," she snapped. "You know he loses track of things. You know he's not as on the ball as you. Not since–"

She didn't finish her sentence. Didn't even trail off, just stopped dead. Seth didn't need to ask what she meant.

"I haven't seen it," he said, "but I still don't see why I have to come and just sit there."

His mother spoke with angry patience, enunciating every syllable. "Be. Cause. I. Want. To. Go. For. A. Run." She dangled the running shoes she was holding. "I get precious little time to myself as it is, and you know Owen gets upset if he's left there alone with Miss Baker–"

"He's fine," Seth said. "He puts it on because he likes the attention."

His mother sucked in her breath. "Seth–"

"If I do it, can I stay over at Gudmund's tonight?"

She paused. His mother didn't like Gudmund much, for reasons she couldn't quite explain herself. "I don't even like his name," he'd overheard her saying to his father one night in the next room. "What kind of name is Gudmund? He's not Swedish."

"Gudmund is a Norwegian name, I think," his father had said, not paying much attention.

"Well, he's not that either. Not even in the way Americans go on about being Irish or Cherokee. Honestly, a whole population who refuse to call themselves after their own nation unless they're feeling threatened."

"You must hear them calling themselves American quite a lot then," his father had said dryly, and the conversation had soured somewhat after that.

Seth really didn't understand it. Gudmund was damn near the perfect teen. Popular enough, but not too popular; confident, but not too confident; nice to Seth's parents, nice to Owen, and always got Seth home by curfew since he'd gotten his car. Like all of Seth's classmates, he was a bit older, but only by ten months, seventeen to Seth's sixteen, which was nothing. They ran on the cross-country team together with Monica and H, which couldn't have been more wholesome. And while it was true that Gudmund's mother and father were exactly the sort of scary American conservatives that tended to horrify Europeans, even Seth's own parents had to admit they were pretty nice people one-on-one.

And though they clearly suspected, his parents had also never found out about any of the trouble he and Gudmund got up to. Not that any of it was actually all that bad. No drugs, and though there was more than occasional drinking, there was definitely no drunk driving. Gudmund was bright and easygoing, and most parents would have been happy to have him around as a friend for their son.

But not, it seemed, Seth's mother. She pretended she had some sixth sense about him.

And maybe she did.

47

"You've got work tomorrow," she said now, but he could already tell she was on her way to a yes in the negotiations.

"Not 'til six," Seth said, keeping his tone as unargumentative as possible.

His mother considered. "Fine," she said curtly. "Now, get up. We need to go."

"Close the door," he called after her, but she was already gone.

He got up and found a shirt to pull on over his head. An hour sitting through Owen's torturous clarinet lesson with onion-smelling Miss Baker so his mother could go run furiously along the coastal path in exchange for an evening of freedom which included a stash of beer forgotten by Gudmund's father (though not behind the wheel of Gudmund's car; really, they were good kids, which made her suspicions all the more infuriating; Seth almost wanted to do something bad, something really bad, just to show her). But for now, it was a fair enough trade.

Any chance to get away. Any chance to feel not quite so trapped. Even for a little while.

He'd take it.

Five minutes later, he was dressed and in the kitchen. "Hey, Dad," he said, taking down a box of cereal.

"Hey, Seth," his father sighed, intently studying the wooden frame for the new counter, a frame that refused to fit, no matter how much sawing went on.

"Why don't you just hire a guy?" Seth asked, stuffing a handful of peanut-butter-flavored granules in his mouth. "Be done in a week."

48

"And what guy would that be?" his father asked distractedly. "There's peace to be found in doing something for yourself."

Seth had heard this sentence many, many times. His father taught English at the small, liberal arts college that gave Halfmarket two-thirds of its population, and these projects—of which there had been more than Seth could count, from the deck at the house in England when he was just a baby, adding a utility room in the garage here, to this kitchen extension his father had insisted on doing himself—were what he swore kept him sane after swapping London for a small coastal American town. The projects all eventually got finished, all eventually pretty well, too, but the peace, perhaps, had less to do with the project than with the medication his father took for his depression. Heavier than the usual antidepressants that some of his friends took, heavy enough to occasionally make his father seem like a ghost in their own house.

"What have I done wrong now?" his father mumbled, shaking his head in puzzlement at a pile of off-cut timber.

His mother came into the kitchen, thudding Owen's clarinet down on the table. "Would someone mind telling me how this ended up in the guest room?"

"Ever thought of asking Owen?" Seth said through a mouthful of cereal.

"Asking me what?" Owen said, coming through the door.

And here was Owen. His little brother. Hair curled up in a ridiculous, sleep-messed pile that made him look way younger than his nearly twelve years, a red Kool-Aid stain around his

49

lips and crumbs from his breakfast still stuck to his chin, wearing regular jeans but also a Cookie Monster pajama top that he was about five years too old and too big for.

Owen. As scatterbrained and messy as ever.

But Seth could see his mother's posture change into something that almost resembled joy.

"Nothing, sweetheart," she said. "Go wash your face and put on a clean shirt. We're almost ready to go."

Owen beamed back at her. "I got to level 82!"

"That's brilliant, darling. Now, hurry along. We're going to be late."

"Okay!" Owen said, blazing a smile at Seth and his father as he left the kitchen. Seth's mother's gaze greedily followed him out the doorway, as if it was all she could do not to eat him.

When she turned back into the kitchen, her face was disconcertingly open and warm until she caught Seth and his father staring at her. There was an awkward moment where no one said anything, and she at least had the good grace to look a little embarrassed.

"Hurry up, Seth," she said. "We really are going to be late."

She left. Seth just stood there with his handful of cereal, until his father, without a word, started sawing slowly on the counter frame again. The familiar yearning to get away rose in Seth's chest like a physical pressure, so strong he thought he might be able to see it if he looked.

One more year, he thought. One year to go.

His final year of high school lay ahead of him, and then

he would go off to college, (maybe, hopefully) the same one as Gudmund and possibly Monica. The location didn't matter so much as long as it was as far as possible from this damp little corner of southwest Washington State.

Far away from these strangers who called themselves his parents.

But then he remembered there were smaller escapes closer to home.

An hour of clarinet, *he thought.* And the weekend's mine.

He thought it more angrily than he expected.

And at the same time, he realized he wasn't very hungry anymore.

10

Seth wakes up on the larger of the two red settees, and once more, it takes him a moment to re-emerge from the–

It really can't have just been a dream.

He'd been asleep this time, he knew, but like the last one, it had been far too vivid, far too *clear*. None of the shifting vagueness of a dream, none of the changes in scene or inabilities to move or speak properly or lapses in time or logic.

He had *been* there. Right there. Again. Living it.

He remembers that morning, as clearly as if he'd just watched it on television. It had been summer, months before the Baby Jesus incident, just after he'd gotten his first part-time job waiting tables at the local steakhouse. Gudmund's parents had flown to California for business, leaving Gudmund to watch over a house that looked out onto Washington's cold, tumultuous ocean. H and Monica had come over for a while, too, and they'd all done nothing, really, except drink some of Gudmund's father's forgotten beer and shoot the shit and laugh themselves incoherent at the dumbest things you could think of.

It had been amazing. Just utterly, utterly amazing, like that whole summer before senior year had been, when everything had seemed possible, when everything good felt like it was just within reach for once, when if he could just hang in there, it really would finally all come together –

Seth feels his chest tighten with a sadness that threatens to rush in like the waves that drowned him.

It had been amazing.

But it was gone.

And was gone even before he died.

He sits up, putting his feet on the dusty hardwood floor of his childhood home. He scratches his fingers through his hair and is surprised to find how short it is, almost military short, way shorter than he'd ever had it in real life. He stands and brushes away the dust from the big mirror hanging over the settee.

He's shocked by what he sees. He looks like a war refugee. Hair buzzed down to almost nothing, his face alarmingly thin, his eyes looking like he's never slept in a safe place in his life.

This just gets better and better, he thinks.

He had come back into the house after peeling the bandages from his skin. By that point, the exhaustion was overwhelming, settling on him like a heavy anesthetic. It had been all he could do to get to the larger settee, shake the dust off the blanket draped along the back, pull it over himself, and fall into a sleep that felt more like being knocked out.

And he had dreamed. Or relived. Or whatever.

It tugs again at his chest as he stands there, so he wraps the blanket around himself like a beach towel and goes into the kitchen again, with a vague thought of trying to scrounge dinner. It takes him a moment to notice that the light from the back window has changed.

The sun is *rising*. Again. It's another dawn outside.

He's slept through almost an entire day and night. Then he wonders again about how time might pass here in hell.

If it did at all. If this just wasn't the same day all over again.

After an easier time with the can opener–he's feeling a little stronger for the rest–he opens a can of beans. They taste unspeakable, and he spits them out. He checks the cabinet for more soup.

There isn't any. In fact, there isn't much of anything, unless he starts eating mummified pasta. Not feeling very hopeful, he turns the knobs on the stovetop to see if he might be able to boil some water, but no gas comes through the elements, and there's no electricity either when he tries to power up the dusty old microwave. None of the overhead lights come on when he flicks the switches, and the refrigerator has a faint smell even with the door tightly shut, so he doesn't risk opening it.

For lack of anything else, he drinks from the taps again. Then he makes an annoyed grunt and gets a glass from the cabinet. He fills it with water that looks almost clear now and drinks it down.

Okay, then, he thinks, trying to keep the fear from rising again. *What's next? What's next, what's next, what's next?*

Clothes. Clothes are next. Yes.

He still can't face going upstairs–he doesn't want to see his old bedroom just yet, not the one he shared with

54

Owen, not in this house – but he goes back to the main room, remembering a cubbyhole under the staircase. Behind the dining table, two small swing doors in the wall lead to a lifeless washer and dryer, silent as sleeping cattle in their stalls. He lets out a cry of delight when he finds a pair of gray sweatpants in the dryer. They're baggy but they fit. There are no shirts to be found, and nothing at all in the washing machine except a smell of ancient mildew, but he finds a sports jacket hanging on a hook. It's tight around his back and the sleeves barely reach past his elbows, but it covers him. He scrounges around on the dark shelves built into the cubby and finds one well-worn black dress shoe and one giant tennis shoe that don't come close to matching but are at least for opposite feet and big enough to wear.

He goes to the mirror in the main room. He looks like a homeless clown, but he's no longer naked.

All right, he thinks. *Next thing.*

Almost exactly at that thought, his stomach rumbles unpleasantly, and not with hunger. He finds himself rushing out back again to a corner of the tall grass for some far more disgusting bodily functions. He cramps painfully, more than what would come from chicken noodle soup and a mouthful of spoiled beans. It's a huge gnawing hunger, so big it's making him sick.

Waiting out the stomach cramps is bad enough, but he feels increasingly uneasy out here in the back, with the pile of bandages still coiled on the deck, the unreasonably tall grass, the barbed wire fencing up on the embankment.

The prison beyond.

As soon as he's able, he gets back inside and manages a halfway-decent wash with some solidified dishwashing liquid and cold water from the tap. There's nothing to dry himself with, so he just waits, wondering what to do *now*.

Here he is. In a dusty old house with no food left in it. With clothes that are a joke. Drinking water that's probably poisoning him.

He doesn't want to be outside, but he can't stay stuck in here either.

What's he supposed to do?

If only there was someone here to help him. Someone whose opinion he could ask. Someone he could share this weird burden with.

But there isn't. There's only him.

And he can see the empty kitchen cupboards.

He can't stay here, not without food, not in these inadequate clothes.

He looks up at the ceiling, thinking for a moment that he could explore the rooms above.

But no. Not that. Not yet.

He stands there, silently, for a long, long while, as the rising sun farther fills the kitchen.

"Okay," he finally says to himself. "Let's go see what hell looks like."

11

As he pulls open the front door, he notices that the switch that keeps it from locking is flipped. He's been in the house all night with an unlocked door. Even though there's no sign of anyone else here, this worries him. He can't let it lock when he leaves, though, or he'll never be able to get back inside. He steps out into the low sunshine, pulling it closed behind him, hoping it at least *looks* locked.

The street is the same as yesterday. Or whenever that was, probably yesterday. He waits and watches. Absolutely nothing changes, so he walks down the steps, down the path where he – Where he what? Woke up? Was reborn? Died? He hurries past the spot and reaches the small gate to the sidewalk. He stops there.

It's still quiet. Still empty. Still a place stopped in time.

He tries to remember more of the neighborhood. To his right is the train station, where there was nothing much more than the station building itself. But to his left is the way to the High Street, where there used to be a supermarket. There had been clothes shops there, too, he thinks. Nothing fancy, but better than what he's wearing.

Left it is, then.

Left.

He doesn't move. Neither does the world.

It's either go left or stay inside and starve, he thinks.

For a moment, the second choice seems the more tempting.

"Screw it," he says. "You're already dead. What's the worst that can happen?"

He goes left.

He hunches his shoulders as he walks, shoving his hands into the pockets of the jacket, even though they're uncomfortably high. Whose jacket *was* this? He doesn't think he saw his dad ever wear one like this, but then again, who remembers clothes when you're that young?

He looks around furtively as he walks, turning often to make sure nothing's following him. He reaches the street leading up into town. Aside from the huge sinkhole across the middle of it–ablaze with a weed forest of its own–it's the same as everywhere else. Cars on deflated tires, covered in dust, houses with paint peeling off, and no signs of life anywhere.

He stops at the edge of the sinkhole. It looks like a water pipe ruptured somewhere and the ground opened up like you saw sometimes on the news, usually with journalists in helicopters hovering over, saying nothing much for very long spaces of time.

There are no cars down in it and none stopped along the edge either, so it must have happened long after the traffic ceased.

Unless the traffic never started, he thinks. *Unless this place didn't exist until I–*

"Stop it," he says. "Just stop it."

He has a fleeting, almost casual thought, about how there is so much plant life in this place, all these weeds and ridiculous grasses, all growing completely out of control and unchecked, like down here in this really quite huge hole.

So you'd think there'd be–

And before he can even think the word *animals,* he sees the fox.

It's frozen there, down at the bottom, tucked in amongst the weeds, its eyes bright and surprised in the morning sun.

A fox.

A real, live, *living* fox.

It blinks at him, alert, but not quite afraid, not yet.

"What the hell?" Seth whispers.

There's a small bark, and three baby foxes–pups? No, *kits,* he remembers–climb playfully over their mother, before freezing, too, when they see Seth standing there above them.

They wait and watch, looking ready to run, ready to respond to whatever Seth does next. Seth wonders what he'll do next, too. Wonders also at the reddish brown faces and the bright staring eyes of the creatures. Wonders what they mean.

It's a long time before he moves away from the sinkhole, but the fox and her kits never stop staring at him, even as he heads back up the street.

Foxes, he thinks. *Actual foxes.*

At the very moment he thought about them.

Almost as if he'd called them into being himself.

He hurries up toward the High Street now, his head still down, eyes glancing around even more suspiciously. Every moment, he expects something to come jumping out of the bushes, out of the unkempt lawns or weedy cracks in the pavement.

But nothing does.

He feels himself tiring again, quickly, too quickly, and when he reaches the High Street, he almost collapses on a nearby bench, panting from the effort of walking up a short hill.

It makes him angry. He spent three years on the cross-country team at Boswell High, the hobby and habit of running having been picked up from his mother, something that should have brought them closer together but had somehow not. Granted, he wasn't a particularly serious competitor, Boswell regularly got beaten quite badly, but still. There's no way he should be out of breath walking up one stupid road.

He looks around. The High Street is really just a long, skinny town square, blocked off at each end by metal posts. His mother would shop here with him and Owen when every square inch was covered in stalls selling sugared almonds and popcorn; homemade candles and bracelets that were meant to cure arthritis; ethnic clocks and paintings even toddler Owen thought were ugly.

There's nothing here now. It's a vast, empty space, with the now-familiar proliferation of weeds and abandoned-looking buildings lining either side, just like any other street.

Seth waits a moment before getting up from the bench.

He didn't create the fox. He *didn't*. It was just hidden there in the weeds, and he saw it, that was all. He's thought of plenty of things since he's been here, his parents and Owen, Gudmund and H and Monica, even his uncle when he saw the painting over the hearth, and none of *them* had suddenly appeared.

There were wild plants, and this seemed for all intents and purposes to be England, so why wouldn't there be foxes? Foxes were English. He remembers seeing them when he lived here, sloping across the street with their oddly adult air of detachment. So of course, there'd be foxes. Why not?

But foxes had to eat. Seth's eyes pore over the trees that grow from brick boxes up the High Street, looking for birds, maybe, or squirrels or rats. They must be there. If one fox was here, there had to be more animals, more *something*.

Didn't there? If he just didn't actually *create*–

"Hey," he says, stopping this line of thought but feeling unsatisfied.

"Hey," he says again, not sure why he's saying it, wanting to say it once more.

And louder this time.

"Hey!" he says, standing up.

"HEY!"

He shouts it again and again, his fists clenched, his throat raking from the effort. He keeps screaming until he's hoarse, until his voice actually breaks.

It's only then that he realizes his face is wet from more crying.

"Hey," he says, whispering it now.

No one answers.

Not a bird or a squirrel or the fox or her kits.

No one answers from any quarter.

He's alone.

He swallows against the pain in his throat and goes to see what he can find.

12

The stores along the High Street are all locked. The sun is brighter now, and Seth has to shield his eyes against the windows to see inside. Some–the doughnut shop, the Subway Sandwich, something called Topshop–seem to have been cleared out, just empty racks and barren shelves, packaging strewn across the floor, naked mannequins lined up against the wall.

But they're not all empty. The thrift store looks full, should he ever need a tea set and a bunch of moldy paperbacks, as does a place that seems to sell only wedding dresses, but he can't really see that as a practical option for an outfit, even in hell.

And then his heart quickens as he looks through the glass of the outdoor supply store next to it.

"No way," he says. "No *way*."

He can see backpacks inside and camping gear and who knows what else that might be insanely useful.

Suspiciously useful, he has a moment to think, but he pushes that thought away, too. There were outdoor stores all over the world. There just were, so why not here?

The glass door is locked, and he looks around for something to break it with, finding some loose bricks in one of the tree stands. He picks one up, but even in this empty, empty place, the prohibition against what he's about to do is so strong, all he does is toss the brick up and down in his hand a few times. He's played baseball and basketball in gym class, the first boring him nearly to death, the second being almost kind of fun in a run-around-and-shout kind of way that other people took seriously enough that it meant he didn't have to get too involved. But he knows he can at least *throw* something, even if not particularly skillfully or especially far.

But still. A brick through a store door.

He looks around again, and once again, he's alone.

"Here goes nothing," he whispers.

He rears back and throws it as hard as he can.

The shattering sound is loud enough to end the world. Seth instinctively ducks down, ready to make excuses that it wasn't him, that it was an accident–

But of course there's no one.

"Idiot," he says, smiling, embarrassed now. He stands again, the feeling of having *done* something, anything, making him actually swagger a little up to the now gaping door.

Where a flock of screeching darkness comes hurtling out past his head at blindingly fast speed. He falls to the ground, protecting his head with his hands, shouting in wordless terror–

And as quick as it came, it's passed, the world silent again except for his racing breath.

He looks up and sees the flock gathering itself into a panicked ball as it disappears over the roof of the shuttered-up bookstore.

Bats.

Bats.

He laughs to himself before getting up, kicking away the broken glass that still stands in the door, and crouching his way inside.

It's a cave of treasures.

He grabs a backpack off a display. Next to it, he finds a whole wall of flashlights, which excites him at first, but there are no batteries to be found anywhere. He takes a large one anyway, long and heavy enough to feel like a weapon even if it never produces light. He finds a bunch of dried-up food rations nearby, too; terrible-looking stuff, freeze-dried pot roast, soup with inflatable dried vegetables, that sort of thing, but it's better than nothing, and he also finds a little stack of butane camp stoves to cook it all on, hoping they won't blow up in his hands the first time he tries to use one.

The store seems more tightly sealed than his house, and there's less dust covering everything. A row of first-aid kits is practically clean, and he stuffs one in the backpack, then pauses. He takes another kit and opens it. It's got the usual: bandages, alcohol swabs, but there, right at the back, he finds a packet labeled CONDUCTIVE TAPE. He tears it open with his teeth. A bundle of bandages falls to the ground.

He doesn't even need to pick it up to see that the underside is covered in metallic foil.

He reads the empty packet again, but CONDUCTIVE TAPE is all it says, along with some pictorial instructions for how to stick it to your skin. Nothing to say what it's for or why you'd use it or why the hell you'd ever wrap so much of it around your body.

"Conductive tape," he says.

Like it's so obvious it doesn't *need* an explanation.

He leaves it there on the floor, not wanting to pick it up again, and heads for the clothes racks at the back of the store.

They're so full he laughs out loud. They've even got *underwear*. Granted, it's thermal-insulated so probably a little hot for summer, but he's out of the baggy sweatpants and pulling on a pair before he thinks to mind. The cool cleanness of them feels so good he almost has to sit down.

The rest of the clothes seem to be mainly for mountain-eering and hiking, but there are T-shirts and shorts and an expensive all-weather jacket that he takes. He exchanges the old sweatpants for what are essentially just more expensive sweatpants, but at least these ones don't make him look like a transient. There are also more kinds of socks than he can count.

It takes him a while to find shoes that fit, having to wade through an ammonia-smelling pile of bat guano to get into the stockroom and find a pair his size. But soon enough, he's fully equipped. He grabs up everything and heads out into the sunshine.

Where he's immediately drenched in sweat because it's far too hot to be wearing such heavy clothing.

For a moment, though, he doesn't mind. He just closes his eyes against the sun and takes it all in. He's not naked, he's not in dirty bandages, and he's not completely filthy with dust. He's wearing clean clothes and new shoes and for the first time since he died, he feels almost human.

13

The supermarket at the end of the High Street is deeper and darker than the rest of the stores, but through the glass frontage, Seth thinks he can still see shelves filled with *something*. He shifts the pack on his back and realizes, stupidly, that he's overloaded it with clothes and other supplies. No place to put any groceries. He sets it down and starts to take stuff out that he can come back for, but then something against a wall catches his eye.

That'll do.

It takes him nearly fifteen minutes to get a rusty shopping cart separated from the petrified row of them, but eventually it comes, its wheels even mostly turning if he forces them hard enough.

It's easier to throw a brick the second time, though once inside, the store is much darker than he thought. The ceiling is low, and the aisles block any view of what they might be hiding in their depths. He thinks of the bats again. And what if there was something larger in there than a fox? Did England have big predators? There were mountain lions and bears in the forests back home, but he couldn't remember a single dangerous thing anyone ever mentioned as living in England.

He listens to the silence.

Nothing. Nothing at all beyond his breathing. No hum of electricity, no sound of things rustling. Though, he supposes, the smashing of the doors could have silenced anything in here.

He waits. But still there's nothing.

He starts to push the unforgiving cart down the aisles.

The produce section is completely empty. The bays yawn open, with only a few shriveled husks of unidentifiable fruits and vegetables at the bottom, and as he goes from aisle to aisle, his hopes start to sink a little. The shelves do have stuff on them, but they've gone much the way of the things in the kitchen cabinets. Dusty old boxes that crumble upon touch, jars of once-red tomato sauce now blackened within, a section of egg cartons that have clearly been ripped apart by a hungry beast.

But he turns a corner and there's good news. Batteries, lots of them. Many are corroded but some are okay. It only takes a few tries before his big flashlight is working.

Torch, he thinks, shining it down a long dark aisle, seeing piles of flour scattered across the floor. *The English call this a torch.*

He balances the torch on the shopping cart and picks his way through the rest of the supermarket, finding some bottled water but not much else. Eventually, he realizes there's going to be nothing much of use anywhere—not the loaves of bread shrunk to nothing inside their wrappers, not the unplugged freezer chests filled with a black mold that smells like rancid olives, not the packages of cookies and crackers that are so much dust—nothing except the two aisles with most of the cans.

Again, many of them are rusted beyond use or so bulging with bacteria that Seth can practically hear it growing inside, but moving the torch up and down the shelves, he finds plenty that look normal, if dusty. He fills his cart with soups and pastas, with corn and peas, with even, he's delighted to find, custard. There are so many cans, in fact, he'd have to make several trips here to even make a dent in them.

So, enough to feed him. For a while.

For however long he might be here.

The darkness and silence of the supermarket, even with the comfortably heavy torch in his hand, suddenly feels like too much. Too oppressive, too heavy.

"Quit it," he tells himself. "You'll go crazy if you think like this."

But he puts his weight behind the cart and gets himself back out into the daylight.

He's tiring again, he can feel it, and the hunger is a real thing now, almost as bad as yesterday's thirst. He spies some green up around a corner from the market and remembers the little park there, sliding down a hill into a small valley with fountains and paths.

He pushes the cart, grunting at the effort, until he's at the top of the park. It's grown up like a jungle, unsurprisingly, but the basic shape is still there. There's even a little sandbox area nearby. It's about the only place here free of weeds.

"This'll do," he says, and lets his backpack fall to his feet.

He follows the directions on the camp stove, and five minutes later, there's enough butane left in the small canister to heat up a can of spaghetti he opened with a far-less-rusty can opener he also took from the store. It's only when the spaghetti is boiling that he realizes he didn't take any knives or forks. He clicks off the stove and has no choice but to wait for it to cool.

He takes a bottle of water from the cart and holds it up to the sun. It looks clear, clearer than the water from his tap anyway, but even though the seal is unbroken, the water is still half-evaporated away. He cracks it open, the bottle giving a little hiss as he does so. It smells all right, so he takes a drink and looks down at the park below him.

It's familiar, yes, despite the wildness, but what does familiar mean? he wonders. This place looks like a version of his childhood home stuck in time, but that doesn't mean it's actually the same place.

It *feels* real enough. Certainly to the touch, and definitely to the nose. But it's also a world that only seems to have him in it, so how real can it be? If this is just a dusty old memory that he's trapped in, maybe it isn't really even a place at all, maybe it's just what happens when your final dying seconds turn into an eternity. The place of the worst season of your life, frozen forever, decaying without ever really dying.

He takes another sip of water. Whatever *this* place might be, they'd never come all that much to the real version of the park. Sandbox and small play area aside, the steepness of the hill prevented it from being much fun. A big brick wall across the bottom of the main incline made even skateboarders avoid the challenge, so it must have been more a place for High Street workers to take a smoke break.

But there is the pond still, at the bottom, kidney-shaped but surprisingly clear-looking. He would have expected a film of algae across the top, but it actually looks cool and inviting on a hot summer day. There's a rock in the middle that was usually covered with ducks preening themselves. There aren't any today, but the sun is so bright, the day so clear and warm, that it somehow seems like ducks might swoop in at any moment.

He looks up, half thinking that his thoughts might create them. They don't.

He's hot in his over-warm hiking clothes, and the pond looks so inviting that he has a fleeting impulse to jump in, have a refreshing swim, have something even like a bath and just allow himself to float, suspended in water –

He stops.

Suspended in water, he thinks.

The terror of it, the sheer awful *terror* that never seemed to stop. Fear was bearable when you could see an end to it, but there was no end in sight out in those freezing waves, those pitiless fists of ocean that cared nothing for you, that tipped you over and down in a kind of callous blindness, filling your lungs, smashing you against rocks –

He reaches around to where his shoulder blade snapped. He can remember the pain of it, can remember the irrevocable *snap* of the bone breaking. He feels a little sick at the thought, even though his shoulder here, in this place, works fine.

Then he wonders where his body is.

In whatever world this isn't, out there where he died, where is he? He wonders if he's washed ashore yet. He wonders if they even know to look for him in the ocean or on the beach, because he wasn't supposed to be there, *no one* was supposed to be there at that time of year. Freezing winter on an angry, rocky coast? Why would anyone be *near* the water, much less *in* it?

Not unless they were forced.

Not unless someone forced them.

He feels another pain in his stomach, an unease at the memory of his last moments on the beach that makes him feel even sicker. He screws the cap back on the water bottle and forces himself to return to the spaghetti, now cooled enough to eat. He makes a mess of it, tipping it into his mouth and slopping it onto one of his new T-shirts, not caring much.

He wonders how his parents found out. Would he have been gone long enough to be missed before his body was found? Would they have been surprised by policemen showing up at the door, carrying their hats under their arms and asking to come in? Or would they have been worried by his absence, growing more worried by the hour, until it became clear something had gone wrong?

Or if time worked the same here as it did there – though the warm summer here and the freezing winter *there* put that into question, and he had no idea how long that first purgatorial bit on the path had lasted, but still—he might have only died late the day before yesterday or even early yesterday morning. It's possible they haven't even noticed yet. His parents might think he's at a friend's house for the weekend, and between Owen's clarinet lessons and his mum's running and his father's decision to start redoing the bathroom, they might still be unaware that he's gone at all.

They never had noticed him all that much. Not after what happened.

In fact, maybe, secretly, they'd have some guilty happiness that it wasn't *Owen* who had drowned. Maybe they'd be a little relieved that Seth was no longer a walking reminder of that summer before they moved. Maybe—

Seth sets down the empty can of spaghetti and wipes his mouth with his sleeve.

Then he wipes his eyes with his other sleeve.

But, he thinks, *it's possible to die before you die.*

There's no one walking through the park, no one in this world at all who can see him sitting on the edge of the sandbox, but he lowers his face down to his knees, as he can't help but weep once more.

14

"*I mean, for God's sake, just look at them*," Monica said as they lay on a hill out of the sight line of their cross-country coach, watching the cheerleaders practice on the football field. "*How can anyone's boobs be that perky without surgery?*"

"*It's the autumn chill in the air*," H said, ironically quoting something Mr. Edson, their English teacher, had said that morning. "*Makes everything firm up.*"

Monica slapped him upside the head.

"*Ow!*" H protested. "*What'd you do that for? You're the one who said to look at them!*"

"*I didn't mean you.*"

It was the second week of their senior year, early September. By mutual agreement, they'd taken a well-known shortcut on their running route, hiding in almost plain sight near the practice finish line, and giving themselves twenty minutes before they were expected back. Remarkably for this time of year, the sun was shining in a clear blue sky, though the wind coming in off the ocean gave the air an extra snap.

Days like this you could almost call beautiful, *Seth thought.*

"The chill firms them up?" Gudmund asked H, stretching back on the grass incline. "Is that why you have a permanent boner all autumn?"

"All year more like it," Monica mumbled.

"As long as you kids stay safe," Gudmund said.

Monica gave him a look. "Like I'm going to have his baby."

"Hey!" H said. "That's not nice."

"There they go again," Seth said.

They all looked back over the field, and sure enough, Boswell High's own blonde and brunette terrors were back at it. Though that wasn't fair, Seth thought. Most of them were actually pretty nice. They all watched, though, as Chiara Leithauser, one of the less nice ones, left the pack and started walking back toward the main school building.

"Where's she going?" Gudmund said.

"Forgot to give Principal Marshall his after-school hand job," H sniggered.

"Oh, please," Monica said. "Chiara's serious about that chastity shit. Won't even let Blake Woodrow put his hands on her bra."

Gudmund shrugged. "Good for her."

Monica laughed, but when he didn't reply, she scanned his face closely. "You mean that, don't you?"

Gudmund shrugged again. "At least she's got principles. What's wrong with that? Somebody's got to counterbalance all us amoral types."

"That's what we can tell Coach Goodall when he catches us," Seth said as they caught sight of the cross-country coach across the field, looking annoyed at his watch, wondering *why his senior runners were quite so overdue from their first long training run.*

"There's nothing wrong with anyone having principles," Monica said. "But there is something wrong with using them to beat four kinds of crap out of everybody else."

"They're only her opinions," Gudmund said. "You don't have to listen to them."

Monica's mouth opened to reply, and then it dropped open farther in amused astonishment. "You like her."

Gudmund put on an ostentatiously innocent face.

"You do!" Monica nearly shouted. "Jesus, Gudmund, that's like loving a concentration-camp guard!"

"I'm not saying I like her, don't be stupid," Gudmund said. "I'm just saying I could get her."

Seth looked over at him.

"Get her?" H asked. "You mean like—" and he made a thrusting motion with his hips that caused a horrified silence. "What?" he said as they all stared at him.

Monica shook her head. "Not in a million years. It's like she's got a limited lifetime supply of fun, and she isn't going to waste any of it on high school."

"Those are the easiest ones to get," Gudmund said. "All their morals are balanced way up high. One push knocks 'em right over."

Monica shook her head again, smiling at him, like she always did. "The shit you talk."

"You know what we should do?" H said, suddenly enthusiastic. "We should have like a bet, right? Where Gudmund has to sleep with Chiara Leithauser by like, spring break or

something? 'Cause you could totally do it, bro. Show her where the wild things are."

"From someone who can't even find a map to the wild things," Monica said.

"Hey!" H said to her, his voice low and aggrieved. "What did I say about telling them our business?"

Monica huffed and turned her back.

"What do you think, Sethy?" Gudmund said, trying to steer the moment away from an argument. "Think I should take that bet? Go for Chiara Leithauser?"

"What," Seth said, "and then secretly find out she's got a heart of gold and actually fall in love with her and then she dumps you when she finds out about the bet but you prove yourself to her by standing outside her house in the rain playing her your special song and on prom night you share a dance that reminds not just the school but the entire wounded world what love really means?"

He stopped because they were all looking at him.

"Damn, Seth," Monica said admiringly. "'The entire wounded world.' I'm putting that in my next paper for Edson."

Seth crossed his arms. "I'm just saying a bet over Gudmund having sex with Chiara Leithauser sounds like some piece of shit teenage movie none of us would watch in a million years."

"Truer words, never spoken," Gudmund said, standing up from the grass. "She doesn't deserve me, anyway."

"You're right," Monica said. "Dating the best-looking, richest, and most popular guy in school must be punishment enough."

H made a scoffing sound. "Blake Woodrow isn't that good-looking."

They all stared at him again. "I am so sick of you guys doing that!" he said. "Not everything I say is stupid. Blake Woodrow has a girl's haircut and the forehead of a caveman."

There was another pause before Monica nodded. "Yeah, okay, I'll give you that."

"And Gudmund could totally get her if he wanted," H said, getting up to join the rest of them.

"Thanks, man," Gudmund said. "From you that's almost a compliment."

"But you're not even going to try?" H said hopefully.

Monica hit him again. "That's enough. I may hate her, but she's not a prostitute. Quit talking about her like she's someone you can just take off a shelf." She looked at Gudmund. "Even you."

"I wasn't serious, you feminist," Gudmund said, smiling. "I only said it was possible. If I wanted to."

Monica stuck her tongue out at him before setting off across the field and onto the track, H on her heels, both of them trying to look as if they'd been running for the past half hour.

Gudmund glanced at Seth, who was watching him seriously. "You don't think I could?"

"Monica would be so jealous she'd probably choke to death," Seth said as they started running back across the field, too.

Gudmund shook his head. "Nah, Monica and I are like brother and sister."

"You flirt that much with your sister? She wants you so bad, it's like she's got a permanent toothache."

"Jeez, are you sure she's the jealous one, Sethy?" Gudmund punched Seth playfully on the shoulder. "Homo," he said.

But he said it with a grin.

They ran toward the now-shouting Coach Goodall and—

15

Seth snaps his head up.

The world is still the same. The sun still in the same place. The park still wild beneath him. It doesn't even feel like he dozed off.

He groans. Are they going to come every time he closes his eyes? All the things that are most painful in their different ways, whether because they're too bad or because they're too good?

Hell, he reminds himself. This is hell. Why *wouldn't* it suck?

He gathers his stuff and pushes the cart back toward the High Street, beginning to feel tired again.

"This is stupid," he says, sweating profusely under the insulated clothes, the backpack on his shoulders, and the weight of the cans in the cart. He stops by the doors of the supermarket, swaps the spaghetti-stained T-shirt for a fresh one, then unloads half the cans onto the ground to come back for later.

He wipes the sweat from his brow and takes another

drink of water. Nothing has moved down the High Street. The glass from where he broke into the outdoor store is still lying there, glinting in the sun. The bats have flown off to who knows where. It's all just weeds and silence.

Lots and lots and lots of silence.

He feels it again. A strangeness. A threat. Something not right with this place beyond all that's so obviously wrong.

He thinks again about the prison. It sits out there, unseen, like it's waiting for him. A huge, heavy thing, almost like it has a gravity all its own, almost like it's pulling at him to–

Maybe he'll take the food back to the house now.

Yeah, maybe that's what he'll do.

He grows more and more tired as he pushes the cart back down the main road, unreasonably so, like he's getting over being really sick. By the time he makes it to the sinkhole–the fox and her kits long gone–he feels like he's run a marathon and has to stop and take in more water.

He turns down his own street. The cart grows heavier as he approaches his front path, and as much as he doesn't feel like he should just leave it on the sidewalk, he's too tired to bring it all in just now. He takes his backpack, the torch, and a couple cans of food and heads into the house.

The door swings open again under his touch, and he holds up the torch, halfheartedly ready to swing it should he meet anyone who needs clobbering. The hallway is still shadowy, and the light from the torch guides his way in. As he heads down the hall, he thinks he might just heat up some custard next, if it's still good in these cans. He hasn't had custard since –

He freezes.

The torch has caught the stairs. It's the first time he's properly looked at them, the first time a proper *light* has been on them, and he sees –

Footprints.

In the dust coming down the stairs.

He's not alone. There's somebody else here.

He backs up so quickly his new pack catches the door, shutting it behind him, and for a moment he panics at being trapped inside with whoever it is. He scrambles around and gets the door open, running back down the front steps, dropping the cans of custard, looking behind him to ward off whoever might be there –

He stops by the shopping cart, panting heavily, holding the torch out like a club, shaking with adrenaline, ready to fight.

But there's no one.

No one comes running out after him. No one attacks him. No sound at all from inside the house.

"Hey!" he calls. "I know you're in there!" He grips the torch even tighter. "Who's there? Who is it?"

And again, nothing.

Well, of course, there's nothing. Because even if there was someone, why would they identify themselves?

Seth looks up and down the street, heart pounding, wondering what to do. All the terraced houses, with their doors

shut and their curtains pulled. Maybe *every* house was hiding someone. Maybe this place wasn't empty after all. Maybe
they were just waiting for him to –

He stops. Waiting for him to *what*?

This road, these houses. You couldn't have a world with
people in it and have this much stuff undisturbed. You just
couldn't. There were no other tracks in the dirt, no plants
broken, no paths cleared. People had to go out, and if they
didn't, they had to have stuff brought to them.

And nobody but Seth has come down this street for a
very long time.

He looks back at his front door, still open from where
he fled.

He waits. And waits.

Nothing changes. No sounds, no movement, not even
any animals. Just the bright-blue sky and plenty of sunshine
to make a mockery of his fear. Eventually, he starts to calm
down. All that was true is still true. Even in his day or two
(or whatever) here, he's seen nothing, not one thing to indicate anyone else.

Not yet, anyway.

But still he waits.

Until finally, the adrenaline starts to fade and his exhaustion returns. He *has* to lie down, that's all there is to it. He
has to eat, as well. He has to get over this weakness that's
making everything here so hard.

And the final truth of it is, where else is he going to go?

Keeping the torch in front of him, he walks slowly down
the path, up the steps, and to the doorway. He stops there,

shining the light down to the staircase. Now that he's looking, he can see the footprints pretty clearly, coming down from the very top step, some places with a clear print, some with the dust smeared like the person was stumbling down the stairs.

Down, but not back up. They're only facing one direction.

"Hello?" he calls again, more tentatively this time.

He edges inside, toward the doorway to the main room. Heart thumping loudly, he turns the corner, ready to club someone with the torch.

But there's no one there. Nothing's been disturbed, other than where he disturbed it, in either the living or dining areas, nothing moved in the cubbyhole, everything in the kitchen just as he left it. He even looks out the back, but it's the same, too, the metallic-sided bandages still lying in their heap, unmoved.

So the footprints could have been there for who knows how long, he thinks, relaxing a little. They could have been there since before he –

He stops.

Stumbling down the stairs, he thinks, the words suddenly making a kind of sense.

He goes back and stands over the bottom step. He's looking at prints of feet, *bare* feet, not shoes.

He kicks off a sneaker and peels off his new sock. He places his foot by the lowest, dusty footprint.

They match. Exactly.

• • •

85

He looks, for the first time, up the staircase. There's been something about the thought of going up there that's made him wary ever since he first arrived. That cramped attic bedroom he shared with Owen when they were small. Those nights he spent there, alone, wondering if they were ever going to get Owen back, and then wondering if he'd live when they did.

But he's already been up there, it seems.

He woke up on the path outside, and the reason was obviously because he'd *stumbled* down the stairs, in those horrible, confused moments after he died. He'd come down the hallway, out into sunlight, and collapsed onto the path.

Where he woke up.

But clearly not for the first time.

He shines the torch up the stairwell but doesn't see much past the bathroom door at the top of the landing, shut tight. The bathroom is over the kitchen, and the landing turns from it, to the office and his parents' bedroom over his head and the attic another floor up.

What was he doing up there?

And why had he run from it?

He shucks off the backpack, dropping it to the floor, then he places his foot on the bottom step, avoiding his footprint. He takes the step up. And then another. Holding the torch in front of him, he reaches the bathroom door. There's a sliver of light underneath it, so he opens it, shedding sunlight on the landing from the bathroom window.

The bathroom floor is the same terrible burgundy lino-leum that his mother always hated but his father had never gotten around to replacing. There are no footsteps across the dust of it, nothing's been disturbed here. He leaves the door open for light and turns back to the landing. Across which his bare, smeared footprints are walking toward him.

He takes care, without knowing precisely why, to avoid stepping in them as he crosses the landing. The office is first on his right, and he looks inside. It's exactly how he remembers it, down to the ancient filing cabinet his mother refused to allow to be shipped to America and a hilariously bulky old-fashioned computer. He flicks the light switch without much hope or success, but like the bathroom, nothing in the office has been disturbed.

There are no footprints coming from his parents' bedroom either, but Seth opens the door anyway. Inside, the bed is made, the floor is clear, the closet doors are shut tight. Seth goes to the curtains and looks down on the front walk. The shopping cart is still out there, unmoved, unbothered.

He heads back out to the landing and confirms what he suspected all along. His footsteps come down from the upper floor, from the attic where his bedroom was.

And they don't go back up.

However this started, it started up there.

He shines the torch up the second flight of stairs. There's only a small landing up top as the house narrows to the peak of its roof. The door to the attic bedroom is there.

It's open.

Seth can see a dim light coming through it, no doubt from the skylight that served as the bedroom's only window.

"Hello?" he says.

He starts up the second flight, torch still out in front of him. He can feel himself breathing harder. He keeps his eyes on the door as he climbs, stopping on the last step. The sweat on his palms is making the torch slippery in his hands.

Dammit, he thinks. *What am I so afraid of?*

He takes another deep breath, raises the torch until it's practically over his head, and leaps through the doorway and into his old bedroom, ready to fight, ready to be fought–

But there's no one there. Again.

It's just his old bedroom.

With one big difference.

There's a coffin sitting in the middle of the floor.

And it's open.

16

Everything else is the same.

The crescent-moon wallpaper is still on the walls, the water stain still spreading through it under the skylight in the sloped ceiling. He thinks he can even see the face patterned there that he always used to scare Owen with, telling him that if he didn't fall asleep in the next *one minute,* the face would eat him alive.

Their beds are there, too, unbelievably small against two corners, Owen's little more than a cot, really. There's the shelf with all their books, very roughly used but still favorites. Below it is their box of toys, piled with plastic action figures and cars and ray guns that shot out little more than loudness, and on Owen's bed is a whole array of stuffed toys – elephants, mostly, they were his favorite – every single one of which Seth knows is across the ocean in his brother's bedroom.

And taking up the middle of the room, on the floor in the space between the beds, sits the long black coffin, the lid opened like a giant clam.

• • •

The blind is down over the skylight, making the light vague in here, but Seth doesn't want to step past the coffin to raise it.

It takes him a moment to remember that the torch has other uses than as a weapon. He shines it on the coffin. He tries to remember if he's ever actually seen one in real life. He's never been to a funeral, not even in ninth grade when Tammy Fernandez had a seizure on school grounds. Nearly everyone went to that one, but Seth's parents weren't going to be swayed from an overnight trip to Seattle. "You didn't even *know* her," his mother had said, and that was that.

This coffin, though, is definitely shining back at him, and not like polished wood might. It shines back almost like the hood of a really expensive car. In fact, *exactly* like the hood of a really expensive car. It even seems to be made of a kind of black metal. The corners of it are rounded, too. Seth's curiosity gets the better of him, and he moves closer. It's strange, stranger than even at first glance. Sleek and expensive looking, almost futuristic, like something out of a movie.

Definitely a coffin, though, as the inside is all white cushions and pillows and –

"Holy shit," Seth says, under his breath.

Crisscrossing the bedding are streamers of metallic-sided tape.

They look as if they've been torn and pulled against, as if someone was tied down by them and that person struggled and pulled with all their might until they were free.

Free to stumble blindly down the stairs before collapsing on the path outside.

• • •

Seth stands there for a long, long time, not knowing what to think.

An ultra-modern coffin, big enough to hold the nearly fully-grown version of him, yet here in the room he left as a child.

But no coffin for Owen. And nothing for his parents.

Just him.

"Because I'm the only one who died," he whispers.

He puts his hand on the open lid. It's cool, just how he'd expect the metal to feel, but he's surprised to find a thin layer of dust on his hand when he takes it away. The inside, though, is almost a blazing white, even in the low light from the blind-covered window. It's cushioned with contoured pillows on all sides, vaguely in the shape of a person.

There are torn metallic bandages–"conductive tape"–all the way down the length of it. And tubes, too, big and small, some disappearing into the sides of the coffin, their stray ends having left stains here and there against the whiteness of the pillows.

He thinks of the abrasions along his body and how it hurt to pee.

Had the tubes been connected to *him*?

Why?

He crouches down, shining the torch underneath. The coffin sits on four short rounded legs, and from the very middle of the bottom of it, a small pipe goes straight down into the floor. Seth touches it. It seems slightly warmer than the rest of the coffin, like there might even be power running into it somehow, but he can't be sure.

He stands up again, hands on his hips.

"Seriously," he says loudly. "What the *hell*?"

He angrily flips up the blind on the skylight. Annoyed, he looks down again to the street below.

To all the houses that line it.

All the houses that look as closed up as this one.

"No," he whispers. "There can't be."

The next instant, he's running back down his stairs as fast as his exhaustion will let him.

17

He heaves a garden gnome as hard as he can at the front window of the house next door. It flies through with a satisfyingly loud smash. He clears away the remaining shards with the torch and climbs inside. He remembers nothing about the people who lived here when he was a child, except maybe they had a pair of older daughters. Or maybe just one.

Either way, there might have been people here who died.

Their front room is as dusty and untended as the one in his own house. The layout is more or less the same, and he walks quickly back through their dining room and kitchen, finding nothing out of the ordinary, just more dusty furniture.

He runs up the stairs. There's only one landing in this house – the owners not bothering to make the attic conversion – and Seth is in the first of the bedrooms before he can even stop to think.

It's a girl's room, probably a teenager. There are posters for singers Seth's distantly heard of, a bureau with some tidied-away makeup on it, a bed with a lavender bedspread, and an obviously much-loved and cried-upon Saint Bernard plush toy.

No coffin, though.

The story is the same in the master bedroom, a stuffier, overcramped version of his parents'. A bed, a chest of drawers, a closet full of clothes. Nothing that shouldn't be there.

He uses the torch to push open the access hatch to the attic. He has to leap a few times to catch the lower rung of the ladder, but it finally clatters down. He climbs up, shining the torch into the open space.

He falls back rapidly from a congregation of surprised pigeons, who coo in alarm and flap wildly out through a hole that's come open in the back roof. When it all calms down – and Seth wipes the pigeon mess from his hands, suddenly less happy to discover there are birds here – the torch and the light from the hole reveal only packed up boxes and broken appliances and more startled pigeons.

No coffins with anyone inside.

"All right," he says.

He tries the house across the street, for no particular reason taking the same garden gnome with him to smash through the front window.

"Jesus," Seth says as he climbs inside.

It's phenomenally messy. Newspapers piled in every corner, every clear space heaving with food wrappers, coffee cups, books, figurines, and dust, dust, dust. He picks his way through. Each room is the same. The kitchen looks like something from a hundred years ago, and even the staircase has things piled on each step.

But the rooms upstairs, including the attic, only have mess in them. No coffins.

The house next door to that one was clearly owned by an Indian family, with brightly colored cloths draped over the furniture and photographs of a bride and groom wearing traditional Hindu outfits.

But nothing else, no matter how many rooms he checks.

He begins to feel a harsh desperation as he heaves the same gnome through the house next door to that one. And the house next door to *that*.

Each one dusty. Each one empty.

He is growing more and more tired now, the exhaustion getting harder to fight. In what could be the tenth or twelfth house–he's lost count–he can't even throw the gnome hard enough to break the window anymore. It bounces to the ground, its eyes leering up at him.

Seth leans heavily against a white wooden fence. He is filthy again, covered in the dust of a dozen houses. A dozen *empty* houses. Not a single one even making space for a bafflingly shiny coffin in any of their rooms.

He wants to cry, mostly out of frustration, but he checks himself.

What has he found out, after all? What new thing has he learned?

Nothing that he didn't think before.

He's alone.

However he ended up here, wherever that coffin came from and however he ended up inside it, there aren't any for his father or his mother or his brother. There aren't any in the houses up and down the street. There are no signs of anyone in the sky or on the train tracks or on any of the roads.

He really is alone in whatever hell this is.

Completely and utterly alone.

It isn't, he thinks, as he trudges back toward his house, *the most unfamiliar feeling in the world.*

18

"Shit, Sethy," Gudmund said, his voice as serious as Seth had ever heard it. "And they blame you?"

"They say they don't."

Gudmund rolled up on one elbow in the bed. "But that's not what they think."

Seth shrugged in an offhand way that more or less answered the question.

Gudmund lightly placed the palm of his hand on Seth's bare stomach. "That blows," he said. He ran his hand up Seth's chest, then back again to his stomach and carrying on farther down, but gently, tenderly, not asking for anything more again just yet, merely letting Seth know how sorry he was through the touch of his hand.

"Seriously, though," Gudmund said, "what kind of country builds a prison next to people's houses?"

"It wasn't really next to our house," Seth said. "There was like a mile of fencing and guards before you got to the actual prison." He shrugged again. "It's gotta go somewhere."

"Yeah, like an island or the middle of a rock quarry. Not where people live."

"England's a crowded place. They have to have prisons."

"Still," Gudmund said, his hand back up to Seth's stomach, his index finger making a slow ring on the skin there. "It's pretty crazy."

Seth slapped the hand away. "That tickles."

Gudmund smiled and put his hand back in exactly the same spot. Seth let it stay there. Gudmund's parents had gone away again for the weekend, and a stinging October rain swarmed outside, spattering the windows and raking the roof. It was late, two or three in the morning. They'd been in bed for hours, talking, then very much not talking, then talking some more.

People knew that Seth was staying over at Gudmund's – Seth's parents, H and Monica – but no one knew about this. As far as Seth knew, no one even suspected. And that made it feel like the most private thing that could ever happen, like a whole secret universe all on its own.

A universe that Seth, as he did every time, wished he never had to leave.

"The question, of course," Gudmund said, idly pulling at the hair that tracked down from Seth's belly button, "is whether you blame you."

"No," Seth said, staring up at Gudmund's ceiling. "No, I don't."

"You sure about that?"

Seth laughed, quietly. "No."

"You were just a kid. You shouldn't have had to face that by yourself."

"I was old enough to know better."

"No, you weren't. Not to have that kind of responsibility."

"It's just me, Gudmund," Seth said, catching his eye. "You don't have to pretend to be all wise. I'm not a teacher."

Gudmund took the rebuke with grace and kissed Seth lightly on the shoulder. "I'm just saying, though. You were probably as weirdly self-contained back then as you are now, right?"

Seth nudged him playfully with his elbow, but didn't disagree.

"And so your parents were probably happy they had this strange little kid who acted like an adult," Gudmund continued. "And your mom thought—against her better judgment, we'll give her that—she thought it's only a few minutes and it's an emergency, so our little Sethy can watch our little Owen for just a second while I run back to the whatever—"

"The bank."

"Doesn't matter. It was her mistake. Not yours. But it's too big and awful to blame herself, so she blames you. She probably hates herself for it, but still. It's a bullshit bad deal, Sethy. Don't buy into it."

Seth said nothing, remembering that morning more clearly than he wanted to or ever usually tried to. His mother had delivered a curse word so loudly when they got back to the house that Owen had grabbed Seth's hand in alarm. It turned out she'd managed to walk all the way home without realizing she'd left a thousand pounds sitting on the counter at the bank.

Seth wondered now, for really the first time, what that money could have been for. Everything was done electronically, even then, cards and PINs and debits from your bank *account. What was she going to do with all that cash?*

"I'll be right back," she'd stressed. The bank wasn't the one on the High Street, it was off of it and up, a lesser bank his mother had never taken them to before on any other errand. "I'll be ten minutes tops. Don't touch anything and don't open the door to anyone."

She'd practically sprinted back down the hall to their front door, leaving Seth holding Owen's hand.

Ten minutes came and went, and Seth and Owen had only moved from their spot to sit down on the floor beside the dining-room table.

Which is when the man in the strange blue jumpsuit knocked on the kitchen window.

"I let him in," Seth said now. "She specifically said not to open the door to anyone, and I did."

"You were eight."

"I knew better."

"You *were* eight."

Seth said nothing. There was more to the story than just the opening of the door, but he couldn't tell even Gudmund that part. He could feel his throat straining, felt the pain rising up from his chest. He turned away and lay there on his side, shuddering a little at the effort of crying and trying not to.

Behind him, Gudmund didn't move. "I gotta tell ya, Sethy," he finally said. "You're crying and I don't really know how to handle that." He stroked Seth's arm a few times. "I really don't know what to do here."

"It's okay," Seth coughed. "It's okay. It's stupid."

"It's not stupid. It's just . . . I'm an idiot about these things. Wish I wasn't."

"Don't worry about it," Seth said. "Just the beer talking."

"Yeah," Gudmund said, agreeing even though they'd hardly had four bottles between them. "The beer."

They were quiet for a second, before Gudmund said, "I can think of a few things that might make you feel better." He pressed his body against Seth's, his stomach against Seth's back, reaching around to grab parts of Seth that responded with energy.

"That'll do," Gudmund said happily into Seth's ear. "But seriously, though, why does there even have to be a problem? He survived and they caught the guy and Owen's a nice kid."

"He's not the same, though," Seth said. "There are neurological problems. He's all . . . scattered now."

"Can you really tell that about a four-year-old? That he was one way before and a different way after?"

"Yeah," Seth said. "Yeah, you can."

"Are you sure, because–?"

"It's all right, Gudmund. You don't have to fix it. I'm just telling you, okay? That's all. I'm just saying it."

There was a long silence as he felt Gudmund's breath in his ear. He could tell Gudmund was thinking, working something out.

"You've never told anybody else, have you?" Gudmund asked.

"No," Seth said. "Who could I tell?"

He felt Gudmund hold him tighter in acknowledgment of the importance of the moment.

"It's nothing I can change, right?" Seth said. "But imagine there's this thing that always sits there in the room with you. And everyone knows it's there and no one will ever say a single goddamn word about it until it becomes like an extra person living in your house that you have to make room for. And if you bring it up, they pretend they don't know what you're talking about."

"My parents found the wrong gender of porn on my touchpad last year," Gudmund said. "Guess how many times they've talked about it with me since?"

Seth turned to look at him. "I never knew that. I'll bet they went ballistic."

"You'd have thought so, but it was just a phase, wasn't it? Nothing that churchgoing and pretending it never happened wouldn't make go away."

"Aren't they suspicious about me coming over all the time?"

"Nah," Gudmund said, grinning. "They think you're a good influence. I tend to play up your athletic abilities."

Seth laughed.

"So we've both got messed-up parents who just don't want to know," Gudmund said. "Though, I admit, yours are a bit worse."

"It's not anything, really, good or bad. It just is."

"It's enough of an anything to make you cry, Sethy," Gudmund said softly. "And that's not something that can be any good." He squeezed Seth again. "Not something I like to see anyway."

Seth didn't say anything, didn't feel like he could without his voice cracking just that second.

Gudmund let the silence linger for a moment, then he said, brightly, "At the very least, it made you guys move out here from England. And if you hadn't, I'd never have learned about this."

"Quit tugging on it," Seth said, laughing. "You know what a foreskin is."

"In theory," Gudmund said. "But to think that I used to have one of these and someone had the nerve to chop it off without even asking—"

"Stop that," Seth said, smacking Gudmund's hand away again, still laughing.

"You sure?" Gudmund moved an arm underneath Seth and pulled him back into a full embrace, nuzzling his neck.

"Hold on," Seth whispered suddenly.

Gudmund froze. "What?"

"Just that."

"Just what?" Gudmund asked, still frozen.

But how could Seth explain it? Just what?

Just Gudmund's arms around him, holding him there, holding him tightly and not letting him go. Holding him like it was the only place that could ever have existed.

Just that. Yes, just that.

"You're a mystery, you are," Gudmund whispered.

Seth felt Gudmund reach for something off the bed and turned to find Gudmund holding his phone up above them.

"I told you," Seth said, "I'm not taking any pictures of my—"

"Not what I want," Gudmund said, and he snapped a picture of the two of them from the shoulders up, just together, there on the bed.

"For me," Gudmund said. "Just for me."

He brought his face around to Seth's and kissed him on the mouth, taking another picture.

Then he put down the phone, pulled Seth even closer, and kissed him again.

19

Seth opens his eyes on the settee and can barely breathe from
the weight on his chest.

Oh, Jesus, he thinks. *Oh, no, please.*

Once more, it was so much bigger than a dream that he
puts his hands to his face to see if the scent of Gudmund's
body is still there. That it isn't—but that he can *remember*
the smell, of salt and wood and flesh and something intensely
private—makes the weight feel so much heavier.

"Shit," he says, his voice cracking as he sits up. "Shit,
shit, shit, shit, shit, shit." He leans forward into himself and
rocks slowly back and forth, trying to bear how bad it feels.

The *ache* of it. The ache of missing Gudmund is so great
he can barely stand it. Of missing how safe being with him
felt, how easy it was, how funny and relaxed. Of missing the
physical stuff, of course, but more than that, the intimacy,
the closeness. Of missing just being held like that, cared for.

Maybe loved.

But also the ache of missing something that was his own.
His own private, secret thing that belonged to no one else,
that was no part of the world of his parents or his brother or
even his other friends.

Gone.

Isn't dying once enough? he thinks. *Am I going to have to keep doing it?*

But then he thinks, *No. Because you can die before you're dead, too.*

Oh, yes, you can.

So why not after?

He had been with Gudmund again. And waking feels like death, like a death worse than drowning.

I can't take this, he thinks. *I can't take this.*

He's slept through the night again, it seems. The light around the blinds has the bluish tint of early dawn. He doesn't want to get up, feels like he can't, but the pressure on his bladder finally forces him up the stairs to the bathroom. Yesterday, after the episode of housebreaking and trying to avoid just exactly this kind of dream-filled sleep for as long as he could, he'd gotten the creaking pipes to work in the sink and shower. He'd then refilled the long dried-out toilet with glasses of water, and it had worked on the first flush, a victory that made him almost embarrassingly happy.

He goes to it now and does his morning business. Then he washes himself in the cold water of the shower, using the hardened block of dishwashing liquid from downstairs as a sticky bar of soap. He gasps as he sticks his face again and again into the brutal coldness of the water, trying to snap himself into wakefulness.

Snap him hopefully from the weight still pressing down on him, ready to crush him if he lets it.

He dries himself off with one of the new T-shirts and heads back down to the main room to put on a clean set of clothes. He'll need to get more of these, too, ones more suited to warm weather, and maybe some lanterns for nighttime. He needs more food as well. He'll unload the cart from outside and then refill it, taking more time to get better things.

Yes. That's what he'll do.

Keep moving, he tells himself again. *Don't stop. Don't stop to think.*

But he stands there for a minute, over the backpack of clothes, feeling the empty house around him, feeling the doorway to the kitchen and the farther door that leads outside onto the deck.

The same door that he'd opened for the man in the jumpsuit.

And the attic upstairs where he'd waited, by himself, on all those terrible, terrible evenings while the hunt for the man and Owen was on, all those evenings when his parents could barely bring themselves to look at him or each other, when his dad started taking the go-away pills he never quite gave up.

Seth hadn't told Gudmund everything, even when he could have, even when the chance was there for –

For what? Forgiveness? Absolution?

If he could have taken forgiveness from anyone, he could have taken it from Gudmund. He could have done it right then, and even now he isn't sure why he didn't.

He remembers being there, lying in bed with Gudmund, being held as close as it was possible to be, having shared a story he'd never told anyone besides his parents and the police.

His chest begins to ache again, dangerously so, and he says, "Right. *Right.*"

He heads outside to start bringing food in from the cart, trying as hard as he can not to cry again.

He makes three trips to the supermarket before the morning is through. It's mostly cans and the few bottles of water that look tolerable, but he's also found some sugar that's not too hard to chip chunks out of and some dried meats vacuum-packed in plastic that may not be too petrified to eat. He's found a couple bags of flour, too, though he doesn't really know what he might do with them.

He gathers a few camping lanterns from the outdoor store and finds some more clothes at a small Marks & Spencer around the corner from it. The shirts and shorts are boring enough to make him look like his father, but at least he's not having to wear snow gear in midsummer, which makes him wonder what will happen if he's still here for whatever passes for winter in hell.

When the sun's in the middle of the sky, he uses the camp stove to heat up more spaghetti. He does it at the same spot in the park where he ate yesterday, looking down the hill again at the grass and the crystal clear pond beyond.

He nearly drops the can when he sees a pair of ducks sunning themselves on the rock in the center of it. There's nothing special about them as ducks per se, just plain brown ones, squabbling quietly to each other.

But still. There they are.

"Hey!" Seth shouts down at them, without thinking. They fly off almost immediately, quacking in alarm. "Hey, come back!" he calls after them. "I brought you here. *I* did that!"

They disappear over some trees.

"Ah, well," he says, taking another bite of spaghetti. "It's not like I could shoot you for dinner."

He looks up. Could he? Well, he'd need a gun first, and he thinks immediately of the outdoor store –

And then he remembers this is England, or at least his mind's version of it. You couldn't buy a gun here anything like how easy it was in the U.S., where he could actually have got one at the local shopping mall, going to McDonald's before and seeing a movie after. His parents were appalled, and talked about it for years with joyous European indignation, while never allowing one in the house. The result being that Seth has barely seen a gun up close, much less shot one.

So that ruled out hunting, probably, at least in the short term. His can of spaghetti, though, is suddenly looking a lot less appetizing than a roast duck. Not that he'd know how to roast it. Or if you even could on a butane camp stove.

He sighs and takes another bite, using the spoon he remembered to bring this time. He's tired but not as tired as he was the day before. He wonders if he's finally catching up on the sleep you need when you first die, which, granted, must be an exhausting thing to happen. Probably the most exhausting thing that ever *could* happen.

He looks back down to the now-empty pond and notices something new. The tall grasses up and down the hill are swaying a bit in the breeze. More than a bit, actually. They're being blown by a wind Seth can now feel against his face. He looks up.

For the first time, there's something in the sky. Clouds. Great big puffy ones. Great big puffy *black* ones scurrying this way.

Seth can't believe his eyes. "It rains in hell?"

He barely makes it back to the house before the skies open up. The storm is a summer one, and Seth can still see blue sky on the horizon, so it won't last, but boy, does it pour. He watches it from the doorway of his house as it quickly soaks the dusty streets to mud and streaks dirt across the windows of the dead cars.

The smell is outrageously good. So clean and fresh, Seth can't help but step out into it, letting it drench his upturned face, squinting as the drops hit his eyes. The rain is surprisingly warm, and he suddenly gasps, "Idiot!" He races back inside to grab the hardened bar of dishwashing liquid. How much nicer would this be than the freezing cold shower he had this morning—

He jumps back out the front door, but the rain is already tapering away, blowing out of the neighborhood as quickly as it came.

"Damn," he says. The wind up high must be blowing something wicked because the rain clouds are leaving like they're being chased by a mob, out past the back of Seth's house and carrying on to–

Where?

Yeah, where *would* they be going?

How big *is* hell?

Big enough for weather, obviously. The sun is back out, the breeze dying down, and steam already rising as the mud dries back into dust on his street.

A street he's been up and down several times but not much beyond.

Maybe it's time to do some exploring, he thinks.

20

He feels tired again after the morning's exertions but resists taking a nap, dreading the vivid dreams even more after last night's. Instead, he packs the backpack with a few supplies and a bottle of water and heads out for a walk.

He takes a moment to decide which direction. To the left is all the High Street stuff he's seen several times already. Of course there are neighborhoods behind that, sprawling for miles before, if he remembers correctly, changing into farmland as they head east.

To the right is the train station.

I could walk all the way to London on that track, he thinks, and that's somehow vaguely cheering. What does it matter if he has no phone to show him maps and no Internet to look things up? If he follows the train tracks one way, he could walk all the way to London.

Not that he's going to. It's bloody miles.

He stops. Bloody. He actually thought "bloody miles." His parents didn't even say bloody anymore, American slang having almost thoroughly obliterated everything but his mum's insistence that he call her "mum."

"Bloody," he says, testing it out. "Bloody, bloody, bloody." He looks up. "Bloody sun."

It's shining down brightly again, even hotter than before, the mud almost already thoroughly dried. This certainly isn't the cold, damp English weather his parents always complained about. Nor is it really what he remembers from living here, though the memories of an eight-year-old about weather might not be the most reliable. But still. It's a lot hotter than he's been led to believe. With the steam rising from the ground, it's almost tropical. Which is a word no one ever used to describe England.

"Weird," he says, then he resettles his backpack and heads to the right, toward the train station.

The roads he crosses are the same as everywhere else, dusty and empty. He thinks it's going to be worth starting some kind of systematic look through the houses, a more thorough search through the ones whose windows he's already smashed and then spreading out across the neighborhood. Who knows what useful stuff could be found? More cans of food, maybe, tools and better clothes. Maybe one or more of them has a vegetable garden –

He stops in his tracks. *The allotments,* he thinks.

Of *course.* A whole huge field of private little gardens, tucked away behind a . . . what was it? He tries to remember. A sports center? Yes, he thinks that's what it was, a sports center on the other side of the train tracks, with a field of allotments behind it. Sure there'd be weeds, but there'd have to be edible things still growing there, right?

He quickens his step, remembering almost automatically

to turn up the long concrete stairway that runs between two apartment buildings–*blocks of flats,* he remembers. The English terms keep coming, and he wonders if his accent will return as well. Gudmund was always trying to make him "talk British," always wanting him to say–

He stops, the feelings of loss coming again, strong. Too strong.

Keep going, he thinks. *As long as you can.*

The stairway reaches a sidewalk that leads up to the train station, which rests on top of a little rise. He can see the station building now. To get to the allotments, he'll have to walk through it, cross the bridge between platforms, and go out the far side. He's almost feeling excited about it as he passes through the entrance, hopping over the ticket gates without a second thought, and up the short stairs to the first platform–

Where there's a train waiting.

It's a short one, just four cars, a commuter train meant to shunt people back and forth to the city up the tracks, and he half expects passengers to start emptying out the doors or for the train to start pulling slowly away from the platform.

It doesn't, of course. It just sits there, silent as a rock from the earth, covered in the dust of this place. There are weeds growing up all along the cracks of the platform and even some in the gutters along the train's roof. Like the cars on the streets outside, it hasn't moved in a long time.

"Hello?" he calls. He walks across the platform to look

in through a window, but it's mostly dark, the windows so badly dusted over they block out most of the afternoon sun. He pushes the open button on the closest door, but there's no power running through it and it stays firmly shut.

He looks down the length of the train. At the front, the door to the driver's compartment has come open. He walks to it, takes the torch out of the backpack and sticks his head inside the driver's compartment. There's only one seat behind the controls, which surprises him. He'd have thought there'd be two, like in airplanes. The screens on the dash are all either cracked or dusted over, dark without power.

There's a door inside to the rest of the train, and it's open, too. Seth steps up into the compartment and shines the light through the inner doorway, down the central aisle of the first car.

It smells. Animals have clearly been in here. There's a fug of urine and musk, and the dust on the linoleum floor of the aisle is disturbed and streaked in any number of unpleasant ways. He can imagine all kinds of foxes huddled under seats now, watching him with his torch, wondering what he'll do.

What he does is look around, almost overwhelmed with memories. The sun is bright enough for a dim light through the filthy windows, many of which are scratched with unintelligible graffiti, but there's enough to see the blue cross-hatch pattern on the cloth of the seats. He runs a hand down one, burring the fuzz with his fingertips.

The train. The *train*.

He hasn't been on a train since he left England. Not once. Americans on the west coast didn't take trains. They drove. Everywhere. This is literally the first time he's set foot on board a train since they crossed the ocean.

And everything the train had meant when he was young! Trips up to London and all the city had to offer a boy of six and seven and eight. The zoo, the Wheel, the wax museum, the other museums that were less interesting because they had no wax. Or down the other way, too, to the coast, with its castles on hills and the great big white cliffs that his mum wouldn't let him or Owen anywhere near. And the pebbly beaches. And the ferries to France.

Trains *always* went somewhere amazing when you were eight years old. They were a way out of the same houses and the same faces and the same shops. It seems embarrassing now, to have been so excited by a simple train journey that millions of people took every day, but Seth can feel a little smile spread across his face as he steps farther down the car, shining the torch on the overhead racks and the assort- ed blocks of seats, two here, three there, and at the back of the car, the little boxed door to the horrible train toilet that Owen, without fail, would need to use within five minutes of the train leaving the station in whatever direction.

Seth shakes his head. He'd almost forgotten trains existed. Looking at it now, he can't believe how exotic they seemed to him as a little boy.

Still, though, he thinks. *A train.*

Which is when the door to the bathroom crashes open and a monster comes roaring up the aisles straight for him.

21

Seth yells in terror and runs back down the aisle, risking a quick look back–

A huge, black *shape* hurtles toward him –

Screeching and roaring in what sounds like rage –

Two eyes staring back at him in unmistakable malevolence –

Seth flies into the train driver's compartment, slamming into the control panels, crying out at a pain in his hip. He scrambles over the driver's seat, and there's a terrible moment when the strap of his backpack gets caught, but gets loose as the shape comes smashing inside.

Seth leaps out the door of the train and takes off, tearing down the platform, dropping the torch and leaving it behind. He looks back again, just as the shape comes rocketing out of the compartment, sending the door swinging back and forth violently. The thing turns and comes after him.

Running a lot faster than Seth is.

"Shit!" he yells, pumping his arms and trying to remember his cross-country form, though that was for long distances, not for sprinting, and he's still not even remotely fully recovered from –

There's a squeal behind him.

(a squeal?)

As he turns up the steps to the bridge over to the other platform, he takes another look back.

The shape is the biggest, ugliest, dirtiest wild boar he's ever seen.

A wild boar? he thinks, charging up the stairs. *A wild BOAR is chasing me?*

The boar rages down the platform and up the steps behind him, and Seth can see it's got a pair of filthy, splintered-looking tusks that would happily tear the stomach right out of him.

"SHIT!" he screams again, running across the flat part of the bridge, but he's so tired, so weak still, that he's not going to outrun the boar. It's going to catch him before he reaches the stairs that go down the other side.

I'm going to be killed, he thinks, *by a PIG. In HELL.*

And the thought is so stupidly outrageous, so insanely angry-making, that he almost misses the chance to save himself.

The bridge is a corridor above the tracks, covered on both sides by square panels of frosted glass, broken by a metal guardrail at waist height. Right near the stairs at the other end of the bridge, two of the upper panels have fallen out in succession.

Leaving a space just big enough for someone his size to climb through.

The boar squeals again, barely five feet behind him, and he's not going to reach the windows, he's not going to reach them, he's not–

He leaps for them and can actually feel the boar slamming its head into the bottom of his feet as he jumps. The momentum nearly carries him all the way out, and there's an impossible few seconds where it seems like he's going to fall straight back down to tracks twenty feet below, but he catches the upright support between the windows, manages to get one foot on the metal strip, and—swinging his free arm and leg wildly into the air—keeps his balance by a whisker.

Just before he's nearly knocked off it again by the boar slamming into the wall at his feet.

"ALL RIGHT! ALL RIGHT!" he shouts, and there's nowhere to go but up. He grabs a gutter above him and pulls himself up to the roof of the bridge. The boar keeps slamming against the railing as Seth hooks a leg up and rolls himself, panting heavily, onto the roof, his backpack lurched uncomfortably beneath him.

He just lies there for a moment, desperately trying to catch his breath. The boar is still going at it, grunting and squealing and ramming its weight against the inside wall of the bridge, knocking out another glass panel, which tumbles to the tracks, smashing into a thousand pieces.

Seth leans back over the side and looks down at the boar, who snuffles angrily up to him. It's enormous, so much bigger and taller and wider than any normal pig, it almost seems like a cartoon. It's hairy, too, and blackened by a thick layer of dirt. It squeals loudly at him.

"What did I ever do to you?" Seth asks.

The boar squeals once more and starts re-attacking the bridge.

Seth rolls onto his back again, looking up into the sky above.

He thinks he can remember stories about them breaking free from boar farms and going feral, but he'd never thought they were actually *real*. Or even if he was remembering it right.

But, you know, once again, *hell,* he supposes.

He keeps lying there, waiting for his breath to return to normal and his heart to slow down. He scoots the backpack out from under himself and gets the bottle of water. Down below, he can at last hear the boar giving up. It snuffles and snorts, making a defiant last grunt, and he hears its amazingly heavy tread back across the bridge beneath him. He can see it come down the bottom of the stairs to the platform before it disappears behind the train, no doubt returning to whatever den it's made for itself in the train's toilet.

Seth laughs. And then louder.

"A boar," he says. "A *bloody* boar."

He drinks the water. He's looking out the way he came, and the view isn't bad. He stands, balancing on the slightly curved roof of the footbridge, and he can even see the top floors of the stores on the High Street. His own house is too low to see, but he can see the neighborhood leading down to it.

To the left, behind where his house is, is the start of the cleared areas that lead farther down to the prison.

He stares at them for a moment. The fences and walls are all still there, with some of the empty spaces between them actually free of all but the sparsest of weeds. He can't see the prison itself. It's down in a small valley and behind a row of thick trees and more barbed wire and brick.

But he knows it's there.

Just the presence of it strikes a weird chord through his stomach. Like it's watching him back. Watching to see what he'll do.

Waiting for him to come to it.

He turns away, thinking he'll see if he can find the allotments from here, find an easy way to get to them. He raises his hand to shield his view from the sun—

And sees that everything on the other side of the tracks—the sports center, the allotment fields, dozens upon dozens of streets and houses stretching to the horizon—has burnt to the ground.

22

The land slopes down on the other side of the train station, spreading out into the shallowest of valleys with barely perceptible rises several miles to either side. It stretches back and back, street upon street, toward Masons Hill – whose name Seth remembers now – the only real rise for miles around, a wooded lump on the landscape, with one sheer side that falls fifty feet to the road below, a place where youths were routinely rousted for dropping rocks on passing cars.

Everything between the train station and that distant hill is a blackened ruin.

Some blocks are nothing more than ash and rubble, others still have husks of brick, their roofs and doors gone. Even the roads have buckled and bent, in some places indistinguishable from the buildings they separated. There's a stretch of ground where Seth is pretty sure the sports center was, and he can see what looks like the remnants of a large square hole that could have been its swimming pool, now filled with charcoal and weeds.

Though not as many weeds as the streets behind him, he notices. And not as tall. There are weeds and grasses scattered through the rest of the burn, now that he thinks to look for them, but they're far scraggier than the ones on his own street, and some of them are just plain dead.

There's no sign at all of the field where the allotments were. He thinks he can see where his memory tells him it should be, but amongst all the ash and burnt timber and blasted concrete, it could also just be his imagination trying to make it be there.

The destruction stretches on for what must be miles, as far both to the left and right as he can see in the hazy sunshine. The fire – or whatever it was; destruction this big may have even been some kind of *bomb* – stretches all the way back to Masons Hill, stopping around its base much like it stops at the rise where the train station sits. Too much bare concrete to cross to actually burn down the station.

He's looking at a wasteland. One that seems as if it might as well go on forever.

It explains all the dust, is the first thing Seth really thinks. The layers upon layers of it, covering nearly everything in the streets behind him. It's not just dust – it's ash, dropped from whatever this huge fire was and never cleaned away.

It's also, in a way that troubles him more than he can really say, a *past* event. Something caught fire, or was blown up, or whatever happened, and then that fire raged out of control before burning itself out some time later, taking most of this neighborhood with it.

Which means that there was a time *before* the fire, a time *of* the fire, and a time *after* the fire.

He thinks he's being foolish feeling troubled about this – there are weeds growing everywhere, obviously, and the food didn't rot in an instant – but those things were just time, time passing in stillness.

But a fire is an event. A fire *happens*.

And if there was an event, then there was also a *was* for it to happen in.

"When, though?" Seth says to himself, shielding his eyes from the sun and scanning up and down the ruins.

Then he turns back to his own neighborhood on the other side of the tracks.

What if the fire had happened over there rather than here? What if his own house had burnt down, not all these empty ones of strangers?

Would he have woken up at all?

On the other hand, he thinks, *is this my mind trying to tell me something?*

Because the blackened ground feels like a barrier, doesn't it? Feels like a place where hell stops. He's gone out exploring and reached an area that might as well have a sign on it saying, DO NOT PASS.

The world, *this* world, suddenly feels a whole lot smaller.

He suddenly doesn't feel much like exploring anymore today. Silently, he drops his backpack through the window of the bridge and climbs down after it. He heads back down the stairs, taking care to tread quietly when he retrieves the torch so as not to disturb that huge, alien boar from the train.

Then he shoves his hands in his pockets, hunches his shoulders down, and trudges on home.

23

"What do you expect us to say?" his mother asked, angrily. "How do you expect us to react?"

His father sighed and crossed his legs in the other chair facing Seth. They were in the kitchen, which—and Seth wondered if they even knew they did this—was where they always had their serious talks with him, especially when he got in trouble.

He was in here way more often than Owen ever was.

"It's not that we,"—his father looked up in the air, trying to find the right word—"mind, Seth—"

"What are you talking about?" his mother snapped. "Of course we goddamn well mind."

"Candace—"

"Oh, I can already see the thinking here. You're already halfway to forgiving him—"

"Why is it a question of forgiveness?"

"Always just this laissez-faire approach, not giving a damn as long as you can do your precious little projects. It's no wonder he's acted like an idiot."

"I'm not an idiot," Seth said, arms crossed, looking down at his sneakers.

"What the hell do you call it?" his mother demanded. "How exactly is this situation not one big idiotic catastrophe for you? You know what they're like here—"

"Candace, that's enough," his father said, more strongly now. His mother made a sign with her hands of sarcastic surrender, then stared firmly at the ceiling. His father turned to look at him, and Seth realized with a shock how rare it was for his father to look him straight in the eye. It was like having a statue suddenly ask you for directions.

The thing was, though, Seth couldn't even say that his mother was wrong. About it being a catastrophe. The pictures had been found. Had gotten out. From an impossible source, one they'd never expected. But then they'd been stupid to ever think they wouldn't, because how could you keep anything for yourself in this uselessly connected world?

"Seth," his father continued, "what we're trying to say is that . . ." He paused again, thinking how to phrase it. For a horrible moment, Seth thought he was going to have to help him along, say the words for him. "Whatever . . . choices you make, we're still your mum and dad, and we'll still love you. No matter what."

There was a long, uncomfortable silence at this.

No matter what, Seth thought, but didn't say. "No matter what" had happened eight years ago. It had come and gone, and it turned out it hadn't been true then, either.

"But this . . ."—his father sighed again—" . . . situation you've got yourself into—"

"I knew we couldn't trust that boy," his mother said,

shaking her head. "I knew he was bad news from the moment I met him. Right down to his stupid name—"

"Don't talk about him that way," Seth said, quietly but the anger in his voice shocked both his parents into silence. He'd only been able to see Gudmund today for just enough time to tell him, to warn him, before Gudmund's parents had thrown Seth out of their house. "Don't you ever talk about him in any way, ever again."

His mother's mouth dropped open. "How dare you speak to me like that? How DARE you think you can—"

"Candace—" his father said, trying to stop her as she rose from her chair.

"You can't possibly think you're going to see him again."

"Just try and stop me," Seth said, his eyes burning.

"Enough!" his father shouted. "Both of you!"

There was a moment of stand-off as Seth and his mother locked eyes, but she eventually sat back down.

"Seth," his father said, "I'd like you to think about maybe taking some antidepressants, or even something stronger—"

His mother let out a cry of exasperation. "That's your answer to this? Disappear into oblivion like you do? Maybe you can both do silent DIY projects for the rest of your lives."

"I'm just saying," his father tried again, "Seth is obviously struggling with something—"

"He's not struggling with anything. He's crying for attention. Can't bear that his little brother needs more care than he does, so he goes and does something like this." She shook her head. "Well, you're only hurting yourself, Seth. You're the one who's going to have to go to school next week, not us."

Seth felt a twisting in his gut. She'd nailed exactly what had been worrying him.

"You don't have to go if you don't want to," his father said. "Not until this blows over. Or we can change schools—"

His mother gave another exasperated gasp.

"I don't want to change schools," Seth said. "And I'm not going to stop seeing Gudmund."

"I don't even want to hear his name," his mother said.

His father looked pained. "Seth, don't you think you might be a little young to be taking decisions this enormous? To be doing these . . . things with . . ." He trailed off again, not quite able to say "another boy."

"And all this when you know how much we've got to deal with for Owen right now," his mother said.

Seth rolled his eyes. "You always have to deal with Owen. That's what your whole stupid life is. Dealing With Owen."

His mother's face hardened. "You have the gall to say that? You, of all people?"

"What's that supposed to mean?" Seth spat back at her. "'Of all people'?"

"All we're saying," his father said, talking loudly over them both, "is that you could have come to us. You can come to us with anything."

And there was another long silence that none of them bothered to fill, as perhaps they all wondered if that was true.

Seth looked down at his feet again. "What's wrong with Owen now?" he asked, unable to stop himself from putting all his anger into the last word.

His mother's answer was to rise quickly to her feet and leave the kitchen. They heard her stomping upstairs, heading straight for Owen's room, heard him start an excited explanation about the new video game he'd gotten at Christmas last week.

Seth looked at his father in confusion. "What's she so mad about? How does any of this hurt her?"

His father frowned, but not at Seth. "It's not entirely you. Your brother's scans came back."

"The ones because of his eyes?"

Owen's eyes had started a strange twitching a few weeks back. He could see something when it was directly in front of him, like his computer games or his clarinet, but walking anywhere had become a wild hazard of knocking things over or simply falling all the way down to the ground. He'd given himself four bloody noses in the past ten days.

"The neurological damage," his father said. "From . . . from before."

Seth looked away, almost automatically.

"It was either going to get worse or better as he grew," his father said.

"And it's got worse."

His father nodded. "And will continue to do so."

"So what happens now?"

"Surgery," his father said. "And cognitive therapy. Almost every day."

Seth looked back up. "I thought you said we couldn't afford that."

"We can't. Insurance only covers so much. Your mum's

129

going to have to go back to work to help with the costs and it's going to eat badly into our savings. We've got rough times ahead, Seth."

Seth's mind was reeling, for his brother, for their money troubles, for the fact, he was ashamed to think, that he had college tuition payments starting in the fall that were going to need some of those very savings and if they weren't there—

"So, this whole thing with you and your friend?" his father said. "Not the best timing in the world."

Laughter rang down the staircase. They turned to look, even though there was nothing to see. Seth's mother and Owen, sharing something between the two of them, just like they always did.

"When is it ever good timing?" Seth asked.

His father patted him on the shoulder. "I'm sorry, son," he said. "I really am."

But when Seth turned back around, his father had broken eye contact.

24

It's raining again the next morning when Seth wakes, though
it takes him a few minutes to notice because of how the
dream is still ringing through him.

He lies motionless on the settee. He still hasn't slept in
any of the beds upstairs; his own in the attic is far too small
for him now, even if he wanted to use it, which he doesn't,
and sleeping in his parents' bed just feels too weird, so he's
stayed on this dusty couch, under the terrified eye of the
horse above the mantelpiece.

Dreaming.

The weight in his chest has grown heavier, almost too
heavy to move.

The greatest thing with Gudmund had been the secrecy
of it all. When they were together like that, they had been
their own private universe, bounded just by themselves, a
population of two. They were the world, and the world was
them. And no one deserved to know, not his mum and dad,
not his friends, no one, not then, not yet.

Not because it was wrong–because it definitely wasn't
that–but because it was *his*. The one thing that was entirely his.

And then the world found out, his *parents* found out.

Those two photos Gudmund took, painfully innocent compared to what some of the boys at school sent their girlfriends, but so private, so something that no one else should have seen, that Seth burns even now with anger and humiliation.

His mother had been right. Going back to school had been a nightmare. The whole world changed in an instant, collapsed to a place where Seth almost didn't even live. After Christmas vacation was over and he'd stepped back onto school grounds, there had been only him and everyone else. Far away. Beyond reach. The school tried to clamp down on the worst of the abuse, but they couldn't catch it all. And the whispers were everywhere; his phone vibrated constantly, even throughout the night, with jeering texts. Nor did he dare look on any social networking, where the picture – and accompanying comments – seemed to be everywhere. His private universe exposed to the egged-on scorn of all.

But he couldn't leave. Gudmund was still out of school while his parents decided what to do about him. And Seth had to be there, for whenever he came back. He had to bear it, alone.

"Self-contained," Gudmund had described him, but what that really meant was that it felt like he'd had a private burden to shoulder for as long as he could remember, and maybe not all of it even to do with what happened to Owen. Worse, it had been accompanied by an equally hard lifelong yearning, a feeling that there had to be more, more than just all this weight.

Because if there wasn't, what was the point?

That had been the other great thing about Gudmund since that surprising spring night at the end of junior year when they had become more than just friends. It was suddenly as if, for the briefest of moments, the burden had been lifted, like there was no gravity at all, like he had finally set down the heavy load he'd been carrying—

He knows he should stop this thinking, knows he should get moving, keep himself occupied with simply surviving this place, but he feels like he's at the bottom of a well, with sunshine and life and escape all miles away, no one to hear him, even if he could call for help.

He's felt like this before.

He lies there, listening to the rain, for a long, long time.

Eventually, biology again forces him to get up. He has a pee, then stands at his front door. The rain pours, rivulets coursing everywhere through the mud. He wonders for a moment why it doesn't just wash away, but he sees that the street is slowly becoming a stagnant flood, great ponds forming at blocked drains, everything swirling together in a muddy mess.

It's nearly as warm as it was yesterday, so he gets the block of dishwashing liquid, leaves his clothes in a heap, and uses the rain as a shower right there on the front path.

He lathers himself up, making a soapy mop of his buzzed-off hair, then closes his eyes and lifts his face to the rain to let it all rinse off. Almost idly, he tries to see if playing with himself will have any results, but the weight on his chest is too heavy, the memories of everything too much. He gives up and just crosses his arms, letting the soap slowly wash off him, the suds slopping down to the brown water gathering on the footpath.

Have I done this? he thinks, pulling his arms tighter around himself. *Have I brought this rain? Have I made this place even more miserable?*

He stands there, motionless, until he begins to shiver.

The rain isn't that warm after all.

It rains all through the day, the flooding on the street getting bad down at one end, but most of it near his house draining slowly into the sinkhole before it gets too deep. He hopes the fox and her kits are all right.

He heats up a can of potato soup. While it cooks, he looks out to the back garden, watching the rain come down on the deck and the now-soaking pile of bandages. The sky is a uniform gray, impossible to separate out any individual cloud, just solid rain from horizon to horizon, however far away those horizons might be. When the soup is hot, he takes two mouthfuls before losing his appetite and leaving the rest by the switched-off camp stove.

There's no television, of course. No computer. No electronic games. For lack of anything better, he takes a book from the bookcase. It's one of his father's, one Seth has already read part of years ago, sneaking it from the shelf in America when his father wasn't looking. It was far too old for him at the time and, he smiles wryly, is probably too old for him *now*. There's large quantities of good-spirited sex, metaphors that run on just for the hell of it, and plenty of philosophical musing about immortality. There's also a satyr who features heavily, which Seth remembers was the thing that got him caught. He'd asked his father about "satire," having heard *that* word said out loud and assuming it was the one he was reading. After a lengthy, baffled explanation, his father had said, "Why on earth are you asking?" and that had been the end of that reading adventure. He remembers now that he'd never actually been able to sneak it off the shelf again to find out what happened in the end.

So he reads on the settee, letting the rain continue and the day pass outside. At some point in the afternoon, he grows too hungry not to notice and heats up a can of hot dogs, eating half and leaving the rest beside the cold can of potato soup. When dusk comes, he lights one of the lanterns he took from the outdoor store, sending stark shadows around the room but illuminating enough to see the pages.

He forgets about dinner.

A book, he thinks at one point, rubbing his eyes, tired from so much focused reading. *It's a world all on its own, too.* He looks at the cover again. A satyr playing pan pipes, far more innocent-looking than what it got up to in the story. *A world made of words,* Seth thinks, *where you live for a while.*

"And then it's over," he says. He's only got about fifty pages left; he can finally find out what happens in the end.

And then he'll leave that world forever.

He folds down a corner to mark his place and sets the book on the coffee table.

• • •

It's fully dark now, and he realizes he's never seen this place at night. He picks up the lantern and stands in the front doorway again, keeping out of the rain, which seems lighter now but still steady.

He's amazed at the unyielding blackness. Not a single other light is shining back at him, not a streetlight or porchlight or even that glow that's always on the horizon from the gathered lights of a city.

Here, there's nothing. Nothing but darkness.

He flicks off the lantern, and for a moment, the world disappears completely. He stands there, breathing into it, listening to the rain. Slowly, slowly, his eyes begin to adjust to a dim light, which can only be the moon behind the clouds. The neighborhood starts to resolve itself into house fronts and gardens, the mud now swirled in rivers and deltas on the sidewalk and street.

Nothing stirring, nothing moving.

And then, suddenly, a break in the clouds, shining starlight that's faint but like the blowing of a trumpet compared to the darkness. Because it's so dark, Seth can see more stars in the small rip in the sky than he thinks he's ever seen in the whole expanse of it. The break widens, shining more, and Seth can't quite figure out the strange streak of faint white he's seeing across it, as if someone's spilled –

Milk.

The Milky Way.

"Holy shit," he whispers.

He's seeing the actual Milky Way streaked across the sky. The whole of his entire galaxy, right there in front of him. Billions and billions of stars. Billions and billions of *worlds*. All of them, all those seemingly endless possibilities, not fictional, but *real,* out there, existing, right now. There is so much more out there than just the world he knows, so much more than his tiny Washington town, so much more than even London. Or England. Or *hell,* for that matter.

So much more that he'll never see. So much more that he'll never get to. So much that he can only glimpse enough of to know that it's forever beyond his reach.

The clouds close up again. The Milky Way vanishes.

25

It's late, later than he's ever stayed up here. He's feeling tired, but he doesn't want to sleep. He doesn't think he can take another memory or dream or whatever. They've grown increasingly painful, and he knows, without wanting to think about it too closely, that there's worse to come.

He flicks the lantern on again as he goes back inside. He pauses for a moment, wondering what to do, then, on a whim, heads up the staircase. He's not interested in the attic–the thought of the coffin up there, in the blackness of the unlit night, freaks him out more than a little–but there's the office, isn't there? His mum's, mainly–his dad had one at the college–but with all the family files.

He sets the lantern on the desk and, without much hope, tries the computer. Of course nothing happens. The huge tower unit and the hilariously non-flat monitor–he can't remember the last time he saw one of those–stay as inert and dark as they were before.

He looks through some of the papers scattered on the desktop, coughing a little at the raised dust. It's mostly old bills, but there are a few scraps of paper, some with what he instantly, almost shockingly, recognizes as his mother's handwriting.

DCI Rashadi? he reads on one. He remembers the name, though he hasn't heard it in eight years. The policewoman who stayed with them during the hunt for Owen, the one who was so kind when she gently repeated questions of Seth. Below her name, there's a phone number with *Masons Hill* and *police dogs* written under it, which is less familiar. There weren't any searches in that part of town, Seth doesn't think. Owen was found in an abandoned warehouse. An anonymous tip had come in, the source of which was never traced, but the police had found Owen and the prisoner –

The prisoner –

The prisoner.

Seth can't remember the prisoner's name.

He reads the notes again. *DCI Rashadi* makes sense, as does another page with the names of *PC Hightower* and *PC Ellis,* who were the first officers to arrive after his mother's frantic phone call.

And they were hunting for –

Seth frowns. How could he possibly have forgotten the name of the man who took Owen? The name of the man from whom Owen had barely escaped with his life? The name of the man now rotting forever in England's highest security prison because of a multitude of crimes, not just breaking out of jail and kidnapping Owen?

"What the hell?" Seth whispers.

He can't remember it. At *all*. It's like there's a pure blank spot in his memory. Everything around it is still there. He'll never forget the man's face, for one thing, or the prison jumpsuit.

Or the things he said.

But his name.

His name, his name, his name.

Forgetting it is *impossible*. He'd heard it over and over and over again as the manhunt went on. He'd even said it in that dream with Gudmund –

Hadn't he?

But it's not there. It's just not there, no matter how much he pursues it.

He reaches for the top drawer of the filing cabinet. There has to be something in there, clippings of the man's arrest or official police statements or –

He stops with his hand on the drawer handle. There's a picture frame face down on top of the filing cabinet. Dust has gathered on the back of it, but even as Seth lifts it up into the lantern light, he knows what it is.

There they all are. Him, his mother and father, and Owen, with – of all people – Mickey freaking *Mouse*. Seth smiles at it. He can't help himself. They'd taken the train to Disneyland Paris. The sixteen-year-old part of him would like to scoff and say that the trip was stupid and that the park was only for little kids and the rides were lame and nothing at all like the roller coasters he ended up going on in America –

But that wasn't how it had been. It had been bloody brilliant. And that was it exactly, *bloody* brilliant. From their lives before anything changed. From their lives when anything had seemed possible.

From their lives before Owen had disappeared for three

and a half days with the convicted killer whose name refuses to surface in Seth's head. Three and a half days of policemen and policewomen—though it was usually policewomen, like Officer Rashadi—sitting in their house every hour that Owen was gone, trying to reassure his parents even when such a thing was clearly impossible. His mother was alternately rageful and scarily calm. His father spoke in a slur brought on by the medication he'd been given after he'd been unable to stop crying on the first day.

Neither of them spoke to Seth much. In fact—he tries to remember—they might not have spoken to him at all.

He'd spoken far more to Officer Rashadi. She was small, with her hair pulled back behind a cloth, but something in her manner had immediately silenced his mum's demands and his father's anguished crying within five minutes of her walking through the door. Seth had liked the way she didn't talk to him in a funny adults-for-kids type voice, liked how it sounded as if every word she said was true.

With the lightest of touches, she'd questioned him again and again about what had happened, saying that if he could remember anything more, no matter how small or stupid, he should tell her because who knew what might help his brother?

"The man had a scar on his hand," Seth had said the fourth or fifth time they talked. He'd made a circle with his thumb and forefinger to show her how big the scar was.

"Yes," Officer Rashadi said, not writing it down in her notebook. "He had a tattoo removed."

"Is that important?" Seth asked. "Or is it stupid?"

141

She'd just smiled at him, her front two teeth slightly crooked but bright as moonlight.

He remembers all of that now but can't remember the name of the man they were talking about, as if that information has somehow been erased from his memory altogether.

He looks down at the photo again. Owen and Mickey are in the middle, Owen smiling so wide it looks physically painful, and his mum and dad on either side, grinning with slight embarrassment but also, he can see, having a great time in spite of themselves.

And there's Seth, smiling, too, looking at Mickey a little more shyly and keeping his distance–he remembers being freaked *way* the hell out by the giant brightness of the suit and the grin that never changed and the weird *silence* of Mickey in person, though he supposes it would have been even weirder if Mickey spoke French.

In the photo, there's a little gap between him and his family, but he's not going to put too much emphasis on that. Just an accident of photography, where he'd probably stepped back from Mickey just as it was taken.

Because he's still smiling. He still is.

He doesn't know what's to come, Seth thinks, putting the picture back on top of the filing cabinet.

He doesn't look back at it as he leaves the office and shuts the door behind him.

26

He spends the time until dawn keeping himself active so he doesn't fall asleep. He digs himself deep into a new book – the one about the satyr still sitting there unfinished on the coffee table – and when he's in danger of nodding off, he gets up and paces the room. He fixes himself a can of spaghetti, but again eats only half before setting it beside the unfinished soup and hot dogs from earlier.

Dawn comes with a slight let up in the rain. It's now more mist than anything, but still coming down, muddy water swirling everywhere outside.

Seth starts to feel weirdly hyper from the lack of sleep, and he thinks that what he'd most like to do is go for a run. Cross-country season was long over when he drowned, and he'd only been able to get in a few runs in the bad weather they'd had over the winter.

His mum had kept up her running, though, almost out of spite. The worse the weather, the better she liked it. She'd come back soaking wet, her breath making clouds in the air. "*Jesus*, that's good," she'd growl, panting heavily just inside the doorway, swigging her bottle of water.

It had been years since she'd asked Seth to join her.

Not that he would have said yes.

Well, maybe. Probably not. But maybe.

But he misses it, the running. Trapped in this house, he misses it more than ever. Misses the rhythm of it, the way his breathing eventually just slotted into place, the way the world kind of fell *toward* him, like he was standing still and the whole planet was turning underneath him instead.

It was solitude, but it was solitude that wasn't lonely. Solitude that could sort things out. And he hadn't had that in ages.

No wonder everything had gotten so screwed up by the end of that winter.

He looks again out the front window. The mist is still there, the world still gray.

"Next time the sun's out," he says, "I'm running."

He's stuck inside through the day and into the evening. The clocks in the house, of course, are all stopped, so he can only guess how quickly time is passing.

More than anything, he doesn't want to sleep. He tries stupid things to keep himself awake. Singing at the top of his lungs. Attempting to perfect a handstand. Trying to remember all fifty states (he gets up to forty-seven, goes absolutely crazy trying to remember Vermont, gives up).

He gets colder as the night draws in again. He lights every lantern and makes his way upstairs to his parents' bedroom to steal more blankets. He wraps them around himself and paces up and down the main room, trying to think of something, anything, to keep his mind occupied, to stave off both sleep and boredom.

And loneliness.

He stops in the middle of the main room, the blankets wrapped around him like robes.

The loneliness. In his accumulating exhaustion, the terrible loneliness of this place swamps him, just like the waves he drowned in.

No one here. No one at all besides him. *No one.*

Forever.

"Shit," he says under his breath, starting to pace faster than ever. "Oh shit, oh shit, oh shit."

He feels like he's underwater again, fighting for breath. His throat chokes shut, just like it did as he was forced under yet another freezing wave. *Fight it,* he thinks, panicking. *Fight it. Oh shit, oh shit—*

He stops in the middle of the floor, only dimly aware that he's letting out a slight moan. He even raises his head, like he's reaching for air that's getting farther and farther away.

"I can't take this," he whispers into the shadowy darkness above him. "I can't take this. Not forever. Please—"

He flexes and unflexes his hands, pulling at the blankets that suddenly feel like they're suffocating him, dragging him farther down. He lets them drop to the floor.

I can't hold it back, he thinks. *Please, I can't hold it back—*

And then he sees in the lantern lights that the blankets have swept the dust away in a pattern on the floor as he paced. The polished floorboards are actually glinting back at him slightly.

He nudges a bunched-up blanket with his foot, leaving a stripe of clean floor beneath it. He pushes it farther along the floor to the wall, wiping away more dust. He picks up the blanket. The underside is filthy, so he folds it to a cleaner side and pushes it along the wall to the hearth.

He looks back. A big stripe of the floor is now relatively clean.

He folds the blanket again and follows the wall around the room, then the floor around the settees, folding and refolding as necessary until he cleans almost the entire floor. He tosses the dirty blanket into the middle of the kitchen and picks up another, folding it into a square and wiping down the dining-room table, coughing some at the dust he churns up, but once again, the surface mostly shines back at him.

He wets the corner of a smaller blanket in the sink and scrubs away the heavier dirt on the dining table before moving to the inert television. Every time a blanket gets too dirty, he piles it in the kitchen and gets another. Soon enough, he's upstairs in the linen cupboard, taking out painfully stiff towels and sheets and using them to wipe down the hearth and windowsills.

A kind of ecstatic trance overtakes him, his mind on nothing but his actions, which are manic, focused, seemingly unstoppable now that he's set them in motion. He cleans off the bookcase shelves, the slats in the doors to the cubbyhole, the chairs around the dining-room table. He accidentally breaks a bulb in the overhead light as he tries to rid them of cobwebs, but he just wraps the glass in a blanket and adds it to the pile.

He wipes away the remaining dust from the mirror hanging

over the settee. Dirt still clings to the glass, so he picks up one of his wetted rags and presses harder on the mirror, scrubbing away in repeated motions, trying to get it clean.

"Come on," he says, hardly aware that he's speaking aloud. "Come *on*."

He steps back for a second from the effort and stands there panting. He raises his arm to go back to it—

And in the lantern light, he sees himself.

Sees his too-skinny face, his short cropped hair, sees the dark whiskers sprouting below his nose and under his chin, though not so much on his cheeks, where he's despaired of ever being able to grow a beard.

Sees his eyes. Sees how they're the eyes of someone being hunted. Or haunted.

And in the mirror, he sees the room behind him. A hundred times more livable than it was before he started on this frenzy, a frenzy he can't really explain to himself.

But there it is. A clean or at least clean*er* room. He's even cleared the dust from the terrible, terrible painting of the dying horse. He looks at it now in reflection, its eyes wild, its tongue like a spike of terror.

And he remembers.

This cleaning. This straightening out of things. This frenzy of order.

He's done it before. To his own bedroom back in America.

"No," he says. "Oh, no."

It was the last thing he did before he left his house.

The last thing he did before he went down to the beach.

The last thing he did before he died.

27

"Don't you think I hate it, too?" Gudmund whispered fiercely. "Don't you think it's the last thing I want?"

"But you can't," Seth said. "You can't just . . ."

He couldn't say it. Couldn't even say the word.

Leave.

Gudmund looked back nervously at his house from the driver's seat of his car. Lights were on downstairs, and Seth knew Gudmund's parents were up. They could discover he was gone at any moment.

Seth crossed his arms tightly against the cold. "Gudmund–"

"I finish out the year at Bethel Academy or they don't pay for college, Sethy," Gudmund practically pleaded. "They're that freaked out about it." He frowned, angry. "We can't all have crazy liberal European parents–"

"They're not that crazy liberal. They'll barely even look at me now."

"They barely looked at you before," Gudmund said. Then he turned to Seth. "Sorry, you know what I mean."

Seth said nothing.

"It doesn't have to be forever," Gudmund said. "We'll meet up in college. We'll find a way so that no one–"

But Seth was shaking his head.

"What?" Gudmund asked.

"I'm going to have to go to my dad's college," Seth said, still not looking up.

Gudmund made a surprised move in the driver's seat. "What? But you said–"

"Owen's therapy is costing them a fortune. If I want college at all, it has to be on the faculty family rate where my dad teaches."

Gudmund's mouth opened in shock. This hadn't been their plan. Not at all. They were both going to go to the same college, both going to share a dorm room.

Both going to be hundreds of miles away from home.

"Oh, Seth–"

"You can't go," Seth said, shaking his head. "You can't go now."

"Seth, I have to–"

"You can't." Seth's voice was breaking now, and he fought to control it. "Please."

Gudmund put a hand on his shoulder. Seth jerked away from it, even though the feel of it was what he wanted more than the world.

"Seth," Gudmund said. "It'll be okay."

"How?"

"This isn't our whole lives. It isn't even close. It's high school, Sethy. It's not meant to last forever. For a goddamn good reason."

"It's been–" Seth said to the windshield. "Since New Year, since you weren't there, it's been–"

He stopped. He couldn't tell Gudmund how bad it had been. The worst time of his life. School had been nearly unbearable, and sometimes he'd gone whole days without actually speaking to anyone. There were a few people, girls mostly, who tried to tell him they thought what was happening to him was unfair, but all that did was serve to remind him that he'd gone from having three good friends to having none. Gudmund had been pulled out of school by his parents. H was hanging out with a different crowd and not speaking to him.

And Monica.

He couldn't even think about Monica.

"It's a few more months," Gudmund said. "Hang in there. You'll make it through."

"Not *without you*."

"Seth, please don't say stuff like that. I can't take it when you say stuff like that."

"You're everything I've got, Gudmund," Seth said quietly. "You're it. I don't have anything else."

"Don't say that!" Gudmund said. "I can't be anyone's everything. Not even yours. I'm going out of my mind with all this. I can't stand the fact that I have to go away. I want to kill someone! But I can take it if I know you're out there, surviving, getting through it. This won't be forever. There's a future. There really is. We'll find a way, Seth. Seth?"

Seth looked at him, and he could now see what he hadn't seen before. Gudmund was already gone, had already put his mind into Bethel Academy, sixty-five miles away, that he was already living in a future at UW or WSU, which were even farther, and maybe that future included Seth somehow, maybe that future really did have a place for the two of them—

But Seth was only *here*. He wasn't in that future. He was only in this unimaginable present.

And he didn't see how he'd ever get from here to there.

"There's more than this, Sethy," Gudmund said. "This sucks beyond belief, but there's more. We just have to get there."

"We just have to get there," Seth said, his voice barely above a whisper.

"That's right." Gudmund touched Seth's shoulder again. "Hang in there, please. We'll make it. I promise you."

They both jumped at the sound of a door slamming. "Gudmund!" Gudmund's father shouted from the porch, loud enough to wake the neighbors. "You'd better answer me, boy!"

Gudmund rolled down his window. "I'm here!" he shouted back. "I needed some fresh air."

"Do you think I'm an idiot?" His father squinted into the darkness where Seth and Gudmund were parked. "You get back in here. Now!"

Gudmund turned back to Seth. "We'll e-mail. We'll talk on the phone. We won't lose contact, I promise."

He lunged forward and kissed Seth hard, one last time, the smell of him filling Seth's nose, the bulk of his body rocking Seth back in the seat, the squeeze of his hands around Seth's torso—

And then he was gone, sliding out the door, hurrying back into the glow of the porchlight, arguing with his father on the way.

Seth watched him go.

And as Gudmund disappeared behind another slamming door, Seth felt his own doors closing.

The doors of the present, shutting all around him, locking him inside.

Forever.

28

It takes Seth a moment to realize he's on the floor. He doesn't remember lying down, but he's cramped and stiff, like he's been there for hours.

He sits up. He feels lighter.

Like he's almost empty.

The weight from the dream feels like it's in the room somewhere, and he's distantly aware of it, but of himself, he feels—

Nothing. He feels nothing.

He gets to his feet. The sleep has returned some of his strength. He flexes his hands, rolls his neck, stretches.

Then he sees that small beams of sun are pouring through the cracks in the blinds.

The rain has stopped. The sun is back out.

And he promised himself a run, didn't he?

Keeping his mind clear, he changes into a pair of shorts and one of the new T-shirts. His sneakers aren't proper running shoes, but they'll do. He debates whether to take one of the bottles of water but decides to leave it behind.

He skips breakfast. He's barely eaten in the last day and a half, but there's a purpose in his chest that feels like it's feeding him.

It's the same purpose he felt when he went down to the beach.

He lets the thought slide through his head and out the other side.

There is nothing this morning.

Nothing at all.

Nothing but running.

He goes to the front door. He doesn't shut it behind him.

He runs.

It was cold, possibly below freezing when he left his house that afternoon, having meticulously cleaned his room without really knowing why, without somehow even really being aware of doing it, just getting everything in its right place, neat and tidy and final, so nothing was left undone.

His mother had taken Owen to therapy and his father was working in the kitchen. Seth walked down the stairs to the living room. His eyes caught that horrible painting by his uncle, the horse, in terror, in agony, but stilled, forever, watching him go, watching as he closed the front door behind him.

It was a good half hour walk to the beach, the sky threatening snow but not delivering. The sea that day wasn't as monstrous as it often was in winter. The waves were shallower, but still reaching, still grabbing. The beach as rocky as ever.

He stood there for a moment, then he started to take off his shoes.

• • •

Seth runs toward the train station, leaving footprints in the drying mud, his legs creaking and groaning from lack of this kind of use. He turns up the stairs between the blocks of flats, heading to the station.

His first sweat is on, the drops stinging his eyes as they drip from his forehead. The sun is blazing down. His breathing is heavy.

He runs.

And as he runs, he remembers.

He runs faster, as if he might escape it.

There was sand there, between the rocks, and he stood on a little patch of it to remove first one shoe and then the other. He set them carefully together, then he sat on a rock to take off his socks, folding them and tucking them deep inside his shoes.

He felt . . . not quite calm, calm wasn't the right word, but there were moments, moments when he wasn't focused on the precise folding of his socks when he felt almost faint with relief.

Relief because at last, at last, at last.

At last, there didn't have to be anymore, didn't have to be anymore burden, anymore weight to carry.

He took a moment to try and shake off the tightening in his chest.

He breathed.

• • •

Seth leaps over the ticket barrier at the train station and pounds up the steps to the platform. He doesn't look at the train as he heads for the bridge over the tracks. He hears nothing from the boar, no doubt sleeping away a hot day in the confines of its den.

Up the steps, across the bridge, and down the other side.

He took off his jacket, because that seemed right, too. He was only wearing a T-shirt underneath, and the wind stung his bare arms. He shivered more as he folded up his coat and placed it on his shoes.

He felt present there, but also separate at the same time, as if he was watching himself from a height, looking down on a shoeless, coatless boy, staring at the sea.

Like he was waiting.

But for what?

Whatever it was, it never come.

And then, "I'm ready," he whispered to himself.

He found, to his surprise, with a sudden upsurge of grief that nearly knocked him flat, that he was telling the truth.

He was ready.

He began walking toward the sea.

He leaps over the gate at the other side of the train station and out the far exit. He pounds down the incline toward the first main road, wincing at the strain on his feet, but his muscles seem to be awakening, returning to the memory of themselves, returning to the memory of running –

He takes the first running steps into the destroyed neighborhood.

Everything around him is dead.

The cold of the water was shocking, brutally so, even in those first steps, and he couldn't keep himself from gasping. A wave of gooseflesh marched up his arms, the thin black hairs standing almost vertical. It felt for a moment as if he had already started to drown ankle-deep in five inches of water.

He knew then that if the water didn't get him, the cold would.

He forced himself to take another step.

And another.

It's so quiet, all he can hear are his footfalls and his breathing. In this first street, everything's been flattened, so there's only blackened ground reaching out on either side. He kicks up clumps of ash into the air, some of it drying now in the sun and making a trailing cloud.

He turns his gaze forward again.

Toward Masons Hill.

His feet – almost blue with cold – went numb as they stepped from rock to rock. Each new shock as he waded in deeper was like a knife slicing into him, but he pressed on. The water reached his knees, his thighs, darkening his jeans to black. There was a long shallows, but he knew it deepened suddenly a little farther out to depths that had to be swum. He also knew there was a current, one that would take an unsuspecting swimmer and smash them into the rocks that loomed down the beach.

He was so cold now that it felt as if his skin had been dipped in acid. A larger wave splashed across his T-shirt, and he couldn't help but call out. He was shaking uncontrollably and had to force himself to keep moving forward.

Another wave came, larger than the last and he almost lost his balance. Another followed that. He wouldn't be able to stand for much longer, his feet and toes gripping hard on the submerged rocks, the tide pulling forward and back. He readied himself to let go, to plunge in, to begin the swim out into the farther cold, out into the terrible, terrible freedom that awaited.

He was here. He had made it this far. There was so very little distance left to go, and he was the one who had brought himself here.

It was almost over. He was almost there.

He had never, not once in his life, felt this powerful.

Down another street, the concrete frames of some houses are still standing, though burnt through, inside and out. Not just houses, but storefronts and larger structures, too.

All blackened, all empty, all dead.

His throat is burning, and he thinks he should have brought water. But the thought is fleeting and he lets it go.

Masons Hill remains firmly on the horizon, and that's all he needs.

He feels empty. Emptied of everything.

He could run forever.

He feels powerful.

Then a wave, larger than any before, engulfed him, plunging him under the freezing water. The cold was so fierce it was like an electric shock, sending his body into a painful spasm. He was afloat, twisting underwater, narrowly avoiding cracking his skull on an outcropping.

Coughing, spluttering, he broke the surface as another wave crashed down. He surged up again, his feet scrambling for purchase, but the undertow was already pulling him out fast. He spat out seawater and was thrust under by another wave.

(He fought; despite everything, he was fighting–)

The cold was so enormous it was like a living thing. In an impossibly short time, he was unable to make his muscles work properly, and though he could still see the empty shore in the seconds he had above water, it receded farther and farther into the distance, the current pushing him toward the rocks.

It was too late.

There was no going back.

(He felt himself fighting anyway–)

• • •

Seth picks up his speed, his breath starting to come in raking gasps, pushing the memories away, not letting them take root.

I'll make it, he thinks. *I'll make it to the hill. Not far now.*

Another street, and another street more, empty buildings all around, reaching up like tombstones, his breath getting louder in his lungs, his legs growing weaker.

I'll make it. I'll run up to the top –

Here is the boy, running.

Here was the boy, drowning.

In those last moments, it wasn't the water that had finally done for him; it was the cold. It had bled all the energy from his body and contracted his muscles into a painful uselessness, no matter how much he fought to keep himself above the surface –

(And he did fight in the end, he did –)

He was strong, and young, nearly seventeen, but the wintry waves kept coming, each one seemingly larger than the last. They spun him round, toppled him over, forcing him deeper down and down.

He doesn't think about his final destination as he runs, not in words. There is only intention. There is only a lightness.

The lightness of it all being over. The lightness of letting it all go.

· · ·

Then, without warning, the game the sea seemed to have been playing, the cruel game of keeping him just alive enough to think he might make it, that game seemed to be over.

The current surged, slamming him into the killingly hard rocks. His right shoulder blade snapped in two so loudly he could hear the crack, *even underwater, even in this rush of tide. The mindless intensity of the pain was so great he called out, his mouth instantly filling with freezing, briny seawater. He coughed against it, but only dragged more into his lungs. He curved into the pain of his shoulder, blinded by it, paralyzed by its intensity. He was unable to even try and swim now, unable to brace himself as the waves turned him over once more.*

Please, was all he thought. Just the one word, echoing through his head.

Please.

Please, he thinks—

There is the sheer drop on one side of Masons Hill. He can see it in the distance.

Fifty feet down to concrete below—

Please—

The current gripped him a final time. It reared back as if to throw him, and it dashed him headfirst into the rocks. He slammed into them with the full, furious weight of an angry ocean behind him.

But it didn't make him free.
    He woke up here.
    Here where there is nothing.
    Nothing but a loneliness more awful than what he'd left.
    One that is no longer bearable –

He is nearly there. One last turn. One more long street, and he'll reach the base of the hill.
    He turns a corner –

And in the distance, far down the road in front of him, he sees a black van.
    And it's moving.

29

He stops so suddenly he falls, burying his hands in inches of ash.

A van.

A van that's driving away from him.

A van that's being *driven*.

It's going slowly, heading off into the distance, kicking up a low cloud of ash behind it, but there it is, solid as the world.

There's someone else in hell.

Seth staggers upright, waving his arms over his head before he can even think if it's a good idea or not.

"Wait!" he shouts. "WAIT!"

And almost immediately, the van stops. It's far enough away that it shimmers in the heat rising from the drying ash, but it definitely stops.

It definitely heard him.

Seth watches, his heart racing, his lungs laboring for air.

The door to the van opens.

And a pair of hands slap themselves over Seth's mouth from behind and drag him off his feet.

PART 2

PART 2

30

The hands bend Seth back so far he can hardly keep his balance. He tries to fight but finds himself so weakened – by lack of food and sleep, by the running, by the sheer weight on his chest – that all he can do is stumble backward, trying not to fall –

Despite how strangely small the hands seem –

They're pulling him off the street, toward the shell of a collapsed structure that may once have been several stories high but is now a place of broken concrete walls and surprisingly dark shadows.

Someone might do anything to him if they got him inside there.

He drops his weight to the ground, falling to the ash-covered pavement and taking his attacker with him.

"Ow!" a voice shouts, and Seth rolls back, fists up, ready to fight whoever it is that's suddenly materialized out of seeming thin air –

But it's just a boy.

• • •

He can't be more than eleven or twelve and is a good foot shorter than Seth. No wonder it felt so awkward; it was like a monkey hanging on to a giraffe.

"No!" the boy whispers in obvious panic. "We have to get off the street!"

He's already rising, looking past Seth down to the van. Seth turns, too. In the shimmering heat, he isn't sure whether he can see a figure, standing next to it—

The boy grabs Seth's T-shirt. "Come! You must!"

Seth smacks his hands away. "Get off me!"

"No, you *must*," says the boy, and Seth notices he speaks with an accent, maybe eastern European. Behind him, Seth can see a bike discarded in the ash at the front of the burnt-out building. The boy turns and calls, "Regine!"

A tall, heavyset black girl, much closer to Seth's age, maybe even older, emerges from the shadows of the building, pedaling her own bike. Seth can see past her to a band of sunlight at the back which must be the opening they rode through. Clearly out of breath, the girl glares at Seth. "Jesus *Christ,* you run fast."

"Who are you?" Seth demands. "What the hell—"

"We have to go!" the boy insists, pointing down the road. "The Driver!"

They all look. The door to the van has shut. The van is moving again, turning around in a circle.

So that it can come back this way.

The girl jumps off her bike, her face newly terrified. "Tommy! Hide!" she shouts. The boy takes the bike from her, grabs his own, and drags them into the darkness of the

168

structure. The girl takes two fistfuls of Seth's shirt, trying to pull him there, too.

She's *much* stronger than the boy.

"Get your hands off me," Seth says, struggling.

She brings her face close to his. "If you don't hide with us *right now,* you're going to die."

"She is not lying!" the boy says, popping up from behind a low wall in the structure, worry all over his face. "Please come!" He disappears behind the wall again, which seems to conceal a small, impromptu cave made out of fallen concrete slabs. He pulls the bikes in after him.

The girl is still yanking on Seth's shirt, so hard it's starting to tear. He resists her and looks down the road again. The van has made its way through the circle. It's starting back down the road after them.

What the hell? he thinks. *Seriously, what the hell?*

The girl makes a frightened yelp, lets him go, and flees into the structure.

And that's what makes Seth finally move. Her fear.

He runs after her into the darkness.

The shadows inside are so deep and black, Seth goes sun-blind for a minute.

"Quickly!" the girl says, pulling him down after her, over the low wall and into the small alcove, made even smaller by the boy and the bikes. Seth takes a moment to wonder why *he* never thought of finding a bike.

"This is ridiculous," he says. "It'll see us—"

"It'll think we followed our tracks back out," the girl says, "if we're lucky."

"And if we're not lucky?"

She holds up her finger to stop him.

And he can hear it now, too.

The engine of the van. Almost here.

The boy lets out a whimper. "It is coming."

The boy and the girl press back farther into the blackness of the little alcove, which now seems pathetically small to protect all three of them, tight against the bikes, sweating, panting, trying not to make a sound.

The van stops outside. Seth hears the door opening.

An arm moves across his chest. The boy, reaching for the girl. She takes the boy's hand and holds it tightly.

No one breathes.

Seth hears footsteps, crunching across the ash. One person, Seth thinks, just one pair of feet.

And then he sees it, stepping into the shadows of the structure.

Impossibly in this heat, every inch of its skin is covered, fingertip to neck, in a black, synthetic-seeming material, almost like a wetsuit. Its face is hidden by a sleek helmet with features molded for nose and chin, but completely blank otherwise, just a smooth, metallic blackness.

Like the coffin on the top floor of Seth's house.

Seth hears a slight breath at his right. In the shadows, the boy has his eyes squeezed shut and his lips are moving furiously, like he's reciting a prayer.

The figure stops almost directly at their feet, its side

turned to them. It only has to look in the right place, it only has to bend down and take one farther glance—

It steps past the alcove, out of Seth's line of sight. He feels the girl exhale, but she holds her breath again as it walks back the other way. It stops once more, looking at the disturbances in the ash, disturbances that Seth is sure will lead it right to them. In its hand, Seth sees it's holding an ominous black baton, one that looks for all the world like a serious, serious weapon.

The figure—the Driver, the boy called it—is inexplicably terrifying. It's got a man's shape, but something about the blackness of its clothes, something about the way it holds its body—

Isn't quite human, Seth thinks.

There is no mercy in it, that's what it is. Nothing to appeal to. It might kill you, like the girl said, but it would do so without you ever being able to convince it not to and without you ever knowing why you were dying.

It steps toward their alcove.

Seth feels the boy's hand grip the girl's more tightly across his chest—

But the Driver stops. It's motionless for a second, then it steps back, walking quickly out of sight. Seth hears the door to the van slam, hears the engine rev, hears the van drive off.

"Thanks be to God," the boy whispers.

After waiting another moment to be sure it's gone, they crawl out of the alcove. The boy and the girl stand in the slanted sunlight, the boy looking sheepish, the girl defiant.

"Who are you?" Seth asks. "And what the hell was *that*?"

They look at him for a moment. Then the boy's face scrunches up with tears. The girl rolls her eyes, but she opens her arms. The boy falls into her, grabbing on to her tightly, weeping into her embrace.

31

"Who *are* you?" Seth asks again, still staring. "What's going on?"

"He's kind of emotional," the girl says, holding the boy. "I think it might be a Polish thing."

"That's not what I meant."

"I know that's not what you meant." She lets go of the boy, whose chin is still wobbling. "We're good, Tommy. We're good."

"Safe?" the boy asks.

The girl shrugs. "As safe as we can be."

She's English, Seth notices, and her eyes are tired and baggy, her clothes that same combination of brand new and ash-covered as his own. She's quite tall, taller than Seth, and her hair is pulled tight across her scalp by a clip at the back of her head. As for the boy, he's so short it's almost comical. Seth notes, too, the way his hair is that same spectacularly messy pile that Owen always wore. For a moment, he feels an unexpectedly deep pang for his brother.

"I'm Regine," the girl says. "This is Tomasz." She pronounces the names Ray-zheen and Toh-mawsh. Both she and the boy look at Seth expectantly.

"Seth," he says. "Seth Wearing."

"You're American," Regine says. "That's a surprise."

"How do you know he is American?" Tomasz asks her.

"The accent."

Tomasz smiles bashfully. "I still cannot tell. You all sound the same to me."

"I was born in England," Seth says, his confusion growing again. "I was born *here*. Wherever the hell here is."

The girl starts pulling the bikes out of the alcove. "You'll have to ride with him," she says to Tomasz. Tomasz groans loudly but takes a bike from her. "Come on," the girl says to Seth. "We really can't hang around."

"You expect me to come with you?" he says.

"We don't have time to fight about this. You can come with us or not—"

"Regine!" Tomasz says, shocked.

"—but if you stay here, the Driver will find you and you really will die."

Seth doesn't answer. He doesn't know *what* to answer. The girl stares back at him, and he sees her looking at his running clothes, his lack of water, sees her considering the *way* he was running, furiously, with purpose. She glances behind him, out to the landscape.

Out to Masons Hill.

It's close, so close he could dash out of here right this second and run up it—

But that intention is less clear now. That feeling of release

174

is gone, for the moment. The feeling that would have driven him up to the top.

To the edge of the sheer cliff.

They stopped him. In the nick of time.

And he considers this, too.

A boy and a girl, appearing from nowhere, stopping him just before he started up the hill, just before he met the black van.

Which also appeared from nowhere.

Did he call them into being? Did he make them arrive?

Just in time?

But Tomasz and Regine. Preposterous names, foreign, even here.

And the van. And the Driver.

What was that all about?

"Are you real?" Seth asks, quietly, almost to himself.

The boy nods a sympathetic yes.

"I know why you're asking," the girl says. "But the only answer I've got is that we're as real as you are."

Seth breathes. "What if that doesn't feel very real at the moment?"

The girl looks like she's understood him. "We really do need to get going. Are you coming?"

He doesn't know what he should do, what he's *supposed* to do. But there's no denying that—whoever they are, whatever they might be—they feel a lot safer than the Driver does.

Seth says, "All right."

32

Regine's bike kicks up clumps of drying ash as she goes. Seth rides a short distance behind her, standing on the pedals. Tomasz sits on the bicycle seat, gripping Seth around the torso tighter than is probably necessary.

"I do not like this," Tomasz says. "You are too tall. I cannot see."

"Just hold on," Seth says.

They ride through ashy streets, sticking close to where Regine and Tomasz's original tracks are, watching for the van around every corner.

"Who *was* that?" Seth asks. "*What* was that?"

"Explanations later," Regine answers.

"She saw it before," Seth hears from behind his back. "She saw what it does."

"Explanations *later,*" Regine says again, pedaling harder.

They ride around another corner, and another, making their way to the train station. The bicycle tracks in the ash are parallel to Seth's footprints on the journey out. "You were following me," he says.

"We were trying to catch you," Tomasz says.

"How did you know where I was?"

"*Later,*" Regine snaps as they turn the last corner. "We've got to get away from – SHIT!"

The black van is there, waiting for them.

Regine swerves so hard she falls off her bike. Seth struggles to keep his own balance as Tomasz leaps off to help her. The van is down the road at an angle to them, clearly anticipating they'd come out from one of three streets. They've taken the one it obviously expected the least, but it's already revving its engines to make the turn after them.

Though now that he's got a full view, Seth sees that "van" isn't the right word for it at all. Sleek and unearthly, its corners are rounded, its windows tinted so dark they almost seem of a single piece with the van itself. There are no other identifying marks on it at all. Even the ash and dust don't seem to be sticking to it. It's just a hard, cool piece of blackness in the gray landscape.

Just like the helmet the Driver was wearing.

Just like the coffin in Seth's house.

"The bridge!" Regine shouts, righting her bicycle, not even pausing when Tomasz leaps on the seat behind her. "Before it can turn!"

She pedals off, unsteadily at first, but with increasing speed. She veers away from the front of the van, the quick dart of the bicycle skating past the bulkier vehicle, but that isn't a matchup they're going to win for long. Seth rides after her, leaping up on an ashy sidewalk to avoid the van swerving at him.

Seth can see the bridge she means. Down from the train station, the tracks go over a brick archway. It's half collapsed onto the road below, but there's a space on the right big enough for a bike to go through.

But not big enough for a van.

Seth pedals past Regine, who's struggling with the weight of Tomasz. There's a surge in engine noise, and when they look back, they see that the van has made its turn.

And is coming after them, at full speed.

"We are not going to make it!" Tomasz calls.

"Hang on!" Regine yells, her legs pumping frantically.

Seth looks back again. The van is bearing down on them. Tomasz is right. They aren't going to make it.

Without stopping to think, Seth veers hard to the right, sending up a wave of ash and turning back the way he came.

"What are you *doing*?" Regine screams.

"Go!" he yells back. "Just go!"

He rockets past them in the opposite direction, heading straight for the van.

"NO!" he hears Tomasz cry, but he keeps on, picking up speed.

"Come on," he says as he rides toward the van. "Come on!"

It doesn't stop or veer.

Neither does Seth.

"COME ON!" he screams.

They're fifty feet apart—

Thirty—

The van's engine revs—

And right before impact, it pulls violently to the

left, hitting a cracked curb and skidding into the burnt foundations of a house.

Seth makes another hard turn in the ash. "Go! Go! Go!" he yells at Regine and Tomasz, who've slowed to watch him. She starts pedaling again and disappears into the narrow opening under the bridge. Seth hurtles after them. They hear the engine revving again, but they ride without looking back, through the darkened dip under the bridge and out the other side.

"Will it come after us?" Seth shouts.

"I don't know!" Regine says. "We should get to your house and hide."

"*My* house?"

"The next crossing point is a bunch of streets north," Regine says, Tomasz still hanging on to her. "We don't think it knows where you live—"

"How do *you* know where I live?"

"We'll hide the bikes," she continues, ignoring him. "It usually doesn't come over to this side at all—"

"Usually?"

Regine grunts in annoyance as they turn another corner. "There's a lot we don't know."

"But we do know some things," Tomasz says.

"Like what?" Seth says.

"Like we were right to follow you," Tomasz answers cheerfully. "Because you saved us."

"What did I save you from?" Seth asks as they finally start slowing their pace. "What was that thing?"

Tomasz looks at him and says, "Death. It was death."

33

"Not actual death," Regine says as they hide the bikes in an overgrown garden two streets up from his house. "We call it the Driver."

"*Maybe* actual death," Tomasz says.

Regine rolls her eyes. "Not a skeleton in a cloak with a . . ." She makes a motion with her hands.

"Scythe?" Seth suggests.

"Scythe," Regine agrees. "But it'll kill you."

"How do you know?"

"This isn't the time to explain," she says, leading them off down the sidewalk in the direction of Seth's house. "We've got to get inside."

"But who *are* you?" Seth says, following. "Where did you come from? Are there more of you?"

Regine and Tomasz exchange a glance. It's enough to give him the answer in an instant. He's surprised at how sudden his disappointment is. "There aren't. Are there?"

Regine shakes her head. "Just me and Tommy. And whatever's driving that van."

"Three of us. That's *it*?"

"Three is better than two," Tomasz says. "And much better than one."

"We figure there have to be more people out there somewhere," Regine says. "It doesn't make sense otherwise."

"Yeah," Seth says. "Because everything else here makes so much sense."

Tomasz frowns. "But sense is what it does not make."

"Try not to use irony," Regine says to Seth. "He doesn't understand it."

"I do, too!" Tomasz protests. "In my language, *plenty* irony. I could tell you story of the dragon of Krakow who –"

"We need to get inside," Regine says. "I don't think the Driver considers us much of a threat unless we get too close, but –"

"Too close to what?" Seth asks.

They both look at him, startled. Regine cocks her head at him. "Where do you think you *are*?"

Seth says, simply, "Hell."

"Yes," Tomasz says. "What *I* say."

"Well," Regine says, pressing on down the sidewalk, "that's one way of putting it."

They make their way carefully, walking on the least dusty bits of sidewalk, trying to disguise their footprints, but anyone looking for them could still find them pretty easily.

They'd have to be looking, though.

"Whatever that . . . *thing* is," Seth says, "it's never come this way before. Trust me. Nothing's driven down these roads for years."

Regine hmphs. "I'll still feel better when we're in the house."

"Do you have any food there?" Tomasz asks. Regine shoots him a glance. "What?" he says. "I am hungry."

"Just cans," Seth says. "Soups and old beans and custard."

"Exactly what we're used to," Regine says.

They turn the corner at the far end of Seth's street. "That one there, yes?" Tomasz says, pointing.

Seth stops walking again. "How do you know that? Have you been spying on me?"

Tomasz's smile falters and even Regine looks uncomfortable.

"What?" Seth says.

Regine sighs. "Tommy saw you standing on top of the train station bridge a few days ago."

"She did not believe me," Tomasz says. "Said that I imagined you." He smiles again. "I did not."

"We're in a house a couple miles from here," Regine says, gesturing northward, "but we were out gathering food and Tommy said he thought he saw someone."

"We looked for very long time in rain that never stopped," Tomasz says, nodding. "Got very wet."

"And then we, uh," Regine says, and she actually seems to blush, "we saw you showering. In the rain. Out in front of your house."

Tomasz grins even wider. "You were pulling on your willy!"

"Tommy!" the girl snaps. Then she frowns at Seth. "Well, you *were*. And we weren't going to say hello when you were *busy,* and we were hungry and wet, so we went back home and thought we'd come back when things weren't so . . ."

"Private," Tomasz stage-whispers.

"*Rainy,*" Regine says.

Seth feels a burning in his throat. "I thought I was alone here. I thought I was completely alone."

"That is what I thought, too," Tomasz says solemnly. "Until Regine finds me." He smiles again, shyly this time. "And now you make three."

"So we got here this morning," Regine says, "only to find that you were running very, very fast toward something in particular." She crosses her arms. "Almost like you had somewhere to go. Something to do."

There's a silence, which Seth doesn't fill.

"And we could not let the Driver catch you," Tomasz says. "So we followed. And here we all are." He shrugs. "Still outside."

Seth waits a moment without saying anything more, then heads down the street, leading them toward his house. He's embarrassed about the shower business, but not as much as he could be. Something's still not right about this. These two just *happened* to be there when he was running toward the hill, just *happened* to stop him before he made contact with the black van, just *happened* to find the perfect place to hide from the Driver?

He sneaks a peek back as he turns up the path to his front door.

A short, happy Polish kid and a big, suspicious black girl.

Did he create them? Because they're just about the last and weirdest thing he'd pick to create.

He swings open the front door, and they follow him inside. Regine takes a dining chair and Tomasz slumps on the settee. "This is a very terrible painting," he says, staring up at the panicked horse above the mantel.

"I'll make something to eat," Seth says. "It won't be much. But while I do, you have to tell me what you know."

"All right," Regine says. "But first you have to tell *us* something."

"And what's that?" Seth says, heading toward the kitchen.

And he hears her ask, "How did you die?"

34

"What did you say?"

"I think you heard the question just fine," Regine says, looking at him firmly, as if setting him a challenge. A test he has to pass.

"How did I die?" Seth repeats, looking back and forth between her and Tomasz. "So you're saying . . . You're saying this place really is—"

"I'm not saying anything," Regine says. "I'm just asking how you died. And your reaction tells me you know exactly what I mean."

"I got struck by lightning!" Tomasz volunteers.

Regine makes a loud scoffing sound. "You did not."

"You do not know," Tomasz says. "You were not there."

"Nobody actually gets struck by *lightning*. Not even in Poland."

Tomasz's eyes widen in indignation. "I was not *in* Poland! How many times I have to say? Mother came over for better working and—"

"I drowned," Seth says, so quietly he thinks they may not have heard him.

But they stop bickering immediately.

"Drowned?" Regine says. "Where?"

Seth furrows his brow. "Halfmarket. It's a little town on the coast of–"

"No, I mean, *where*? The bathtub? A swimming pool–?"

"The ocean."

She nods, as if this makes sense. "Did you hit your head?"

"Did I hit my–?" Seth says, and then stops. He touches the back of his skull where it smashed into the rocks. "What does that have to do with anything?"

"I . . ." Regine starts, then looks down at the freshly swept floor Seth left behind this morning. "I fell down a flight of stairs. Cracked my head on a step on the way down."

"And you woke up here?"

She nods.

"It was the lightning for me!" Tomasz says happily. "It is like getting punched on your entire body all at one time!"

"You did *not* get struck by lightning," Regine says.

"Then you did not fall down stairs!" Tomasz says, upset bending his voice, a tone Seth recognizes from a hundred and one fights with Owen.

"So you both . . . ?" Seth doesn't finish the sentence.

"Died," Regine says. "In a way that caused a specific injury."

Seth feels the back of his head again, where he hit it on the rocks. He remembers the horrible finality of that collision, could swear he still feels the bones breaking, in a way from which there was no return.

Until he woke up here.

There are no broken bones now, of course, that was another place, another *him,* and all he can feel is the still-brutal shortness of his hair, something that Regine and Tomasz have clearly been here long enough to outgrow. There's nothing else unusual, just the inward curve of his neck leading up to the outward curve of his skull.

Regine looks at Tomasz. "Show him," she says.

Tomasz leaps up from the settee. "Lean down, please," he says. Seth stoops to one knee and allows Tomasz to take his hand. He splays Seth's fingers so the first two are a particular distance apart. Tomasz sticks out a little nubbin of tongue as he concentrates, and once more, he reminds Seth so much of Owen, Seth feels his chest contract.

"Here," Tomasz says, placing Seth's fingers on a particular stretch of bone just behind his left ear. "Can you feel that?"

"Feel what?" Seth says. It's exactly where his head struck the rock, but there's nothing unusual there, nothing but a stretch of –

There's something. A rise in the bone so slight as to almost not be present, so slight he didn't feel it seconds ago when pressing in exactly the same place.

A rise in the bone.

Leading to a narrow notch in that same bone.

"What?" Seth whispers. "How . . . ?"

He *swears* it wasn't there before. But there it is now, subtle but clear, the rise and the notch almost like a completely natural extension of his skull.

Almost.

"That's where you hit your head?" Regine asks.

"Yes," Seth answers. "You?"

Regine nods.

"And that is where the lightning punched me!" Tomasz says.

"Or whatever happened," Regine mumbles.

"What is it?" Seth asks, feeling around on the same spot on his right side to see if there's another one. There isn't.

"We think it is a kind of connection," Tomasz says.

"Connection to what?"

Neither of them answers.

"Connection to *what*?" Seth says again.

"What have your dreams been like?" Regine says.

Seth frowns at her. Then he has to look away, feeling the vividness of his dreams in a way that causes his skin to flush.

"The dreamings," Tomasz says, patting Seth's back sympathetically. "They are not easy."

"Like you're not just seeing it all again," Regine says. "Like you're actually *there,* back in time somehow, reliving it."

Seth is surprised to find his eyes filling, his throat choking. "What is it? Why does it happen?"

She glances at Tomasz, then back at Seth. "We're not sure," she says carefully.

"But you have an idea."

She nods. "The things you dream. They're important?"

"Yes," Seth says. "More than I want them to be."

"Some of it is good," Tomasz says. "But good in painful way."

Seth nods.

"But that, all that–" Regine makes a gesture in the air,

capturing in a single twist of her fingers all the dreams he's had–"all that is not your whole life."

"What?"

"There's more. There's much, much more." She gets a grim set to her mouth. "And you've forgotten it."

For some reason Seth can't quite put a finger on, this makes him angry. "Don't tell me I've forgotten," he says, fierce enough to surprise everyone, even himself. "I remember too much, is the problem. If I could forget some of these things, then . . ."

"Then what?" Regine says. "You wouldn't have *drowned*?" She says the word with a sarcastic snap, challenging him with her eyes.

"Did you fall down those stairs," he hears himself saying. "Or were you pushed?"

"Whoa," Tomasz says, taking a step back. "Something has happened. I have missed it. Why are we fighting?"

"We're not fighting," Regine says. "We're getting to know each other."

"People who are getting to know each other share information," Seth says. "All you're giving me are riddles and hints about how much more you know than I do." He stands, his voice rising with him. "Why do I have a brand-new notch in my head?"

Tomasz starts to answer, "It is not brand–" but Seth keeps going.

"Why did I crawl out of a coffin in the house where I grew up?"

Regine looks surprised. "You grew up here? In this house?"

But Seth is barely listening. "And where is everyone else? Who are you, anyway? How do I know you're not working with that thing in the van?"

This causes a lot more outrage than he was expecting.

"We are NOT!" Tomasz shouts.

"You don't know anything!" Regine says.

"Then tell me!"

"Fine!" she says. "Tomasz isn't the first person I saw here. He was the second."

Seth feels strangely victorious. "So there *are* others?"

"Only the one, before I found Tomasz."

"And thank the Holy Mother she did," Tomasz says, nodding vigorously. "Was in very bad way."

"But before then," Regine says, "there was another. A woman. I knew her one day. *One day*. And then I watched her die. She pushed me to safety and let the Driver catch her so it wouldn't catch me. I watched it kill her. That baton has some kind of charge in it. It kills you. And then the Driver takes your body away."

Tomasz frowns at Seth. "She does not like to talk about it."

"So, screw you," Regine continues. "How do we know *you're* not–"

She stops.

Because they've noticed the sound.

A distant purring, a sound of wind that isn't the wind.

The sound of an engine.

Growing louder as it approaches.

35

They turn to the windows, though the blinds are still down and nothing can be seen of the street beyond.

"No," Regine says, standing up. "It never follows this far. If we get away, it always stops."

The sound of the engine grows louder, two, maybe three streets away.

And getting closer.

Tomasz scowls at Seth. "You were shouting! It heard you!"

"No, it didn't," Regine says. "It's just searching, street by street, trying to find us. Now, be quiet."

They're silent, but there's a shift in the sound as it obviously turns a corner—

And starts driving down the road to Seth's house.

But Seth is thinking.

They only heard the engine after he spoke the words. After he accused them of working with it.

And now here it is.

I did this, he thinks. *Did I do this?*

"Our footprints are all over," Tomasz says. "It will know we are here."

"It's driving," Regine says. "It may pass by too quickly to notice—"

But she doesn't finish.

Because the engine has come to a stop right outside.

Seth feels Tomasz's hand slip into his own, gripping it the way Owen did every time they had to cross a street. Seth can feel the tension vibrating up from the little, stubby fingers, can see the nails that are bitten painfully down to the quick, can see the wide-open, terrified eyes looking back up from Tomasz's face.

So much like Owen.

"It'll pass," Regine says. "It'll drive on and out. Just nobody move, okay?"

They don't move. Neither does the sound of the engine.

"What is it *doing*?" Tomasz asks, his voice a desperate whisper.

And Seth sees again the craziness of his hair, an avalanche of wiry tangle. Again, just like Owen's. Seth looks at Regine, his mind racing.

Everything about this world has felt small. Everything has felt like he was hiding in a tiny pocket of a place with walls that pressed in from every side, in the form of memories he couldn't shake, a burnt-out wasteland that made a border, and now these two, showing up just in time to stop him from going any farther, bringing him back to this same stupid house at the very moment he tried to leave it for good, and who knows, maybe even bringing this van after them.

"Something about this isn't right," he says.

"What?" Tomasz asks.

Seth squeezes Tomasz's hand, then lets it go. "I'm going to find out what it is."

"You're *what*?" Regine says.

He starts to cross the sitting room toward the blinds. "I'm going to check and see what's happening."

Tomasz moves over to Regine and holds her hand now.

Seth stops and looks at them curiously. "You're not here, are you?" he says, the words coming out, unexpected.

Regine frowns. "Beg pardon?"

"I don't think you're really here. I don't think *any* of this is really here."

The engine still thrums outside.

"If we're not here," Regine says, holding his stare, "then neither are you."

"You think that's an answer?" Seth says. "You think that's proof?"

"I don't care what you think. If you let that thing see us, we're dead."

But Seth is shaking his head. "I feel like I'm beginning to understand. I'm finally beginning to understand what this place is." He turns back to the window. "And how it works."

"What are you doing, Mr. Seth?" Tomasz says. "You said you were just going to check."

"Seth, please," Regine says, and he hears her say to Tomasz, "Go, run, there's got to be a back way–"

"There's nothing to run from," Seth says. "There's nothing here that can hurt me, is there?"

193

With an almost casual swipe, he pulls up the blinds. The sun blasts into the dim room, and Seth squints in the brightness –

And the Driver punches a fist through the window, slamming it into Seth's chest, sending him flying across the room with seemingly impossible force.

36

He lands in a tumble at the feet of Regine and Tomasz, who are fleeing to the kitchen. His chest feels as if it's had a hole punched through it, knocking every bit of air out of his lungs. The Driver smashes out the rest of the glass in the window, throws away the blind in a violently efficient motion and steps over the low window ledge into the sitting room, its feet hitting the floor with a dead *thump* that feels unnaturally heavy.

It stands there, arms out slightly, feet apart, its sleek featureless head angled so it seems to be looking down at Seth, still curled on the floor, struggling for breath. He can hear Regine and Tomasz as they battle with the door to the back garden, but there's only high fences and deep grass out there. Nowhere for them to run away from this faceless, horrible, man-shaped *thing*.

There's no escape. For any of them.

The Driver moves toward Seth, its steps booming against the floorboards. As it walks, it makes a reaching motion with its arm, and the black, steely baton seems to just appear in its hand. The Driver swings it once, as if to test it. It crackles in the air, emitting a dangerous-sounding *hum,* tiny spots of light flowing from it as it moves.

Seth's thoughts jar and tumble as he pushes himself back. *What a stupid time to be wrong,* he thinks, and *Here it is, my death* and *They just have to pull on it to make the lock work* and *Will it hurt? Oh, God, will it hurt?* and he's trying to scoot away and the Driver comes on, implacable, baton at the ready—

He is dimly aware of Tomasz in the kitchen saying, "We cannot, we *cannot,*" and Regine calling out "Tommy!" but all he can see is the merciless, empty face looking back at him, coming for him—

"No," Seth starts to say—

The Driver leaps, raising the baton to bring it down with a final, terrifying authority—

And is knocked to the ground by a full bookcase tumbling into it.

Seth cries out in surprise, but Tomasz is already running from where he overbalanced the bookcase as Regine scoots her hands under Seth's arms to help lift him. They drag him into the kitchen, and Seth can see the Driver throwing the bookcase off itself with improbable strength. Tomasz slams the kitchen door behind them, and Regine helps him tip the refrigerator against it.

"Do you have a key?" Tomasz shouts, pointing at the door to the deck. "Please say you have a key!"

"It's open," Seth gasps, his chest still throbbing. "Pull on it, wiggle the switch."

There's a crash as the Driver throws its weight against the kitchen door, nearly knocking the refrigerator away on its first try, but Regine's already got the back door open. She grabs Tomasz's hand and yanks him outside, yelling, "Come on!" to Seth.

He staggers to his feet as a second crash comes, knocking the top half of the kitchen door from its hinges. But it holds. For the moment. Gasping, still hunched over at the pain in his chest, Seth dashes out the back door after them.

They've already disappeared into the grass by the time he makes it onto the deck. He can see Regine's head above the stalks, but Tomasz is only a current running through them, like fish near the surface of a lake.

Seth stumbles past the heap of silvery bandages–still there, still where he left them–and into the grass as he hears a more definitive crash from inside the house.

"Tell me there's a way out," Regine shouts back at him.

Seth doesn't answer.

"Shit," he hears her say.

They stop next to the ancient bomb shelter, its door long gone, its innards piled high with shards of pots and about eighteen million coat hangers. The back fence is high and wooden with no easy place for footholds, and the embankment on the other side only runs steeply up to another fence, impossibly high with barbed wire across the top.

"Where exactly *is* this?" Regine says.

"The prison grounds," Seth gasps. "There's another fence beyond that and another beyond that–" He stops because Regine and Tomasz are looking at each other in surprise. "What?"

"The *prison*?" Tomasz says.

"Yeah," Seth says. "So what?"

"Oh, hell," Regine says. "Oh hell, oh hell, oh hell."

"HERE!" Tomasz shouts, pulling at a loose board on the lower corner of the fence. Regine and Seth go to help him, Seth wincing as he bends down, and they yank back two, then three boards. Tomasz scrambles through to the other side. They pull off a fourth and Regine pushes Seth through.

He turns to help her.

But she's looking back at the deck.

Where the Driver now stands.

Through the hole in the fence, they can see her looking at it, see her turn back to face them.

See her eyes calculating.

See her not moving.

"What are you doing?" Tomasz says, alarmed.

"Go, both of you." She looks at Seth. "Take care of Tommy."

"NO!" Tomasz shouts, lunging back for the hole, but Seth instinctively stops him.

"Regine, that's crazy!" he says.

"I'll slow it down," she says. "You can get away."

"Regine!" Tomasz cries, pulling against Seth's arms.

There's a tearing sound as the Driver starts ripping through the tall grass, slowly now, almost leisurely, as if it knows it's got them.

"Go!" Regine shouts. "Now!"

"Regine−" Seth says.

And Tomasz breaks from his arms, evading Seth's grasp as he dashes back through the hole in the fence, avoiding Regine, too, as she tries to step in front of him. "Tommy!" she shouts.

But Seth can see him reaching into his pocket, see him pull out a small plastic cartridge, see his stubby fingers working frantically –

See the flame of a cigarette lighter as it dances in the air. "Tommy?" Regine asks.

Tomasz drags the lighter along the edge of the tall, willowy grass, still brittle even after the rainfall, still *very* ready to burst into flames wherever Tomasz touches the lighter. He flicks it off. "Come!" he shouts at Regine, dashing back through the hole in the fence.

Regine looks at the rising flames, spreading so quickly that billowing smoke is already hiding the Driver. Seth sees her wait, motionless, for the smallest of seconds, but then she follows Tomasz through. They turn right, down the embankment, hoping there's a way out at the end of the fences.

And they run like hell.

37

"That's my lighter, you little thief," Regine says as they run, Seth continually looking over his shoulder for the Driver, but the flames are now burning so high he can see them over the tops of intervening fences.

"That'll spread," Seth says. "Everything here will burn just like the other side of the tracks."

"Sorry," Tomasz says.

"I want my lighter *back*," Regine says.

The space between the back fences and the steep embankment is too narrow to run on comfortably. They're having to move as fast as they can with one foot flat on the ground and the other up a steep slope.

"It's not following us," Seth says, looking back again.

"Not yet," Regine says.

They reach the end of the row of houses, bursting out into the parking lot of a small block of flats down from the sinkhole. Seth veers left, away from his own street.

"No!" Regine calls, out of breath. "We have to get away from the prison. There's no chance of losing it if we don't."

Seth stops. "What? Why?"

But she's already running in the other direction, up toward the sinkhole and the High Street, Tomasz right behind her.

"That'll take us right by it!" Seth calls after them, but they don't stop. "Dammit!" he shouts and goes after them, grabbing his still aching chest—

Still aching, but—

They run to the edge of the sinkhole and stop, crouching down. Tomasz peeks around the corner of an overgrown shrub. "Nothing," he says. "The van is still there, but nothing else. Just lots of smoke."

"Come on then," Regine says. She dashes across the street, Tomasz after her, both exposed to the van for a quick, horrible second. Seth follows, glancing toward his house, but nothing is moving. They hide in the bushes on the other side of the street. "My chest," Seth says, hand on his heart. "It's—"

"We will go back to *our* house," Tomasz says. "We can help you there."

"Too far to go on foot with that thing after us," Regine says. She turns to Seth. "Do you know anywhere to hide?"

Seth looks up to the High Street, thinking past all the smaller stores he's been into and out of, all the way to the supermarket at the top of the hill.

"As a matter of fact," he says.

"Dark in there," Tomasz says, peering through the glass door of the supermarket after they've raced up the High Street.

"It's perfect," Regine says, nodding at Seth. "Good one."

Seth looks back in the direction of his house, where smoke is still rising. "Do you think we killed it?"

"Death itself cannot die," Tomasz says.

"It's just a man in a suit," Regine says. "It's not death. We shouldn't even call it an 'it.'" She ducks inside and is lost in shadows almost immediately. Seth makes to follow her, but Tomasz remains firmly in place, biting his lip.

"Is dark," he says again.

"Come on!" Regine calls from inside.

"We'll be in there with you," Seth says to him. "And you've got the lighter."

Tomasz takes it out of his pocket, turning it over in his fingers. "Is not mine. Is Regine's. She ask me to hold it for her." He glances up at Seth. "As way out of temptation."

"She said you stole it."

Tomasz shrugs. "People ask for what they need in different ways. Sometimes by not even asking for it at all. What my mother always say."

Regine comes stomping out of the darkness. "I'm serious, Tommy. The only thing in here that'll hurt you is me if you don't move your short little ass."

"You smoke?" Seth says.

She stares at him. "That's what you want to talk about? Are you kidding me with that shit?"

"Come on, Tommy," Seth says, turning to him. "We really do need to get inside."

Tomasz looks surprised. "You called me Tommy."

"I did."

"I prefer Tomasz, please.'

202

"*She* calls you Tommy."

"Is allowed. Is Regine. For you, Tomasz I like better. Is making more sense this way."

He follows Seth and Regine into the darkness of the store. They walk back through the silent aisles, their feet sliding on the dust of ancient food scattered everywhere.

"This'll do," Regine says, turning to Tomasz. "Give me the lighter."

"No," Tomasz says, shaking his head. "You are done for the smoking, you said. No more smoking for me, says Regine."

"It's still *mine,* and I need to see if Seth here's going to die of a punctured lung."

"I will do it," Tomasz says. He flicks on the lighter, holding it above his head to light the aisle.

"Not so high," Regine says. "It can be seen from the front."

"Oho," Tomasz says. "All the advice now, but there is nothing when Tomasz is lighting the grass on fire and saving all our lives. Oh, thank you, Tomasz, thank you so much for your clever idea which lets us get away. Ow!"

He drops the lighter and sticks two burnt fingers in his mouth.

"Yeah," Regine says. "Thanks so much, genius."

"You are welcome," Tomasz says through a mouthful of fingers. Regine starts patting around the floor in the gloom to find the lighter again.

"Why is this particular lighter so important?" Seth asks.

"Because it works," she says, finding it and flicking it on. "These things are basically alcohol. You know how many hundreds I tried before I found one that wasn't evaporated? Now, take off your shirt."

Seth blinks at her.

"Your chest, stupid," she says. "You're walking and talking, so I'm guessing you're fine, but we might as well see."

Seth hesitates, suddenly shy.

Regine frowns. "We've already seen you showering."

"And more!" Tomasz says.

Regine switches the lighter to her other hand. She gives him a mischievous look. "I'm not asking you out on a date or anything."

"It wouldn't matter if you did," Seth says, the words coming out almost as a reflex. "I don't date girls."

Her face drops immediately. "You mean you don't date *fat* girls."

"No, that's not–"

"I can see you thinking it. How can she still be so fat in a world where there's hardly any food? How fat must she have been to start with?"

Seth starts to argue but stops. He *didn't* think that. But it does beg a larger question. "How long have you been here?"

"Five months, eleven days," Tomasz says.

"Long enough," Regine says at exactly the same time.

There's silence for a moment, as Seth doesn't know what to say, so finally, he just says, "No, I meant I don't date *girls*. Any girls."

Regine holds up the lighter to look at him, understanding now. "So what you're saying is, if we're going to repopulate the planet, it's up to me and this little Polish person?"

"What?" Tomasz says, confused. "What are you saying? I am not following."

"He dates boys," Regine says.

"*Does* he?" Tomasz says, fascinated. "I have long wondered how this works. I have *many* questions for you—"

"Just let me see your chest before he goes off on one," she says to Seth. "*Please.*"

In the light of the flame, all they can see on Seth's skin are the beginnings of a bruise and maybe some redness.

"How can this be?" Tomasz says. "It knocked you all the way across the room."

"I know," Seth says. "I thought I'd have ribs sticking out my *back*."

Regine shrugs. "Maybe it didn't hit you that hard?"

Seth gives her a look.

"I don't know," she says. "Just be happy." Her voice has gone irritable again, and she starts making her way down the aisle, deeper into the store. "Is there anything here to drink?"

"You could be a little friendlier, you know," Seth says. "We're all in this together."

She faces him, the flame shining off her sweaty cheeks. "Are we now? Because I thought me and Tommy weren't really here. And if we're not, then there's not a lot of point being friendly to you, is there? Not when you make brilliant moves like the one back at the house that nearly got us all killed. Thank God for us not being there, eh?"

"But we are okay!" Tomasz says. "Thanks to myself."

"Well, if I knew what was going on," Seth says, "instead of all this stupid mystery–"

"You want answers?" she says challengingly.

"Regine," Tomasz says carefully. "He is maybe not ready."

"Nope," she says. "He asked. So I'll tell him."

"Tell me what?" Seth says.

She stares at him, the flame flickering between them. "This world? This hell you think we're in?"

"Regine," Tomasz says. "Stop."

But she presses on. "This isn't hell, Mr. You're Not Here So I Hope You Don't Mind If I Kill You. Everything you're remembering, everything you're dreaming, every stupid little bit of life you can ever recall living?" She leans into the flame until her eyes look like they have their own fires burning in them. "*That* was hell."

"It was *not*," Tomasz says, firmly.

"It was and you know it," she says. "But this here"– she gestures to encompass the store, the empty streets beyond, the Driver, which is still undoubtedly out there somewhere looking for them–"this is the real world. This here. *This.*"

She slaps Seth across the face. "Hey!" he shouts.

"Feel that?" she says. "That's as real as it gets, baby."

Seth puts his hand up to the sting spreading through his cheek. "What'd you do that for?"

"You didn't die and wake up in hell," she says. "All you did was *wake up.*"

She clicks off the lighter and heads into the darkness.

"Wake up from what?" Seth says, going after her.

She stops in front of the bottled water, her eyes wide. Without a word, she and Tomasz start searching through the bottles, holding them up to the lighter flame, discarding the discolored or empty ones.

"Don't you have a supermarket in your neighborhood?" Seth asks, a little shocked at how vigorously they're attacking the shelves.

"The big one near us is totally empty," Regine says.

"Which leaves only small corner shops and markets called Something Express," Tomasz says, drinking out of a bottle.

"But you're only a couple miles away," Seth says, taking a bottle and drinking, too, only realizing as he does how thirsty he is. "Didn't you come looking?"

"Not with the Driver on patrol," Regine says. "It's all been undercover, house to house and keeping quiet and trying not to be seen. Which we did fine until today."

"If that was my fault, then I'm sorry, but I'm getting a little tired of–"

"I need a smoke," Regine says.

"No!" Tomasz says. "You will die! Your lungs will be as dark as your skin! Your brain will grow out of your eyes in tumors!"

"Well, that'll be something to see," she says, and heads back to the front of the store.

Through the doors, they can still hear the engine cutting across the silence of the neighborhood, but it's comfortably distant sounding and nothing's hovering around the entrance waiting to grab them.

"As long as we're not by the prison," Regine says, going to the cigarette counter, "I'm guessing it doesn't care as much."

"What's so special about the prison?" Seth says. "And what do you mean about me waking up?"

"Hold on," Regine says from behind the cigarette counter. Most everything looks like it's been torn to bits by rats, but after some scavenging, she finds a nearly whole pack of Silk Cuts. She rips it open like it's the first Christmas present she's ever received and taps out a cigarette.

"Regine," Tomasz says, disappointed.

"You have no idea," Regine says. "I mean, seriously, you don't even have the first clue."

She uses the lighter for its original purpose, the end of the cigarette sparking up in the gloom. She takes a deep, deep breath, holding the smoke in, and they can see her close her eyes tight against it, tears coming down first one cheek, then the other.

"Oh, Jesus," she whispers. "Oh, sweet holy shit."

Tomasz looks seriously at Seth. "It will kill her."

"I thought you said we were already dead," Seth says.

"No," Regine says. "Not dead. Tommy's wrong there." She coughs and takes another drag, leaning one hand on the counter in what seems like nearly debilitating relief. "What a stupid day."

"Regine," Seth says impatiently.

"All right," she says. "All right." She takes another drag. "I'm going to tell him, Tommy. You okay with that?"

Tomasz drags one foot across the floor, drawing a line in the dust. "He will be shocked," he says. "He will not want to know." Tomasz looks up at him seriously. "I did not believe it. I still do not very much."

Seth swallows. "I'll take that risk."

"Okay, then," Regine says, taking one more drag, then stubbing the butt out on the counter, pulling out another to light up. She looks at Seth, holds out the pack, offering him one.

Seth absentmindedly gestures at the running shorts and running shirt and running shoes he's still somehow wearing. "Runner," he says. "We can do pretty much anything *except* smoke."

Regine nods. And then she begins.

"The world," she says, "is over."

38

"Over?" Seth asks. "What do you mean, over?"

Regine sighs, the smoke curling out of her. "We *think* it's over because we wanted it to be over."

"We?"

"Everyone. All of us."

Seth starts to ask more, but she stops him. "Did you used to go online? Before you woke up here?"

He gives her a confused look. "Of course, I did. What kind of question is that? You couldn't get through life without your phone or your pad."

"And that's true everywhere, it seems," Regine nods. "Even Poland."

"I was not *in* Poland," Tomasz says, irate. "How many times I have to say? Mother came over for work. And Poland is online quite fine, thank you very much. Very *advanced* country. I am tired of you always–"

"*Anyway,*" Regine says. "We think that sometime, eight or ten years ago, if you go by the dates on the stuff you find here, everyone went online." She blows out another long line of smoke. "Permanently."

Seth furrows his forehead. "What do you mean, permanently?"

"Oh, *I* know!" Tomasz says. "It means a thing like choosing to do it forever and forever."

"I know what the word means–" Seth says.

"Everyone left the real world behind," Regine says, "and moved to one that was entirely online. Some completely immersive version that didn't look like being online at all, so much like real life you wouldn't know the difference."

But Seth is already shaking his head. "No, that's insane. That kind of crap only happens in movies. You'd always be able to tell the difference. Real life is real life. You wouldn't just forget about it."

"Ah!" Tomasz says. "She has theory about this, too. She thinks we made ourselves forget. That way we worry less and we don't miss it."

Seth frowns at him. "You said you didn't believe her. You said this was hell."

Tomasz shrugs. "It is. But hell you make for yourself is still hell, maybe."

"And you expect me to believe this?"

"I don't care what you believe," Regine says. "You asked for the truth, and this is it, the best that makes sense. We stuck ourselves in those coffins–"

Seth starts. "You guys woke up in them, too?"

"Oh, yes," Regine says. "They're not coffins, though, really. All those tubes, all that metallic tape stuff. It's to keep us alive, isn't it? Keep us fed, take our waste away, keep our muscles from dying, all while our minds think we're somewhere else."

211

"I couldn't even see when I got out of the coffin," Seth says. "In fact, I didn't even know there *was* a coffin until I went back upstairs a couple days later."

"Upstairs?"

"It was in the attic. In my old bedroom."

Regine nods, as if this confirms something. "I woke up in my sitting room," she says. "As confused as you were. Didn't even move from where I fell for at least a day or two."

Seth looks down at Tomasz, but Tomasz doesn't offer his own story, just drags his toe along the floor once more. "Rain is coming," he says.

They look out. Clouds are indeed rolling in fast from a distant horizon. Another weirdly tropical storm on the way.

"It is quiet, too," Tomasz says.

Seth listens. The sound of the engine has gone while they were talking. There's only the wind, blowing in the rain clouds that will at least finish any fire. *Another convenient thing*, he thinks.

"What you've said is impossible," he says. Regine makes a tutting sound, but he continues. "But everything here is impossible, too. The emptiness. The dirt. The world growing old with no one in it."

"Except us," Tomasz says.

"Yeah," Seth says. "Because that's the question, isn't it? There weren't any other coffins in my house or any of the houses on my street. If the world put itself to sleep, where *is* everyone?"

Neither of them answers.

And Seth realizes he already knows. It has all the inevitability of a story.

212

"The prison."

Tomasz studiously avoids his eye. Regine ignores him, too, but then finally gives him a resigned look.

"We can't," she says.

"Can't what? You don't even know what I'm going to say."

"Yes, I do, and I'm telling you we can't."

"We really, really cannot," Tomasz says, pleadingly. "*Really.*"

Seth is annoyed at their sudden resistance. Ever since he's been here, the prison has loomed. In the distance or over a hill or even just the knowledge of it out there somewhere, unseen. The source of everything that set his life down a path away from the one that could have been good, that could have been happy.

He's avoided it, by sheer, gut instinct.

But now that they're telling him he can't go, it suddenly seems like the one thing he must do, the obvious thing. Because if this is a place his head made up so he could accept his death or if it really is some kind of hell where he's been sent, then either of those things would mean the prison is important. A place where answers might be found.

But also, if Regine is somehow right and this *is* the real world, then that means it's where his family is.

Right now.

"Show me," he finally says. "Take me to the prison."

39

"Oh!" Tomasz says, pulling the mass of his hair with two fists. "I *knew* this! I knew this would happen."

"It's too dangerous," Regine says. "The Driver won't let us anywhere near it."

"But it obviously isn't at the prison all the time," Seth says. "It goes out patrolling or whatever."

"It'll know you're there and it'll do more than punch a hole in your chest."

"A hole that's healed oddly rapidly, don't you think?" Seth thumps his chest, then winces at the bruise. "We could find a way in."

"Please do not make me," Tomasz says. "Please do not. Not again."

"Again?" Seth says.

"I woke up there," Tomasz says unhappily. "So many coffins. And you do not know who is in them or what they are dreaming or if they are even alive." He's holding his hands together, *wringing* them, the first time Seth's ever seen the word actually demonstrated. "And my mother."

"Your mother?" Seth asks when Tomasz doesn't continue.

But Tomasz says nothing, just shuffles over to Regine,

who stubs out her cigarette and embraces him so he can cry again against her stomach. "He was running from the Driver when I found him," she says. "We barely got away. It was a week before I could convince him I wasn't an angel or a devil."

"I know the feeling," Seth says. "What did he mean about his mother?"

"Not everything is your business. I'll tell you what we know and what we think, but there's stuff that's private."

"You're saying everyone's at the prison?"

"Well, not everyone in the *world,* obviously. But a lot of people from this town. There've got to be other places, but who knows where they might be? Or what's guarding them."

"But we could—"

"We're *not* going to the prison. It's the one place here you don't go."

"You went there when you found Tomasz."

She stops at that. "Becca had been killed. That woman I met. I didn't know what else to do."

He looks at her now, more closely. "So you went to a place you knew was dangerous?"

She picks a bit of ash off her tongue and asks him, deceptively simply, "Where were you running to this morning?"

There's a long silence at this. Regine brings the still-snuffling Tomasz to the front of the cigarette counter, and they sit down on the floor against it. Tomasz leans into her, closing his eyes.

"Why would everyone be there," Seth asks, "if I was at my house?"

Regine shrugs. "I was at *my* house. Maybe they just ran out of room. Or time. Maybe some people had to make do with what they had."

"Seems like a pretty inefficient way to arrange things."

"Who says it was arranged? Maybe they were in a rush and had to cut corners."

"How do you mean?"

"Have you *seen* the world?" she asks, raising an eyebrow. "Where are all the animals? Where did all this dust and mud and decay come from? That's way more than just eight years' worth. When did that fire on the other side of the tracks happen, before or after? What's with all this freaky weather?" She shrugs again. "Maybe the world was just getting too bad and we finally had no choice but to leave it entirely."

Lightning flashes so bright they all jump, even Tomasz with his eyes closed. The world holds its breath, then a long roll of thunder peals, quickly followed by the pounding of rain against the glass, hurling itself against the storefront as if all it wanted to do was come in and seize them.

Tomasz falls asleep with his head in Regine's lap. Seth gets some cans of food and sits next to Regine. They eat with plastic spoons, trying not to wake Tomasz. The rain keeps slamming down outside, so hard it's like they're underneath a waterfall.

"I don't remember rains like this," Regine says. "Not in England. It's like a hurricane."

"There's too much wrong with your explanation," Seth

says, struggling to swallow his room-temperature spaghetti. "Why would I be in my house, but not my parents or my brother?"

"I don't know. We're having to guess at everything. Like how is it that the coffins are powered through that one connection at the bottom, but there's no electricity anywhere else?"

"Yeah, I saw that, too."

"And this." She taps the back of her head. "A connection point that doesn't pierce the skin?"

"But if that kind of technology is here," Seth wonders, thinking of the metallic strips, too, "why didn't we have it in the online world? Why didn't we bring it with us?"

"Maybe we wanted things simpler, easier."

"Your life was simple and easy?"

She gives him a harsh look. "You know what I mean."

"Well, it's certainly simpler and easier having you here to explain it all to me. Pretty useful, wouldn't you say?"

"Back to the me and Tommy aren't really real thing? You want me to slap you again? Because I'd be more than happy to."

"The rain that puts out the fire and also traps us here so we can talk," he continues. "A chest injury that heals fast enough for me to get away. It all just sort of works, doesn't it?"

"People see stories everywhere," Regine says. "That's what my father used to say. We take random events and we put them together in a pattern so we can comfort ourselves with a story, no matter how much it obviously isn't true." She glances back at Seth. "We have to lie to ourselves to live. Otherwise, we'd go crazy."

Tomasz shifts on her lap, sleeptalking in Polish: "*Nie, nie.*"

217

Regine moves her hand to wake him, but he settles back down.

"He's having one of those dreams, isn't he?" Seth asks.

"I expect so."

"What do *you* dream about?"

"That's private," Regine says sharply.

"Fine, sorry, just you mentioned your father . . ."

They eat in grumpy silence for a few minutes.

"So what about this?" Seth says, thinking. "If the whole world is online, how did dying make us wake up here? Wouldn't we just reset or something?"

"I don't know," Regine says again, "but people still died there, didn't they? My Auntie Genevieve died of pancreatic cancer. And my father . . ." She clears her throat. "But if it was meant to be real, *so* real we'd forget we ever lived anywhere else, then even death would have to work, wouldn't it? Maybe our brains couldn't accept it otherwise. You die online, you die for real, because that's life."

"But *we* didn't die for real." Seth's getting angry again, thinking about what happened to Owen, what happened with Gudmund, what happened to *him*. "And why would we do that anyway? Why would we live in a world where that shit still happens? If we were supposedly in a place so perfect we forgot we moved there–"

"Don't look at me. My mother married my bastard of a stepfather in that perfect world, so I have no idea." Her hand goes unconsciously to the back of her neck. "What I do know is that if you give a human being a chance to be stupid and violent, then they're going to take it, every time. No matter where they are."

"But how did we end up here, then?" Seth persists. "How come this world isn't filled with people who died and just woke up?"

"We were supposed to die in this world, too, I think. But I fell down the stairs and hit my head in a certain spot. You drowned and hit *your* head in the exact *same* spot. Tommy–" she looks down at him, still sleeping–"well, Tommy says he got struck by lightning, but I'm guessing that whatever it was is something he doesn't want to remember, so fair enough, but still, the same spot. Some malfunction right at the point of connection that overloads the system and instead of killing us, disconnects us." She shrugs, suddenly out of energy. "Or that's what we think anyway."

She runs her hand lightly over Tomasz's wild hair. "It was his idea, actually, even though he keeps saying he doesn't believe it. Lots of good guesses in that funny little head." Tomasz presses himself closer against her, sleeping on.

"But if everything that happened to us isn't real," Seth says, "if everything we know was just some online simulation–"

"Oh, it was real, all right," she says. "We lived it; we were there. If you go through something and put up with it even if you want to get away from it more than anything in the whole world, then it was definitely bloody real."

Seth thinks back to Gudmund, thinks back to the smell of him, the *feel* of him. Thinks back to everything that happened this past year, good and bad and very, very bad indeed. Thinks back to what happened to Owen, to the frantic days when he was missing, to every small bit of punishment he received from his mum and dad in the years that followed.

It sure *felt* real. But if it was all somehow simulated, how could it have been?

And if he was here, right now, where was Gudmund?

"We shouldn't go back to our house until dark," Regine says. "We could take turns sleeping, one of us keeping an eye out."

At the thought of this, Seth feels how tired he is. After staying up nearly all night, after the run, after the adrenaline rush of the day, it suddenly becomes some sort of miracle he's even managing to keep his eyes open.

"All right," he says. "But when I wake up–"

"When you wake up," Regine says, "I'll tell you how to get into the prison."

40

"You have to forgive me," Monica said on his front step before even saying hello. "I didn't mean it. I was just so angry and—"

Seth stepped out into the cold, closing the door behind him. "What are you talking about?" he said. "What's going on?"

She looked at him fearfully. Yes, there was no other word for it. She was frightened of what she had to tell him. He felt his stomach turn to ice. "Monica?" he said.

Instead of answering, she looked up into the sky, like help might be found there. Stupidly, Seth found himself looking up, too. It was freezing, had been for the weeks leading up to Christmas, but without any snow falling. The sky was a collection of gray smears, like the snow was too angry to fall.

He looked back at Monica to find her crying.

And he knew.

Because it could only be one thing, couldn't it? It could only mean that the one good thing in his life was about to end. All that was left was finding out exactly how it was going to happen.

"You and Gudmund," she said quietly, her nose running in the cold air, her breath coming out over her scarf in white puffs. "You and fucking Gudmund."

She looked almost childlike in her ultra-thick winter coat and knitted hat with the red reindeer across it that she'd worn in cold weather from when it was far too big on her growing head until now when she didn't even wear it ironically. It was Monica's red reindeer hat, as much a part of her as her hair or her laugh.

"It makes sense," she said. "Looking back. If you'd asked me before, I'd have even wished it." She smiled at him, her eyes sad. "Wished it for you, Seth. Something that could make you so happy."

"Monica," Seth said, his voice barely audible. "Monica, I don't—"

"Please don't say it's not true. Don't do that. Before everything turns to shit, please don't pretend it wasn't a real thing."

He frowned. "Before everything turns to—"

"Hello, Monica," his mother's voice boomed as she came out the front door. Owen clattered out behind her, wrapped up like a mummy, thermos in one hand, clarinet case in the other. "Why are you making her wait out here, Seth?" his mother asked. "You'll freeze to death." She smiled at Monica, a smile that disappeared when she saw Monica's face. "What's going on?"

"Nothing!" Monica said, forcing cheerfulness and wiping her nose with her glove. "Just a winter cold." She even coughed into her hand.

"All right," Seth's mother said, clearly not believing her but using a tone that said she was willing to be fooled. "All the more reason to go inside then. The kettle's still hot."

"Hi, Monica!" Owen said cheerfully.

"Hey, Owen," Monica said.

Owen waved the thermos. "We made hot chocolate."

"Yeah," Monica said, forcing a laugh. "You still got some on your mouth there, kiddo."

Owen just smiled back and didn't even attempt to wipe the chocolate from his lips.

"Seriously," Seth's mother said, pulling Owen toward the car. "Go inside. Much warmer." She waved as she got into the driver's seat. "Bye, Monica."

"Bye, Mrs. Wearing," Monica said, waving a single glove.

Seth's mother watched them both with a serious look on her face as she and Owen drove away.

"She calls it a kettle," Monica said.

"Monica," Seth said, pulling his arms around himself, and not just because the cold air was cutting straight through his flimsy shirt. "Tell me."

She waited again, almost dancing in place with what was obvious reluctance. "I found some photos," she finally said. "On Gudmund's phone."

And there it was, simple as that, the world ending almost quietly.

"I'm so sorry, Seth," Monica said, crying again. "I'm so sorry—"

"What did you do?" he said. "What the hell did you do, Monica?"

She flinched, but she didn't look away. He'd remember that. She'd been brave and sorry enough to not look away when she told him what she did.

But also, damn her. Goddamn her forever.

"I sent them to H," she said, "and everyone else I could find from school who was on Gudmund's phone."

Seth said nothing, just found himself stepping back, as if he was losing his balance. He half fell onto the stone bench his parents kept by the front door.

"I'm sorry," Monica said, crying more. "I've never been more sorry about anything in my life—"

"Why?" Seth said quietly. "Why would you do that? Why would you—?"

"I was angry. So angry I didn't even think."

"But why?" Seth said. "You're my friend. I mean everyone knows you like him but—"

"Those pictures," she said. "They're not . . . They're not sex, you know? And sex, I could understand, I guess, but . . ."

"But what?"

She looked him in the eye. "But they were love, Seth."

She stopped, and he didn't ask what she meant, why love was so much more painful to see.

"I loved him first," she said. "I'm so sorry, that is such a shitty reason, but I loved him first. Before you."

Even in his free fall, even in what felt like the first tip of the world crashing down on him—everyone knowing his most private thing, his friends, his parents, everyone at school—all he could think about was Gudmund, how it

224

would still be all right if Gudmund was all right, how he could put up with everything, with anything, *if Gudmund was there with him.*

He stood. "I need to call him."

"Seth—"

"No, I need to talk to him—"

He opened his front door and—

41

Seth wakes. He's curled against the cigarette counter, using some stiff old kitchen towels they'd found for a pillow. He feels the dream washing from him, and he tries not to let it take him down with it.

One conversation on a doorstep. A few words from Monica while he shivered there. That had been the beginning of the end.

The end that had brought him here.

But why had he dreamed that? There'd been worse in all that had happened. He'd *dreamed* worse while he'd been here. And why had it ended where it had? He'd opened the door and—

He can't remember. He remembers frantically trying to find Gudmund, of course, but exactly what happened after he went inside—

It feels important, a little. Something there. Something just out of reach.

"Bad one?" Regine asks, standing over him.

"Did I cry out?" he asks, sitting up. He's still, amazingly, wearing his running gear. It's starting to smell sour.

"No, but they're usually bad, aren't they?"

"Not always."

"Yeah," she says, sitting down next to him and handing him a bottle of water, "but if they're good, they're good in a way that feels really, really bad anyway."

"Where's Tomasz?" he asks, taking a drink.

"Finding a private place to go to the toilet. You wouldn't believe how much of an old lady he is about that. Won't even say the word out loud. Just disappears, does his business, and never mentions it again. I swear he cried when he saw all the toilet paper they've got here."

The rain's stopped outside, and night is beginning to fall over the pedestrianized part of the street down from the supermarket. Still no sound of the engine, no sign of smoke in the air. The world is quiet again, save for the two of them breathing here.

"I was thinking about what you said," Regine says. "About why we'd put ourselves in an online world that was so messed up." She nods toward the glass. "Maybe compared to how the real world was going, it *was* paradise. Maybe all we wanted was a chance to live real lives again, without everything falling apart all the time."

"So you really believe all that?" Seth asks. "That this is the real world, and everything else was a dream we were having with other people?"

She takes in a long breath. "I miss my mother," she says, looking out into the dusk. "My mother when I was young, not who she turned into, not who she became after she married *him,* but from before. We used to have fun, just the two of us. We used to laugh and sing really badly." She raises an eyebrow at him. "You know how all black women are

227

supposed to have amazing voices? Like the world won't let us run things or get any real power or be president or anything, but that's okay because we can all sing like a choir of angels?"

"I never said—"

"Well, we can't. Take my word for it. Me and my mama, God, we sounded like two lonely moose." She laughs to herself. "Doesn't matter, though, does it? When it's just you and your mama."

Seth stretches out his legs. "But you say all that wasn't real."

"You're purposely misunderstanding," she says, sounding frustrated. "I was there. My mama was there. Even if we were fast asleep in different places. It was real. If it hadn't been real, why didn't we sing beautifully?"

"There's always beauty," Seth murmurs. "If you know where to look."

"What?"

"Nothing. Something someone I once knew used to say."

She looks at him closely, too closely. "You had someone. Someone you loved."

"None of your business."

"And you're wondering if it was real. You're wondering if you really knew . . . *him,* I'm guessing?"

Seth says nothing. Then he says, "Gudmund."

"Good Man? That some kind of nickname?"

"Gud*mund.* It's Norwegian."

"Yeah, okay, so you're wondering if Norwegian Gudmund was real, aren't you? You're wondering if all those wonderful times really happened. If you were really there. If *he* was really there."

Seth's mind goes again to the smell of Gudmund on his fingertips. To the tapping of Gudmund's fingers on his chest. To the kiss from those pictures, the pictures that everyone saw —

"He was," Seth says. "He had to be."

"Yeah, that's what I said," Regine says. "That's what it all comes down to, doesn't it? They have to be, or where does that leave us?"

It's grown darker, even in the short time they've spoken, the shadows in the store bleeding out to cover them.

"Here's what I think," Regine says, lighting a cigarette. "I think I'm the only real thing I've got, except maybe Tommy. Even here, in this place, because who's to say *this* isn't some simulation, too, some other level we'll wake up from. But wherever I am, whatever this world is, I've just got to be sure I'm me and that's what's real." She blows out a cloud of smoke. "Know yourself and go in swinging. If it hurts when you hit it, it might be real, too."

"It hurt when you hit *me*."

"That's interesting," Regine says, reaching above her to the counter, "because I didn't feel a thing." She flicks the lighter on to show him the piece of paper she's brought down. "I've made a map back to where Tommy and I are staying."

"But aren't we —"

"It's so you can find your way back to us after you go to the prison."

• • •

229

"Don't tell Tommy," she says, lowering her voice. "Tell him you're going back to your house to change clothes and you'll join us later." She looks at him sternly. "I mean it."

"I believe you."

He takes the map from her. He recognizes a road, peeling away from this side of the train tracks and heading north. There's an X drawn on a side street and a number written below it for the address.

"You've got to add three to everything," Regine says. "It's actually three streets more north than that one and for the real address you add three to the first digit and three to the second. If you get caught, I don't want it to find us."

"What about the prison?" he asks. "The main entrance is way on the other side from my house."

"You can't get in that way," Regine says. "It's boarded and locked up like you wouldn't believe, like they didn't want anyone to get in or out no matter what happened. Which is probably true, I guess. What you want to do is–"

"What is that?" Tomasz's voice comes to them out of the darkness, his tone suspicious.

"Map back to your house," Seth says quickly.

"Why are you not coming with us?" The flicker from the lighter is enough to reflect his obvious worry back at them.

"If you didn't burn my house down, I need to change clothes," Seth says, and mimes smelling his armpit.

"Then why are we not coming with *you*? There is safety in numerals."

"Numbers," Seth says. "Safety in numbers."

"Yes," Tomasz frowns, "because grammatical right-ness is exactly what we are talking about at the present moment."

"I want to get back," Regine says. "Too risky hanging around, all of us outside."

"But *he* will risk it."

"That's his choice," Regine says, standing up.

"*I* do not choose this," Tomasz says. He opens and closes his hands into stubby little fists, the same way Owen used to when he was nervous about something, Seth remembers. Owen would stand there, impossibly vulnerable, so that you either wanted to pick him up and tell him everything was going to be okay or start slapping him for being so ridiculously available for harm.

"I'll be back before you know it," Seth says, then he says. "I promise."

"Well," Tomasz says, perhaps unconvinced. "That is good." He looks at Regine. "We should take supplies. Water. And food. And toilet paper. I found birthday candles, also. For when we are having birthdays."

There's a beat as they both stare at him.

"What?" he says. "I like birthdays."

"How old *are* you both, actually?" Seth asks, curious.

Regine shrugs. "Before I woke up, I was seventeen. Who knows how old I really am? If time is even the same here as there."

"Really?" Seth asks. "You don't think–"

"No way of knowing one way or the other."

"I am fourteen!" Tomasz says.

Seth and Regine look down on the mighty, mighty shortness of him and laugh out loud.

"I *am*," Tomasz insists.

"Yeah," Regine says, "and you were struck by lightning and Poland is paved with gold and chocolate. It's time to go."

Regine and Tomasz take bags from the cash registers and fill them with what supplies they can carry, then they all head back out onto the High Street. There's still no sound of the engine, but they walk cautiously into what is now almost full night.

"Will you be able to find us in the dark?" Tomasz says, sounding worried. "We will leave a candle burning outside–"

"No, we will *not*," Regine says. "He'll find it, don't worry."

"I still do not see why we cannot wait for him–"

"I just need time to gather my stuff," Seth says. "Some of it's private. It might take a while."

"But still–"

"Sweet Jesus, Tommy," Regine snaps. "He probably just wants to wank again in the last moment of privacy you'll ever give him."

Tomasz looks at him, astonished. "This is true?"

Seth can see Regine laughing silently in the moonlight. "I have a brother, Tomasz," he says. "Wherever he is now, we grew up in that house. Before we moved to America."

Regine has stopped laughing, and Seth can see her light another cigarette, pretending not to listen.

"While we lived there, something bad happened to him," Seth says. "Something that made him different, not right. And in an important way, it was my fault."

"It was?" Tomasz whispers, his eyes wide.

Seth glances down the street. The sinkhole's ahead of them, his own road next to it. He's only intended to mollify Tomasz, but the truth of his words cuts sharper than he expects. "Whatever this place is, real or not, my house is dangerous because of how close it is to the prison. And if I'm not coming back, I want to say good-bye to it." He looks at Regine. "I want to say good-bye to the brother I had there before all the bad stuff happened."

"And this needs to be done privately, yes, I see," Tomasz says, nodding gravely.

Seth smiles, despite himself. "You remind me of him. You're like a version of what he might have been. If he was Polish."

"I thought you were going to say he was like the version of your brother that wasn't right," Regine says, taking another puff of smoke.

"That is *not* nice," Tomasz says. "For myriad reasons."

"We're going to get the bikes," Regine says, "so we'll see you tonight, yes?"

"I'll try not to be long, but don't worry if I—"

He nearly falls backward onto the sidewalk as Tomasz lunges into him with a hug. "Be safe, Mr. Seth," Tomasz says, his voice muffled against Seth's shirt. "Do not let death get you."

Seth's hand hovers over the springy mess that is Tomasz's hair. "I'll be careful."

"Leave him be," Regine says. Tomasz backs away, letting Regine approach. "I'm not going to hug you," she says.

"I'm okay with that," Seth says.

"I wasn't asking for your approval." She lowers her voice. "Don't even bother with the main entrance. That's what I was going to tell you earlier. Follow the train tracks down to the far side of the prison. You'll see a big section where the walls have fallen in."

"Thanks," Seth whispers back.

"You're making a huge mistake," Regine says. "You're not going to find whatever it is you're looking for and you're going to get yourself killed in the process."

He grins at her. "Nice to know I'll be missed."

She doesn't grin back.

"What are you two talking about?" Tomasz says.

"Nothing," Regine says, then lowers her voice again. "Just think about maybe keeping your promise to Tommy."

Seth swallows. "I'll think about it."

"Yeah, right," she says, turning away from him. "Nice knowing ya."

Tomasz waves happily again in the moonlight, but Regine doesn't look back as they disappear into the darkness.

"Nice knowing you, too," Seth says to himself.

Then turns and starts walking toward the sinkhole.

Walking toward his home.

42

The van is gone from the front of his house. From where Seth is hiding down the road, he can see the ruts it made in the mud as it turned around and drove away. He waits, but nothing moves, not even a cloud passing in front of the moon in the newly clear sky, the weather changing so quickly it's like it's on fast forward.

Somewhere out there, many streets away, Regine and Tomasz are riding northward, their bikes overladen with food and supplies. He takes a moment to wish for their safety. And the wish feels like as much of a prayer as this place can allow.

He moves out into the street, slowly, cautiously, trying to see any sign of the van or the Driver lying in wait, but nothing leaps out at him as he goes. The house looks unchanged as he approaches, aside from the shattered glass of the front window. It's too dark to see through the broken blinds, and he curses himself for not taking one of Tomasz's birthday candles to light. He'll have to go pawing around in the dark for his lantern, and who knows how much damage the fire caused before the rain stopped it? There might be no lantern left to find, no clothes to change into.

No trace of the stuff left over from his family.

What is *that stuff, anyway?* he wonders, considering Regine's explanation of everything. Is it his memories reconstructing a place or is it actually the same physical house from when his family moved to America?

Or when they *chose to believe* they moved to America, when in fact they just lay down in sleek black coffins and welcomed a new version of what was real?

He remembers the move, though, the stress and anxiety of it. Owen hadn't been out of hospital very long and was still deep in rehab to get his motor skills functioning properly. The doctors were always hesitant to say how much was damage from his injuries and how much was psychological trauma, but his mother had been insistent on a change. It wasn't too soon, she'd said, and even if it was, surely a new environment with entirely new stimuli – and entirely new doctors, for that matter, who weren't so bloody useless – could only help her younger son. Plus, she couldn't stand living in this house for *one moment longer.*

Seth's father had come up with a surprising solution. A small liberal-arts college on the dark, wet coast of Washington, where he'd once spent a semester as a young visiting professor, had answered an inquiry and said yes, as a matter of fact, they *did* have a place for him to teach, should he want. It was even less money than he made in England, but the college was so desperate for staff, they'd provide a housing stipend and moving expenses.

Seth's mother hadn't hesitated, not even at the remote location, two hours' drive from the nearest cities. She'd started packing boxes before his father had even accepted the job, and they were gone from England in a bewildering tornado of a month, moving to Halfmarket, a place that may not have been under a permanent winter's night but sure felt that way.

Seth shakes his head now, rejecting the idea that the whole experience had somehow just been online. His mum had been too angry about everything, his father too unhappy, Owen too injured, and Seth too ignored. If it was all fake or programmed or whatever the hell it was, why wouldn't they be better? Why wouldn't they be happier?

No, it didn't make sense.

Well, okay, it made *more* sense than any other explanation so far, but still. The world might have done that, gone online to forget itself, but his parents? They wouldn't have chosen that. Seth sure as hell wouldn't have chosen those things to happen to him.

Unless they hadn't *had* a choice?

He stops before his front door.

Maybe the Driver wasn't really guarding the people in the coffins from outside interference. Maybe it was there to make sure no one ever woke up. It didn't look fully human, so maybe it wasn't. Maybe it was a robot. Maybe it was an alien and they'd forced humans to—

"Crap sci-fi," Seth mutters to himself. "Life is never actually that interesting. It's the kind of story—"

He stops again.

It's the kind of story where everything's explained by one big secret, like everyone going online and what's real and what's not being reversed. The kind of story you watched for two hours, were satisfied with the twist, and then got on with your life.

The kind of story his own mind would provide to make sense of this place.

He pushes open the door. It isn't locked, never has been. The Driver could have walked in and killed them before they'd had a chance to run anywhere. And that would have been the end of *that* story.

Instead, they survived. In unlikely ways. The Driver had waited outside until Seth saw it, then taken its time coming into the house after punching him in the chest – he rubs the area now, still bruised, but not nearly as bruised as it should be – before taking its time again to chase them through the grass.

And everything else, too. An outdoor store to provide every bit of equipment he needed. A supermarket stocked with enough food to keep him alive. Rain that not only washed him, but showed up just in time to put out a fire that clearly – as he finds the lantern and flicks it on – hadn't even reached the kitchen.

Everything inside is just as they left it. It smells of smoke, but that's all. He climbs over the tumbled fridge and goes out to the deck. The tall grass is all burnt away, but the deck is intact, if blackened at the end. The pile of his original bandages is still there, too, the metallic strips reflecting the moonlight almost more than they should be able to.

He goes back inside, has a quick cold wash at the sink, and dresses in warmer clothes. He finds his torch, and that quickly, he's ready to go.

But he takes one last look around the sitting room and finds himself doing what he told Tomasz he was going to do.

"Good-bye, Owen," he whispers. "Good-bye, house."

As he steps out the front door, pulling it shut behind him, he wonders if it really is the last time he'll ever see it. He feels unexpectedly sad about that.

However real this house is, it's meant something.

And then he remembers Regine's words.

I'm the only real thing I've got, he thinks.

And then he remembers what else she said.

"Know yourself and go in swinging," he says out loud.

It's time to go to the prison.

Because, real world or not, maybe there are answers there.

43

He heads toward the train tracks on a path that's become familiar. The moon is bright enough that he doesn't need to turn on the torch. It's completely quiet as he goes. No crickets. No owls. Still no wind, despite the earlier rain.

He keeps alert as he walks, ready to run at any movement, but he makes it to the passage between the blocks of flats without incident. He reaches the train station and treads quietly through it past the train, wondering all the while if boars are nocturnal. He hops lightly down onto the tracks and looks in the direction of the prison.

The tracks are strangely empty. There are tall weeds here and there, but it's mostly just gravel and strangled-looking grass that barely reaches his ankles. He can still see the rails shining in the moonlight for much of their distance south. Maybe years of pesticides to keep them clear were hard to fight.

On the right, there's a brick walkway, possibly for train repair crews, that still seems in pretty good shape. Seth makes his way over to it and heads out of the station building. To his left, over the low fences, he can see some of the burnt neighborhood. It's too dark to make out any details, just shadows on the landscape that could be tombstones. He sees no signs of movement, just empty desolation, with the silhouette of Masons Hill on the horizon.

He knows from memory that this track goes all the way to the ocean, though they'd only gone a couple times, and frankly, it was about as appealing as the seashore in Half-market. All rocks and cliffs and outlandishly cold water. But before the train would reach there, he remembers, as it pulled out of the station heading seaward, it would start its journey by passing great rows of fences and walls, chain link and brick, cornered by towers poking out of the surrounding trees. An architecture designed to hide itself within its own folds: the prison.

In the moonlight, he can already see one of the towers through the treetops in the distance. It's probably not even a ten-minute walk from here, when it should be, he feels, something that took hours.

Ten minutes seems way too easy.

And not nearly enough time to work himself up to it.

He keeps heading down the brick walkway, gripping the torch like his own version of the Driver's baton. He checks back to make sure a boar isn't after him, and he sees the bridge over the tracks, on top of which he caught his first glimpse of the burnt-out neighborhood, and from where Tomasz saw him for the first time, too.

He wonders if they were worried when they found out someone else was here. Frightened, even. For him. *Of* him. And what had they thought when they found him showering? In an intimate way. He feels himself blush, though Regine had seemed as embarrassed as he was and Tomasz took it in the same enthusiastic stride as he did everything else.

Seth feels a pang again at letting Tomasz go. He pictures him now, waiting at their house, cheerfully expecting Seth along any minute. And Regine, thinking she knew better. And maybe she did.

Tomasz and Regine. A boy and a girl come to stop him before he reached Masons Hill, before he ran straight into the arms of something dangerous. A boy and a girl to give him answers to all the questions he might have, though leaving just enough unexplained to let the mystery seem plausible–

"You need to stop this," he says. "This kind of thinking will drive you crazy."

Her slap was sure real. The hug from Tomasz and the faint, familiar stinkiness of a boy that age was *tangibly* real, felt on Seth's skin and smelled through his nose.

And yes, okay, Tomasz was a lot like Owen, just like a helping figure his brain might have conjured up to help him . . . accept death or move to a different consciousness or whatever the point of this place was, if it even had a point, then that might have made sense.

But he wouldn't have made Regine up. She wasn't like anyone he knew, not anywhere. Not that accent, not that attitude.

No, they were real. Or real enough.

But then Gudmund–

"Stop it," he tells himself again. He keeps on walking. Through the trees between the tracks and the prison, he can see that he's nearing the corner of the fifteen-foot-high brick wall. The outermost of the prison defenses.

He'll take it as it comes, he thinks. If it's a big opening and he can see through it, he'll have a look. If it seems safe enough to enter, well, then, maybe that's what he'll do. If it doesn't, he can always come back another night. All they've got here is time, don't they? There'll always be another chance –

A hundred feet along the brick wall from where he's standing, he sees a light.

Electric light. For that's clearly what it is, an odd, blank whiteness different than flickering firelight and much too strong to be coming from a torch or a gas lantern. It's filtering through some trees, through what should be – if the wall continues through the foliage – solid brick. It's shining out, low enough not to have been seen from his house.

Seth listens all around him, for other footsteps on the brick, the thrum of an approaching engine, even the snuffling of the boar. But there's nothing except him and his breathing. The light is silent, too, no rumbling of a generator, no whine of burning filament. The harsh shine of it comes on him unexpectedly through the leaves as he continues on. He squints into the glare, holding up a hand to shade his eyes. He's reached the break in the prison wall.

Regine was right. The opening here is huge. The outer wall has been ruptured, but so has every row of fencing inside it, including the wooden walls of what look like some kind of holding room, now nearly flattened. From this point, there's a straight open line, right into the very heart of the prison.

The light itself is nothing more remarkable than a streetlight-size bulb attached to what he can see now is an inner fence, torn open and collapsed. The light illuminates bricks from the outer wall tossed in almost casual piles and the twisted chain link of the fences within fences behind it.

It looks as if something enormous broke through. As if something rose up from the center of the prison and went straight through everything in its path to get out.

But how? Seth wonders. *What could have done this?*

Whatever did it, though, whenever it might have happened, now there is only quiet, and the single light showing the way to the heart of the prison.

He stands there, unsure. The ground angles down through the broken walls and fences. He can see maybe a hundred feet before it returns to blackness.

There could be anything down there. Anything at all. People sleeping in their coffins. Or no people, just empty rooms. Or there could be a single figure, dressed all in black, waiting for him.

If it's a test, Seth doesn't know what the right answer is.

To go in, or to leave it all unknown.

He grips the torch firmly again.

"I'll just see," he says. "That's all I'll do. I'll just see what's next."

He steps forward into the darkness.

44

He moves through the first random scatters of bricks. Some roll and tumble as he bumps them but settle immediately back into silence once they fall.

The outermost wall, the brick one, is the tallest, which makes obvious sense. There are three rows of chain link next, all with barbed wire—of a sharper, uglier kind than on regular keep-out fences—stretching across the top. He has to take great care to get past a particularly messy tangle of it, but after that, he's through and next to the light itself, hanging down, almost broken off, from the third stretch of chain link.

Other light fixtures hang along the fence to either side, but this is the only one still working, a heavy plastic housing attached to the fence with a burning bulb still inside. No hint of where the electricity to run it is coming from. Seth wonders, in momentary panic, if the fence itself might be electrified, before remembering he's grabbed it several times on the way through.

He heads farther in. The light is behind him now, facing the other way. It starts to grow darker, everything turning to shadow. The trees have all stopped, as it's obvious they would. Why would you give prisoners something to climb? The ground keeps angling down, the prison built at the bottom of what Seth thinks must be meant by a "dell."

He can see a bit of it in the moonlight, a complex of buildings spreading down the hill in front of him, some behind farther rows of fences, others stretched along a little service road. There are also wide expanses of empty space, covered in weed-broken asphalt, which might have been prisoner exercise yards. The three main buildings at the bottom are five stories high, marking off three sides of another empty square. It's too dark to see them clearly.

Dark, he thinks. *As in no other lights.*

The rest of the prison is quickly resembling everything else in this world. Abandoned, silent, still. He walks through thick grass again, though it isn't as tall as in his own back garden. As ever, there are no rustlings of birds or nighttime creatures.

He stops on the last of a little rise. He's well inside the prison grounds now, and the row of breakages in the fences has ended. The moon is still bright and clear, and his eyes adjust enough to let him see it all before him.

There is nothing happening here. No sign of any activity, not even the sound of an engine running. No sound of anything, like there would have to be – you couldn't keep that many people alive, even if they were asleep, without there being *some* noise. Tomasz said he woke up here and was trapped with countless coffins behind countless doors and walls, but there's nothing here now. If possible, it's even more dark and still and silent than the rest of this world. Even the air is stale, like the inside of a locked room.

246

Nothing. Really nothing. So much so that a thought wanders into Seth's head.

Did they?

Did they *lie* to him?

Were they *trying* to keep him away? If so, they hadn't tried very hard. In fact, he almost thought they'd talked about it in such a way to make sure he'd come here to look.

By himself.

"No," he says out loud. "They may have been a lot of things, but they weren't–"

A shaft of light pours out across the small square as the door to one of the three main buildings opens.

The Driver steps out into the night.

Seth drops to the ground. There's nowhere to properly hide, no building close enough to run behind. He can only press himself down into the grass and hope it's tall enough to block the view.

The Driver is still some distance away, five hundred feet or so, silhouetted against the light from the doorway. It stands there looking out, as if it's sensed something and is coming to investigate. It moves down the steps and into the courtyard, its footfalls echoing heavily across the small dell.

Seth tenses, preparing to run. It must know he's here. It could probably see quite easily in the dark–

But then the Driver returns to the door and closes it. The light vanishes, and in the temporary blindness that follows, Seth holds his breath, straining to listen. He waits to hear footsteps again, but there's nothing. Has the Driver moved to a softer part of the square, something covered with grass? Maybe it's coming for him right now, on a new silent kind of footing –

And then a step. A clear step, just like when it came through the window of his house, a *thunk* of surprising weight.

And then another. And another.

The sounds of the footfalls are bouncing between the three buildings, confusing any sense of where it's going. Is it coming toward him? Walking away? Seth risks raising his head farther above the grass, but all he can see is the glowing purple spot on his retina left by the light from the door.

Step. And another.

Growing louder, unquestionably.

There's no choice. He's going to have to run as fast as he can back to the tracks, make his way out somehow, run toward –

But then he realizes he can't run to Regine and Tomasz. He'd bring the Driver right to them.

Step. Step.

"I'm sorry," he finds himself whispering, to Tomasz, to Regine, to himself, not knowing what to do, where to go. "I'm so sorry."

He stands to run.

And he hears the engine of the van start up.

He drops back down. Out there in the darkness somewhere, the engine noise grows in an oddly smooth way, as if the volume on it had been turned down and is slowly being raised again. It's somewhere off to the side of the three buildings, maybe even–

Yes, *there*. Headlights, coming from around the corner of the farthest building, the one the Driver walked out of. The van moves across the square and turns down the main drive through the center of the prison.

Away from Seth.

It heads toward the southern entrance, the one Regine said was locked down. The Driver obviously has a way out into the world to patrol it, fulfilling whatever mysterious role it's been assigned or taken on for itself.

Whatever it is, it's leaving. The engine noise doesn't quite disappear, but it grows more distant, distant enough for Seth to feel slightly safer. He spares a thought again for Regine and Tomasz, out there in the world, hiding somewhere while the Driver prowls.

"Be safe," he whispers. "Be safe."

He looks down toward the buildings again, toward the doorway–now shut tight, not a peep of light escaping from behind it. His night vision has returned. He can see the square in the moonlight now. See the buildings in their silent darkness.

See how they seem unattended.

The engine is still faintly whining in the distance, though it sounds so smooth, so efficient, that in a world with other cars, with any other sounds *at all*, you'd never hear it coming.

But still, it's an engine that's moving away.

The prison, for the moment, is possibly unguarded.

Seth rises. First to his hands, then with a deep breath, to his feet.

Nothing happens. Silence continues to unroll. The engine noise is now so distant sounding as to almost not be there.

Seth thinks, he *feels,* that he's alone here.

And if it's a story he's telling himself or a path he's supposed to be on or just another convenient thing that's happened to lead him forward, well, does it matter, he wonders? Does any of it really matter?

Because he wants to know, more than anything, what's behind that door.

45

He sneaks down to the nearest building of the three around the square, stopping to look in a window. It's got prison bars on it, but inside, there's only darkness. He flicks on the torch. Nothing happens until he hits it a few times, rotates the aging batteries, and hits it a few times more. It flickers to life with a light barely bright enough to read by, but it's better than nothing.

Through the dusty wired glass that sits just behind the bars, all the torch illuminates is an empty corridor, stretching away from him. He can see the heavy-looking doors to rooms—*cells,* of course they are, actual prison cells. The doors have smaller barred windows set in them and none of them is leaking any light.

It's a dead place, as dead as everything else.

The next window has a number of its wired glass panes broken out, but inside is more of the same. Another stretch of corridor, another row of darkened, empty cells, no indication of life or movement or activity.

No indication of any coffins, that's for sure.

Before he can check the third window, the last before the corner of the building, the torch goes out and refuses to light again, no matter how much he curses over it. He sighs, but he doubts there was much more to see anyway. Prisons probably didn't bother much with variation. He makes his way instead to the corner of the building, the one that leads on to the square.

It's a concrete expanse, broken by the usual weeds pushing up through cracks. There's not even the remnants of anything else – old benches, concrete planters, nothing – just an empty space that would have been completely bare before things started growing up through it. Another exercise yard, maybe, or perhaps just a clear area where there was nowhere for a prisoner to hide.

Each of the buildings looks the same. Ugly and square and unyielding. Not a curved line to be seen. One main front door to each and rows of evenly spaced windows, bars and heavy locks on every conceivable thing that might open.

Looking around, Seth wonders for a moment where the man who took Owen was kept. The prisoner whose name he *still* can't quite bring to mind, no matter how many ways he tries to approach it.

Had the prisoner ever been in this square? Almost certainly. And had no doubt spent his empty time in one of these very cells. When he escaped, maybe he had hidden behind this same corner where Seth now stands.

Seth remembers that the prisoner hadn't been regarded as a flight risk. The police said that even though he had occasionally been kept in solitary confinement, that was for his own protection, not for what trouble he might cause or that he might try to escape. He'd been a model prisoner. That's what the officers kept saying to his parents on those awful nights when Owen was still missing, as if it was somehow supposed to be comforting rather than what it actually was, an apology for taking their eye off him at the most important moment.

Seth orients himself in the dark, mentally placing the train tracks on one side and looking up toward what must be the direction of his house.

The prisoner had been given a pass that day, that's the story that emerged, one that allowed him to move freely from one part of the prison to another, to tend to the grounds, as he'd shown a talent for gardening. Yes, the memories are coming back to Seth now (but his name? What was his freaking *name*?). The prisoner had arranged it somehow so that one set of officers expected him to be in one place and another expected him to be somewhere else, so that for just long enough, no one was looking for him.

The police assumed he must have had help, but Seth can't remember anything ever being explained beyond that. The prisoner had created a hole in time, a shaded, hidden chain of moments that allowed him to go—Seth turns a bit more, getting it right—*that* way, and sneak through fences and duck past guards (who may or may not have been looking away on purpose) until there was only one more fence to climb.

The fence into Seth's backyard.

Seth spits onto the grass, his stomach sour. He had opened the door to the man. No matter what happens in the rest of his life, he will always have opened that door.

It wasn't your fault, Gudmund had said. *You were eight.*

And oh, how Seth wanted to believe him.

He stares into the darkness, up toward where the prisoner had entered Seth's life and taken Owen from it, returning him injured and broken.

Seth is angry now, remembering it.

Angry, and suddenly a whole lot less afraid.

He steps into the square and heads for the door where the Driver emerged.

It looks the same as the doors in the other buildings. No light comes from any crack or seam, nor through the windows on either side. Seth holds the torch up as he approaches, ready to swing it if he must at anything that might sneak up on him.

But there's nothing, still. Just empty space and silence. All those barred windows looking down on him. Deserted, dirty buildings watching his progress.

The door is up a few steps and recessed a little, and as he moves to it, the moon is angled so that he's stepping into shadow. He hits the torch a few more times, fruitlessly, then feels around in the darkness for some kind of handle on the door, finding one, never expecting in a million years—

It opens.

With a simple click of a lever, the door swings under his touch, pulling outward with an easy silence that seems as strange as the smoothness of the van's engine. If ever a door should creak loudly, it should be one on the front of a darkened, empty prison, but it glides open like something hydraulic and modern.

Before he's ready, before he ever expected, Seth is standing in front of an open doorway.

A doorway so dark it might be an entry on to deepest space.

He thumps the torch again, but more out of nervous energy than expectation.

He squints, trying to see something, *anything* in the black.

But there really is just . . . emptiness.

Nothingness.

A blank on the world.

Seth goes back down the steps. He walks to the window to the right of the door and peeks inside. The shadows are deep here, too, but he can see a little bit, enough to suggest that this building is like the last one, corridors and cells and the dust of years.

But the doorway to the entrance is still just deepest black, unnaturally so, like the rules of light and space are suspended in that single rectangle.

He can see *nothing* beyond it.

"It's a trick of the light," he whispers to himself. "A trick of the moon."

But he stands for a moment longer, the world holding its silent breath, the empty nothing of the doorway staring back at him.

He reaches for the anger in him again. The anger at the prisoner who just walked away from here and ruined everything. It helps. He goes back up the steps, nearing the darkness, nearing the doorway.

The silence is almost deafening now, so solid that Seth

begins to almost doubt it. Surely he should hear *something*. A breeze. The shushing of blown grass down the hillside. A creak as the building settles.

But there is only this void. Waiting for him to step through.

There could be anything beyond it, anything at all. It could be an entryway to a whole other *world*, for all he knows—

"Which is stupid," he whispers, still staring into the blackness.

But out here, alone, in the dark, his mind begins to reel with possibilities.

Because maybe this place is a journey.

And maybe this door is its final stop.

Because if there is death anywhere here, it can only be beyond this doorway.

Maybe it *is* this doorway.

And if this place really is a kind of hell, maybe you have to die to leave it.

Maybe it's as simple as walking through a door.

As long as it's the right door.

And almost without trying, he begins to think about that day on the beach—

No, a voice in his head says. *No.*

But still, he thinks of that day, that *last* day, when he had calmly walked into a freezing, wild ocean and had *un*calmly been battered to death against a rock.

And woken up here.

Stop this, he thinks. *Stop it—*

But he thinks about this morning, too—though that it's still the same day he left to go running toward Masons Hill seems ridiculous, it was weeks ago, lifetimes.

He thinks about that feeling again.

It's dangerous to do this, to think this way, he knows. Dangerous to revisit a place that most people never got to, most people never *wanted* to get to.

Is this what he died for? Was this what he'd been asking for all along? Was this what Tomasz and Regine and the Driver and all the convenient things had been leading him to?

Do I want this? he thinks.

Do I still want this?

And he realizes that he doesn't really know for sure.

Here is the chance—

Here is the doorway.

He lifts his hand and reaches through.

46

The surge of light is so bright it's almost a physical assault. He squeezes his eyes shut like he's been punched and stumbles back down into the square, ready to run –

But not quite yet.

He holds up a hand to shadow his eyes and opens them into the tiniest slits he can manage. The doorway, so solidly dark just seconds before, is now equally solidly white.

No. Not quite solid.

There's something just inside.

Another door. A second door. Made of milky-white glass.

And it's open.

Seth cautiously goes back to the front steps. The light seems to radiate not from any particular source but from every surface inside: the inner door itself, the walls beyond, and he can also now see the stairway going down from it deeper inside. All white, all seemingly made of glass.

It is absolutely *nothing* like the insides of the buildings around it.

He can hear something now, too. A *hum* of . . . what?

Electricity? It must be, to generate a light this powerful. But also more. A *hum* suggesting further power, coming from down those stairs, but like the silent door opening, like the engine of the van, it's a clean sound, sleeker and newer than any power source he's ever heard.

Seth stops at the outer threshold. He leans down and reaches in a hand, touching the floor. It feels exactly how it looks, like a white pane of glass, and the air inside is cooler than out here.

He stands. The light is so naked, such an unmistakable signal in this dark night, he feels dangerously exposed. He looks around nervously. Surely some alarm must have been tripped. Surely the Driver must be making its way back here even now.

But he only hears the low *hum*. Nothing else.

No sound of the engine.

And without another thought, without letting himself disappear into another self-debate, he steps through the outer doorway.

Nothing happens. No sounds, no blaring sirens objecting to his presence, nothing. He looks back out onto the square, floodlit by all this brightness. Whatever he's going to do, he needs to hurry.

It's two steps to the inner door, and he takes them. Nothing still happens. The white glass stairs beyond it go down a flight and turn back on themselves, heading farther down. He can just about see the bottom of the second flight, where they reach what could possibly be another corridor.

Again, it's nothing like the rest of the prison. It's like he's stepped into an entirely different building, an entirely different place altogether. Even the door has no latch, no way to open or shut it, or lock it either. It's essentially just a panel on invisible hinges, unlike any door he's ever seen. Except maybe on television. In shows about the future.

He puts a foot inside the second doorway. Nothing changes. He takes the first step down. Then another, and another. He glances back into the darkness, but there's still nothing. He keeps going, trying to make his footfalls as quiet as he can, listening for any other sounds.

But there's only him, and that low *hum*.

He pauses at the turning. The same white walls and steps lead down to a short corridor with a door at the end. It's closed. Seth continues on toward it, noticing that the under-side of the stairwell is made of the same glassy material as everything else. This whole room could have been carved out of one solid block of milk-colored glass. He reaches the bottom and stops before the door. It's like the one above, flat, featureless, and generating its own light.

He reaches out, but before he even comes into contact with it, it opens. He jumps back, but stops as he sees that it's merely sliding smoothly into the wall, as if it's simply responded to his presence by performing the most likely task he might ask of it. Beyond it, there's just another white corridor with a turn at the end.

But the *hum* is louder.

He waits for another moment. Then another. But still, nothing happens. No one comes. He sees that the light down the new hallway is different, more than just the glow from the walls. Something changes beyond the turn.

Seth swallows. He swallows again.

Now or never, he thinks.

It doesn't work. He doesn't move.

It'll be nothing, he thinks. *It won't be what Tomasz and Regine think. It won't be what I imagine. It won't be stupid aliens, that's for sure.*

But he's afraid, more than he was outside.

Because *something* is clearly down here.

He steps through the door.

He moves down the corridor.

He turns the corner.

And looks out.

Over a vast, vast room, as deep as an airplane hangar.

Which contains hundreds, *thousands* of shiny black coffins.

47

The room doesn't match the stairwell. The walls and floor are a kind of polished, shiny concrete that looks spotlessly clean. Milky panels of light shine down on the coffins at intervals from the ceiling.

Over an area that stretches farther than he can see.

He's on a rise, a small platform edging out from the door slightly above the floor of the larger room. Beyond, there are rows upon rows upon rows of coffins. They pull away from him, pushing into the distance, carrying on through faraway passageways into suggestions of deeper, even larger rooms beyond.

This place is *much* bigger than the prison above it. There are wide aisles down the center of the room, stretching as far into the depths as the coffins. *Wide enough for a van to drive through,* Seth thinks. Well, they had to get the coffins down here somehow, didn't they? There could be any number of unknown doors back there, opening out at different points into the world above, but . . .

"How can this be?" he whispers. "How?"

The *hum* comes from here. He can see no source for it, no cables along the floor or any kind of separate machinery that's not a coffin, but the sound is certainly this place, these things, operating however they're supposed to be operating.

With people inside. Asleep.

Living their lives.

The platform he's standing on has a short staircase at one end. He makes his way down to the shiny concrete floor, again expecting an alarm to warn him away or someone demanding to know what the hell he's doing here.

He approaches the nearest coffin. It's shut tight. He half expects it to pop open under his touch, like the door did, but nothing changes. He has to look for several long moments to even find the seal. The metal feels cool, but neither artificially cold nor hot. He moves around it, but everything's the same as the one at his house, including–he kneels down to check–a small tube in the middle disappearing into the shiny concrete floor.

How can this possibly work, though? he thinks, doubt creeping back in. *How can this possibly be real?*

Because how did people have babies, huh? He turns around the room, the coffins stretched out before him like an army of the dead. And how did everyone stay healthy? How did they even get fed? He and Regine and Tomasz were maybe not prime athletes, but they were still functional human beings who could walk and lift things. He'd been weak for a bunch of days, sure, but his legs could still hold him up after years of lying down.

No, he thinks. *No, this can't be.*

He wanted something, he realizes now. Wanted an answer other than the ones he'd been given. Wanted to find out this whole world had some purpose, some *particular* purpose. For him.

He doesn't want the explanation to be the obvious one.

He sticks his fingers on the seal of the coffin, trying to find purchase. He can just about slide his fingernails – untrimmed since he woke, but yeah, how about that, how did everyone's fingernails not grow? – into the seam. It doesn't budge much, but he presses hard and lifts up.

The lid rises half an inch, an inch –

Before slipping from his grip and shutting again, pinching his fingertips painfully. He shakes his fingers out and tries again. And once more.

"Come on," he grunts. "Come on!"

The lid opens so suddenly and so high, Seth loses his balance and falls hard to the floor, knocking his elbow on the concrete. He unleashes a long, loud shout of the worst curse words he knows, holding his elbow close to his chest until the pain ebbs.

"Shit," he says, more quietly. More mildly, too.

Still breathing hard, he looks up to the now-open casket. He's below the edge of it and can't see inside, but already the underside of the lid looks like the one from his house, with tubes and strips of metallic tape, though this one has pulses of light moving along the length of it.

He drags himself to his knees, unbending himself slowly up and up, the pain in his elbow still throbbing, as the bed of the coffin comes into view.

He's surprised. He shouldn't be, he knows it, but he's surprised at what he sees.

Because, of course, there's a person lying inside.

A man.

A living, breathing man.

The man's body is wrapped like Seth's was when he woke, bandages around legs, torso, and chest. His genitals are exposed, and Seth can now see why. There are tubes connected to the man's penis and another running down between his thighs, held there by medical adhesive tape. Seth remembers the marks on his own body. Marks where tubes must have gone into him exactly the same way. Taking away his waste, just like Regine and Tomasz had guessed.

Almost every other inch of the man is covered, down to his fingertips and almost his entire face. Seth doesn't remember those bandages, but he does remember that horrible vague period after he died. That sense of disoriented panic. It had been a different kind of frightening, almost worse than the death itself, but whatever his mind had been doing, his body had been tearing bandages away from his hands and face, as he crawled out of the coffin and found his way downstairs. He wonders now how he made it without breaking his neck, how he knew where to go when he was so blind.

Instinct, he supposes. A memory he didn't even know he possessed.

The only thing not covered on the man's face is his mouth, which has a guard fitted between his teeth with a tube attached to the end of it, supplying food or oxygen or water, Seth guesses, but who could say for sure? Who could say for sure about *anything*? Did the metallic tape on the bandages provide the programming for the sleeping world? Did they stimulate the muscles so they wouldn't atrophy? Did the tubes for waste also do the work of reproduction somehow?

Who knew? Who had the answers?

The man gives no sign at all of knowing that anything's different, that someone is standing over him. His only movements are the slow rise and fall of his chest as he breathes. The top of the man's head isn't covered, and his hair is as brutally short as Seth's. The man's neck is uncovered as well, and Seth finds himself reaching for it, touching the skin there, lightly, gently, just to see if it's real.

He's surprised somehow to find that it's warm, the warm, blood-filled skin of a living person. He's even more surprised to find the man has stubble. Low and barely there, but still. How did that not grow into a beard? Did someone *shave* him? Were there drugs that stunted hair growth? How the hell did all of this work?

"And who are you?" Seth whispers. "Did I know you?"

Because all these people were from the same town, *this* town, wasn't that the idea? All the people from the houses out there in the neighborhood moved to a single spot. So this man could have been a next door neighbor or a friend of his parents or –

"But I moved away, didn't I?" Seth says. "Or in the imagined world, we did. And who knows where you imagined *you* went."

266

He stares down at the man, uncomfortable at his sheer vulnerability. He looks like a patient lying there. Someone recovering from an indescribably terrible accident. Kept asleep because being awake was too painful and the recovery too long—

And then a notion takes Seth. A crazy one, an impossible one.

He resists it, crossing his arms, still looking down on the man.

But the notion returns.

Because he's roughly Seth's size, isn't he? Pretty close in height and about the same weight, too. The same width across the shoulders and chest, the same skinny legs of a runner, the same color body hair.

"No," Seth tells himself. "Don't be stupid."

But the idea won't leave. The more he looks at the shape of the man through the tightly wound bandages, at the few stretches of skin and body that aren't covered, the more he thinks—

"No," he says again.

But he's moving his hand back to the man's face, back to the bandages there. He gently takes the edge of one and tries to peel it away. It doesn't give. He follows it along, trying to find a seam to start the unwinding, turning the man's head to look for it.

"This is crazy," he mumbles to himself. "How would that make any sense at all?"

But he still needs to see. Needs to know for sure—

Because what if—

What if it *is* him?

What kind of answer would *that* be?

"Shit," he's saying, his anxiety rising, his heart beating faster. "Oh, shit."

He finds the bandage end near the man's left ear and starts peeling it back, working hard to get a start, then peeling more and more of it away. The bandage unwraps a layer across the man's face, and Seth lifts the man's head out of its cushion to unwind it around the back –

Where there's a light blinking under the skin of the man's neck.

Seth freezes, the man's head in his hands. He's suddenly aware, really for the first time, that he's holding a living being, someone sleeping but *breathing,* warm to the touch.

Alive.

Gently, gently, he turns the man's head to get a better look at the blinking light. It flashes on and off, green and sharp, in a regular pulse on a stretch of skin just at the base of the man's skull below his left ear, uncovered by bandages.

At exactly where the bump is on the back of Seth's own skull.

At exactly the point where he hit the rocks and everything here started.

Then he sees something else. He lifts the man's head out farther. In the stretch of bare skin above the bandages on the man's back is one of those quasi-Celtic tribal tattoos, stretching the width of the man's shoulders.

A tattoo that Seth emphatically does not have.

Then of course he sees everything how it always was. The man's hair is really a bit darker than Seth's, and Seth's

268

stubble isn't that thick anyway. The man's torso is clearly shorter than Seth's, now that he looks again, and frankly, as embarrassing as it is, he doubts there's a teenage boy alive who wouldn't recognize his own wang.

This man isn't him.

Of course it isn't him.

And all at once, touching the man feels too private, feels like an *invasion* of another person, almost criminal. He rewraps the bandage around the man's head, saying "Sorry, sorry," re-sticking the start of the adhesive to the spot by the man's ear probably harder than he really needs to. He drops the man's head back onto the cushion –

And that's when the alarm finally goes off.

48

It's not hugely loud, but it's unambiguous, surging in and out like all bad news alarms everywhere. Seth looks around for the source of it but doesn't see anything. He grabs the coffin lid to slam it shut. It swings down but then stops abruptly, finishing the journey in a slow, automatic smoothness, resealing itself and the man inside with a small hydraulic sound, looking as if nothing had ever happened.

The alarm is still blaring, though, and Seth is already running back to the platform to get back up the steps and–

He hesitates.

A display has appeared on the blank white wall, one long, milky rectangle sort of demisting to reveal that it's been a screen all along. It's now covered with words and boxes and symbols of different colors, just like you'd see on any computer pad. The alarm is still blaring, Seth still poised to run, but his eyes are caught–

Because on the screen, in a circular set of graphical symbols, the words CHAMBER OPEN flash in time with the alarm. Seth doesn't even want to consider that this alarm must be alerting the Driver out there, that it can only be racing back here at top speed–

CHAMBER OPEN. CHAMBER OPEN. CHAMBER OPEN. In bright-red letters.

"But I *shut* the chamber," he says and, almost in exasperation, he reaches out and touches the red symbols.

The alarm stops.

He lifts his hand away. The symbols have turned green, and figures and boxes and images suddenly appear on the rest of the display, whirring through their business, seemingly oblivious to his presence. One section shuffles through images of different angles on different rows of coffins, clearly a kind of surveillance, and Seth nearly jumps out of his skin when it shows an image of him standing in front of the display. But the image rushes on, as if his presence isn't a threat.

He looks behind him to see where the camera might be, but there's still only the blank whiteness of the lights, the endless spread of black coffins. Back on the screen, the images keep shuffling through, including what looks like a flash of a large, garage-size door on some distant wall, and he has a momentary unease that the van could come driving right up through here to get him, any minute now, any *second*–

But he can't quite tear himself away. Boxes around the edge of the screen show things like temperature and humidity, others shifting clocks, only a few of which show anything like what the current time might plausibly be before being replaced by other times and then others still. The rest of the boxes contain graphs and displays Seth can't even begin to guess at. What does MODULATION RATE mean? What's BETA

Cycle, Segment Four? And Flow Management could be anything. Flow of what? Managed how? By who?

Seth knows he needs to go, that he may have shut off the alarm, but that doesn't mean the Driver wouldn't have heard a signal of some kind—

But he doesn't go, not yet.

Because the center of the screen is asking him a question.

Chamber Re-actualized? it reads.

Beside it, in the main body of the screen, is a green, graphical map of the coffins—he can tell it's the ones behind him because the stairwell is there—and the coffin Seth opened is highlighted by a pointing line.

Connected to the line is a pop-up window with a picture in it of what can only be the man in the coffin Seth just opened.

It's a head-on shot, like a driver's license or passport. The man isn't smiling, but he doesn't look unhappy. More bored than anything else, like this is just one more bureaucratic photo that needed to be taken.

And his name is written below the picture.

"Albert Flynn," Seth says out loud.

It gives other details, too. Something that could be a date of birth, but not written in a way Seth expects, and possibly height and weight, along with other measurements that aren't clear. There's a box labeled Physical Markers, and Seth touches it. It opens up another box, displaying a picture of the man's tattoo, stretching from shoulder to shoulder and down the backside of either of his arms.

Seth presses the box again and it disappears. He glances up to where the alarm symbol was. CHAMBER RE-ACTUALIZED? it still reads.

"Yes?" he says, and presses it. The symbol and words disappear, and the box with Albert Flynn's face shrinks down to nothing, back into the graphical rows of coffins on the screen.

Seth glances around, worried again at the time that's passing, but he still can't hear anything from the stairwell. The sound of the engine had disappeared deep into the night when he was outside. Maybe the Driver went far from here, traveling down roads that didn't allow for fast passage.

He presses one of the coffins on the graphical display. The face of a woman expands out into a box. Older, more smiley than Albert Flynn.

EMILIA FLORENCE RIDDERBOS.

Seth presses the coffin next to hers. Another face pops up, an older man.

JOHN HENRY RIDDERBOS.

"Husband," Seth automatically says, because how many Ridderboses could there be in the world? He moves to select the one next to John Henry, but he pauses. Yes, husband. Families would have entered here together, wouldn't they? Husbands and wives. Parents and children.

Except Seth woke up alone, in his own home.

But here were two Ridderboses, next to each other in the same row.

"So what about the Wearings, then?" he says, scanning the rest of the read-out, wondering if there's a way to –

There is. A box marked, simply, SEARCH. He presses it. A small keypad display appears, grouped in the normal keyboard arrangement. *So probably not alien then*, he thinks. He types in *Wearing*. He hesitates for a second over the word GO, but then presses it, too.

The graphical display of the coffins rapidly switches and turns, as if an overhead camera is zooming out over the vast rooms behind him before slowing down and closing in on a row, deep in some corner that he'd almost certainly never find.

First one coffin is highlighted, then another, and a list of names begins to emerge.

EDWARD ALEXANDER JAMES WEARING.

CANDACE ELIZABETH WEARING –

Seth doesn't even wait for it to finish processing. He presses his father's name.

And there he is. Younger, obviously so, his hair a completely different style and no streaks of gray. But his eyes have that slightly medicated look that Seth knows all too well. Seth presses his mother's name, and her picture pops up next to his father's. She's younger, too, her mouth pursed in that familiar defensive tightness, leaving no doubt as to who she is.

As simple as that, there they are.

Seeing them is unexpectedly hard. Worse than hard, *painful*. Seth's stomach actually starts to hurt. The unmistakable faces of his parents, younger but immovably them, staring back at him.

And somewhere in the room behind him, too.

He turns to look, but the graphical search had moved so fast he couldn't follow where it went. They could be anywhere, in any part of this vast complex.

Sleeping.

But also not sleeping. Living their lives, lives that to them were completely real. He turns back to the pictures and wonders what they're doing, right now, right this second, in the world of their house in Halfmarket.

Are you thinking about your son? he wonders.

The son who left without explaining or saying good-bye.

Their faces stare back at him from the screen, and he tries not to see accusation there.

Seth has to go. He knows it. It's been too long. The Driver will be on its way, will probably be here any second.

He has to go.

But he keeps looking into the eyes of his mother and father.

Until he finally swallows away the pain in his stomach and taps their pictures lightly, collapsing them back into the grid of coffins. It's time to leave. It's *past* time to leave, but he has to see one more. He reaches over to the list of names to tap—

He stops.

Owen isn't there.

The list of Wearing names is only two long. Edward and Candace, his father and mother.

Seth frowns. He opens the SEARCH box again and re-types his last name. It delivers the same results: Edward and Candace Wearing. He goes back to the SEARCH box once more and types in Owen's full name.

No matches found, the screen tells him.

"What?" Seth asks, his voice getting louder. "*What?*"

He tries again. And again.

But Owen isn't here.

He doesn't believe it, *can't* believe it. He types in his own name, but of course, he isn't here either, because he was in a lone coffin, separate from the main group, out there in his house, on his own. Maybe there hadn't been space. Maybe most of the coffins had been filled by the time his family came to join and other plans had to be made.

Who knows? And frankly, who cares?

Because Owen isn't here. Owen is out *there* somewhere. Out there in this burnt-up, empty world. In his own coffin. All by himself.

Alone, like Seth was.

"How could you?" he asks. "How could you do that?"

His anger rises. He knows it's illogical. That wherever Owen might be physically, he was with his parents, in every way that mattered in the online world. He'd seen it himself for the past eight years.

But still. What if he woke up? What if he was like Tomasz and woke up alone in a strange place, with no one to protect him?

The resolution comes hard and fast, like it's the thing he now knows he must do.

"I'll find you," he says, a new sense of purpose flooding him, a *welcome* one. "Wherever you are, I'll goddamn

276

well find you." He reaches to stab his parents' coffins again, thinking there might be further information, some record of where their youngest son is being kept–

"Ow!"

A static charge shocks him where he touches the screen. It's not much, the pain is negligible–

But the screen has changed. The coffins are all gone, replaced by a few words.

DAMAGED NODE DETECTED, the screen now reads.

SCAN IN PROGRESS, appears below that.

There is a shift in the lights, as one end of the room is suddenly lit by a strange greenish glow. Far too fast to outrun, it moves along the rows of coffins, until it washes over Seth.

And stops on him.

"Oh, crap," he says.

RESTORATION POSSIBLE, the screen says.

RE-ACTUALIZATION BEGUN.

"Shit!" Seth says, not sure what *Re-actualization* means but certain it can't be anything good. He's already turning back toward the short corridor to the stairs, already beginning to run–

When a blinding, debilitating pain shoots through his skull–

Right from the spot on the back of his neck where Albert Flynn's lights were blinking, right from where Seth's own "damaged node" must be–

And everything disappears in a flash of light.

49

"There's always beauty," said Gudmund. "If you know where to look."

Seth laughed. "Gayest thing you've ever said, mate."

"'Mate,'" Gudmund laughed back. "Quit pretending to be English."

"I am English."

"Only when it's convenient."

Gudmund turned back to the ocean. They were up on a cliff that plunged down thirty or forty feet to the rocky waves below. It was the end of one of those noticeably shorter days that said that summer was winding down and the start of the school year was near.

But not yet.

"I mean, just look at that," Gudmund said.

The sun, halved by the ocean's horizon, seemed bigger and more golden than it had any right to be, a huge scoop of butterscotch ice cream melting into the pavement. The sky above it reached out for Seth and Gudmund with dark pinks and blues, the scattered clouds vibrant trumpets of color.

"You turn away from that crappy little beach," Gudmund

said, "away from all the rocks and the waves that won't let you swim, and there's no place to picnic with your nice sandwiches and the wind will blow your whole tedious little family away if you don't keep them tethered to you. But then you look out into the ocean. And, well, there it is."

"Beauty," Seth said, not looking at the sunset, but at Gudmund's profile lit by that same sun.

There were other walkers up on the cliff, other people taking advantage of the day and the sunset, but Seth and Gudmund were momentarily alone, everyone else too far from them to be part of this exact view.

"Gudmund–" Seth began again.

"I don't know," Gudmund said. "I really don't, Sethy. But we've got now, which is more than a lot of people have, right? Let the future take care of itself."

He held out his hand toward Seth. Seth hesitated, checking first if anyone could see them.

"Chicken," Gudmund teased.

Seth took his hand and held it.

"We've got now," Gudmund said again. "And I've got you. And that's all I want."

Their hands still clasped, they watched the sun set–

"Can you tell me anything else?" Officer Rashadi asked, gently but seriously, in that way she spoke to him that was so unlike all the other officers.

"He was short?" Seth volunteered, but he knew he'd already said that. He just didn't want Officer Rashadi to *leave, didn't want this conversation to finish, as this was the most anyone had talked to him in days.*

She grinned at him. "That's what everyone says. But according to the records we have, I'm two inches shorter, and no one ever says that about me."

"You don't seem short, though," Seth said, twisting his fingers together.

"I'll take that as a compliment. But don't you worry. That doesn't mean he'll be harder to find, Seth. Even short people can't hide forever."

"Will he hurt Owen?" Seth blurted out, also not for the first time.

Officer Rashadi closed her notebook and folded her hands together over its cover. "We think he's using your brother to guarantee his safety," she said. "And so he knows that if he does hurt your brother, then there's no chance of any safety at all."

"So why would he hurt him?"

"Exactly."

They sat quietly for a moment, before Officer Rashadi said, "Thank you, Seth. You've been very, very helpful. Now I'm going to see how your parents are–"

They both turned at the sharp thump of the front door slamming open. Officer Rashadi got to her feet as another officer rushed into the sitting room.

"What is it?" Seth could hear his mum calling from upstairs. She rarely left the attic these days, wanting to be near Owen's things. "What's happened? Have you–"

But the new officer was speaking only to Officer Rashadi.

"They've found him," he said to her. "They've found Valentine—"

Gudmund's phone rang and rang and rang. On the second try, it went straight to voice mail.

Seth grabbed his coat. After what Monica had just told him on his doorstep, he had to see Gudmund. There was nothing else that had to happen in the whole wide world. He had to find him. Now. He took the stairs back down to the sitting room two at a time and was at the front door when his father called from the still-in-progress kitchen.

"Seth?"

Seth ignored him and opened the door, but then his father called in a way that brooked no argument. "Seth!"

"Dad, I have to go," Seth said as he turned, but he stopped when he saw his father standing there. He was covered in fine sawdust from the kitchen work, but he held his cell phone in his hand, staring at it in an odd way, as if he'd just hung up.

"That was your principal," his father said, sounding baffled. "Calling me on a Saturday afternoon."

"I really, really need to go, Dad—"

"Said his daughter had been sent a photo of you." His father looked down at his phone. "This *photo*," he said, holding it up so Seth could see.

A silence fell. Seth couldn't move. Neither, it seemed, could his father. He just held up the picture and looked at Seth questioningly.

"He wasn't mad or anything," his father said, slowly turning the phone back and looking down at the photo himself. "Said you were a good kid. Said someone was clearly out to cause you trouble, and he was worried that things might be hard for you come Monday. That he thought we should know. So we could help."

He stopped, but still stood there, quietly.

To his great irritation, Seth felt his eyes fill with tears. He tried to blink them away, but a few escaped down his cheeks anyway. "Dad, please. I need to go. I need to—"

"Find Gudmund," his father finished for him.

Not asking it, just saying it.

Seth felt caught, more caught than he could ever remember, more caught than on the day the man knocked on the window of the kitchen in the house in England. The world had stopped then, and it had stopped right now. Seth had no idea how it would ever start again.

"I'm sorry, son," his father said, and for a heart-sinking second, Seth thought he was saying he was sorry because he wasn't going to let Seth leave but—

"I'm sorry you felt you couldn't tell us," his father continued, looking down at his phone again, at the picture of Seth and Gudmund, just there together, but in a way serious and real and undeniable to anyone who might look. "I can't tell you how sorry I am about that."

And to Seth's astonishment, his father's voice broke as he said it.

"We haven't been great to you," his father said. He looked back up. "I'm so sorry."

Seth swallowed away the thickness in his throat. "Dad–"

"I know," his father said. "Go. Find him. We'll talk later. Your mum won't be very happy but–"

Seth waited a moment, not quite believing what he was hearing, but there was no time to waste. He opened the front door and raced out into the cold air, on his way to find Gudmund–

And it was summer again, it was months before, and Gudmund smiled at him on the cliff's edge, the sunset casting his face in gold.

"There's always beauty," he said. "If you know where to look."

Before the world was swallowed by a bright, white light–

50

Fiery pain grips Seth's head like a burning fist, blocking out everything else. It seems impossible to be able to live with pain this bad, impossible to think there isn't irreparable damage being done. He can hear a distant screaming before he realizes it's coming from his own mouth—

"I don't know what else to do!" a voice says.

"Just turn it off!" shouts another voice. "Turn the whole thing off!"

"HOW?"

Hands that Seth didn't know were holding him lower him to the floor, but there's pain occupying every free space, every free thought, and he can't stop screaming—

"That sound he's making! I think it's killing him—"

"There! Press that! Press anything!"

With such suddenness it feels like he's fallen off a cliff, the pain ceases. Seth vomits across the smoothness of the concrete floor and lies there helpless, his eyes running with water, his throat raw, gasping for air.

A pair of hands grabs him again.

Small hands. And he hears a worried prayer in what can only be Polish.

"Tomasz?" he grunts, and he feels two stubby arms grip him tightly in a hug. He's finding it difficult to focus his eyes, and it takes several blinks to see Regine's face leaning down toward him, too.

She looks ashen, and even in his confusion, he can see that she's terrified. "Can you get up?" she asks, urgency thrilling her voice.

"You must get up, Mr. Seth," Tomasz says, and they try to get him to his feet. Seth's legs won't support his weight, and they have to almost drag him across the floor.

"We must go," Tomasz says. "We *must*."

"How–?" Seth whispers as they get him up the platform and into the corridor, but he can't say anymore. His mind is racing away from itself, filled with images, crashing together in a torrent, a tidal wave come to drown him. He can see Tomasz and Regine, but he also sees Gudmund on the clifftop, sees his father, sees himself as a young boy when Owen was taken, all swirling together, and he can't look away, even when he closes his eyes.

"I guessed that you told an untruth," Tomasz says, starting to pull him up the main stairs. "An untruth *Regine* tried to conceal."

"We came back for him, didn't we?" she snaps.

"And only found him just in time!"

"Again," Seth finds himself mumbling, though his mind still thrums so fast, he's not even sure if he's spoken aloud.

He has. "That's right," Regine says, manhandling him past the turn in the stairwell, pushing both him and Tomasz up toward the inner door. "We're not actually here. None of us are. This is all just something you're imagining."

"Less of the arguing!" Tomasz says. "More of the hurrying!"

They reach the top and guide Seth outside. Every time he blinks, he sees his memories before him, so clear and vivid it's as if he's switching back and forth between this world and that one. Owen and Gudmund and Monica and H and the ocean and the house in England and the house in America. All twisting and shifting so fast, the nausea rises, and as they get him down the front steps of the prison, he vomits again.

"What's . . . happening?" he gasps. "I can't . . . The world is collapsing . . ."

In the spinning of his vision, he sees them exchange a worried look—

Then he sees Tomasz look up in panic. "Regine?"

Seth sees a look of horror cross Regine's face—

But he blinks again, and once more, overwhelmingly, the memories come, him sitting at the table with Officer Rashadi, another officer rushing in and saying they'd found him, they'd found Valentine—

Seth's eyes snap open.

There, right *there*, something he'd missed. Something he can hold on to. He feels the rush of memories ebb for the briefest of moments—

He looks up. He's in Regine's arms. She and Tomasz are trying to get him standing again, but the thing, the important thing, it's right on the tip of his tongue, it's—

"Valentine," he says.

Regine and Tomasz stop for an instant to look at him.

"What?" Regine says.

"Valentine," he says, gripping her arms more tightly. "His name was Valentine! The man who took Owen! The man who–!"

"Seth, can't you hear that?" Regine yells.

Seth stops. And listens.

The engine of the van.

Close, and growing louder, faster than they're ever going to be able to outrun.

Tomasz darts away from them across the square over to where two bikes are piled together. In a panic, Seth moves to follow him, but he struggles to even stay upright and Regine has to grab him to keep him from falling. "We won't make it with you like this," she says. She turns to the other buildings, looking for a place to hide.

"But Tomasz–" Seth says. He sees that Tomasz isn't picking up a bike. He's picking up a satchel tied to the back of one of them, frantically unwrapping something.

"Come on!" Regine says, pulling Seth toward the middle building of the ones that surround the square. The roar of the engine is nearly on them, and Seth can see lights growing in the darkness beyond the building they just left–

"Regine!" he cries.

"I see it!" she says.

Tomasz is running across the square toward them now, carrying something long and metallic, something Seth can't quite make out in the moonlight and shadows. He blinks, trying to adjust his eyes to the darkness –

–and he's lying with Gudmund on the bed, Gudmund's arm reaching up with the phone, taking the photograph, the one of just the two of them together, the private moment caught forever –

"Regine?" he says. "Regine, I think –"

"No, Tommy!" Regine yells.

Seth looks, his vision whirling. Tomasz is still crossing the square, running but not fast enough, fussing with the thing in his hands –

And Seth suddenly sees what it is, so unlikely as to be almost literally unbelievable –

Tomasz is carrying a shotgun.

It's almost as long as he is.

"Tomasz, look out!" Seth yells –

Because behind Tomasz, the black van sails around the corner of the building, roaring into the square –

Bearing down on Tomasz as he runs –

"No!" both Seth and Regine shout –

"Run!" Tomasz cries to them –

The van cuts between them, its wheels screeching to a halt on the concrete, and before it's even fully stopped, the door is opening –

The Driver is getting out –

And hurtling toward Tomasz with unthinkable speed –

"Tommy!" Seth hears Regine scream –

And she's trying to run for him –

But there's no way she'll get there in time –

The Driver holds out its baton, sparks crackling from it, ready to strike—

Tomasz awkwardly points the shotgun—

"NO!" Regine shouts—

And Tomasz pulls the trigger.

51

The bang is much bigger than Seth expects and indeed, there are *two* flashes, one from the end of the gun fired into the chest of the Driver –

And another as the gun explodes in Tomasz's hands.

Through white smoke, Seth sees the two bodies flying away in opposite directions, the spinning shadow of the Driver crashing into the van, nearly tearing off the open door in the impact, before slumping violently to the ground –

But also Tomasz, crying out as he sails back, bits of the gun splintering into the air, smoke trailing from him as he tumbles down onto the hard concrete of the square.

"TOMMY!" Regine yells, bolting toward him. Seth tries to keep up, but he's still unsteady on his feet. He follows her around the front of the van, catching a glimpse of the shadowy figure on the ground, also unmoving. Ahead of him, Regine slides down to the ground next to Tomasz –

No, Seth thinks. *Please, no* –

But then he hears a small coughing.

"Thank God," Regine says as he kneels down roughly next to her. "Thank God."

"*Moje ręce,*" Tomasz says, sitting up, his voice pitifully small. "*Moje ręce są całe zakrwawione.*"

He holds out his hands. Even in the shadows from the doorway light, they can see how burnt they are, strips of torn flesh and blood dripping down his wrists.

"Oh, *Tommy,*" Regine says furiously, gripping him in an embrace so tight Tomasz actually calls out. She lets go of him and starts shouting. "YOU IDIOT! I TOLD YOU IT WAS TOO DANGEROUS!"

"It was for last chance only," Tomasz moans. "And we were on last chance."

Seth looks behind them. The barrels of the shotgun are lying in two separate places among the weeds, the wooden stock now just smoldering embers across a wide area—

—*And the officer has come into their sitting room and he's saying, "They've found Valentine—"*

With a grunt, Seth forces it away, turning back to Regine and Tomasz. She's taken off her coat and is ripping a sleeve, tying it around one of Tomasz's hands.

"Where did you get a *shotgun?*" Seth asks, garbling the words a little. Now that things have slowed down, his head has started to spin again.

"In an attic in a neighboring house," Regine says, tying Tomasz's other hand, ignoring his tuts of pain. "But it was clearly *broken* and *dangerous* and *not something we could ever use.*"

"I tell you this again," Tomasz grunts. "A last chance. When there is no hope."

"You could have died, you little . . ." But Regine can't

finish, and her eyes are wet with furious tears. She glares back at Seth, daring him to say something. Then her face changes. "Are you okay?"

Seth winces, still feeling the memories crowding in, still feeling them whirling through his head.

"It was ready to kill me," Tomasz says, looking at the van. "To kill little Tomasz. But I kill him first, no?"

They all look back at the Driver. They can see a deep hole in the chest of the uniform where it took the full blast of the gun.

"Valentine," Seth whispers, holding on to the name again.

"Why do you keep saying that?" Regine says.

He looks at her, his face pained.

"Seriously," she says, "are you okay?"

"I don't know," Seth says, struggling to stand again.

"You said it was the name of a man," Tomasz says, standing awkwardly too, not using his injured hands. "He took someone called Owen?"

"Owen is my brother," Seth says.

Tomasz makes an *ahhhh* sound of understanding.

Seth can feel all the memories there in his mind, spinning around him like he's in the eye of a hurricane that's pressing in, surging toward him, *wanting* something from him. "Valentine," he whispers again.

"Yeah, okay," Regine says gently. "Valentine. Gotcha." She turns back to Tomasz. "Are you hurt anywhere else?"

"My chest, little bit," he answers, gesturing with his bandaged hands where the gun hit him, "but not so bad."

"He won't be able to ride," Regine says to Seth. "You'll have to help him. Are you up to that?"

"Yeah, I think so," Seth says, still distracted. That name, Valentine, it most definitely is the name of the prisoner who took Owen, the name that for the life of him he'd been unable to remember back at the house, no matter how hard he tried.

Until whatever happened down there with the coffins.

But there's more to it. . . .

The memories grow louder in his head again, surrounding him on all sides.

"Valentine," he whispers again.

"We can lie you down in the house," Regine says. "Both of you." She turns toward the van. "But first . . ."

She starts walking toward where the Driver still lies.

"What are you doing?" Tomasz calls out in alarm.

"Making sure it's dead," Regine says, moving slowly, carefully, ready to run again.

Seth watches her go but hardly sees her, his mind filling again with the beach, the sea, the coldness—

With the police and Owen and Valentine—

With Monica and Gudmund and H—

The tidal wave is coming again, breaking over him, drowning him once more—

"I do not think this is a good idea," Tomasz calls to Regine, shifting nervously from foot to foot—

Something's there, right there, as the memories keep flooding in—

"I'm willing to risk it for one less bad thing in the world," Regine says.

"Seth?" Tomasz asks. "Regine, something is very wrong with Seth."

Regine turns at the worry in Tomasz's voice. Seth presses his hands to the sides of his head, as if to keep it from exploding.

"No," he says. "Oh, no."

In the flood of thought whooshing through his brain, the memories are crowding his vision, fighting for attention, swamping him, pulling him under –

But he can still see what's in front of him, though it's getting harder –

Still see something not quite right –

Still see *movement* –

As behind Regine, the Driver starts to rise.

52

Tomasz calls out something in Polish so horrified there's no need for translation. Regine whips round to the Driver and screams.

"The bikes!" Tomasz yells.

Regine grabs Seth's arm as she runs past him, but his eyes are locked on the Driver, slowly sitting up.

Slowly rising to its feet.

"Go, go, go, go, go!" Regine says, pulling him so hard she nearly knocks him down.

And now he's running, too, though it feels more like trying not to fall than anything else. Tomasz is at the bikes but can't lift them with his injured hands. Regine grabs one and practically throws it at Seth. He catches it by reflex, and Tomasz is already climbing up behind him, wrapping his coat-bound hands around Seth's waist to hang on.

Seth takes one last look back at the Driver.

It's standing next to the van now, balancing with an arm on the broken door. It watches them, facelessly, the visor of its helmet reflecting the moonlight back at them.

An enormous chunk torn from the middle of its chest.

How? Seth thinks in the maelstrom of his brain. *How?*

But then they're riding, as fast as Seth's confused legs can pump the pedals, Tomasz gripping him tightly. Regine darts out of the square in front of him, and he does his best to follow her, struggling to keep his balance.

"Oh, do not fall," he hears Tomasz say behind him. "Do not fall, do not fall."

He focuses on that, trying to keep his overwhelmed mind on the task at hand. Tomasz's wrists are pressed so tight around Seth's middle it's making his sides hurt, but he rides out of the square after Regine and past the first building. Seth listens for the engine, but there's no change in tone or volume, no sign that the Driver is chasing them.

Unless it's on foot, Seth thinks. *Who knows how fast it can run?*

He pushes harder on the pedals.

Regine is ahead of him, fighting her way up the hill on an overgrown concrete path. *Go*, he thinks, forcing his body to work. *Go, go, go, step, pedal, push, go, go, go.*

"You are doing very fine," Tomasz says, as if he can read Seth's reeling mind.

"I'm finding it hard," Seth says, sweat seeping into his eyes as they climb the small hill. "I'm finding it hard to keep . . ."

Keep what? he thinks. *Keep conscious? Keep in this place?*

He doesn't dare blink for what he sees whenever his eyes are closed. Even when they're open, he can still see shadows of it all, one world laid down over the top of another, everyone he ever loved, everyone he ever knew, seeping into the flight of bicycles up a hill—

"It is not following us," Tomasz calls to Regine.

"How is it still alive?" she shouts backs. "How did it just stand up like that?"

"Bulletproof?" Tomasz suggests, but Seth can see Regine shaking her head and he knows what she's thinking. That was something more nightmarish than simply a bulletproof vest or uniform. The hole in its chest was too big.

It should be dead. It should have lain there forever.

But instead, it got back up –

They ride through the collapsed fences until they reach the rubble by the train tracks, where the electric light still burns. There's no path through, so Regine stops and lifts her bike over the tumbled bricks.

Seth and Tomasz do the same, hopping off. Seth grabs the frame of the bike, hoisting it up –

And the world empties.

Sound and noise, memory and image, all of it close in on Seth in a silent crush.

He calls out, strangely softly, and the bike slips from his fingers, clattering down on the bricks, the wheel bending sharply as it crashes.

"Seth!" Tomasz says, shocked. He crouches down by the bike. "Can we bend it back into place?" He looks back up. "Can we –?"

He stops. Because Seth is frozen there, hands out in exactly the same position as when he dropped the bike.

He can still see Tomasz, see the bike, see Regine hurrying back to them.

But he can see everything else, too.

Everything.

He can't stop it.

His mind has filled, in a quiet tumult so enormous he can no longer fight it, no longer even move—

Everything. Everything is there.

"What's going on?" Regine says, her voice echoing faintly in his ears, as if from three rooms away.

"He is stuck," Tomasz says, eyes wide.

Regine steps over to Seth. "Are you there, Seth? Are you with us?"

Her words echo across the miles of everything that's ever happened to him, and any answer of his will take too long to reach his mouth to explain—

He is far from them. So far, he'll never reach them again—

And then Regine takes his hand.

She presses it between her own, squeezing hard, but not untenderly.

"Seth," she says, "wherever you are, it's okay. You can come back from it. Whatever happened to you down there, whatever the world looks like now, that's not how it always looks. That's not how it's always *going* to look. There's more. There's *always* more. Whatever you see, wherever you are, we're still here with you. Me and Tommy."

Seth opens his mouth to try to answer her, but it's like slow motion. His mind and thoughts are so full, there's no room for action, no room for speech.

"Yes," Tomasz says. He takes Seth's other hand, gently, his own still swaddled in the torn-off sleeves of Regine's coat. "Here we are, Mr. Seth. We will be taking care of you. We will be finding you." Seth can see him suddenly smile. "Like we did just now in big prison breakout! Including guns!"

Regine shushes him but keeps staring into Seth's eyes.

"Tell us where you are, Seth," she says. "Tell us where you are so we can come and get you."

Seth can feel both of his hands held by Tomasz and Regine, can feel her warmth and roughness, can feel Tomasz's worry even through the cloth, can even maybe feel their heartbeats, though for Tomasz that's hardly possible—

But still, he's feeling *something* real—

(Isn't he?)

(He is.)

And he feels himself coming back—

Feels it all still spinning, churning, raging like a hurricane—

But the eye of the hurricane returns, too—

Small—

But still—

He looks up at the moon, at the prison behind them, at the silence down the hill—no Driver approaching out of the murk, no increasing sound of the engine, though his brain is still telling him they need to run, to get out of this place, but—

But Regine and Tomasz are here, too.

And he tells them.

Tells them what's happened.

"I remember," he says. "I think I remember everything."

PART 3

53

"Everything?" Tomasz asks. "What do you mean everything?"

"It's all there, I think," Seth says. "Everything that happened. Why we're here. How we *got* here." He frowns. "But it rushes away when I look at it too closely." He reaches out a hand as if to grasp it. "It's just . . ."

"We have to get home, Seth," Regine says when he doesn't continue. "You can tell us all about it when we're safe."

Tomasz turns balefully to the bike with the bent wheel. "This will not go."

"Can you run?" Regine asks Seth.

"I think so," he says.

"Then come on," she says. She abandons her own bike and takes off down the brick pathway alongside the tracks. They follow her, Seth able to keep up better than he expects, Tomasz frequently looking back to make sure he's still there.

"Just go," Seth says. "You won't lose me."

"That is what you said before," Tomasz says, "and you were saying an untruth."

"I'm sorry about that. I really am."

"Apologies later," Regine says. Her breathing is very heavy. They catch up to her easily. "Goddamn cigarettes."

"Also," Tomasz says, "you are quite plump."

Regine slaps him on the back of the head, but she picks up her pace a little. They reach the train station without seeing any sign of the Driver. They climb onto the platform and hurry out the exit, rushing down the steps between the blocks of flats. Instead of turning toward Seth's, they head north, down house-filled streets. After a number of corners, Regine pulls them into a tree-filled front yard to rest and hide for a moment.

They listen, panting. The night is silent around them. No footsteps, not even the sound of the engine, which should have been audible even at this distance.

"Maybe we really did hurt it," Regine says.

"But how did it rise at all?" Tomasz says. "I shot it. With a gun."

"And nearly killed yourself in the process."

"Not being the point right now, even though no one seems to be thanking me. I shot it from one meter. And still it stands?"

"I don't know," Regine frowns and looks at Seth. "You're the one who said you remembered. Do you have an answer?"

"No," he says, shaking his head. "Everything's crowded together. I can't get it into any kind of order yet and it's . . ."

He stops, because when he tries to think about it, it threatens to swamp him again. It seems to be everything he ever knew, but without any way to sort it. It's like having a million instruments playing a million different songs in his head at one time, far too noisy to make sense of. He grips on to the one thing that feels absolutely sure.

"I need to find my brother. That's what I need to do next."

"He is here?" Tomasz says.

"I think so. I feel like I *know* he's out there somewhere. Alone, not with everyone else. And if he wakes up and no one's there . . ." His eyes fill with tears. The other two watch him, warily.

"I understand," Regine says, "but it'll have to wait until morning. That thing could be out there anywhere."

Seth looks into the long, dark night. His head feels so heavy with thoughts and memories that it's hard to even talk to Regine or Tomasz, hard to even feel present. The answers are all there, he's sure of it, he just can't make any sense of them yet —

"Seth?" Regine says.

"Yeah," he says, almost automatically. "I can wait. I need to rest. I can barely stand —"

"That's not what I meant." She pulls down on the back collar of his shirt.

"You are blinking, Mr. Seth," Tomasz says.

"I'm what?" Seth asks, putting his hand up to where they're looking.

"Here," Regine says, guiding him back to the front window of the house. It's filthy, but even through the dust Seth can see it reflect the blinking blue light coming from under the skin of his neck.

"Blue," he says. "Not green."

"What about 'blue not green'?" Regine asks. "Why is that important?"

"I don't know."

Regine sighs. "So when you said you remembered everything, what you actually meant is that you don't remember anything *useful*."

"I opened a coffin. There was a man inside, hooked up to tubes and bandages and everything. He had a green light, right at this same place."

"When we found you," Tomasz says, "the screen said NODE ACTUALIZING. Maybe blue means you are not fully actualized. Maybe that was why all of the screaming."

"Yeah," Regine says, "but what does *actualized* mean?" She glances at Seth. "Let me guess: you don't remember that, either."

"I told you–"

She holds up a hand to stop him, frowning again. "I don't like this."

"Don't like what?"

"Not knowing stuff."

"How is that different from before?"

She gives him a look. "We just found out there's new stuff not to know."

Seth sees Tomasz's lips move as he tries to figure out that sentence.

"Let's get back to our house," Regine says. "I'll feel safer inside."

"It is a long walk," Tomasz says, slightly mournfully.

"Then we'd best get moving," Regine says.

• • •

They sneak down the sidewalk, keeping a careful eye out, following Regine as she turns up one street and then another.

"Blink-blink," Tomasz says, watching Seth's neck as they go. "Blink-blink."

"Yeah, because that won't get annoying," Regine says.

"Trying to see if there is a pattern," Tomasz says.

"Is there?" Seth asks.

"Yes. Blink-blink, blink-blink. But what it means is a question for someone else, I think."

Regine stays ahead of them, leading the way, never quite letting them catch up.

"She is angry with you," Tomasz says to Seth.

"She's been angry every second since I met her," Seth replies.

"No, I mean from before. We are calming now, so she is remembering it. She did not want you to disappear from us. She said it was your right to do what you wanted, but I could tell. She did not want you to go." He turns to Seth. "I did not want you to go either. I, too, am angry with you."

"I'm sorry," Seth says. "But I had to see. I had to know." He looks down at Tomasz. "Thank you for coming for me."

"And *there* is the thank you," Tomasz says with a surprising burst of frustration. "At very long last."

"How did you find me?"

"I knew something was wrong." Tomasz frowns at Regine's back. "She was acting funny, all out with the cows."

"'Out with the cows'?"

307

"Also growing a little tired of making fun of how I speak," Tomasz says under his breath, then more loudly, "Perhaps I have misunderstood. What is the word? Distracted. She was distracted."

Seth drags something up from his whirling memory. "Away with the fairies?"

"Yes! That is it. She was away with the fairies."

"Very similar to being out with the cows."

"And still you make fun," Tomasz complains, "after I am saving your life. Again. So tell me, please, your intricate knowledge of Polish references. Yes, that would be most amusing. Long, long talk now about how much you know about Polish language and the words Polish people use to describe how they feel in picturesque language."

"Where did you learn English? The 1950s?"

"STORY OF RESCUE," Tomasz practically shouts. "Regine was distracted. I figure out why. I say we come to save you. She says no, that is not what you want. I say, Who cares what Mr. Seth wants, Mr. Seth does not know proper danger he is in. I say we take shotgun and we go." He looks at Regine again. "To this last, there was resistance."

"For good reason," Regine says, not turning around. "You could have died."

"And yet here I am," Tomasz says. "I am sorry that I know more about guns than you, but I do."

"Not enough to keep it from blowing up in your hands."

"But enough to stop the Driver from chasing us!" Tomasz holds up his wrapped hands in frustration. "Why is Tomasz never given credit? Why is he never thanked properly for his good ideas? I have saved you now *twice* from the thing that would kill us, but oh, no, I am still little joke Tommy with his bad English and his crazy hair and his too much enthusiasm."

They stop, amazed a bit at his anger.

"Jeesh," Regine says. "Someone needs a nap."

Tomasz's eyes blaze, and he hurls a long trail of furious Polish sentences at them.

"I said I was sorry," Seth says. "Tomasz—"

"You do not understand!" Tomasz yells. "I am lonely, too! You think you are older and you are wiser and you feel things more deeply. You are not! I feel these things, too! If I lose you or you, then I am alone again, and I will not have this! I will not."

He's crying now, but they can see that he's annoyed at himself for it, so they don't try to comfort him.

"Tommy—" Regine starts.

"It is *Tomasz*!" he spits.

"You said it was okay for me to call you Tommy."

"Only when I am liking you." He wipes his eyes and mutters to himself. "You know nothing of Tomasz. Nothing."

"We know you were struck by lightning," Seth says.

Tomasz looks up to him, his eyes full of something Seth can't quite read. Disbelief, for one, looking for teasing in what Seth says, but also fear. And pain. As if he was remembering being struck by lightning all over again.

"I'm not teasing you," Seth says. "I understand loneliness. Boy, do I ever."

"Do you?" Tomasz asks, almost as a challenge.

309

"Yeah," Seth says. "Really, really."

He reaches up to put a hand of truce on Tomasz's back, and as Tomasz ducks into it, Seth's fingers brush the spot on the base of Tomasz's skull–

Which lights up suddenly under his touch–

And the world vanishes.

54

The room is cramped and dark. There are other people here, he can't tell how many, but it's crowded, bodies pressed into bodies, so close he can smell their sour breath and body odor. And their fear.

Their voices are hushed but speaking frantically. He can't understand what they're saying—

But yes, he can *understand them. They're not speaking English, but he can understand every word.*

"Something's gone wrong," a woman's voice says nearby. "They're going to kill us."

"They will be paid," says another woman sternly, trying to calm the first woman but still plainly afraid herself. "The money will come. That's all they want. The money will come—"

"Even if it comes, it won't matter," says the first woman, as other voices around her rise in the same worry. "They're going to kill us! They're going to—"

"Shut your mouth!" roars a new voice, one right behind his head, one owned by the woman whose arms are around him, holding him tight. "Shut your mouth or I will shut it for you."

The first woman stops at the fury in this new voice. She begins a long, loud weeping, hardly better than the words before.

"Don't you listen to her, my little puddle," the voice behind him says into his ear. "Everything has gone according to plan, and there is nothing to be afraid of. This is a little delay. Only that. We will be starting our new life soon. And what a time that will be."

He speaks. They are not his words, not his voice, but they are coming from his mouth.

"I'm not afraid, Mama," he says.

"I know you're not, puddle." She kisses the back of his head, and he knows that she's calming herself, too. He really isn't afraid, though. She's gotten them this far. She'll get them farther still.

"Let Mama hear some of your English," she whispers. "Let me hear your words, and we will make a new home out of them."

And he remembers. Remembers being too poor to pay for English lessons but never questioning why his mama brought home videotape after videotape—not downloaded like at school or even on disc, but played on a massive, ancient machine held together by electrical tape—of black-and-white or flamboyantly colored films in English, a language that both leapt forward into wide-open spaces and then looped back to cramp itself up. They would make a game of it, him and his mama, trying to match the English dialogue to the subtitles.

He was smart, his teachers always said, some even saying "freakishly," and he started picking it up against all odds, practicing it on the few English-speaking tourists who ventured that deep into the country. Even trying his *hand at the moldy old English-language novels someone had donated to the local library.*

He's learned enough, he hopes. They are here. They are inside the borders. They have almost reached the end. He really, really hopes he's learned enough.

"'To lose one parent, Mr. Worthing,'" he says now to his mama, quoting a film, straining hard to remember, for her, "'may be like losing your fortune. To lose both means that no one cares.'"

"Good, good, puddle," his mama says, understanding less than half of it, he knows. "More."

"'You were only supposed to bleed open the doors off,'" he says, "'and blow them away.'"

"Yes, my darling."

"'Of all the jukeboxes in every bit of the world—'"

There is a sudden sharp cry from the women around him—and he remembers now that it is all women and a few children like him—as a lock is loudly undone and the massive metal door begins to open, booming with its own weight. The women make sounds of relief when they see that it's the friendlier of the two men who've brought them this far. The one with the kind smile and sad eyes who speaks to them of his own children.

"You see?" says his mother, standing them both up. "A few words and the world changes."

But the women start to scream as they see that the kind man is holding a gun—

55

A hand shoves Seth hard in the chest, Regine, her full weight behind it. He tumbles to the mud-covered pavement. She stands next to Tomasz, who's looking down at him now, too.

"What did you do?" Tomasz says, horrified. "What did you *do* to me?"

"*Co się stało?*" Seth says.

In Polish.

"What?" Regine says.

"*What?*" Tomasz says, coming over to him. "What did you say?"

Seth sits up, shaking his head. He can still smell the fear in the cramped room, still feel the press of the women against him, the terrible, terrible panic that swept through the group when they saw the man's gun–

"I said–" Seth tries again, in English this time, but he doesn't get another word out before Tomasz strikes him across the face, hard, the cloth wrapped around his hands cushioning it hardly at all.

"You have no right!" Tomasz says, hitting him again and again. Seth, too stunned to defend himself, can already feel his nose bleeding. "That is private! You have no right to be there!"

"WHOA!" Regine shouts, grabbing Tomasz's flailing arms. She wraps her big frame around him, straitjacketing him, but he still looks furiously at Seth.

"That was not yours to see!"

"Would someone tell me what the hell is going on?" Regine says, then she sees the back of Tomasz's neck. "And why is Tommy's light blinking?"

"I don't know," Seth says, pulling himself back up, wiping the blood from his face. "I don't know what happened. I just touched him and—"

"I am right here!" Tomasz shouts. "Do not speak of me as if I am not present!"

"I'm sorry, Tomasz," Seth says. "For both things. I don't know what happened. I didn't mean anything by it—"

"It was not yours to see!" Tomasz says again.

"What was it?" Regine asks Seth, still holding Tomasz close.

"I think . . ." Seth says. "I think it may be private."

At that, Tomasz's face crumples and he *really* begins to cry, buckling at the knees and dropping into Regine's embrace. He speaks long sentences of Polish with his eyes squeezed shut.

"Okay, seriously, what the hell happened?" Regine says to Seth, holding Tomasz to her stomach. "I don't need to know what you saw, but you touched the back of his neck and then you both just froze. Like you left your bodies."

"I don't know," Seth says.

Regine sighs angrily. "Of course you don't."

"Regine—"

"I'm not mad at you," she says. "I'm mad at this whole stupid place. You say you're remembering and you just can't imagine how much I want to know, but all that seems to mean is new pain. That's all that happens in this life. One shitty, horrible surprise after another–"

"You weren't a horrible surprise," Seth says quietly.

"And the weather makes no sense and there's some immortal *freak* in a black suit chasing us and . . . What did you say?"

"I said you weren't a horrible surprise," Seth says. "Neither of you." Tomasz is still snuffling into Regine's shirt, but he turns an eye back to Seth.

Seth wipes his nose. "Listen," he says, but then stops. He runs a hand over his short hair, his fingers finding the rise at the back of his skull, knowing it's blinking, not knowing why, despite the mess of it churning in his brain. Not knowing anything at all, in fact, except that he's here, right this second, with Tomasz and Regine. And it feels like he owes them more than he can ever repay.

"I killed myself," he says.

He waits to make sure they're listening. They are. "I walked into the ocean. I broke my shoulder on a rock, and then that same rock crushed my skull, hitting it right where the light is." He pauses. "But it wasn't an accident. I did it to myself."

Regine says nothing, but Tomasz sniffles and says, "We had a little bit guessed."

"I know," Seth says. "And that day you found me, that day you stopped me from running into that thing in the van,

I . . ." He wavers, but then forces himself. "I was going to do it again. I know Masons Hill. I know where I could throw myself off. And that's what I was going to do."

He tastes blood on the back of his throat and spits it out. "And so when I say you weren't a horrible surprise, I mean it. You were a good surprise, *so* good it's why I doubt it's even true. Even now. And I'm sorry for that. I'm sorry it made me lie to you. I'm sorry it sent me to the prison. And I'm sorry, Tomasz, for seeing what I saw. I didn't mean to."

Tomasz sniffles again. "I know this. But still." He's wearing the saddest face Seth has ever seen, his mouth curled down, his bottom lip out, his eyes too old for his young, young face.

"I did not get struck by lightning," he says.

"We had nothing," Tomasz continues, looking at his feet. "Remember those years when the world lost all its money? Even online, I guess."

Seth and Regine both nod, but Tomasz isn't looking at them anyway.

"We were poor before that," he says. "And it was worse after. You used to be able to cross borders in Europe, but when all economies fell, you could not anymore. No one wanted anyone else. We were trapped, my mama and me. But she found a way. She found a man who says he can smuggle us in on a ship. Give us passports, documents to say we were there before borders close." He clenches his little fists. "It costs us everything we have. *More* than everything, but my mama says it is better life. Makes me learn English, says all will be better."

His eyes narrow. "But it is *not* better. Journey is very hard, very long, and the men who help us, well, they do not help us very much at all. One is nicer, but one is very bad. He treats us very badly. He . . . *do* things. To Mama."

Tomasz turns his fists up and looks at them. "I am too small to help. And Mama says it is all right, we are almost there, we are almost there. And one day we arrive in England. We are all very excited, day is almost here, we have traveled long and hard road, but here we are, here we are, here we are." His face has opened up a little in wonder, but it hardens again. "But there is a problem. Money, always wanting more money, always asking more from people who have none."

He sighs. "But there *is* no more. And the kinder man comes to where they are keeping us. In big metal container for ship. Like we are pigs or trash. The kinder man comes one night."

He looks at Seth. In the moonlight, his eyes are filled with tears again, and Seth realizes what he's asking.

"He shot you," Seth says simply, finishing the story. "He shot you and your mother and everyone else."

Tomasz just nods, fat tears running down his cheeks.

"Oh, Tommy," Regine whispers.

"But I do not know why I am *here*," Tomasz says, his voice wet. "I get shot in the back of my head and I wake up here! And this is making no sense. If we have all been sleeping away somewhere, why do I not wake up in Poland? Why can I not find my mother or anyone else?" He appeals to Seth. "I do not recognize this place at all. I wake up and

I think the men must be after me still and so I am afraid and I say to Regine when she finds me that I have always been here, that Mama and me have been here for long time, but . . ." He just shrugs.

"Maybe you *were* here," Seth says. "Maybe you reached here and they put you in the coffins and . . ."

But it *doesn't* make sense.

Or maybe, he thinks, maybe there hadn't been time to deport anyone anymore. Maybe Tomasz's mother did get here in the real world just before everything ended, when Tomasz was a baby. And maybe they were arrested and the only thing to do was to put them to sleep, making them think they'd never left Poland. That they were back where they started without ever having made the journey.

But if it was someone with the willpower and courage to make that journey once, they might be the sort of person who would be willing to make it again, wouldn't they? If they didn't know they were online, only that they had to get somewhere else, at whatever cost.

Never knowing they had already succeeded and were already here.

It seems almost impossibly cruel.

"Tommy, I'm so sorry," Regine says.

"Just do not leave me alone," Tomasz says. "It is all I wish."

She embraces him again even more tightly.

"What about you?" Seth asks her. "How did you get here?"

"I told you," she says, not looking at him. "I fell down the stairs."

"Are you sure?"

She glares at him, not answering, but Tomasz is looking up at her, too, the same question on his face. "It is all right," Tomasz says. "We are your friends."

Regine still doesn't answer, but a flicker of doubt crosses her brow. She takes in a breath, to explain or deny or tell them to piss off, Seth will never know, because somewhere, in the distance, they hear the engine of the van start up all over again.

56

"Hurry," Regine whispers back to them as they rush from shadow to shadow.

"How far?" Seth asks when they catch up to her, huddled between two cars at the side of a road.

"We're close, but there's a big main road to cross first."

"The sound is distant," Tomasz whispers behind them. "It does not know where we are."

"Has it ever seen where you guys are staying?" Seth asks.

"We do not think so," Tomasz says. "We have always lost it before we got home, but . . ."

"But what?"

"But it's not that big a neighborhood," Regine says. "And your lights are still blinking. In a world this dark, that's going to be noticeable."

"If they were broadcasting some signal," Seth says, "it'd be on us by now, wouldn't it? So that's something at least."

"Something," Regine says. "Not a lot."

She leads them in a crouched run through the parked cars, across a small street and up the sidewalk toward an intersection. It's the main road Regine was talking about, and aside from the usual weeds and mud, it's a massive open space they're going to have to cross. They wait between two small white trucks parked at the edge.

"We should be okay," Tomasz whispers. "The engine is not near."

"You shot it in the chest at point-blank range and it stood up again," Regine says. "We don't know *what* it might be capable of doing. You think it doesn't know we rely on the sound of the engine to tell us where it is? You think it might not use that to screw with us?"

Tomasz's eyes grow wider, and he slips a cloth-covered hand into Seth's.

"We really aren't far," Regine says. "If we can get across—"

She stops, eyes suddenly alert in the moonlight.

"What?" Seth whispers.

"Did you hear something?"

"No, I—"

But he hears it now, too.

Footsteps.

Definitely footsteps.

Far closer than the distant drone of the engine.

The footsteps are slow, quiet, as if they don't want to be heard. But they're coming this way.

Tomasz grips Seth's hand tighter and lets out a very soft, "Ouch," at the pain from the burns. He doesn't let go, though.

"Nobody move," Regine whispers.

The footsteps grow louder, nearer, coming from some-where on their right, maybe from the sidewalk on the other side of the street, hidden by darkness and the cars parked there. They have a strange quality to them, oddly hesitant, stopping and starting, as if having trouble getting up a good walk.

"Maybe we hurt it," Regine whispers, and Seth sees her posture change slightly. She would be happy if it was hurt, he realizes. Happy to face it when she stood a chance of beating it.

"Regine—"

She shushes him, pointing silently with her finger. Seth and Tomasz lean forward.

There's movement in the shadows across the street.

"We should get out of here," Seth says.

"Not yet," she says.

"It's still got weapons—"

"Not *yet*."

Seth can feel Tomasz pulling back, readying himself to run. Seth moves back with him, but Regine stays where she is—

"*Regine,*" Seth hisses through clenched teeth—

"Look," is all she says.

Angry, tense, ready to flee, Seth leans forward to look out onto the wide street again, where the footsteps take their last movements out of shadow and into moonlight.

Tomasz makes a little gasp beside him.

It's a deer. *Two* deer. A doe and her fawn, hesitantly picking their way into the street, ears alert, stopping every little bit or so to make sure the way is still safe. The fawn steps past its mother and takes a mouthful of wild weeds from the road. It's impossible to tell their color in the moonlight, but they don't look skinny or unwell, Seth thinks. There's certainly enough vegetation around to keep them fed. And if there's a fawn, then there must be a stag out there somewhere.

Seth, Tomasz, and Regine watch the pair make their way down the street, their hooves clicking on the tarmac. The engine noise is still in the distance, and it's clear by the flicks of her ears that the doe hears it, but she keeps watch calmly as her fawn feeds itself.

She stops and raises her head higher, sniffing the air.

"She smells us," Regine whispers. The doe doesn't bolt, but she turns from them, pushing her fawn away down the road, disappearing into farther darkness until not even the moon can see them.

"Wow," Tomasz says after they've gone. "I mean, WOW!"

"Yeah," Seth says. "I didn't expect—"

He stops.

Because he can see Regine wipe two stray tears from her cheeks.

"Regine?"

"Let's keep going," she says, and stands to lead them on their way.

They take a long circle to get to the house. The trees are surprisingly thick here in amongst the homes, and the moonlight shines down only in glimpses, as if they're at the bottom of a steep canyon. The drone of the engine stays far away, and when they reach Regine's street, there's no sign of anyone waiting for them.

It's a nicer neighborhood than Seth's, he can see that even in the dark. The houses are stand-alones, not in blocks like his, the gardens more spacious, the streets a bit wider. Despite the decent size and niceness of his own house, Seth remembers it was only affordable to his parents because it bordered a prison.

"This is where you grew up?" he asks, already regretting the surprise in his voice.

"Yeah," Regine says, "and even in online utopiaville, we were still the only black people. So what does *that* tell you?"

They wait at the corner, behind a better model of derelict car.

"I am not seeing anything," Tomasz whispers.

"No," Regine says. "But how would we know? It can probably wait a lot longer than we can."

"Any of these houses will do for a rest," Seth says. "They probably all have empty beds."

"Yeah," she says, squinting down the road, "but they're not my house, are they? I don't think I'm ready to give up my house."

"I really don't doubt that," Seth says, "but–"

"Oh, for the sake of heaven," Tomasz says, standing. "My hands are hurting. I want to wash them. It is there or it is not, and if it is there, then it knows where to find us and it can do that anywhere we try to run. Besides, I am feeling cranky and over-tired."

He marches down the street.

"Tommy!" Regine calls after him, but he keeps on going.

"He's got a point, you know," Seth says.

"Doesn't he always?" Regine grumbles, but she stands and heads after Tomasz. Seth goes, too, and he can see now how right Regine was about the lights. Tomasz's is shining in the darkness like a beacon.

What *did* happen? he thinks. Why did they link up? Why the sudden immersion into what was clearly the worst thing that had ever happened to Tomasz? It made no sense, but at the very least, it's calmed down the torrent in his brain for now, all that information still bubbling but temporarily at bay.

He looks at the back of Regine's neck. *What would happen if I connected to her?* he wonders.

"Tommy, wait," Regine says as they near the front path of a dark brick house, hidden behind the same shadows of wild plants and mud. Regine looks around carefully, turning in a full circle—the same way Seth does when he's being watchful, he notices—but there's still nothing in the darkness that comes after them.

"I think we are fine," Tomasz says. "For now."

Regine breathes out a long, low sigh, still scanning the fronts of the neighboring houses. "For now," she echoes quietly.

57

"Hold on," Regine says at the front door. She pushes it open slightly, removing a small scrap of paper. "To make sure no one's gone in before us. If this had fallen, we'd have known someone was inside."

She disappears into the house, motioning them to wait.

"We have blacked out the windows," Tomasz tells Seth, "to keep from being seen."

After a moment, a light appears from deep within, as if it's coming from around more than one corner.

"Okay," Regine says, appearing again. "Get inside, quick."

Tomasz waits for Seth to pass before bracing the door shut behind them with a chair stuck underneath the handle. They're in a generous sitting room with a staircase leading up and a second doorway to a kitchen in the back.

Right in the middle of the front room sits a dusty black coffin, surrounded by the sofas and chairs as if it was a coffee table.

"Come, there is food," Tomasz says, walking past the coffin and leading Seth to the kitchen. The light shines from there, a lantern tucked into a side cabinet that might have been a pantry. There's a door heading out the back, its seams stuffed with blankets to keep the light from leaking out.

"We sleep upstairs," Regine says. "There are three bedrooms, but one's a storage room now. You can share with Tommy, if you want."

"I usually sneak in to the floor of her room anyway," Tomasz says in a stage whisper.

Regine lights another lantern. She calls Tomasz over to the sink to unwrap his hands. Once the blood is washed away, they look less bad than feared. A few deep cuts and some burns—which cause Tomasz to hiss every time Regine runs the water over them—but he can flex them a little.

"You'll mend," Regine says. Then she takes some old kitchen towels out of a drawer and wraps them around his hands. "We should scrounge up some antibiotics, though, in case they get infected."

Tomasz still looks defiant. "I say again, you are welcome for being saved."

Regine reaches in the cabinets for cans of food. "Nothing fancy, I'm afraid," she says, lighting the flame on a gas camp stove similar to Seth's.

Towel-handed Tomasz sets out some bowls while she prepares the meal. Looking for something to do, Seth pours them mugs of water from the bottles they brought back from the supermarket. No one really says much. Seth's mind is still crammed to overloading, and if he lets it, he can slide off into paralysis, trying to make sense of it all. The effort is constant, difficult, exhausting. He stifles a yawn. Then is too tired to stifle a second.

"Tell me about it," Regine grumbles, handing him a bowl that's half creamed corn, half some kind of noodle-filled chili.

"Thanks," Seth says.

Regine and Tomasz sit on small chairs in the kitchen to eat. Seth sits on the floor. There's almost no conversation, and Seth looks up once to see Tomasz asleep, his head back against the counter, an empty bowl in his lap.

"I knew it wasn't lightning," Regine says, quietly enough not to wake him. "But I had no idea."

"Me neither," Seth answers.

"Why would you?" she says crisply.

Seth makes a frustrated sound. "What is your problem with me? I said I was sorry."

"And I believe you," she says, setting her own empty bowl on the counter. "Can't we just leave it at that?"

"Clearly not."

"And that's actually kind of it. The way you think you have the right to know everything. That it's all about you. I mean, even thinking me and Tommy are here to help you somehow. How self-centered is that? You ever think maybe you're here to help *us*?"

He scratches his ear. "Sorry. I've had less time to get used to here than you." He looks around at the lantern-lit kitchen and their ancient-can dinner. "My father said with enough time you could get used to anything."

"My mother said that, too. And she was right."

Regine says it so bitterly, Seth looks at her, surprised. She sighs. "She was a schoolteacher. Sciences, mostly, but she and my dad were French so she taught that too, sometimes. She was great. Strong and good and funny. And then my dad died and she kind of . . . broke. And got lost somehow."

Regine frowns. "And my stepdad, that son of a bitch, he saw how broken she was and just moved on in. And at first it's okay, you know, not perfect, but okay, and you get used to it. Then it gets a little worse, and you get used to that, too. Then one day, you wake up and you don't have the first freakin' clue how it got that bad."

"My dad broke," Seth says gently. "I think my mum broke a little, too."

"And you."

"And me. People break, I guess. Everyone."

"What finally made *you* break?"

"Now who's the one who thinks everything is her business?"

She hesitates, but then gives him a look that's almost friendly.

He yawns, which makes him wonder what memory will come tonight when he finally goes back to sleep. He hopes it's good, even if painful. Maybe the night he first found out Gudmund felt the same way. Or maybe the time they went camping and Gudmund's parents were in the next tent over so they couldn't do much more than talk and it was great, greater than anything, as they planned out a future together, with college and beyond.

"We can have anything," Gudmund had said. "We can do anything we want once we get out of here. You and me together? No one could *think* about stopping us."

And Seth couldn't even say how thrilling and frightening and true and impossible those words had seemed.

They had talked all night. They had set out the rest of their lives.

It makes his heart hurt to think about it.

"People break," he says again. "But we got a second chance, the three of us."

Regine laughs once. "You think this is a second chance? How shitty was *your* life?" She stands, reaching for Tomasz. "Come on, give me a hand here."

They get the still half-sleeping Tomasz up to his bed, Regine lighting a candle to show their way. She takes some musty blankets out of a closet. "You'll have to make do with the floor."

"That's okay," Seth says, piling them up on the carpet.

"You can have his bed when he sneaks into my room," she says. "He wasn't kidding about that."

Tomasz is already snoring away. Regine looks down at him in her gruffly tender way, and then turns to leave without a good night.

"Thank you for finding me," Seth says. "And maybe try not to be such an asshole about accepting the thanks, okay?"

Regine snorts. "It's hard here. Toughness keeps us alive." She gives a wry smile. "I used to be a really nice person."

Seth smiles back. "I don't believe that for a second."

"Good," she says. "You shouldn't." She looks at him for a moment. "First thing, we can start looking for your brother. If it's really that important."

"It is. Thank you."

"Don't thank me. You'll be doing all the work. Like, where do we even start?"

Seth shakes his head. "Something'll come to me. It's all there, I know it is. I've just got to sort it out."

"Good," she says, "because I'd like some answers, too." She nods good night at him and leaves.

Seth lies down on the floor and wraps a blanket around himself. It's quiet. Even between Tomasz's little snores, he can't hear the van's engine outside, at any distance. Regine and Tomasz have hidden themselves well here, he thinks. And now they've hidden him here with them, too.

His brain is still overloaded with unsorted memories, but for a fleeting moment, before the endless exhaustions of the day catch up with him, he realizes he feels almost safe.

He does not dream.

"Wake up, Mr. Seth," Tomasz says, shaking him by the shoulder. "We have survived another night."

Groggy, Seth opens his eyes to the dim glow just barely filtering in through the blankets that cover the windows.

"There is corn and chili again for breakfast," Tomasz says. "I am sorry for this."

Seth opens his mouth to answer –

But he stops.

Something is different.

Something has changed.

Something –

He sits bolt upright.

"Oh shit," he says.

"What is it?" Tomasz says, alarmed.

"Oh no."

"*What?*"

"It's all there," Seth says, looking up at Tomasz in amazement. "It's all clear now. Falling asleep must have processed it or –"

He stops.

"What is happening *now*?" Tomasz says.

But what can Seth answer? What can he say? All the chaos is now making sense. What he'd forgotten –

Oh no.

He gets up, barely stopping to shove his feet into shoes before hurtling out of the bedroom and down the stairs.

"Wait!" Tomasz says, coming after him. "Where are you going?"

Seth grabs the chair lodged at the front door, but his first confused attempt only manages to stick it more tightly.

"What's going on?" Regine says, coming in from the kitchen, holding a bowl of the horrible breakfast.

"He woke up and went all crazy," Tomasz says.

"Again?"

"I didn't dream," Seth says, grappling with the chair.

"What?" Regine asks.

"I didn't *dream*. I slept and I didn't dream, not one memory, nothing." He feels on the verge of panic now. "I woke up and everything was clear."

The chair finally springs free under Seth's hands and clatters into the sitting room. Seth pulls open the front door.

"Where are you going?" Regine cries, but he's already out, already racing down the pavement, already running down the street.

Because he knows.

He remembers.

Even though this neighborhood is unfamiliar, his feet are guiding him. The large street they crossed last night is a landmark he is suddenly sure of. He runs from Regine's house, not even listening for the van's engine. He's about three miles north of his own house, he thinks, and his mind is mapping out a path for him.

He knows where he's going.

He knows.

"WAIT!" he hears, some distance behind him.

"I can't," he says, not nearly loud enough for them to hear. "I can't."

He keeps running, taking a corner with unhesitating certainty. The blocks start to fall away behind him, and he's running effortlessly, fast, purposeful. Another corner. And another. The roads are edging downwards now, coming around in a direction that'll take him behind the supermarket and out the other side of the small park where he saw the ducks.

"For Christ's sake!" he hears behind him in gasped breaths.

He takes a quick glance to see Regine, pedaling away on a spare bike they must have had at the house, Tomasz clamped on behind her, his bandaged hands wrapped around her middle.

"You are running away from us!" Tomasz shouts with surprising anger. "Again!"

"I'm not," Seth says, shaking his head, not stopping. "Please, I'm not."

"What are you *doing* then?" Regine shouts.

"I remember," he says. "I *remember*."

"Then you'll remember that we're not exactly out of danger, are we?" Regine says, not able to keep up with how fast he's going.

"I'm sorry," Seth says, pulling away. "I have to, I'm sorry."

336

He runs. It's not even a feeling he can name. It's some kind of compulsion, something making him go–

Something he can't believe–

Something he *won't* believe–

The road is angling down steeply now and he reaches the bottom of a hill, whispering, "No. No, no, no."

He turns away from the direction of the duck pond, running up a low rise and down the other side. There are very rich houses here, behind massively overgrown hedges. The road is better too, with fewer weeds breaking through what was probably more expensive asphalt. He passes a kind of community center, then sees a church on a corner and he knows he's near. He can hear Regine and Tomasz distantly behind him as he turns a last corner.

He slows to a stop in the middle of the road.

He's here. He's found it. All of a sudden, too soon. Like the short walk to the prison, this is a journey that feels as if it should have taken much longer.

But here he is.

"No," he whispers again.

Regine and Tomasz pull up behind him. Regine is too out of breath to do much besides hunch over the handlebars, but Tomasz is already off the bike and yelling. "You cannot do this! You promised! You cannot–"

He stops as he sees how frozen Seth is.

As he sees where Seth has brought them.

"Mr. Seth?" he says, puzzled.

Seth says nothing, just steps over a low stone wall into the overgrown field. He knows where to go. He doesn't *want* to know, but he does. The grass is as tall as he is, and he pushes it away in fistfuls. Tomasz follows right behind him, trying to keep up in the grass jungle. Seth isn't sure what Regine is doing because he's not looking back. He's keeping his eyes forward, looking, seeking.

He lets his feet lead him.

There are paths here, hidden behind the grass, and he takes them without hesitation, turning where he needs, orienting himself with a tree and turning again—

And then he stops.

Tomasz comes up behind him. "What is happening? Mr. Seth?"

Seth hears Regine arrive, too. "Regine?" Tomasz asks her. "What does it mean?"

But Seth says nothing. His legs feel weak beneath him, and he kneels down. He reaches forward and parts a stand of grass, breaking it, clearing it away.

To what's underneath.

He reads what he finds.

And he both knows it's true and knows it must be a lie.

But it isn't a lie. It isn't.

Because he remembers it now. He remembers it all.

"Is that—" Regine whispers. "Oh, my God."

"What?" Tomasz says. "*What?*"

But Seth doesn't look back, just keeps kneeling there, reading it.

Reading the words carved into marble.

Owen Richard Wearing.
Taken from this world, aged 4.
His Voice was Musick and his Words a Song
Which now each List'ning Angel smiling hears
Seth has brought them to a cemetery.
To a tombstone.
To the place where his brother lies buried.

60

It was how silent his parents were at the table across from Officer Rashadi that upset him the most. They weren't crying or yelling or visibly distressed in any way. His father sat glassy eyed, staring unfocused at a spot somewhere over Officer Rashadi's shoulder. His mother, head hung low, unkempt hair hiding her face, made no sound, gave no signal she knew anyone else was there.

"This will be no solace," Officer Rashadi said, her voice low, calm, respectful, "but we have very strong reason to believe that Owen didn't suffer. That it happened soon after the abduction and was done very quickly." She reached forward across the table as if to take one of their hands. Neither his mother nor his father responded. "He didn't suffer," she said again.

His mother's voice, raspy, quiet, said something.

"What was that?" Officer Rashadi asked.

His mother cleared her throat and looked up slightly. "I said, you're right. It's no solace."

Seth was sitting on the bottom step in the hallway. Neither Officer Rashadi nor the other officer who'd come in saying that Valentine had been found was watching out for him after they'd sent him from the room. He'd snuck back down and listened.

"We'll take you to see him," Officer Rashadi said. "We're just waiting for the all clear, and then we can go."

His parents still said nothing.

"I'm so, so sorry for your loss," Officer Rashadi said. "But we've caught Valentine, and he'll pay for what he's done, I can promise you that."

"You'll put him back in jail?" his mother said. "So he can read his books and do his gardening and walk right out again whenever he feels like it? Is that your idea of him paying for what he's done?"

"There are other ways, Mrs. Wearing," Officer Rashadi said. "All prisoners are now automatically placed into—"

"Shut up," his mother said. "Just please, shut up. How will anything ever matter again?" She turned to his father, still glassy eyed, as if barely there. "I was going to leave you."

His father didn't seem to have heard her.

"Are you listening to me?" his mother said. "I was going to leave you that day. I'd stashed money away. That's what I went back to get that morning. I'd managed to leave it on the counter of that stupid bank." She turned to Officer Rashadi. "I was going to leave him."

Officer Rashadi looked back and forth between them, but his father wasn't reacting and his mother remained in a kind of terrifyingly still anger, like a leopard waiting to pounce.

"I'm sure that's something that can be worked out later,"

Officer Rashadi said. She paused, then her voice changed slightly. "Or maybe it's something you don't have to work out at all."

The other officer piped up at that and said what must have been Officer Rashadi's first name. "Asma—"

"I'm just saying there may be a way," she said. "A way so that none of this ever happened."

For the first time, she had the attention of both his mother and father.

"The world was changing," Seth says quietly, his eyes still on the tombstone. "Had changed. Become almost unlivable."

"Well, that much is obvious," Regine says. "Just look at this place."

Seth nods. "For a long time, people had been living two lives. And at first, I think, it *was* two. You could do both. Go back and forth. Between the online world and this one. And then people started *staying* online and that seemed less weird than it was even a year before. Because the world was getting more and more broken." He looks back at Regine and Tomasz. The sun is shining behind them, and they're almost in silhouette. "At least it's what I think happened."

Regine hears the question. "I don't remember anything from before," she says. "I'm sorry."

"That's how we made it, I think," Seth says. "So we'd forget there was ever anything else. Your own memories rewritten to make it all work, and then your life was there in front of you. Online. The real one, as far as you ever knew."

Seth turns back to the tombstone. He runs his fingers across the carved letters of Owen's name.

"He died," Seth says simply. "The man who took him murdered him. He never came home."

Seth can sense grief stirring in his stomach, his chest, but the weight of new and old knowledge is still too heavy to deal with, and all he feels at the moment is numb.

"Oh, Mr. Seth," Tomasz says. "I am so sorry."

"I'm sorry, too," Regine says. "But I don't understand. How can this be your brother? You said he was—"

"Still alive," Seth says. "I grew up with him. I sat through his clarinet lessons. Tomasz reminds me of him so much I can hardly look at him sometimes."

"But . . ." He can hear Regine trying to keep the impatience out of her voice. "But he's *here*. He died. In the real world."

"If this *is* real," Tomasz says.

"We're going to have to say it is *sometime*," Regine snaps. "I know I'm real, and that's all I've got to go on. You've got to hang on to something." And then she says it again. "You've got to hang on to something."

"So how can this have happened?" Tomasz says.

Seth doesn't turn away from the tombstone. "My parents," he says, "were given a choice."

"You've heard about Lethe?" the woman from the Council asked them over the same dinner table where Officer Rashadi had broken the news just three nights before.

Seth's mother frowned. "The place in Scotland?"

"No, that's Leith," his father said, his words slurred. He nodded at the woman from the Council. "You mean Lethe." He pronounced it Lee-Thee. "The river of forgetfulness in Hades. So the dead don't remember their former lives and spend eternity mourning them."

The woman from the Council didn't look too happy to have been corrected, but Seth saw her choose to ignore this. "Indeed. It's also the name of the process people have started to undertake when they enter the Link."

"Enter and don't come out again," his mother said, her voice even, her eyes on the table in front of her.

"Yes," said the woman from the Council.

"They just give up their lives," his mother said, but it was a question, too.

"Not give them up. Exchange them. For a chance to make something out of themselves and their futures in a world that hasn't been so damaged." The woman's posture changed to a less formal one, one that seemed to suggest she was going to share something secret with them, off the record. "You've seen how things are. How they're going. And it's only getting worse and faster. The economy. The environment. The wars. The epidemics. Is there really any question about why people are wanting to start over? In a place where at least they've got a fair shot?"

"People say it's as bad as this world—"

"Not even close. You can't stop a human from acting like a human, of course, but compared to what we have now, it's paradise. A paradise of second chances."

"You never get old and you never die," his father said, sounding as if he was quoting something.

"Actually, no," the woman from the Council said. "We can't perform those kinds of miracles. Yet. The human mind can't quite take it. But everything else is fully automated. You'll be under permanent guard. You'll get medical treatment when you need it. Your bodies will remain physically viable, including keeping your muscles toned, and we've just developed a hormone to keep your hair and nails from growing. We're even on the threshold of actual reproduction and childbirth. This really is our best hope for the future."

"What's in it for you?" his mother asked. "Who gains?"

"We all do," the woman from the Council said immediately. "It takes power, sure, but far less than humans walking around do. We shut off everything except the connection to the chambers, and we take what we've got left and put it to proper use. At the very least, we sleep our way through disaster and come out the other side." She leaned forward. "I'll be honest with you. There'll come a day, and soon, when you may not have a choice, when even I don't have a choice. Best to do it now, on your own terms."

His mother looked at her carefully. "And you're saying we'll have Owen back?"

The woman got a funny little smile on her face. It was meant to be kind, understanding, but even Seth, sitting unobserved at the far corner of the table, could see that it was also a smile of triumph. The woman from the Council had won, and Seth hadn't even known they were fighting.

"The simulation programming is a prototype," the woman said. "I want to stress that."

"'Yet'," his father said.

"I beg your pardon?"

"You said 'yet' earlier about miracles. This is the 'yet', isn't it?"

"If you like," the woman said, in a way that made it clear she didn't like it. "But I can tell you two things. One, Lethe will make sure you never, ever know the difference, and two, the results we've had so far in initial testing have been beyond the participants' wildest dreams."

"And we'll just . . . forget this all ever happened?" his mother said.

The woman from the Council's mouth went tight. "Not quite."

"Not quite?" his mother said, suddenly harsh. "I don't want to remember anything. What the hell do you mean, not quite?"

"Lethe is a subtle process, one with amazing properties. But it has to work with what's already in you. It can't erase memories as big and important as what's just happened—"

"Then what's the goddamn point of it?"

"—but what it can do is give you an alternative outcome."

There was a silence. "What do you mean?" his father finally asked.

"Any detail I would give you here would be speculation until we got your nodes implanted and did a full actualization, but I suspect that you would probably remember the abduction of your son—"

His mother made a scoffing sound.

"–but that it would have a much happier ending. He would be found, alive, possibly injured, possibly in need of recovery and rehabilitation–this would be what Lethe would have you believe as you adjusted to the new Owen–but he would no longer be dead. He would be created from your memories of him, and he would grow and develop and respond to you, just as your son would have. For all intents and purposes, he'd be alive again. So much so, you'd never know the difference."

His mother started to speak but needed to clear her throat. "Would I be able to touch him?" she asked, her voice rough. "Would I be able to smell him?" She covered her mouth with her hand, unable to go on.

"Yes. You would. The Link isn't just a variation of the world. It is the world, put into a safe place. Your jobs would be the same, your house would be the same, your family, your friends–the ones who have already entered it anyway, and again, that's going to be everyone very soon. It feels and looks completely real because it is completely real."

"How would we interact with people who aren't in it, though?" his father asked. His mother scoffed again, as if this was the stupidest question she'd ever heard.

The woman from the Council didn't blink. "The same way you interact with people who are in it now. That's one of the cleverest things about it. We've flipped it. When you're there, it's this world that seems online, and that's how you interact with it. You send the same e-mails and messages. And if someone in the real world tries to tell you that you're online, well, Lethe makes you forget again and again."

Her voice turned more serious. "But, and I mean this, we really are nearing a tipping point. Pretty soon these questions won't matter, because there won't be a world here to interact with. We'll all be there, living out happier lives, in a world that isn't already used up."

"I don't want to live here," his mother said. "In this town, I mean. In this stupid country. Can you arrange that?"

"Well, again, we can't just plant you in a whole new life, there'd be no memories to work from, but moving around there is the same as moving around here. If you want to leave, then you can leave."

"I want to leave." His mother looked around the sitting room again. "I will leave."

"The practicalities are simple," the woman from the Council said. "We get the nodes implanted, get your memories actualized, and then we place you in the sleeping chambers. We're reaching capacity in our current facility, but we're expanding all the time. If we need to, we can easily install one here in your own home and move you when space becomes available."

"That easy?" his father asked.

"I could manage it within the week," the woman said. "You could see your son again, and all this pain you feel now would be gone."

His mother and father were silent for a moment, then they looked at each other. His father took his mother's hand. She resisted at first, but he held on and eventually she let him.

"He wouldn't be real," his father whispered. "He'd be a program."

"You wouldn't know," the woman from the Council said. "You'd never ever know."

"I can't take this, Ted," his mother said. "I can't live in a world where he's gone." She turned back to the woman. "When can we start?"

The woman smiled again. "Right now. I brought the paperwork. You'll be amazed at how quickly we can get things moving." She took three large packets out of her briefcase. "One for you, Mrs. Wearing. One for Mr. Wearing. And one for young Seth."

His parents turned to look at him, and Seth was certain they were surprised to find him sitting there.

"The woman from the Council must have been right," Seth says after he's told Regine and Tomasz this story. "There was some kind of tipping point, when the final parts of it happened faster than they expected. No one ever moved me out of my house to the prison." He looks at Regine. "Or you, either. And no Driver ever came to guard me *or* you. Whatever systems they meant to set up, they obviously didn't get all the way done. They had to protect what they could and hope for the best. The world must have been right on the point of collapse." He breathes. "And then it collapsed."

"But," Tomasz says, "you cannot just replace a whole person. Your brother –"

"Yeah," Regine demands, heat in her voice. "Why would my mother marry my bastard of a stepfather if she could have had my father back?"

"I don't know," Seth says. "It's like you said, every time we find something out, there are a hundred brand-new things we *don't* know." He turns back to the grave. "But you can imagine what happened, maybe. It started as a fun thing to dip in and out of. And then people began staying there, leaving the real world behind, and the governments of the world think, *Hang on, this could be useful*. Then people started being *encouraged* to stay, because hey, you'll save us money and resources and maybe, as a bonus, we'll try offering you things that aren't even there anymore. But then maybe everything just got too bad too fast. People were *forced* to stay, like the woman said, because the world became unlivable."

"And now *everyone* is there," Tomasz says. "Even the ones who wrote the programs that made your brother. No one to fix it. No one to make it better."

"No," Seth says, "he never did get better."

"But no one there knows any different," Regine says, still sounding angry.

"I'm not sure that's true, actually," Seth says. "I think they do know, on some level. They feel something's not right but refuse to think about it. Haven't you ever felt like there has to be *more*? Like there's more out there somewhere, just beyond your grasp, if you could only get to it . . ."

"All of the time," Tomasz says quietly. "All of the time I feel this."

350

"Everyone does," Regine says. "Especially when you're our age."

"I'll bet my parents knew," Seth says. "On some level. That he wasn't real, no matter how real he seemed. How can you truly forget making a choice that awful? It was there in how they treated me. Like an afterthought. Like a burden, sometimes." His voice drops. "And I thought they just didn't forgive me for being there when Owen was taken."

"Ah," Tomasz says. "When you said it was little bit your fault."

Seth places his hand on top of Owen's grave. "I've hardly ever told anyone. The police, who told my parents, but no one else." He looks up into the sunshine and thinks of Gudmund. "Not even when I could have."

"What can it matter now, though?" Regine asks. "The truth as you knew it isn't true."

He turns to her, surprised. "What do you mean, *what can it matter*? It changes everything."

Regine looks incredulous. "Everything's *already* changed."

"No," Seth says, shaking his head. "No, you don't understand."

"Then help us to understand," Tomasz says. "You have seen my worst memory, after all, Mr. Seth."

"I can't."

"Won't," Regine says.

"Oh, yeah?" Seth says, growing angry. "How did you die again? Freak accident falling down the stairs?"

"That's different–"

351

"How? I just found out I killed my brother!"

A small group of pigeons flaps out of the grass nearby, startled by Seth's raised voice. Seth, Tomasz, and Regine watch the birds fly off, too small to be a flock, disappearing deeper into the cemetery, into overgrown trees and shadows, until they're nothing but a memory.

And then Seth begins to speak.

61

He was still holding Owen's hand. Their mother had said, "Don't move!" and they'd obeyed her almost to the letter, sitting down on the floor next to the dining-room table when they got tired.

And then came the knocking. Not at the front door, but on the kitchen window at the back, in the garden that led nowhere except to fence after fence.

Where a man in a funny-collared dark-blue shirt was now looking at them.

"Hello, lads," he said, his voice dampened by the glass. "Can you help me out?"

"Seth?" Owen said, worried.

"Go away," Seth said to the man, trying to sound braver than he was. But he was eight and never sure why adults did any of the things they did, so he also said, "What do you want?"

"I want to come in," said the man. "I'm hurt. I need help."

"Go away!" Owen shouted, echoing Seth's words.

"I won't go away," said the man. "You can count on that, lads. I will never, ever go away."

Owen gripped tighter onto Seth. "I'm scared," he whispered. "Where's Mummy?"

Seth had a sudden inspiration. "You'll get in trouble!" he shouted at the man. "My mum will catch you! She's here. She's upstairs. I'll go get her now!"

"Your mother left," the man said, unbothered. "I watched her go. I thought she might pop back in, because who would leave two youngsters like yourselves on their own, even for a few minutes? But no, it really does seem like she's gone. Now, I'm going to ask you again, lads. Unlock this back door here and let me in. I need your help."

"If you really needed help," Seth said to him, "you would have asked for it when Mummy was here."

The man paused, almost as if acknowledging this mistake. "I don't want her help. I want your help."

"No," Owen whispered, still panicky. "Don't do it, Seth."

"I won't," Seth said to him. "I never would."

The man's face was half in shadow from the sun, and Seth had a moment to think how short he must be, if all they could see was his shoulders and head. When their father looked in, he nearly had to lean down.

"I don't want to have to ask again," the man said, his voice a little stronger.

"You have to wait until our mother comes back," Seth said.

"Let me put it this way," the man said calmly, "so that you understand me, okay? If you let me in, all right? If you let me in, then I won't kill you."

And at that, the man smiled.

Owen's little hands squeezed Seth's hard.

The man cocked his head. "What's your name, boy?"

Seth answered, "Seth," before he was even aware he could have refused.

"Well, Seth, I could break that door down. I've done worse in my time, believe me. I could break it down and I could come in and I could kill you, but instead, I am asking you to let me in. If I really meant you harm, would I do that? Would I ask your permission?"

Seth said nothing, just swallowed nervously.

"And so I'm asking you again, Seth," the man said. "Please let me in. If you do that, I promise not to kill you. You have my word." The man put his hands up to the glass. "But if I have to ask one more time, I will come in there and I will kill you both. I'd prefer not to, but if that's the decision you make—"

"Seth," Owen whispered, his face pulled tight with terror.

"Don't worry," Seth whispered back, not because he knew what to do but because that's what his mother always said. "Don't worry."

"I'll count to three," the man said. "One."

"No, Seth," Owen whispered.

"You promise not to kill us?" Seth asked the man.

"Cross my heart," the man said, making the motion across his chest. "Two."

"Seth, Mummy said no—"

"He says he won't kill us," Seth said, standing.

"No—"

"I'm about to say three, Seth," the man said.

Seth didn't know what to do. There was threat every-where, crackling through the dead, stale air of their house, *a place where harm and danger seemed impossible. He could feel it shining from the man like a fire.*

But he didn't understand the threat, not fully. Was it a threat if he didn't do what the man said or if he did? He didn't doubt that the man could break down the door—adults could do that sort of thing—so maybe if he just did what the man said, maybe he would—

"Three," said the man.

Seth leapt into the kitchen, suddenly urgent, fiddling with the lock, shifting its weight so it would open.

He stepped back. The man moved from the window and around to the door. Seth saw that the funny-collared shirt was actually a dark blue jumpsuit. The man was stroking his chin, and Seth saw scarring on the man's knuckles, a strange white puckering like he'd been burnt there.

"Why, thank you, Seth," the man said. "Thank you very much indeed."

"Seth?" Owen said, edging around the doorway from the main room.

"You said you wouldn't kill us if I let you in," Seth said to the man.

"That I did," said the man.

"We've got bandages if you're hurt."

"Oh, it's not that kind of hurt," the man said. "It's more a dilemma than an injury, I'd say."

The man smiled. It wasn't friendly. At all.

"I need one of you lads to come with me on a trip." He leaned forward, hands on his knees, so that he was down on Seth's level. "I don't care which one of you. I really don't.

But it has to be one. Not both, not neither." He held up a single finger. "One."

"We can't go anywhere," Seth said. "Our mum is coming back for–"

"One of you is going to leave this house with me," the man interrupted. "And that's the end of the story."

He stepped fully into the kitchen now. Seth backed into the oven, never taking his eyes off the man. Owen still held on to the door frame, his face bunched up, his skin white with fear and amazement at the stranger in their kitchen.

"Here's what I'm going to do, Seth," the man said, as if he'd just had the best idea in years. "I'm going to let you choose. I'm going to let you choose which of you two comes with me."

62

"Oh, Mr. Seth," Tomasz says. "That is too, too terrible."

"I thought," Seth says, not able to meet their eyes. "I thought if I said he should take Owen, I'd be able to raise the alarm better. I'd be able to explain what happened faster and they could go after the guy and catch him. Owen was only four. He barely had any language at all, and I thought . . ." He turns back to the tombstone. "Actually, I don't know what I thought. I don't even know if that's true or if it's a story I told myself."

"But it was impossible," Tomasz says. "You were a boy. You were *little* boy. How can you choose this?"

"I was old enough to know what I was doing," Seth says. "And the truth is"—he stops, having to swallow it away—"the truth is, I was afraid. Afraid of what would happen to me if I went, and I said . . ."

He stops.

Tomasz steps forward. "If he asks you now, this man."

"What?" Seth says.

"If this man, he comes into your kitchen now, and he asks you this question again. He says to you, I will take you or your brother and you will choose. What do you say?"

Seth shakes his head, confused. "What are you—?"

"You are asked *now*," Tomasz insists. "You are asked right now who to take, you or your brother. What do you say?

Seth frowns. "That's not the same—"

"What do you *say*?"

"I say take me, of course!"

Tomasz leans back, satisfied. "Of course you do. Because you are man now. This is what a grown-up person does. You were not man then. You were boy."

"*You* were only a boy in that room with your mother. You were going to try to protect her. I could feel it."

"I was older. I was not eight. I was not boy."

"You weren't a man. You're not one *now*."

Tomasz shrugs. "There is space in between, no?"

"You don't seem to get it," Seth says, his voice rising. "I killed him. And I'm only just finding this out, don't you see? I always thought they found him alive. Damaged and in need of rehabilitation, which was bad enough. But now. Now."

He turns back to the grave. His chest begins to draw tight, his throat closes shut, and he feels as if he's choking, as if his body has been clamped in a vise.

"Stop this," Regine says, quietly at first, but then louder: "Stop this, Seth."

He shakes his head, barely hearing her.

"You're just feeling sorry for yourself," she says, enough anger in her voice to get through to him.

He turns to her. "What?"

"You can't possibly believe it's your fault.'

359

Seth looks at her, his eyes red. "Whose fault is it then?"

Regine's own eyes widen, as if stunned. "How about the *murderer,* you dolt? How about your mother for leaving you alone in a house when you were way too young to be faced with something like that?"

"She didn't know–"

"It doesn't matter what she knew or didn't know. Her job was to protect you. Her job was to make sure you never had to face any kind of shit like that. That was her *job*!"

"Regine?" Tomasz asks, startled at her volume.

"Look," Regine says, "I can see why you'd think this is your fault, and I can see how your parents might have made you keep on thinking that, but did you ever consider maybe it wasn't about you at all? Maybe your mum just screwed up, okay? And sometimes that even happens to good people. So maybe the way they treated you wasn't *about* you. Maybe it was about *them*. Maybe all that happened is that they forgot you were there because they were too busy with their own crap."

"And you don't think that's bad?"

"Of course it's bad! Don't worry, I'm not trying to take away everything that makes you feel sorry for yourself, since you seem pretty damn good at that!"

"Regine," Tomasz warns, "he has just found out his brother is–"

"But maybe," she keeps shouting, "*maybe* their world didn't revolve around you, Seth. Maybe they thought about themselves as much as you thought about *yourself.*"

"Hey–" Seth says.

"WE ALL DO IT! Everyone! That's what we do. We think of ourselves."

"Not always," Tomasz says quietly.

"Often enough!" Regine says. "So maybe all this tragedy of how you made the wrong decision and your parents punished you for the rest of your life, maybe that's a story you just *want* to be true, because it's easier."

"*Easier?* How the hell is it easier?"

"Because then you wouldn't have to do anything yourself! If it's your fault, that clears everything up. You've done this horrible thing and that's easy. You don't ever have to risk being happy."

Seth stops as if she's slapped him. "I risked being happy. I did risk it."

"Not enough to stop you from killing yourself," Regine says. "Oh, poor little Seth, with his poor little parents who didn't love him. You said we all want there to be more than this! Well, there's *always* more than this. There's *always* something you don't know. Maybe your parents didn't love you enough, and that sucks, yes, it does, but maybe it wasn't because you were bad. Maybe it was just because the worst thing in the world had happened to them and they weren't able to deal with it."

Seth shakes his head. "Why are you doing this?"

Regine makes an angry, frustrated sound. "Because if it isn't your fault, Seth, if it's just a shitty thing that happened to you, well, shitty things happen all the time. Tommy got shot in the head! I—"

She bites her tongue.

"What?" Seth asks challengingly. "What happened to you?"

She looks into his eyes, her own blazing.

He doesn't look away.

"I was thrown down the stairs by my stepfather," she says.

Tomasz takes in a surprised breath.

"He started drinking more," she says, her eyes not moving from Seth's, "and decided that a slap now and then was okay. Then a punch. My mother tried to explain it all away, tried to make it seem normal and bearable, but I fought that bastard. I fought him every stupid time he tried to lay his hands on me. But one day, for whatever reason, he went that extra step. Probably didn't even mean to, the piece of shit, but he did. He wanted to beat me and I was saying no and he knocked me down the stairs and I hit my head and I *died*." She furiously wipes away the tears that have appeared on her cheeks. "And my mother, who I loved more than anything, she didn't stop it either. That was her *job,* and she never stopped him."

She looks around them, into the sun, at the comically tall grass they're all standing in. "And this world? This stupid, empty world? I don't care if it's hell. *I don't even care.* If it's real or not real, if we've all woken up from some online thing or if this is all your stupid imagination, Seth, I don't care. All I know is that I'm real enough. And *Tommy's* real enough. And however much of a hell this *is* . . ." She suddenly quiets, as if the energy's been leached from her. "However awful it is, it's better than there."

63

"I did not know," Tomasz says, taking her hand in his still-wrapped own.

"How could you?" Regine says, wiping her nose with her sleeve. "I never said."

The sun beats down on them, hot again, and Seth notices once more the lack of insect noise. There isn't even any wind. There's just the three of them, in the stillness of an overgrown cemetery.

"Are we not some funny kind of group?" Tomasz says. "Child abuse, murder, and suicide."

"None of which happened for any good reason at all," Regine says.

"Is that why you're so mad at me all the time?" Seth asks. "You think I did it because I felt sorry for myself? While you two had *really* rough times?"

Regine gives him a look that doesn't need words attached to it.

"I didn't kill myself because of what happened to my brother," Seth says. "It was shit and it just got shittier, but it wasn't the reason."

"So why, then?" Tomasz asks.

"Is this from when you said you risked happiness?" Regine asks. "With the guy with the funny name?"

Seth doesn't answer for a moment, but then nods.

"Well," Tomasz says, looking at the tombstone, "if there is more to this story than you thought, maybe there is more to that one, too. Maybe there is always more."

The sun rises higher in the sky. Seth's still reeling from all the things this morning has brought, all the new but strangely familiar hurt waiting to be felt. He's exhausted again, despite the night's sleep. His feelings are knotted together, so tight he can't unwind them. Pain and anger and humiliation and loss and longing.

But maybe more, too.

He looks back at Owen's name and wonders if Tomasz is right. There *was* more to this story.

Was there more to Gudmund?

"I'm not trying to be funny," Regine says after a moment, "but are we going to stand here all day? Some of us were interrupted before we'd eaten breakfast, and some of us would like to get back to that, if that's okay with some *others* of us."

"Yeah," Seth says. "Yeah, all right."

No one says anything as they make their way back through the grass, occasionally bumping into hidden tombstones. They reach the low wall, and Tomasz clambers over.

"Have you ever thought of trying to go back?" Seth asks as Regine moves to step over, too.

She stops. "Go back?"

"Not to your old life, maybe," Seth says. "But if it's all

364

just programming and memory manipulation . . ." He shrugs. "Maybe you could go back and it'd be better."

Her face is still hard, but sad, too. "Knowing what you know, how would you be able to look your parents in the eye? Or your brother?"

"That's not really an answer."

"What is taking such a time?" Tomasz calls from over by the bike, unable to pick it up because of his hands.

"Nothing," Regine says. "Just another unhelpful idea from Seth—"

But Seth doesn't let her finish.

"TOMASZ!" he shouts—

Because he sees the Driver—

Running fast around the corner from the nearby church, its crackling baton already up—

Heading straight for Tomasz.

Tomasz turns and screams, tripping over the bike in his rush to get away. Regine is already sailing over the low wall, pounding into the street, straight for Tomasz.

Seth is right behind her, but they're not going to make it—

Because here the Driver comes, its baton sending flashes and sparks from its tip.

It was waiting for us, Seth thinks. They hadn't heard the engine. It had to have been there all along. But how could it possibly have known—?

Tomasz is yelling in Polish, trying to scramble away crabwise from where he's fallen—

"NO!" Regine is screaming. "TOMMY!"

And Seth hears the anger in her voice, which makes so much more sense now that he's heard her story—

She's protecting Tommy—

Like *she* wasn't protected—

The Driver makes a terrifyingly smooth leap over the bicycle, not slowing its stride as it closes in on Tomasz—

Regine is moving faster than Seth has ever seen her, so fast she's pulling away from him—

But it's too late—

It's too late—

The Driver has reached Tomasz—

Tomasz is raising his bandaged hands to protect his head—

Light streams from the tip of the baton as the Driver swings it down—

And strikes the arm of Regine, who has thrown herself between Tomasz and the Driver.

The end of the baton fires into her skin. She screams inhumanly at the pain of it, her body twisting in agony. Her arm and chest and head are enveloped in a shower of sparks and flashes.

Her scream cuts off halfway through, in a sudden stop that is the scariest sound of all. She falls to the ground, making no effort to protect herself from hitting the concrete.

And lies there.

Lifeless.

64

Seth doesn't think. He doesn't call out or scream her name or make any sound.

He just moves.

The Driver is standing over Regine, and Seth doesn't even consider that the baton is still crackling and flashing in its hand. He races past Tomasz, who's crying out Regine's name, and he leaps at the Driver, throwing his full weight against the faceless black shape of it.

It sees him at the last moment and tries to bring the baton up, but Seth hits it hard, and as they both fall to the ground, the baton is knocked from the Driver's grasp and goes skittering across the road.

They hit the pavement with a hard *whumpf*. Seth lands on top of the Driver and has the air knocked out of him. It feels as if he's thrown himself down onto a pillar of steel. Pain shoots through his ribs, but he ignores it and tries to use his weight to keep the Driver on the ground.

He doesn't know what he's going to do next—

Only that a rage unlike anything he's ever experienced is surging through him like a forest fire.

He throws his fist down, hitting the Driver's throat on the

exposed area beneath its visor. It's like punching the concrete of the sidewalk. He calls out, and the Driver bucks underneath him, throwing him off easily and regaining its feet.

Looking up, Seth has a clear view of its chest, where Tomasz sent the shotgun blast. Some kind of repair seems to have been made, but there's still a cavity that's deeper than it should be.

Deeper than should be survivable, Seth's mind registers.

Tomasz is now curled over Regine a few feet away, wailing into her ear to wake up, wake up, wake up, his face so twisted with disbelief and shock, Seth can barely look at it.

The Driver spies the baton and runs toward it. Seth jumps to his feet throwing himself again at the Driver, knowing it won't work but having to try, having to at least try–

But this time the Driver is ready for him. It spins around, its fists up, catching Seth in mid-leap, knocking him hard across the side of the head, hard enough to drop him to the ground.

Seth's vision disappears in flashes of light. He's dimly aware of the concrete below him, his forehead pressed against it, his suddenly distant body twisted in the fall.

He's unable to move properly, unable to get his arms and legs to do what he wants, but he rolls over just enough to see the Driver hurrying toward the dropped baton with those freakily silky steps it takes.

He sees Tomasz scream out and throw himself at the Driver.

He sees the Driver cuff Tomasz across the crown of his head as if he were no more than an annoying wasp, sees Tomasz crumple to the ground.

He sees the Driver retrieve the baton and turn back to where Seth lies helpless.

Here it is, he has a moment to think. *Here is my death.*

The Driver approaches, closing in fast.

I'm sorry, Seth thinks, but he doesn't know to who or why –

But the Driver stops beside Regine. It makes a complicated motion with its arm, and the baton disappears into an invisible sleeve. Seth tries to make himself rise again, but new pain thunders through his head and he feels as if he might black out. He slumps back to the ground.

All he can do is watch as the Driver kneels and puts its arms beneath Regine's body. It stands, lifting her tall, heavy frame with an ease that would be laughable if it weren't so horrific.

The Driver turns to him one last time, Regine in its arms, its face as unreadable as ever, and the last thing Seth sees before unconsciousness claims him is the Driver taking her body away.

65

"Wake up," he hears distantly, like someone calling from the next street over. "Oh please, please, please wake up, Mr. Seth."

He feels taps on his cheeks, muffled by the bandages still somehow on Tomasz's hands, taps too small to hurt, but large enough to be noticeable.

"Tomasz?" he says. His mouth and throat feel as if they're covered in feathers and sticky toffee.

"It has taken her, Mr. Seth!" Tomasz exclaims, nearly hysterical. "She is gone! We have to find her! We have to –"

"She's . . ." Seth says, barely able to lift his head.

"*Please*," Tomasz says, pulling on his arm. "I know you are hurt, but we have to stop the Driver! It will kill her!"

Seth looks up at Tomasz, squinting at the pain in his skull. "*Will* kill her? It didn't . . . ? She wasn't . . . ?"

"She was gone and out," Tomasz says, "but she was breathing. I swear she was breathing –"

"You *swear*? Tomasz, are you sure you aren't mistaking –"

"Her light was blinking." Tomasz flashes his fingers fast. "Blink-blink-blink-blink-blink. It has never done that before, Mr. Seth. It never come on even once. And it was *red*. Not like ours."

"Why did it take her?" Seth asks, forcing himself to sit up, his head spinning. "What's it doing?"

Tomasz gasps. "Maybe it is going to reconnect her."

Seth looks up at that. "Reconnect her?"

Tomasz grabs the sides of his head with a cry. "I figure it out, Mr. Seth! We are not supposed to be here! You said it yourself. We are a malfunction. We are *accidents*."

Seth breathes through his mouth, trying not to vomit. "And it's trying to fix those accidents. It's a kind of caretaker or something. Putting us back where we belong."

"It will put her back into her old life!" Tomasz shouts. "Where she is supposed to be dead!"

"Why didn't it just kill her here, though? She said it killed the woman she met."

"Maybe Regine only thinks her friend was dead when the Driver took her away."

"Oh, hell," Seth says. "It's going to put her back. . . ."

He thinks of Regine, big, angry, brave Regine, being thrown down the stairs by a man she was trying to fight, a man she shouldn't have *had* to fight.

And she was going to be put right back there. A world where she was dead.

Seth gets to his feet, Tomasz helping. Seth looks down at him, at a face he knows will go to hell and back to save Regine. Save Seth, too, probably.

He isn't Owen, Seth thinks, *but he's Tomasz. And she's Regine. And we're all we've got.*

"Let's go get her," he growls. "And let's put that son of a bitch down once and for all."

• • •

"I think it went to the prison," Tomasz says, grimacing at the pain in his hands as he lifts the bike. "I heard the vehicle start up again and drive away."

"Why wouldn't it go to Regine's house?" Seth asks, concentrating on keeping upright. "That's where her coffin is."

"I do not know," Tomasz says again. "Maybe it is only supposed to look after those in the prison. Maybe it thinks that is where we are supposed to be."

"It was waiting for us here. It was waiting to take us back."

"Yes," Tomasz says. "Maybe it knew you would come here. Maybe it learned your memories when you got zapped."

"Oh, shit, I hope that's not true."

"We are needing to be hurrying now."

"I'm coming," Seth says. He takes a few steps and loses his balance but catches himself.

Tomasz looks at him, worried. "You *must* be okay, Mr. Seth. You must. However badly you are feeling, we have to get her. There is no other choice."

Seth stops for a moment, closes his eyes, and opens them again. "I know," he says. "We're not sending her back to die. No matter what."

He takes a deep breath and forces himself to walk more steadily. He moves faster and then faster again, until he reaches the bike. He swings his leg over the seat, feels himself swoon a bit, but rides it out. "You are okay?" Tomasz asks, climbing up behind him.

"Okay enough."

"Do you know what you are doing?"

"I know how to ride a *bike,* Tomasz–"

"No," Tomasz says, his face pressed into Seth's back, holding on for the journey about to start. "Do you know what you are doing right now?"

"What? What am I doing right now?"

"You threw yourself at the Driver when it attacked her," Tomasz says. "I saw it. You did this knowing you would probably be killed yourself. And now you are going to save her, knowing how strong it is, knowing what it can do. You are going to try and save her anyway."

"Of course I am," Seth says, irritated, trying to get his feet up on the pedals without tumbling the two of them over.

"This is who you are, do you see?" Tomasz continues. "You are not a boy who hands his brother over to a murderer instead of yourself. You are a man who will save his friends. You are a man who does not even *hesitate* to save his friends."

"My friends," Seth says, almost asking it.

Tomasz squeezes him. "Yes, Mr. Seth."

"My friends," Seth says again.

He starts pedaling, fighting to keep the bike level with their combined weight, but pedaling faster and then faster again.

66

"She will be there," Tomasz says, over Seth's shoulder, saying it like a prayer. "We will be in time."

"We'll save her," Seth says. "Don't you worry."

He pedals along, dodging the taller weeds, thumping over deep cracks. They're riding through the neighborhood toward Seth's house and the prison beyond.

"Watch out!" Tomasz says as a startled pheasant flies up from under a blast of weeds. Seth swerves, nearly toppling them, but he's feeling stronger now, focused on a goal. He's going to get them to the train station. They're going to ride down that path beside the tracks and go as far into the prison grounds as they can get—

And then what?

Well, he doesn't know the answer to that yet, but all they need to do now is get there. He speeds up as they turn down the street his own house is on.

Whatever is true, whatever this place is or isn't, whether it's all in his head or whether this really is the way the world turned out, he thinks about what Tomasz said.

His friends.

Yes, that felt right. That felt *real*. Friends that he couldn't possibly make up, with lives that he'd never imagine.

Whatever the other explanations were, Tomasz and Regine felt real.

And then he remembers what Regine said, saying it to himself firmly, like a vow.

Know yourself, he thinks, as they sail past his house.

And go in swinging.

They carry the bike up to the train station, take it over the platform and down to the brick path on the side of the tracks. Tomasz loops his hands around Seth's waist again, and they ride the short distance to the break in the wall.

"Almost there," Tomasz says nervously as they get off once more and take the bike through.

"I don't suppose you have a plan?" Seth asks.

"Aha!" Tomasz says, grinning desperately. "*Now* you are asking. After seeing Tomasz make so many brave escapes and have so many clever ideas. Now you are giving him credit."

"So do you?" Seth says, setting the bike back down on the other side of the maze of broken fences.

"I do not," Tomasz says sheepishly, and Seth thinks he's never looked younger.

"How old are you really?"

Tomasz looks at the desolate sprays of grass growing up in the prison ground. "I was about to become twelve before I woke up. I do not know how old that makes me here."

Seth grips his shoulders, making Tomasz look him in

the eye. "I think it makes you a man here. From what I've seen anyway."

Tomasz just looks back for a moment, then nods gravely. "We will rescue her."

"We will." They get on the bike and race down the hill. The buildings surrounding the square seem smaller in the sunshine as they approach. No hidden shadows that could contain endless spaces.

Nope, Seth thinks, *the endless spaces are all hidden underground.*

"Why would they build it under a prison?" he wonders aloud as they ride. "Of all places, why here?"

"A prison has to be safe, maybe?" Tomasz says. "And this place would have to be, too, for all the people to sleep. It makes a kind of terrible sense."

"When do you think we're going to find anything here that makes good sense?"

"I do not know, Mr. Seth. I am hopeful for soon."

They reach the end of the path, bumping on weedy ground as they approach the first main building. "I can't hear the engine anymore," Seth says.

They get off the bike and peek around the corner into the square, but there's nothing to see, nothing surprising anyway. The buildings look even harder in daylight, more unflinching.

"Do we think she is down there?" Tomasz asks.

"Where else?" Seth says.

Tomasz nods. "Then I will ask you to go in and get her while I try to locate the vehicle."

• • •

"What?" Seth asks after a startled moment. "Are you crazy?"

"It must be around here. This is clearly where it parks."

"And you'll do *what* with it?"

"I do not know! But now we have nothing. It might be *something*."

Seth tries to answer but can't think of anything to say.

"Just keep the Driver away from her," Tomasz says. "I will try to find something to help. And if I cannot . . ." He shrugs. "Then I will come back and we will both go down fighting."

Seth frowns. "We *aren't* going to go down."

"I know you are trying to be brave for me, but we might. That is a risk when you are fighting with death. You do not always win."

"But we're going to today," Seth says firmly. "There's no way we're going to let that thing take Regine. Just no way at all."

Tomasz grins. "She would very much like to be hearing you talk this way. Yes, she would be very much liking this indeed."

"Tomasz, I can't let you–"

But Tomasz is already backing away, still grinning. "How funny that you continue to believe I am in need of your permission."

"Tomasz–"

"Go find her, Mr. Seth. I will not be far behind."

Seth makes an exasperated sound. "Well, don't take any unnecessary risks."

"I think we are in a place where all risks are necessary," Tomasz says, and takes off running.

• • •

Seth watches him go, his stumpy little legs crossing the square and disappearing around the far corner of the building opposite, where the van emerged the last time they were here.

"Stay safe," Seth murmurs. "Oh, stay safe."

He takes a deep breath for courage, then takes another, and runs across the square himself. He's half expecting the Driver to leap out from somewhere, but the sun is shining down on every corner and he sees nothing. He reaches the prison door and listens. There's no buzz of an engine, no sound of footsteps.

No sound of Regine arguing or fighting or struggling.

He opens the door. The milky-glass inner door and stairs are the same, glowing with light. He steps through the first doorway and edges to the second.

Still nothing but the electric hum coming from downstairs.

He crouches low as he takes a few steps down. Then a few more. He reaches the turn in the stairway. His heart is thumping away in his chest, so hard he wonders for a crazy moment if the Driver will be able to hear it too.

And then there's a scream.

Regine.

He runs down the rest of the stairs before he can even think to stop.

67

He pounds through the lower corridor, tearing around the final corner and into the vast room, his blood rushing, his fists actually up, ready to fight.

Go in swinging, he thinks.

But he can't see her. From this little platform, it's just rows and rows of coffins, like before. He sees the one he opened, now closed and sealed like nothing ever happened. The vast room stretches before him, and he remembers the cameras on the display flashing through endless farther distant rooms.

She could be anywhere.

"Regine?" he calls out, his voice swallowed by the huge empty space.

There's nothing. No response. No further screaming.

He turns to the milky panel on the wall to see if he can get it working again. It lights up under his touch, smaller screens within the larger one, scrolling rapidly through information that makes no sense and is often too fast to read anyway, plus changing pictures from the cameras, too, taken from all through the complex.

But at the very center of the screen, one image is remaining steady. An open coffin, somewhere out there in the vastness.

Regine lying inside.

The Driver standing over her, wrapping her in bandages.

"No!" Seth says, pressing the screen wildly, trying to find any information that'll tell him where she is. There's a grid map next to her, like the ones he saw before, but it could be anywhere and the coordinates are written in a way he can't understand. *2.03.881,* it says, which could mean anything. Room two, row three, coffin 881? But what does that tell him?

He looks out at the room, thinking he'll just have to chance it, he'll have to run until he finds her and do whatever he can to stop—

She screams again.

He whirls back to the display. Regine doesn't seem to be resisting the Driver or even know that it's there. Seth watches as she screams once more, the sound reaching his ears separate from the image, coming from deep within the recesses of the huge building.

"You son of a bitch!" he shouts at the image, the Driver going about its business, ignoring Regine's fear, ignoring whatever it is that's happening to her. "I will kill you. Do you hear me? I'll *kill* you!"

He slams his fist on the screen.

And it changes.

Her name pops up in a box. REGINE FRANÇOISE EMERIC, it says, atop a list of facts. Height, weight, her birthday, then a date that could be when she was put online.

And one more date, listing itself as DISCONNECT.

The date she was thrown down the stairs. It has to be. The date there was a mistake and, instead of dying, she woke up here.

ORIGINAL CHAMBER OUTSIDE PROTECTED GRID, he reads. That must be why the Driver brought her here instead of her house. Years too late, it was bringing her inside with everyone else.

Another line pops up, blinking red: LETHE CONNECTION PENDING.

"Lethe?" Seth says. "Why would it . . . ?"

He scans the screen again. There's so much data surrounding Regine's screen it's hard to figure out what any of it means. He presses LETHE CONNECTION PENDING and another screen pops up.

The disconnect date is there and below it, RECONNECTION TIMECODE.

Seth reads it.

Then he reads it again.

"No way," he whispers.

The reconnection date, the time she's being put back online –

It's before her disconnection date.

The Driver is placing her back in time. It's putting her back *before she died*. Only a few minutes, but definitely before.

"How?" Seth says, pressing more and more buttons, trying to find some answer. "How is that possible?"

It's a program, he thinks. *That's all it is. A program everyone's agreeing to, a program everyone's a part of–*

But still just a program.

If Owen was a simulation, then who knew what could go on in there? Who knew if the present and the past were even the same online? He'd relived his own past, after all, over and over again in the dreams. He'd been right there in Tomasz's too.

And if Regine's death had been a mistake in the system –

Maybe the system needed to fix its mistakes.

Maybe it could place her back to a time just before her death, so she'd go through it again, but properly this time.

Be properly killed.

There's a sudden flash of blue on the screen. LETHE INITIALIZED, it blinks. In the image, the Driver has placed a breathing tube in Regine's mouth. Probably how they get Lethe into your body, Seth thinks.

It was going to make her forget. It was going to make her forget him and Tomasz. It was going to wipe all this away from her.

And then it was going to kill her. Just to make the world work.

"The hell you are," Seth says, pressing LETHE INITIALIZED. A screen pops up beside it. PAUSE INITIALIZATION? YES/NO.

Seth stabs YES. "How do you like them apples, you piece of shit?"

In the image, the Driver turns.

And looks right back into the camera.

As if it's looking right into Seth's own eyes.

And then it begins to run.

• • •

Seth listens for footsteps. He hears them, approaching fast, from around a corner on the right, some distance away.

Which is where Regine must be.

Seth's breathing increases, his heart pounding again. He has no weapons. Nothing to fight it with. If it reaches him, there's no way he can overpower it.

But maybe he can outrun it. He used to be a pretty good runner, after all.

He jumps down from the platform, racing down the rows of coffins. All that matters in these immediate seconds is to keep the Driver away from Regine, away from whatever process is about to kill her. He takes a turn at the far end of the room, heading now in the general direction of the Driver's running footsteps. He ducks as he sees it turn the corner. Seth stops by a coffin, ready to run wherever the Driver might chase him.

But the Driver isn't coming for him. It's moving down the central aisle, past him, not even looking—

Heading for the display screen.

"HEY!" Seth shouts, standing up. "OVER HERE!"

But the Driver keeps on. It reaches the platform and immediately starts pressing the display, no doubt recommencing the process on Regine.

Seth looks around frantically for something, *anything* to throw at the Driver, anything to even slightly slow it down. But there's only coffins, stretched wall to wall and around every corner and disappearing into further recesses—

He has a thought. That first coffin he'd opened, now back in place like nothing ever happened—

It's a caretaker, he thinks. *That's what it does. It cleans up messes.*

He reaches down to the coffin he's leaning against and tries to find the seam, struggling like last time to get his fingers into the lid, forcing all his weight up, straining against its resistance –

And he nearly falls over again as it pops open. A short man is inside, wrapped in bandages, lights sailing through his coffin, doing their mysterious processes. Seth looks over at the Driver.

Which is looking right at him.

It turns back to the screen, its fingers flashing wildly over the display.

The coffin in front of Seth starts to close.

"No!" Seth says, trying to catch it. But it comes down with implacable force, no matter how much he struggles against it. The Driver goes back to programming whatever it needs for Regine.

"Shit!" Seth lets go of the lid. But then he gets an idea. He reaches into the closing coffin and grabs the man's arm. He drapes it over the lip of the lid and steps back. The lid keeps closing, closing, closing, threatening to crush the man's arm –

But as soon as it touches the man's skin, it springs back open.

"Ha!" Seth says, triumphant, and looks up.

The Driver is looking at him again.

And it starts to move toward him.

"Have to fix them all, don't you?" Seth shouts, scampering away. He stops at another coffin. He's got a sense of the lid now, and this one pops open easier and faster. It's an old woman, and he drapes her arm over the lip, too.

He sees the Driver at the coffin of the man, putting him back in place, then pressing a particular spot on top of the coffin that lights up a small display across the metal surface. The coffin closes immediately.

Seth looks down at the coffin next to him and presses the same spot. The display appears on the coffin's lid. "So *that's* how it works," he says. There's a box labeled OPEN FOR DIAGNOSTIC? He presses it. The lid lifts, revealing the sleeping body of a middle-aged black man. Seth takes the man's arm, drapes it over the lip, and runs away as the Driver approaches.

Seth moves fast down rows of coffins, stopping randomly and opening first one, then another, repositioning the inhabitants and moving on. The Driver is behind him, tending to each coffin in turn.

It's doing it faster than Seth can. It's catching up.

Seth rushes to the next and opens it. It's a tiny, pale woman. "I'm so sorry," Seth breathes to her, and he reaches his arms under her, lifting her out of the coffin and setting her gently onto the floor. Her coffin starts beeping and flashing with warning lights, some of them running along the tubes still attached to her. Seth takes a handful of them and hesitates a moment.

"It's to save my friend," he says to the woman's unconscious form. "You probably won't remember anything anyway."

He yanks the tubes on the coffin end. They come out surprisingly easily. Sprays of gels and liquids fly out in a wave as other tubes spark, one of them burning Seth's hand. He hisses and drops the tube—

And barely avoids the Driver as it arrives next to him, its baton up and blazing, ready to fall—

Seth tumbles out of the way, the baton smashing into the floor and leaving a scorch mark. The Driver stands over him as he moves back, the baton ready again—

But it turns to the woman. She's now in an increasing puddle as the liquids from the disconnected tubes spill across the floor.

Seth takes his chance, jumping to his feet and starting to run. "I'm sorry!" he shouts back at the woman as the Driver picks her up, places her back into the coffin, already reconnecting tubes and pressing panels with blinding speed—

Seth keeps running. He turns the corner the Driver had come around and slows down, amazed at what he sees.

Stretching in front of him are more coffins than seems possible, so many it'd take him hours to even partially count them. The wide passageways connecting the rooms stretch farther back than he can even see, turning around other corners, too, to delve who knows how much deeper beyond.

He starts running again, scanning right and left, looking for an opened coffin, but all he sees are innumerable closed ones, polished and clean and humming away with their individual lives being lived inside. The Driver clearly did its job with brutal efficiency.

Seth hazards a look back. It hasn't followed him yet, but it can only be a matter of seconds. Seth nears the end of this second area and is about to cross into a third. He stops and opens another coffin, pressing its pad expertly now, lifting the lid with ease.

There's a woman inside.

She's holding a baby.

The woman is bandaged like everyone else, but the baby is wrapped up tight in a blanket that looks made of blue gel. Tubes run from it to the mother, but her arms are around the infant, holding it close, pressing it to her.

Like any mother and baby.

We're on the threshold of reproduction and childbirth, the woman from the Council had said.

Well, they'd clearly managed to cross that threshold before everything went bad. Conception happening through the tubes, mothers giving birth while they were still sleeping, who knew how it exactly worked?

Children were being born.

Hope for the future, the woman from the Council had said, and here it was.

They'd believed there was a future.

He hears footfalls again.

The Driver is running, somewhere behind him.

Seth takes one last look at the woman and baby and closes their coffin. He opens the next one over. Inside is a chubby teenage boy. Seth yanks out tubes in three or four handfuls, then reaches under the boy's shoulders to pull him out of the coffin–

The sound of footfalls enters the room, and Seth can see the Driver hurtle through the passageway, running fast.

A jolt of adrenaline gets the boy out and onto the floor. Seth sets him upright against the coffin, tearing out a few more tubes for good measure.

"Sorry," he says to the boy and takes off running again.

As he passes out of this second room, he turns back—

And sees the Driver stop by the teenage boy.

But not go to him.

It keeps on looking at Seth, obviously conflicted.

There's a terrifying moment when it looks like it may keep on coming—

But then it goes to the boy to put him back. Seth keeps running, thinking that the Driver must somehow be learning, and that next time this trick of taking someone out may not work, that he's got to find Regine, he's got to do it quickly, he's got to—

And then he hears her scream again.

"Regine!" he shouts.

The sound came from the next room after this one, he's sure of it, down through the wide passageway at the far end. She's got to be in there. She's *got* to be.

He hears the scream again. "No," he says, sprinting now. "No, no, no, no, no—"

He sails through the passageway. He has no idea now where he is in relation to the surface. This series of rooms seems impossibly big, impossibly *deep*. His mind keeps telling him that it makes no sense. When was it built? Why was it built *here*?

She screams once more.

And he sees her.

Off to his right, down a row, nearly to the far wall. Her coffin is open, and he can see her lying there.

See her struggling.

She wasn't struggling before.

"Regine!"

Unlike everyone else in the coffins, she's still half-dressed, the bandages wrapped around her upper body and face, but her jeans and shoes still on, as if getting her memory erased was the most important thing, and why wouldn't it be?

It's the one thing that makes all this possible, Seth thinks.

But she seems to be fighting it, fighting against the bandages over her eyes, fighting the tube in her mouth, a tube doing nothing to stifle her screams –

"I'm coming!" he shouts.

He reaches her and pulls the tube out. It sends her into a spasm of distressed coughing.

"Regine?" he cries. "Regine, can you hear me?"

She screams, terrifyingly loud. Her hands are frantic, slapping at him, not in any coordinated way, just flailing around, striking wildly at the air.

"Can you *hear* me?" he shouts again. She jerks away from him, clearly in terror, and screams as loud as before.

"Oh, shit, Regine," Seth says, distraught. He looks back across the rows of coffins, down the wide central passageway that links this large room to the one he just came out of and

389

onto who knows how many beyond it the other way. No sign of the Driver yet, but there's no way it can be far behind.

"I'm sorry," he says, and with one hand he grabs Regine's wrists, forcing them down. She's strong and he can barely hold her there, the force just making her more upset. "I'm sorry, I'm sorry, I'm sorry," he says, and he slips his free hand around her neck, trying to find the end of the bandages.

"You'll see me! It'll all make sense. I promise–"

His hand brushes against the rapidly red-blinking light on her neck–

And in an instant, he's gone from the world.

68

"You're nothing," the man says. "You're fat. You're ugly. And too bloody monstrous for any boy to ever look at you."

"Lots of boys look at me," she says, but she's got fear in her stomach. She can see his fists clenched at his side. She's big, but he's bigger, and she knows he's not afraid to use those fists, like he used them on her mother just now, knocking her once across the kitchen table when the tea was too cold, a knock that sent Regine running up the stairs, him roaring after her.

He's usually slow when he's drunk, but she's taken too long to grab her phone and her money, and when she left her bedroom, there he was, blocking the top of the stairs.

"No boy ever looks at you," he spits at her. "You slut."

"Let me pass," she says, clenching her own fists. "Let me pass or I swear to God . . ."

He smirks. That stupid pink face of his, all lit up with ugly, drunk delight, that lank blond hair that always looks dirty, no matter how often he washes it. "Let you pass or you swear to God you'll what?"

She says nothing, doesn't move.

He steps back, gesturing grandly with one hand and

bowing in a sarcastic way, giving her leave to go down the stairs. "Go on then," he says. "Be my guest."

She breathes through her nose, every nerve awake. She just has to get past him, that's all. Take a slap or duck a punch or maybe nothing at all, maybe as drunk as he is—

She rushes forward suddenly, surprising him. He jerks back at her momentum, exactly what she was hoping for, and she steps around the banister past him, getting a foot on the top step—

"Ugly bitch!" he shouts—

She feels the punch coming before it even lands, feels the air displace behind her—

She tries to duck, but her positioning is all wrong—

His fist connects—

She falls—

She's falling—

The hard stairs coming up to meet her too fast, too fast, too fast—

And she screams—

"You're nothing," the man says. "You're fat. You're ugly. And too bloody monstrous for any boy to ever look at you."

"Lots of boys look at me," she says, but she's got fear in her stomach. She can see his fists clenched at his side. She's big, but he's bigger, and she knows he's not afraid to use those fists, like he used them on her mother just now, knocking her once across the kitchen table when the tea was too cold, a knock that sent Regine running up the stairs, him roaring after her.

He's usually slow when he's drunk, but she's taken too long to grab her phone and her money, and when she left her bedroom, there he was, blocking the top of the stairs.

"No boy ever looks at you," he spits at her. "You slut."

"Let me pass," she says, clenching her own fists. "Let me pass or I swear to God . . ."

He smirks. That stupid pink face of his, all lit up with ugly, drunk delight, that lank blond hair that always looks dirty, no matter how often he washes it. "Let you pass or you swear to God you'll what?"

She says nothing, doesn't move.

He steps back, gesturing grandly with one hand and bowing in a sarcastic way, giving her leave to go down the stairs. "Go on then," he says. "Be my guest."

She breathes through her nose, every nerve awake. She just has to get past him, that's all. Take a slap or duck a punch or maybe nothing at all, maybe as drunk as he is—

She rushes forward suddenly, surprising him. He jerks back at her momentum, exactly what she was hoping for, and she steps around the banister past him, getting a foot on the top step—

"Ugly bitch!" he shouts—

She feels the punch coming before it even lands, feels the air displace behind her—

She tries to duck, but her positioning is all wrong—

His fist connects—

She falls—

She's falling—

The hard stairs coming up to meet her too fast, too fast,
too fast—

And she screams—

"You're nothing," the man says. "You're fat. You're ugly.
And too bloody monstrous for any boy to ever look at you."

"Lots of boys look at me," she says, but she's got fear
in her stomach. She can see his fists clenched at his side.
She's big, but he's bigger, and she knows he's not afraid to
use those fists, like he used them on her mother just now,
knocking her once across the kitchen table when the tea was
too cold, a knock that sent Regine running up the stairs, him
roaring after her.

He's usually slow when he's drunk, but she's taken too
long to grab her phone and her money, and when she left her
bedroom, there he was, blocking the top of the stairs.

"No boy ever looks at you," he spits at her. "You slut."

"Let me pass," she says, clenching her own fists. "Let
me pass or I swear to God . . ."

He smirks. That stupid pink face of his, all lit up with
ugly, drunk delight, that lank blond hair that always looks
dirty, no matter how often he washes it. "Let you pass or
you swear to God you'll—

69

Seth is suddenly back in the room with the coffins, gasping for breath. Regine's thrashings have jerked her head away from his hand, breaking their connection.

She screams again.

And no wonder, Seth thinks with horror. She's caught in some kind of loop, reliving the moment, reliving the *worst* moment.

She's dying over and over and over again.

He can still feel her fear, still feel the pain of the punch, the terror of the slipping, the disbelief at the fall –

He's got to find a way to get her out of there –

"Seth?" she says.

He freezes. Her voice is weak, desperate, afraid. Her head is still bound in the bandages, but she's stopped struggling.

"Seth, is that you?"

"I'm here," he says, grabbing her hands so she can feel him. "I'm here, Regine. We've got to get you out of here. Now."

"Where are we? I can't see. There's something on my eyes –"

"You're wrapped up. Here." He turns her head to grab the seam at the back and starts unwrapping her. "We're underground. Under the prison."

"Seth," she says as he reaches the level of her skin and starts slowly unsticking the bandage from her eyelids. "Seth, I was –"

"I know," he says. "I saw it. But we've got to –"

And then he hears footfalls again. He turns to look. The Driver runs through the entrance to this room.

It sees them.

And it stops.

Stops right there in the central passageway and stares at them with its empty face.

"Oh, no," Regine whispers. She's peeled the last of the bandages away and can see what he's seeing.

Seth looks around them. There's nowhere to run. They're backed into a corner, and Seth can tell from Regine's face that she knows it, too.

"You go," she says, her voice rough, her eyes filled with water, more vulnerable than he's ever seen her. "I don't think I can. I feel so weak. You get out of here."

"Not a chance. Not even a little chance."

"You came here to save me," she says, shaking her head. "That's enough. Really, you don't even understand how much that's enough. To have you *choose* to do that –"

"Regine –"

"You broke that loop somehow. You've already saved me –"

"I'm not leaving you here," he says, raising his voice.

The footfalls begin again. The Driver is walking toward them, slowly. It takes out its baton, sparks flashing.

"It knows," Regine says. "It knows it's won."

"It hasn't won," Seth says. "Not yet."

But even he doesn't really believe that.

He feels something at his hand. He looks down. Regine has taken it in her own. She squeezes it, tight.

He squeezes back.

The Driver is halfway down the wide central aisle now, the black screen of its helmet focused purely on them. Seth knows, somehow, that it's not going to let him get away. Not this time. It won't stop no matter what he does to any of the coffins. It will come to him first and it will run faster than him and it will be stronger than him and there will be nothing he can do to stop it.

But he'll try. He'll try anyway.

"Is Tommy safe?" Regine asks quietly.

"He ran off. Said he might have an idea."

"So he's bound to come in for a last-minute rescue, huh?"

Seth can't help but grin crazily back at her. "If this was all a story my brain was putting together, yeah. That's exactly how this would end."

"For the first time ever, I'm hoping you might be right about that."

The Driver has reached the end of their row. It stops once more, seeming to savor how trapped they are.

Seth grips Regine's hand even harder. "We'll fight," he says. "All the way to the end."

Regine nods at him. "Until the end."

The Driver makes a snapping motion with its hand. The baton doubles in length, the sparks and lights flashing from it even more dangerously.

Seth plants his feet, ready to fight.

"Seth?" Regine says.

He looks at her. "What?"

But he never hears what she says—

Because a whining sound fills the room, low at first, but increasing—

The Driver hears, too, turning toward the passageway that extends deeper into farther rooms—

Where the sound is coming from—

Swiftly growing louder—

They see the Driver make to run—

But not fast enough—

As the black van flies out of the deeper passageway, slamming into the Driver at extraordinary speed, so fast one of its legs is knocked right off its body. The van pushes it down the wide central aisle, not stopping until it smashes into a far wall, trapping the Driver against it.

The Driver struggles for a moment longer. The van's wheels spin fruitlessly against the concrete floor, sending up spirals of smoke, crushing the Driver into the wall.

And then it collapses across the hood of the van, dropping the baton, which goes clattering across the floor.

The Driver lies still.

The wheels of the van slowly stop turning.

Seth and Regine watch, dumbfounded, as a small figure climbs out the still-broken door.

"Is everyone all right?" Tomasz asks.

PART 4

70

Tomasz throws his still-bandaged hands around Regine's waist and embraces her like he might never let her go. "I am glad," he says. "Oh, how I am glad."

"I'm glad, too," Regine says, pressing her face against his wild, wild hair.

Seth watches, still stunned, as Tomasz disentangles himself from her, then hugs Seth so hard it squeezes the breath out of him. "And you! You said we would save her and we did!"

"You did it mostly," Seth says, looking back across the rows of coffins at the crashed van, at the motionless Driver still hunched across its hood. "Right in the nick of time." He looks back at them both. "Again."

Tomasz glances at Regine. "He is back to believing we are made up."

"He may have a point," Regine says. "How the hell did you manage to find the van and then drive it underground?"

"Was not the hell hard," Tomasz says. "We thought it was parked around the prison somewhere. It was only matter of finding it."

"And getting it started," Seth says. "And driving it –"

"Well, okay, so a few weird things happen when I do find it, I confess," Tomasz says. "The door is still off and I sit down in it and it starts automatically. I do nothing and it just starts. And then screens start lighting up, asking me questions I do not understand – and not because of language barrier but because they do not make sense. Numbers that mean nothing, camera views of huge rooms with all these coffins –"

"Yeah," Seth says. "I've seen those."

"And then there is this blinking box that says NAVIGATE TO DISTURBANCE? Like that, like a question, so I figure DISTURBANCE can only be you and so I say, yes, pressing box to NAVIGATE and then car just takes off! I am nearly falling out while it speeds away." Tomasz mimes the turns with his body, this way and that. "And we zoom through the burnt-out neighborhood until we get to big underground carpark entrance and before I know it, we are driving down and down and down."

He holds out his hands as if to say the rest is self-evident. "And here I am, in these rooms. And there is the Driver, standing in the middle of the path, and I take the steering so the van cannot steer away and I have to lean down to press my foot on the drive faster pedal and then *bang,* it is hit." He claps his hands to make the bang. "And then we hit the wall." He rubs the top of his head. "Which was hurtful."

"You did great," Regine says.

"Yeah," Seth agrees. "More than great."

Incredibly great, he thinks. *Suspiciously great.*

But then again, unlikely didn't always mean impossible –

"I don't suppose anyone's seen my shirt," Regine says.

"Here," Tomasz says, squatting down behind the coffin and grabbing a bundle of cloths. "It is much torn up. I am sorry."

"Never much liked it anyway," Regine says, wrapping the remnants around her.

"And you are okay?" Tomasz asks her.

She's silent for a moment and Seth thinks she won't want to talk about it, but then she says, "Seth saw it. Seth saw my death."

Tomasz turns to him, eyes wide. "Just like you saw mine."

"Lucky me," Seth mumbles.

"I could feel you there," Regine says.

"You could?" Seth asks, surprised.

"Yes!" Tomasz says. "I knew you were there, too. I could feel you with me as I lived mine."

"And somehow," Regine continues, "just knowing you were there was kind of enough, in a way." She rubs her eyes wearily with the palms of her hands. "I don't know how to explain it. It was awful. Seeing that bastard again. Having to *live* it again." She looks at Seth. "But then I knew you were there. And I knew . . . I guess I just knew that someone remembered who I was."

Tomasz nods. "This is the best thing of all."

"And it wasn't okay that it was happening," she says. "It was as scary as it had ever been. But somehow, it felt like, if it had to happen, then at least knowing you'd tried to stop it, knowing you'd made that big effort . . ."

She frowns. He can see her eyes welling again, see her reflex irritation at the fact.

"I understand," Seth says.

She looks at him, almost accusingly. "Do you?"

Seth nods. "I think maybe I finally do."

They walk through the coffins toward the main central aisle, Seth in the lead, Tomasz in the middle, Regine at the back, still clutching the shreds of her shirt around her.

Nothing around the van or the Driver moves.

"Leg," Tomasz says, pointing to the dismembered limb. It's been torn off at the thigh, a viscous dark liquid pooling around it on the floor. A liquid that definitely isn't blood.

"Mechanical," Regine says. "Way more advanced than anything we had in the other world."

"Yeah," Seth says thoughtfully.

"I hate it when you sound like that," she says. "All suspicious-like."

They approach the van slowly. There are sparks and smoke coming from where the Driver is slumped. One of its arms looks dislocated, and its head is twisted at an angle that could, *should*, indicate that it's broken.

"Oh, boy," Tomasz says, and they see him find the baton under a nearby coffin.

"Careful with that," Regine snaps.

Tomasz rolls his eyes. "And still everyone thinking they are my mother. How many times I have to save your lives? How many–OW!"

He drops it as a bolt of electricity licks out and shocks him in the face. When the baton hits the floor, something triggers inside it and it folds back down into its smallest state.

"You all right?" Regine asks, trying not to laugh.

"Stupid thing," Tomasz says, holding his cheek.

The new folded-down version of the baton seems inert, though, so he picks it back up. They don't stop him when he puts it in his pocket. If anyone's earned the right to it, it's probably Tomasz.

They watch the van burn, coughing a little now at the smoke. The viscous fluid spills in larger quantities across the hood, dripping into pools down the side. The Driver seems clearly dead, but Seth notices how slowly they're all moving, as if at any second they expect it to surge back to life and attack them.

That's what would happen if this were a story, Seth thinks. The villain who wouldn't stay dead. The one who has to be stopped over and over again. That's what would happen if this were all just my mind trying to tell me something.

Except.

Except, except, except.

"I need to know," he says.

"Know what?" Regine asks.

"What's under its visor. I want to look at the face of the thing that wouldn't stop chasing us." He starts walking toward it. "I want to know exactly what it is."

Which is when the van explodes.

71

The low sparks arc up suddenly bright, catching on a pool of the liquid beside the van. There's a surprisingly soft *whoompf*–

And everything disappears in a fireball.

They're blown back, flames washing over them as they fall–

But the first flash dissipates quickly, and as they tumble to the floor, it's already receding, the most gaseous fumes burnt off in the first rush, the main fire reduced to the liquid fuel on the front of the van, burning surprisingly bright and hot.

The Driver now unreachable behind flames.

"You've got to be kidding me," Seth says, coughing.

But Tomasz is already on his feet, looking around in panic at the coffins. "The people! They will burn! They–"

An intensely strong rain of water thunders down on them from newly opened ports in the ceiling. They're drenched in seconds, the downpour bouncing off the sleek, shiny coffins. The fire is out almost instantaneously, but the spray of water continues. Billows of smoke and steam come rolling off the van, filling up the room. They breathe it in.

"It tastes like poison," Tomasz says, wincing.

"It probably is," Regine says. "None of that seems to be made of anything as simple as metal."

Seth's still staring at where the Driver was, now vanished behind the steam and smoke.

"I wanted to see what it looked like," he says. "Under-neath."

"We beat it," Regine says, shivering in the water. "Isn't that enough?"

The poisonous-tasting steam fills the passageway back to the prison entrance. "We will have to go back the way I came in," Tomasz says.

Regine holds out her hand for him. He takes it. They look at Seth expectantly.

"Yeah," he says, still watching the churning smoke. "Yeah, all right."

They head back up the central aisle. The overhead water stops in the next room, but when Seth looks behind them, there's still nothing to see. They walk deeper and deeper, past row upon row upon row of coffins. Seth keeps checking back, but many, many rooms later, when they finally reach a ramp back up to the surface, their defeat of the Driver has long been lost to sight.

They don't speak much as they climb, Seth in particular keeping his thoughts to himself. The ramp is circular, and he sees the dust and mud of the world above begin appearing in small layers the higher they go.

"Could you remember who you were?" he asks Regine as

they slowly spiral up. "I know you said you felt me there, but could you remember this place?"

"Yeah, actually, I could," she says. "I mean, being back there was just so *unfair*. I kept thinking, I can't die here. If I die here, I die there. So I did remember this place."

"I think time may work differently there," Seth says. "The past can be closer than it is in real life. And maybe *everything* happens, all the time, over and over."

Regine looks at him. "I get it. What you're asking."

"What?" Tomasz says. "What is he asking?"

Seth keeps walking. "The display said it was starting the Lethe process on you. The one that makes you forget."

"But it didn't," Regine says carefully. "Or it hadn't yet. I remembered everything. So that means—"

"That means," Seth says, stopping her but not elaborating.

"That means *what*?" Tomasz says. "I am not happy with not being told what this means."

"Shush," Regine says. "Later."

She keeps watching Seth, her eyes demanding. He stays quiet, though, as they walk up and up, this end of the storage facility clearly far deeper underground than the way he came in.

He's thinking about all that's happened, about *how* it happened. Everything that's led them to this place, the three of them walking up this ramp, into daylight—and here it is, at the exit, warming them, Regine audibly sighing in pleasure—every single event that's occurred to bring them, *him*, here, right now.

And as he looks out into the sun over the ash of the

burnt-out neighborhood, he's surprised—though maybe not so much—that a possibility is forming in his mind.

Because this place might be one thing.

Or it might be another.

Or it might even be something completely unguessed.

But he thinks he knows what he needs to do next.

"You ready to go home?" Regine asks.

She's asking Tomasz, but Seth has to stop himself from answering.

72

Tomasz spends most of the long walk back to Regine's house repeatedly recounting how he rescued them, each time becoming slightly more heroic, until Regine finally says, "Oh, please, you found a parked car and you sat down. That's basically it, isn't it?"

Tomasz looks horrified. "You *never* appreciate–"

"Thank you, Tommy," Regine says, suddenly smiling. "Thank you for finding a parked car and sitting down and coming to the rescue at the very last minute. Thank you very, very much for saving my life."

His face goes all bashful. "You are welcome."

"You have my thanks, too," Seth says.

"Ah, you did well yourself," Tomasz says, generously. "Keeping the thingy person busy until I could drive in like a hero."

"I'm just amazed you were tall enough to reach the accelerator," Regine says.

"Well," Tomasz admits, "it was not easy. Much stretching."

They find their way to the train tracks, then follow them north. Regine repeatedly pats her pockets as they go, never finding what she's looking for. She sees Seth watching and glares at him. "Don't you think after dying a hundred times in a row I deserve one measly cigarette?"

"I'm not saying anything."

"*I* think you do not," Tomasz says. "I think you have cheated death many times this day, so why not do it once more?"

"No one's talking to you," she says. But not as harshly as she might have.

After a good hour's walk, under the partially collapsed railway bridge and over toward the supermarket—Seth suggests they stop at his house, but Regine is still shivering, despite the sun, and wants to get out of the bandages as quickly as possible—they cross the road where they saw the deer and turn up to Regine's house.

"I keep expecting it to pop out," Regine whispers as they approach her front walk. "Like it can't possibly be this easy."

"You think this was *easy*?" Tomasz says.

"That's what'd happen if this was a story," Seth says. "A last-minute attack. By the villain who's never really dead."

"You so need to quit saying shit like that," Regine says.

"You're thinking it, too," he says.

She looks defiant. "I'm not. I still know I'm real. That trip back online was all the proof I needed."

They keep on, and indeed there's nothing surprising awaiting them at Regine's front door. Inside, it's the same sitting room as before, Regine's coffin in the middle, sofa and chairs cramped around it. She heads upstairs to change, and Tomasz goes into the kitchen to make some food.

Seth sits down on the sofa, the coffin in front of him. He listens to Tomasz in the kitchen, clanking plates, swearing in Polish when the little gas stove doesn't light on the first couple of tries. Upstairs, Regine is in the bathroom, running some water, taking all the recovery time she needs.

These two funny, difficult people.

He hears them and his heart hurts a little.

But he pushes on it and realizes it's not a bad hurt. Not bad at all.

He smiles to himself briefly. And then, after a moment, he taps a finger on the coffin like he did down in the prison.

After a few tries, a display lights up, broken but readable.

A little while later, Tomasz comes out of the kitchen with some steaming bowls in his hands.

"Special occasion," he says, handing one to Seth. "Hot dogs, creamed corn and chili con carne."

"You're making a joke, but for an American, this is almost a barbecue."

"Ah, yes, I keep forgetting you are American."

"Well, I'm not really anythi–"

"REGINE!" Tomasz shouts at ear-splitting volume. "Dinner is ready!"

"I'm right *here*," Regine says, coming down the stairs in fresh clothes, pressing a towel against her hair.

"Is in the kitchen," Tomasz says. "Keeping warm by lit stove."

"Good way to burn the whole house down."

"You are *welcome*," Tomasz singsongs after her.

They eat in silence for a while. Tomasz finishes first, burping happily and setting his plate on a side table. "So," he says, "what are we going to do now?"

"I'd like to sleep for a week," Regine says. "Or a month."

"I was thinking we could go back to the supermarket," Tomasz says. "We never got back there. So much food and things for taking."

"Yeah, I could use some more–"

"Do not say cigarettes!" Tomasz interrupts. "You are living now. We have saved you. Let the end of the smoking be a celebration."

"Actually, you know what?" Regine says. "I think maybe we *are* in need of a celebration."

Tomasz looks over, surprised. "You mean?"

She nods. "I mean."

"You mean what?" Seth asks as she takes her plate into the kitchen.

"Well," she says, "not everything goes bad after years and years, does it?"

Seth glances at Tomasz, who's grinning madly. "What's she talking about?"

"Celebration!" Tomasz says, then his face gets serious. "Though we have not had much to celebrate until now."

Regine reappears in the kitchen doorway, a bottle of wine in one hand and three coffee mugs in the other. "We don't have refrigerators, so I hope you like red."

She opens the bottle with an alarmingly rusty corkscrew

and pours a full mug for her and Seth, half a mug for Tomasz. "Hey!" he protests.

"Give him some more," Seth says. "He's earned it."

Regine looks skeptical but fills Tomasz's mug, then they raise them in an awkward toast. "To being alive," Regine says.

"Again," Seth says.

"*Na zdrowie,*" Tomasz says.

They drink. Tomasz spits his right back into his cup. "Bleck!" he says. "People *like* this?"

"Haven't you had communion wine?" Regine asks. "I thought Poles were Catholic."

"We are," Tomasz says, "but I always believed communion wine was flavored to be hard to drink, otherwise, why such a small taste? But *real* wine . . ."

He doesn't finish the sentence, so Regine does. "Is supposed to taste like grape juice?"

He nods. "It does not." He sniffs at his mug and takes another drink, a small sip this time. "It is terrible," he says. Then he sips it again.

Seth drinks his own. He's had wine at dinner with his mum and dad, much to the scandalized chagrin of his friends' decidedly non-European parents. He never much liked it, too vinegary, but here, now, this feels like less a drink than a ritual, and he's happy to have it.

Regine doesn't drink much, though. She holds it in front of her awhile, then sets it down on the table.

"Don't you like it?" Seth says. "It's not bad. A little heavy, but–"

"*He* drank," she says. "His breath, it always stank of . . .

Even in the memory, it stank. I didn't think it would bother me, I've had it before, but."

"But," Seth agrees. He sets his own mug down. Tomasz does too.

Regine scratches at a non-existent spot on her pants. "Is he down there, you think? I guess I didn't really believe it till now but . . . He's gotta be, doesn't he?"

"My parents are," Seth says. "I saw them on a display screen. They're in there somewhere. Living their lives."

"And my mother, too," Regine says. "Carrying on with a dead daughter and a shit husband." She coughs away some emotion, but there's a dark question on her face and she says no more.

"My mother is dead," Tomasz says, matter-of-factly. "But I find a new family! A brother and a sister."

"*Step*brother," Regine says, grinning as Tomasz makes to protest. "All right, half-brother. Adopted."

"Oh," Tomasz says, "I am thinking we are *all* adopted."

"I saw a baby in there," Seth says at this. "In one of the coffins. With its mother."

They stare at them. "But how is *that* possible?" Tomasz asks.

"There are probably ways, if you think about it," Seth says. "But however they did it, they believed in the future." He leans forward and places his hands on the coffin in front of him. "Listen."

Tomasz simply looks at him, but he can see Regine tense, see her bracing herself.

"Right," he continues. "Okay. I saw both of your deaths. I

didn't mean to, but I did." He taps the coffin, no longer looking them in the eye. "I think it's only fair I tell you about mine."

He begins to talk.

He tells them everything.

Including the end.

73

"You've got a visitor," his mother said curtly through his bedroom door on a Saturday morning.

"Gudmund," he said to himself, his heart lurching in his chest enough to make him light-headed. He hadn't seen him since that night a few weeks back, when Gudmund had promised they wouldn't lose contact, when he promised there was a future, if they just held out for it.

Since then, though, Gudmund's cell phone had either been confiscated or had its number changed, and there were no answers at any of his e-mail addresses. But surely he could have borrowed someone's phone at his new school or set up a fake e-mail account. You couldn't keep people from communicating these days, not if they wanted to.

But there'd been nothing.

Until now.

He practically bounded out of bed to the door, opening it–

And finding Owen blocking the way.

"Hi, Seth," his brother said.

Seth placed a soft hand on Owen's chest to push him back. "Outta the way. I've got–"

"I wrote a song on the clarinet."

"Later, Owen."

Seth thumped heavily down the stairs, turning into the living room, his eyes bright, his voice too loud, saying, "Christ, Gudmund, I never thought I'd—"

He stopped. It wasn't Gudmund.

"H," Seth said. He felt his skin getting hot and knew an embarrassed blush was starting up his neck.

But it was an angry blush, too.

H hadn't spoken to him, hadn't even acknowledged his existence since the pictures had come out. The worst of the abuse at school had settled down some, but there was still the minefield around him that felt as if no one could approach him, even if they wanted to. Seth knew H had always been the weakest of them, the one who'd suffer the most by association when it turned out that his two closest male friends were doing each other.

But he'd always been good-hearted, too, hadn't he? Beneath all the stupid jokes and goofing around, Seth had always thought H was basically decent. Which made the exile particularly painful.

"I'm not him," H said, hunched there on the sofa, sitting underneath that awful painting by Seth's uncle that used to scare him as a little kid. H hadn't even taken off his coat. "I haven't seen him."

They were alone. Seth's mum had disappeared to who knew where, and his dad was still working on the kitchen.

The silence stretched, until H finally said, "I can go, if you want."

"Why are you here?"

"I need to tell you something," H said. "I need to tell you something that I don't even know if you need to know. But."

"But what?"

"But maybe you do."

Seth waited for a moment, then went to the chair that faced the couch and sat down. "It's been shit, H."

"I know."

"I thought you were my friend."

"I know–"

"I didn't do anything to you. We didn't do anything to–"

"That's bullshit. You lied."

"We didn't lie."

"You lied by not telling. Though it's not like anyone with eyes couldn't see it."

"See what?" Seth said warily.

H looked him in the eye. "That you loved him."

Seth felt his face flushing again, but he said nothing.

H started turning his gloves over in his hands. "I mean, I *didn't* see it. Because I'm a total idiot. But looking back, I mean. Looking back, it's obvious."

"And how was I supposed to tell you a thing like that? If this is the way you were going to react?"

"That's not–" H said, raising his voice, then looking around and lowering it again. "That's not why. That's not why I've been acting like I have."

"Really."

H sighed. "Okay, a little, but not for any major freaky-outy reasons or anything. It's not easy for me either, you know? Everyone thinks I'm a fag now, too, don't they?"

"No, *they don't. You've been dating Monica for ages—*"

H got a funny look. "*Yeah, well.*"

"*What?*"

"*I'm not seeing her anymore.*"

Seth was surprised. "*Well, good. She's the one who made this whole mess. If it wasn't for her—*"

H interrupted him. "*Seth.*"

Seth stopped. A faint sick feeling started to swirl in his stomach at the way H had said his name. "*What?*"

"*Didn't you ever wonder how she got those pictures?*"

"*What do you mean?*"

H fidgeted with his gloves again, turning them, folding them. "*You think Gudmund just left his phone lying around for her to find? You think he was that stupid? The Boy Wonder?*"

"*You're saying . . .*" *Seth started, but had to try again.* "*You're saying he gave it to her—?*"

But H was already shaking his head. "*No, Seth, that's not what I'm saying.*"

"*Well, what* then?"

H took a deep breath, reluctant. "*You know how she always flirted with Gudmund, right? And he'd flirt back?*"

"*Yeah, she was totally in love with him.*" *He saw H wince.* "*I mean, sorry, man, no offense, she was with you and that was good, but you know . . .*"

"*Yeah.*" *H nodded sadly.* "*I know.*"

"*That's why she did it. She even told me. She found out about me and Gudmund and was jealous and—*"

"*She found* out, *because she was sleeping with him, too.*"

The words hung in the air, almost in physical form,
almost as if Seth could see them.

See them, but refuse to read them.

"What?" he finally managed to whisper.

"She told me," H said. "Finally. Last night." He
frowned. "When she was breaking up with me. Said she
found the pictures when she grabbed his phone one night
to take a photo of them." H was now wringing his gloves
so tightly they were in danger of tearing. "And they fought,
I guess. And I guess he said he was only sleeping with her
because she needed him to. That he cared for her as a friend
and didn't know how to handle it so he just gave her what
she wanted because he thought, well"–H shrugged–"that
was what she wanted."

Seth felt like everything had frozen around him. Like
there was never going to be anything that moved ever again.
Like it was only ever going to be cold.

And empty.

I can't be anyone's everything, Gudmund had said on
that last night. Not even yours, Seth.

That was Gudmund's biggest fault. That he couldn't be
anyone's everything.

But that he'd try anyway.

"Why are you telling me this?" Seth said.

"Because it's true. Because I thought, I don't know."
H sighed. "I thought it might make it easier for you that he's
gone."

"It doesn't. It doesn't at all."

H ran his hand through his hair, agitated. "Shit, Seth, I'm telling you because why does everybody have to lose every-body? We were friends. And people messed up, okay? They didn't say shit they should have said and did shit they shouldn't have done but Jesus, people need, you know? I know that. They need things and they don't know why, they just need them. I don't even really care that she slept with him. I only care that she broke up with me because who do I have now?"

He looked at Seth, and Seth saw how lost he was.

"I had three good friends, three best friends, and now what do I got? I got nobody. I got a bunch of brain-dead idiots who think I'm half-fag and won't shut up about it."

Seth sank back slowly in the chair, still reeling. "What are you doing here, H?"

H made a frustrated sound. "I don't know. I thought you should know, I guess. The truth. Like I said, I thought it might make it easier."

Seth said nothing to this, found he couldn't even really look at H, and after a minute, H got up. He waited again to see if Seth would say anything, and when he didn't, he put the gloves back on.

"I think he really did love you, though," H said. "At least that's how it seemed to her."

And then H left. Seth heard the front door open and close again.

He was alone.

After a while, he didn't know how long, he got up and climbed the stairs, though he was hardly aware of doing so. Owen was still waiting outside his bedroom door, holding his clarinet.

"Can I play you my song now?" he asked, smiling wide, his hair a really astonishing mess.

Seth went past him into his bedroom.

"I wrote it for you because you've been so sad," Owen said and raised the clarinet to start playing. Seth shut the door on him. That didn't stop him. A surprisingly melodic set of notes repeated themselves several times, way too fast, but Seth barely heard them, just sat on the edge of his bed.

He felt empty.

But also strangely calm. He heard his mother take Owen to therapy but sat so quietly on his bed, he didn't even think she knew he was still home.

He was hardly aware of making a decision to start cleaning his room.

Making a decision to then put on his coat.

Making a decision to go to the ocean.

74

Tomasz looks ashen. "Oh, Mr. Seth," he says. "You learned you could trust no one. Is very bleak lesson."

"No," Seth says, "that's not quite—"

"I'm sorry," Regine interrupts, obviously trying to contain her confusion, "but I don't see why that was the last straw."

"What?" Tomasz says. "But the Good Man was not who Seth thought he was."

"Look, I don't mean to *downplay* it or anything but—"

"But Tomasz got murdered," Seth says, "and you got shoved down the stairs. All I did was get my heart broken."

"Do not underestimate the broken heart, though," Tomasz says. "My heart was broken, waking up here, without my mama. Was very painful."

"I'm not saying it didn't hurt," Regine says, "but it seems a little—"

"Extreme," Seth says. He taps the coffin again, gathering his thoughts. "You know that feeling we talked about, that there had to be more? More life beyond the crappy ones we were living?"

"Yeah," Regine says hesitantly.

"Well, I thought I *had* more. I thought Gudmund was

my more. It didn't matter how crap everything else was. The stuff with Owen, the stuff with my parents, even later with the stuff at school. I could live with *all* of that, because I had him. He was mine and no one else's. We lived in this private world, that no one else knew about and no one else ever lived in. That was my more, do you see? That was the thing that made it all bearable."

"But it wasn't just yours," Regine says, sounding like she's understanding.

"I thought Gudmund being taken away was the worst thing that could ever happen to me," Seth says, "but it wasn't. The worst thing was finding out he was never really all mine in the first place. And so, for a moment, for a terrible, unbelievably shitty afternoon in a shitty little town on the shitty, freezing coast of Washington, I had nothing. There wasn't anything more, and the one good thing that was mine wasn't mine after all."

He takes a thumb to wipe the tears from his face. He clears his throat, embarrassed.

"You miss him," Tomasz says.

"More than I can say," Seth says, his voice rough.

"But I can understand this," Tomasz says to Regine. "Why it would feel so bad to lose someone so important. Why it would feel so bad you would want to walk into the ocean. Can you not?"

"I can understand pain," she says. "Feeling so bad you want to get out. Believe me, I understand that. I've looked into the darkness. You aren't the only one."

"I never said I was," Seth says.

"But the difference is that I think you never do it. Even if you're tempted, even if you're really close, because who knows? There *might* be more."

"But–" Tomasz starts.

"No, she's right," Seth says. "There was more, even for me. More than I thought, more than I could see for myself. I mean, look at Owen. Even if that world was a lie, then part of that's still true for my parents. Something terrible happened to their son. Why wouldn't that affect them? And not even be about me?"

"But for your Good Man, though?" Tomasz asks. "Where is the more?"

"The more is in the things that made him so safe, that made him so *good*. They were exactly the same things that made him be with Monica, weren't they?" He smiles sadly to himself. "Gudmund couldn't stand to see people he cared about suffer. And he didn't know how to stop their suffering, so he offered himself."

"And you're wondering if that's all he did for you," Regine says.

"That's the big question, isn't it?" Seth says. "And that was my big mistake. When I remember it, when I see it clearly, like what I just told you, I know that wasn't true. H said so, *Monica* said so, and I couldn't hear it. Gudmund loved me back." He brushes his cheek again. "It was everywhere, in everything he said and did, every memory I've had of him since I've been here."

"Which does not make it easier," Tomasz says.

"Except it does, though, in a way. For one minute

I stopped believing it and that was enough to make everything seem impossible, but it *wasn't* impossible. And that isn't even all. I mean, in those last days, my dad apologized to me, said he was sorry he hadn't been there for me. Something I chose to forget because it didn't fit in with how shit everything was. And even H on that very last morning."

"He was offering you friendship," Regine says.

Seth nods. "He was lonely. He missed me, missed his friends, and telling me about Monica was probably, for H, the biggest act of friendship he could have done." Seth has to clear his throat again. "I wanted so badly for there to be more. I *ached* for there to be more than my crappy little life." He shakes his head. "And there *was* more. I just couldn't see it."

Regine sits back. "And that's why you've got more to tell us, isn't it?

Seth doesn't respond.

"Tell us what?" Tomasz says. No one still answers. "Tell us *what*?"

Regine never stops looking at Seth. "That's why he's about to tell us he's going back."

"He is WHAT?" Tomasz says, standing up.

Regine just keeps a challenging gaze on Seth.

"Is she right?" Tomasz demands. "Tell me she is not right."

"Yeah, Seth," Regine says, "tell Tommy I am not right."

Seth sighs. "She's right, but—"

"NO!" Tomasz shouts. "You want to go back? You want to *leave* us? Why?"

"I don't want to leave you," Seth says, firmly. "That's kind of the whole point—"

"You want to go back, though!" Tomasz's face crumples. "You always have. Since you arrived. One way or another, you have always wanted to leave us." He makes a frown so sad, Seth can hardly bear to look at it. "I do not want you to leave us."

"Tomasz," Seth says, "when Regine went back, she *remembered*. She remembered who she was and how she got there." He turns to Regine. "Didn't you?"

She looks uncomfortable. "Vaguely, though. Not enough to change anything. Not enough to not make anything happen."

"Are you sure?"

She opens her mouth to answer, but then stops. "I never even thought about that. I just knew what had to happen and that I had to do it."

"I think you had *some* Lethe," Seth says. "It was starting to work but hadn't got very far. But if you were to go back there with no Lethe at all—"

"It is too late," Tomasz says. "You are already dead there."

"What's dead there, though? There was a malfunction. A *simulation* of me died. A simulation that knew a whole lot less than I do now."

Tomasz is shaking his head. "I do not see how it can work. How you will not just go back and die there and then die here and be lost to us."

430

"I'm not sure, either," Seth says, "but doesn't it feel like it *might* work? Regine went back and remembered who she was. And then, Tomasz, we got her out again."

Tomasz starts to argue, but then his eyebrows raise, in surprise and a little delight. "You mean, you would come back?"

Seth looks at him, then looks at Regine, who's still staring at him, hostile, he can see, but maybe hopeful, too.

"Absolutely, I'd come back," he says.

75

Tomasz licks his lips, and Seth can almost *see* him thinking. "But how would you do it, though?"

"Well," Seth says, starting up the display on Regine's coffin, "I've been thinking about it. This one's broken. Regine must have damaged it when she came out of it."

"I thought I was fighting someone," Regine says. "Lots of kicking and pushing."

"Yes," Tomasz says, "that sounds like you."

"But I've been reading this," Seth says, tapping the display. "Half of it doesn't make sense, but it looks like putting someone back in there isn't actually all that difficult." He presses a box, and the coffin creaks open, not smoothly like the ones in the prison did. Regine and Tomasz come round to look. Seth picks up a particular tube. "This is Lethe, I think."

"You *think*?" Regine says.

"You had it in your mouth. I think you breathe it in. And when I interrupted the process, you didn't get the full amount. You got just enough to make you aware without being able to fight it."

"But if you went back without breathing in the tube . . ." Tomasz says.

"Maybe you'd remember everything. Maybe you'd remember who you were and where you were and maybe, *maybe,* you'd be able to do what you used to do when the online world first started. Go in and out as you pleased."

But Regine is already shaking her head. "There's no way you can be sure that'd happen. You'd probably just go back and die over and over again like I did, and even if you didn't, how do you know you wouldn't get stuck? I don't remember any doors marked EXIT."

"I'd have the two of you here," Seth says.

"We could pull you out if anything went wrong," Tomasz says.

"You don't know that we could," Regine says. "Not if you were all the way in. We had to *die* to get here."

"I got *you* back. And people used to go back and forth all the time. We could try really brief trips to start—"

"If you could even get it to work. And why? Why go back at all? It's not real."

Seth takes a deep breath. This is the big question. He wonders if he's as sure as he thinks he is. "Because I know more now," he says. "It felt like the world had closed down to nothing, but that wasn't true, was it? I mean, it's not perfect, but I was wrong about how hopeless it was. By accident, we all got a second chance. I want to take it."

"And you want to see your Good Man again," Tomasz says.

"Yes. I can't lie. My body is here, but he's across an ocean and a continent, so if I want to see him again, I have to go back. And I want to find him somehow. Tell him I understand. Find H, too. Even Monica."

"But you're dead there," Regine insists. "You died last week or whenever it was. I've been dead there for months—"

"But it's also *winter* where I live there. It sure as hell isn't winter here. Like I said, maybe time doesn't work the same way. You went back *before* your death. And if you could go back knowing enough to change things—"

"Then all of those people who went to your funeral are just going to go, *Whoops, our mistake*?"

"They changed the memories of everyone who knew my brother to make it seem like he hadn't died. Don't you think it could be re-adjusted even easier for a real live person? I mean, there's got to be glitches all the time, people remembering stuff they shouldn't—"

"Could we go back to any time?" Tomasz interrupts. "I could go back before my mama talked to the bad men. I could save her. . . ." He falters. "But of course she died there properly. She would be dead for real for a very long time."

"I'm sorry, Tomasz," Seth says. "I don't think it would work, anyway. There was a specific time on the panel when the Driver put Regine back in the coffin, and it's the same one here." He turns on the display again and points to a date. "I can't find any way at all to change it. I think we've only got a loophole because it needed to fix a mistake. That's what its job was, after all."

"You're making a lot of assumptions," Regine says.

"If you've got a better explanation, I'm willing to hear it."

She sighs. "I wish this *was* all happening in your head."

"Look," Seth says, "I may be completely wrong, but don't you think it's worth a try? Can you imagine what it would be like if we *could* go back and forth from there to here? We could tell people. We could remind them of who they were."

"They wouldn't want to hear it," Regine says.

"Some of them wouldn't, but others might. And if we found a way to wake them up–"

"They wouldn't want to come," Regine says. "Why the hell would they want to leave a world where everything works for one where everything's dead?"

"Your mother might want to. If we could find a way in and out, maybe–"

He stops because she looks like she wants to hit him. "Don't you talk about my mother," she says. "Don't you promise things about her that can never be."

"I didn't mean–"

But she's sitting back down in her chair, blinking away angry tears. "People are harder to save than you think. And you keep forgetting they went there for a reason. The world is over."

"It is not over," Tomasz says. "The world is healing itself. There are deers. There is us."

"The *world* is half a burnt-out neighborhood and another one covered in mud," Regine says. "No, what'll happen is Seth'll get back there, everyone will be *so* happy he isn't dead, and he'll have all his *real* friends back, his *real* family, and he'll just–"

She stops dead, frowning ferociously.

"I'll just what?" Seth asks. "Forget about you? Is that what you think?"

"Why wouldn't you? Why wouldn't anyone?"

"Because, you idiot," he says, finally snapping back. "The reason I killed myself was because I was certain there wasn't anything more. That there was never going to *be* more. That I was alone and unhappy forever."

"Yes, yes," Regine says, acting grandly bored, "and now you've learned your valuable lesson about how people aren't spending all their time just thinking about poor old Seth and all his terrible, terrible problems."

"No," Seth says, firmly, "what I've learned is that there actually *is* more. There's you guys. You guys are my more."

"Oh, now, see," Tomasz says to Regine. "This is very nice thing for him to say."

"Saying it is all well and good," Regine persists, "but what if you go back and die? Are we supposed to give you a nice funeral because you *like* us?"

"Look, I know it's a risk–"

"A risk with your life."

"A risk worth taking. Look, I want both. I want them *and* I want you. Now that I know there's more? I want to *have* more. If there really is more to life, I want to live all of it. And why shouldn't all of us? Don't we deserve that?"

There's a long silence while Tomasz and Regine exchange looks.

"It may not even work," Seth says again.

"But it may," Regine says.

Seth sighs. "Make up your mind, Regine–"

"It would change everything, wouldn't it?"

"And what's wrong with that? Don't you think things *need* changing? Don't you think people need to wake up? Literally? If we could figure out a way to get in and out, maybe we could figure out ways to change other things, too." He looks at her. "Make it better."

But Regine looks skeptical. "Well, *you've* gone all heroic."

"You're the one who's been trying to get me to face reality. You yell at me for thinking this is all in my head—"

"Oh, you're finally believing this is real, are you?"

Seth makes a scale-like motion with his hands. "Sixty-forty."

"What if I told you it *was* all in your head?" Regine says. "And that we were just making it easier for you to accept your death?"

"Then I'd keep my eyes open, remember who I was, and go in swinging."

Regine is surprised into silence by hearing her words said back to her.

"There's more than this," Seth says. "So let's go find it."

"Well," Tomasz says, after a moment, "I do not know about either of you, but I am feeling *very* stirred up!"

76

They decide to make a first try that afternoon. Seth is eager to go, but even he can see the sense of a nap after the morning they've had.

None of them can sleep, though.

"Forget it," Regine finally says, rousting Tomasz and Seth from their bedroom. "Let's just go and you can fail and then we can all get some proper rest."

"That's the spirit," Seth says.

They start gathering things to take to Seth's house, which seems the most likely place to try first. They'll see if his coffin is less broken than Regine's and go from there.

"I like what you say about changing the program, maybe," Tomasz says. "I could learn to do that."

"It's pretty sophisticated," Seth says.

"And I am *very* clever. I am sure I could figure it and *shazam*! Tomasz saves the world again."

"You could probably save the world just by combing that hair," Regine says, handing Tomasz a bottle of water. "It was shaved when I found you. How can it be such a briar patch?"

"Male hormones," he says, knowledgably. "I am

approaching my growth spurt. I will shoot up even taller than the two of you."

"Yeah," Regine says. "You just keep telling yourself that."

Having lost or broken all of their bicycles, they set out walking.

"Just think," Tomasz says to Seth as they go. "This may be the last time you see this house. If you die."

"That's kind of the point of the two of you coming along," Seth says, "to try and make sure that doesn't happen."

"Oh, we will do our best, Mr. Seth, but it may not be good enough."

"What happened to *Tomasz saves the world again*?"

Tomasz shrugs. "I am bound to muck it up one of these times."

"Do you have a plan for when you get back there?" Regine says, crossing the main road. "What if you open your eyes and you have a broken shoulder and can't save yourself?"

"You started there at the top of the stairs," Seth says, "a little bit before the malfunction. Maybe I'll start before I get too cold to swim. Maybe I'll even start on the beach and can just not go in."

"It may not be as easy as you think. I was overwhelmed by it. It's hard to change something you've already done."

"Would you really like me not to do this at all? Not even try?"

She pulls her mouth tight. "I just want to make sure you've considered everything."

Seth grins. "I really came late to the guardian angel sale, didn't I? To get the pair of you."

"I think we have done just fine, thank you very much," Tomasz says.

"I don't believe in guardian angels," Regine says seriously. "Just people who are there for you and people who aren't."

"Yes," Tomasz says. "Yes, I agree with this."

"Just people," Seth says, finding he agrees, too.

They walk down the empty High Street where Seth first really saw this world, past the supermarket where he got so much needed food and the outdoor store where he got so much needed equipment.

And there is the thought again, never quite disappearing. How everything he needed to survive, food, shelter, warm weather, has been provided. How these two not-guardian angels have saved him at the last minute, over and over. How he's learned vital information just when he needed it, to take just the right steps, toward . . .

Toward what? Acceptance? Going back? Dying?

"Well," he says, almost to himself, "we'll know in a minute."

"We will know what in a minute?" Tomasz asks as they approach the sinkhole, the weeds growing out of it like slowly crashing waves.

"If this *is* my brain telling me a story—"

"Not this again," Regine mutters.

"If this was a movie or a book, right?" Seth says. "If this was some kind of story I was telling myself, then it'll be waiting for us."

440

Tomasz and Regine stop when they realize what Seth means by "it."

"This is not an amusing thing to say, Mr. Seth," Tomasz says.

"It's dead and gone," Regine says. "There's no way it'll be there."

"All I'm saying is that's what would happen if this was my brain trying to make sense of stuff," Seth says. "The Driver would be there, half-burnt, insane with revenge, waiting for one last attack before we do whatever it is we're going to do."

"But that is okay, though," Tomasz says, brightening. "Because in that story, there is always one last fight, and the hero always wins."

"Hey, yeah," Seth says. "I like that version."

"The fighting's over, do you hear me?" Regine says. "There's not going to be anymore."

"I'm just saying–"

"Well, *quit* just saying. You say way too much."

Seth holds up his hands in surrender. "It was just a thought. Nothing's going to happen. We killed it. It's gone. The end."

But they're all quiet as they take the final turn into Seth's street.

Which is empty. No van. No figure. Just the same old parked cars and weeds and mud. Regine exhales in relief, then she scowls at him. "Got us all scared," she snaps. "Fool."

Tomasz laughs. "For one moment there, I really thought–"

441

And the Driver steps out from where it was crouched between two parked cars. Its helmet is melted into a nearly unrecognizable shape, its missing leg replaced with a thinner, newer metallic lattice.

It grabs Tomasz with two melted, crackling fists, lifts him from the ground, and hurls him nearly all the way across the street, where he slams into the side of a car, tumbles to the ground, and doesn't get back up.

77

I do not believe this, Seth thinks even as Regine is screaming Tomasz's name, even as the Driver is grabbing her arm and forcing her down. *I do not believe this is happening.*

He goes in fighting anyway.

He throws himself at the Driver –

But even in his split-second leap, he can see that it doesn't have the same effortless strength as before, that it's struggling against Regine's resistance –

He tackles it mid-chest, and they fall to the sidewalk. The Driver thuds beneath him, and this time, it's like landing on a bag of metal shards. Seth doesn't let go, though.

This isn't happening, a part of his brain keeps telling him. *This would only be happening if none of this were* –

"Shut up!" he growls as if it was the Driver talking to him. He strikes it across the helmet, but his fist glances off the melted facade, sticky black tar coating his knuckles. He rears back to strike it again –

The Driver's arm shoots up and grabs him around the neck. It jerks him to one side, thumping his head into the door of the car beside them –

But Seth anticipates the move, and the Driver *isn't* as

strong as it was before. He checks its arm motion before he gets the full brunt of the car door on his head.

It's still got a hand around his throat, though, and when thumping Seth doesn't work, it starts to squeeze—

Seth hears a call to his right and a shadowy figure blocks out the sun. Regine is bringing down an enormous rock on the Driver's head—

The Driver sees it coming (*How?* Seth has a mad moment to think, *With what eyes?*) and moves its head to one side. The rock catches it with a glancing blow, and the Driver uses its free hand to grab Regine by her foot. She stumbles back into some weeds behind her. With a cry, Seth pulls himself away, freeing his neck from the Driver's hand and punching again with his own—

His fists fall on hard metal sections, all sticky with the tarry substance. The Driver makes to strike him back, but Seth blocks it with his arm—

And though the Driver is obviously weakened, it's not exactly *weak*. The punch feels like it nearly breaks Seth's wrist, and his recoil from the pain is enough to let the Driver land another blow. It catches Seth on the side of his head, rolling him onto the sidewalk—

Where the Driver begins to rise—

And this time Regine is on it again. She clubs it with another rock across the back of its head. It spins around and grabs her arm, squeezing it enough for her to cry out and drop the rock. It punches her, hard, in the face, sending her back over the low stone wall of an adjacent front garden.

She stays down.

The Driver turns to Seth. There's only the two of them now.
Seth gets to his feet.

And a terrifying but somehow *true* thought enters his head.

I'll win, he thinks, dancing back as the Driver approaches. *That's how this story goes, doesn't it? The enemy makes a surprise return just before the end, facing the hero one last time—*

And the hero wins.

It takes a step toward him. Then another.

"You piece of shit!" Seth shouts. "You're nothing! You're just a hunk of plastic that's got big ideas!"

The Driver swings for him again, but Seth jumps out of the way. It's stumbling a little on its replacement leg, the thinner metal of it creaking at the knee. There's a definite scraping as the Driver moves forward. When Seth knocked it to the ground, it must have snapped something.

Yes. Oh, yes.

"Not really fixed, are you?" Seth shouts, dodging another punch. "You're breakable. And I'm guessing, *out of warranty!*"

Another punch dodged, another step.

Seth looks left and right, trying to find some ammunition, something to fight it with, but he can't see where Regine got those rocks.

But maybe there's a way to at least stop it. And if he can stop it, then—

I'll beat it, Seth thinks again. *That's what happens. That's the end of this story.*

The Driver swings again, and Seth moves out of the way once more.

But he sees the way forward now.

"You," he says, dodging one more blow, timing what he's about to do, "are nothing more"–dodge, step–"than an obsolete"–dodge, step–"malfunctioning"–dodge, step–"JANITOR!"

He leaps toward the Driver's punches–

Putting all his weight behind his right foot–

Aiming for the Driver's creaking knee–

He hits it, full-on.

The leg snaps in two.

The Driver falls into the car next to it, shattering its window, but not reacting in time to catch itself before falling to the pavement. Seth leaps past it, swerving out of its reach. He picks up Regine's first rock, the larger one, staggering under its weight. Jesus, that girl is *strong*.

He turns back to the Driver, which is struggling to rise, the broken half of its leg lying uselessly in front of it. Seth gives a grunt and lifts the rock up high, above his head. He starts to yell, growing louder as he races toward the Driver–

Who looks up at him, the melted helmet facing Seth, as blank and unknowable as ever–

"I win!" Seth shouts. "This story is finished!"

He surges forward–

Heaves the stone back to throw it–

The Driver's arm moves in a flash, faster than any living thing possibly could—

And Seth feels cold steel plunge deep into his front—

The stone clatters down in front of him, dropping harmlessly to the pavement—

Because the broken-off leg of the Driver is now sticking out of Seth's stomach.

78

Seth collapses to the sidewalk, lying on his side, gasping, the steel both cold and somehow also burning all the way through his body. He grabs it instinctively, and his hands come away drenched with his own blood, which spills onto the mud and weeds. He twists his neck and sees that the metal shaft has gone all the way through him. The end of it is sticking out his back.

He glances up the sidewalk in shock.

The Driver has pulled itself upright on its one leg.

It balances with a hand on the parked cars lining the pavement.

It half hops, half drags itself forward.

It's coming for Seth.

It had seemed so clear. The Driver was right where it was supposed to be, right where Seth half expected it to be.

And if that was true, then everything else had to be true, too.

He would defeat the Driver after it came back from the dead one last time. He would beat it, and then he'd go triumphantly into . . .

What?

He doesn't know. The certainty's gone.

Because here he is, the Driver's latticed metal leg protruding from just below his rib cage, sticking out his back in a nightmare of pain and impossibility that his brain can't even process, except to focus on the fact that he's bleeding everywhere.

That he's dying.

And that, at last, he desperately doesn't want to.

"Please," he hears himself whispering, trying to push himself back along the sidewalk. "Please."

The horrible *wrongness* of the metal through his body is too much to contemplate. Because it means there's no getting out of this one. No last-minute heroics. No Tomasz or Regine leaping to the rescue. It doesn't matter if anyone stops the Driver; there's nothing they can do before he bleeds to death.

It's too late.

He coughs, and there's blood in his mouth.

And the Driver pulls itself closer.

"Please," he says again, but his strength is deserting him rapidly. And the *pain*. There's no way he can move to lessen it, and for a moment, for a terrifying moment, he feels himself blacking out.

The world goes inky and dark—

—*and there is Gudmund, taking Seth's hand, in a world that's just the two of them, and they're watching TV, something unimportant and forgettable, but Gudmund has reached over and taken Seth's hand for no other reason than that he wants to, and there they sit, together—*

But the pain returns.

And precious seconds have passed.

He's still on the pavement.

Still with the metal shard stabbed all the way through him.

Still bleeding.

Still dying.

And the Driver only needs one last scraping hop to reach him.

It stands over him, looking down.

And Seth hears nothing, no sound of Regine or Tomasz stirring, no last-minute roar of an engine, no calls of his name or cries of victory.

There's just him and the Driver.

At the end.

"Who *are* you?" he gasps.

But the Driver, of course, makes no answer, just raises a cracked and melted hand to end Seth's story once and for all.

It doesn't punch him, though. It does something much worse. It grabs the end of the leg sticking out of Seth's stomach.

Seth cries out in an agony so overwhelming, he wonders if he's going to black out again, *hopes* for it, thinks he can hear himself *begging* for it—

The Driver twists the leg, and impossibly, the pain increases. Seth's whole torso feels like it's being dunked in burning acid, like every muscle is snapping from the bone in metal cords.

"STOP!" he screams. "PLEASE! STOP!"

The Driver does not stop. It twists the leg once more in the other direction, as if testing the best way to cause Seth the most pain–

And just like the first time Seth saw it, hiding in the burnt-out neighborhood with Tomasz and Regine, there is nothing to appeal to there, nothing human, no mercy to be asked for or given–

The Driver changes its grip on the leg, fixes a hard fist around it–

"No," Seth says, sensing what's coming. "NO! PLEASE!"

It yanks the leg out of him in one terrible, final movement, and Seth loses his mind for a bit, the horror of just the motion of it passing through his back and out his stomach, the terror that all his guts must be spilling out onto the sidewalk (though when he looks there only seems to just be blood, blood and more blood), the utter certainty that his death is really here, that this really is it, that there will never be anything more–

And then the Driver is pushing him over onto his back. He can no longer really breathe, the blood he's coughing up choking him just like the seawater did.

He's drowning in it–

(And maybe that, finally, is it–)

(Maybe that's what this has all been–)

(Maybe he never stopped drowning–)

The Driver effortlessly pulls Seth's hands away from the wound, and though Seth's brain is telling him to resist, to fight back, he doesn't have the strength to do anything at all–

He is at the Driver's mercy–

451

And the Driver has none to offer –

It leans over him now, raising its arm above Seth, its hand clenching into a fist –

Seth wishes so many things were different, wishes he knew that Regine and Tomasz would be okay, wishes only that he could have stopped the Driver for *them* –

A line of spikes shoot out from the Driver's knuckles, sharp and needle-like –

Seth sees sparks start to flash between them, small arcs of electricity casting from one to the other –

This is it, he finds enough strength to think –

This is it –

No –

Bolts of electricity shoot from the Driver's fist –

For a split second, the pain is worse than should be humanly possible –

And then there is only nothingness.

79

"Eat up," says his mother, setting the dish in front of him. "It's not your favorite, but it's what we have."

The table where he's sitting is absurdly long, too long to fit in any normal room, and the clink as she sets the plate down echoes into the milky whiteness beyond. This is no place. No place he's ever seen. No place that ever existed.

"It's my *favorite*," Owen says, reaching across the table with a spoon and dishing out the steaming hot food onto his own plate.

"Tuna-noodle casserole?" Tomasz says, sitting next to Owen. "I have not heard of this."

"It's great!" Owen says, serving some to Tomasz.

"Isn't that the food you hate most, Seth?" H asks, in the chair next to him.

"Is it?" his father says, down at the end of the table.

"It is, I'm afraid," Gudmund says, leaning forward on Seth's right. "I mean, he really, really hates it. Cooked tuna is about the worst taste in the world. And then you mix it with onions—"

"He's right," Monica says as Owen spoons some casserole onto her plate, too. "It's disgusting."

"And that's what the Internet age has done for us," his mother says, sitting down. "Anything you don't like is automatically disgusting and anyone who may like it themselves is an idiot. So much for a world full of different viewpoints, huh?" She takes a bite. "I think it's delicious."

"Taste has become opinion," his father agrees, picking up a newspaper and opening it. "When any fool knows they're two different things."

"Still," Tomasz says, frowning at his plate, "neither my taste nor my opinion of this is either of them very positive."

"You can have some of mine," Gudmund says to Seth, offering his plate, which has the chicken mushroom pasta that's Seth's favorite.

"Or mine," H says, offering the same thing.

"I want to get in on this action," Monica says, lifting her plate across the table and offering it to Seth as well, the tuna-noodle casserole replaced on her plate with the same pasta.

"I do not have that," Tomasz says, his own plate now filled with a red savory-smelling mixture of meats and vegetables, "but this is my favorite from when I was a little boy."

His mother shakes her head. "Everyone thinks they know what's best. Everyone."

And then a voice behind him says, "Sometimes you need to find out that you don't, though."

He turns. Regine is there, a little away from the table, the light behind her making a silhouette. She is different from the others. Apart. He senses that she's waiting for something.

Waiting for him somehow.

He squints into the light. "Is that what I'm supposed to find out?" he asks her, his voice raspy, as if it hasn't been used for years and years and years. "Is that what all of this means?"

Regine steps out of the light and it dims behind her, becomes a swath of stars against a night sky, the Milky Way blazing. She stands in front of him, the same big, awkward Regine he knows her to be.

Except she's smiling. It's a don't-be-an-idiot smile.

"Don't be an idiot," she says as the voices behind him fade.

"This isn't a memory," he says. "Not like the others."

"Well, obviously."

He looks back to the quiet dinner, everyone still eating and talking around one table. All the people he knows. Gudmund glances back at him. And smiles.

"It doesn't feel like a dream either," Seth says, his heart aching.

"There you go again," Regine says, "expecting me to have all the answers for you."

"Is this death?" He turns to her. "Have I died? At last?"

She just shrugs.

"What am I doing here?" Seth asks her. "What has all this been about?"

"Hell if I know."

"But haven't you been leading me somewhere?" He gestures to the room, to the guests at the table again, Gudmund still watching him carefully, a look of concern crossing his face. "What does it all mean?"

Regine chuckles. "Are you serious? Real life is only ever just real life. Messy. What it means depends on how you look at it. The only thing you've got to do is find a way to live there."

She leans down until her face is close to his. "Now, make hay, dickhead. While the sun still shines."

80

He opens his eyes.

He's still on the pavement. The Driver is still over him. The sparks still coming from the needles on its fist—

But they're dying down, dampening, receding.

Stopping.

Seth takes in a breath.

He *can* take in a breath.

He coughs up some blood and has to spit it messily out—

But he can breathe. His lungs feel wet and heavy, like he has a terrible cold, but they're working. He breathes again. And once more.

And it's easier.

"What's happening?" he asks. "Am I dead?"

The Driver remains motionless. The needle-like protrusions disappear back into its knuckles, but it stays looming over Seth. He tries to scoot away and pain shoots through his rib cage. He puts a hand on the wound—

But something's different.

He's still covered in blood, but it's no longer spilling out of him in a great rush.

"What . . . ?" Seth says.

The Driver seems to be regarding him, watching to see what he'll do—

As if it's waiting.

The pain is still terrible as Seth pulls up his blood-soaked shirt where the Driver's leg pierced him, and below, on his skin—

Is the wound, set in the curve just below his ribs. It's horrific to see, a wound that looks impossible, that looks fatal—

That looks as if it's sealing itself.

Seth glances up in bafflement at the Driver, still motionless, still watching him, then back down at the wound. There are little sparks flashing within it, *inside* his skin somehow. He can feel the shocks of them as they fire—

As they seem to be stitching the wound shut.

It still hurts, *a lot,* but even as he watches, the torn layers of his skin are coming together, like little fingers reaching for one another. After a moment, there's no trace of bleeding at all.

He cries out as he feels the sparks moving deeper into his body, and he realizes he can feel them working on the exit wound on his back, too. He puts his hand there but has to pull it away when he's shocked by the sparks.

And still the Driver watches him. However it is that it manages to watch, Seth feels *watched.*

"What have you done?" he gasps, turning again at the pain in the wound—

The pain as it seems to be healing—

"What have you *done*?" he says again, and his voice is full of emotion. "I don't understand."

458

He curls forward at another shock in his body, arms around his middle, but he finds he can bear it. He looks back up at the Driver, and his own eyes are clouding with tears.

"Why?" he whispers, and then he says again, "I don't understand."

The Driver makes no sound, no sign that it's even heard him. It's as mysterious and unreadable as ever, its face as blank and empty as a void.

The shocks in Seth's body seem to be dissipating. He looks down at the wound again. The scar is ugly, purple, painful to the touch. But it *is* a scar. His mortal wound has healed.

He looks at the Driver again and repeats his question from earlier. "Who *are* you?"

The Driver makes no response. Balancing on its one leg, it pulls itself up on the parked car, rises over Seth again, and regards him. Seth licks his lips, tasting the drying blood there. He's too weak to run, too weak to fight anymore. All he can do is wait and see what the Driver does next.

Seth has absolutely no idea what that might be.

And then the Driver twitches, its whole fractured body twisting oddly in one violent jerk –

It raises its arm as if reaching out for something –

But there's nothing in front of it, nothing to reach for, Seth is still on the ground at its feet –

A point of light appears in the middle of the Driver's

chest, just a small white spot at first but then exploding out in a shower of sparks so wild that Seth scoots back on the sidewalk, grunting at the ache still running through his torso.

The Driver shakes, its back against the parked car, as if it's being held there somehow. The lightning surrounds it, diving into and out of its body, causing it to spasm all over, its seams and joints starting to buckle. There's a buzz in the air now, a whine that increases as the bolts surge through the Driver, increasing in density and speed, a web of pure electricity being woven around it—

Seth moves to get himself to safety. He drags himself behind the stone wall where he can see Regine still lying—

He looks back—

A huge *CRACK* tears the air—

The Driver disintegrates.

It blasts outwards in burning, melting little pieces—

Seth curls down to avoid the shrapnel, pulling himself onto Regine to protect her—

But not before he sees the Driver's helmet shattering into fragments and circuitry and unknowable materials that might have even once been flesh—

And then there is only quiet. Just the pitter-patter of little bits of Driver falling to the ground, like noxious rain. Seth uncurls himself and looks over the wall.

The Driver is gone.

Burning, melting parts of it cover everything—

But it's gone. It's really gone.

And rising from the seat of the car the Driver had been leaning against is Tomasz, a ludicrous strip of hair completely burnt away from the top of his head.

He's holding the baton.

"Well," he says, "that is not what I expected."

81

Seth gets slowly to his feet, his middle aching, glancing down at Regine to make sure she's still breathing, before he goes to Tomasz.

"I crawled in the other side," Tomasz says, getting out of the car. "And stabbed it in the back."

"Yeah," Seth says, breathing heavy. "Yeah, I can see that."

Tomasz half stumbles over to him, still wobbly from being thrown through the air so far. He leans into an embrace with Seth, and Seth hugs him back, getting a close-up view of the almost even stripe of hair missing from the top of Tomasz's head.

"I saw it *kill* you," Tomasz says, his voice cracking. He puts a hand on the tear in Seth's shirt. "I saw it do this."

"Yeah," Seth says. "I don't know either."

"I thought you were dead."

"Me, too. I think maybe I *was*—"

Tomasz looks across the stone wall and cries out. "Regine!" He runs to her, Seth following.

"I think it just knocked her out," Seth says as they kneel down next to her. There's an ugly swelling coming up around her right eye where the Driver punched her. There don't seem to be any other wounds, though, no blood on the back of her head.

"Regine!" Tomasz shouts, almost directly into her ear—

A wince crosses her face. She parts her lips, and a low moan escapes. "*Seriously*, Tommy," she says. She says something else, but it's lost in Tomasz's cries of relief. He throws himself across her in a hug, which she accepts for a minute, then says, "Get the hell off me."

Seth pulls Tomasz back, and they wait next to her as she slowly sits up. "What happened?" she asks.

"I wish I knew," Seth says. He looks around at all the little bits of burning Driver scattered around them.

"I killed it," Tomasz says, but he doesn't say it in his usual way that's asking for more credit. "I stuck the baton in its back." He takes the baton out of his pocket. It's completely fried, the end cracked and broken. "I think it overloaded."

"The Driver is dead?" Regine asks.

"If it was even alive to begin with," Seth says.

She shoots him an angry look that causes her to wince again. "I swear to God, if you say one more philosophical thing to me—"

"It saved my life."

This stops her. "It what?"

"It killed him first," Tomasz says, his voice still edged with worry.

"It did this to me with its leg," Seth says, pulling up his shirt to show her the bruised, purple scar. "But then it took it out of me and did . . . *something*. Something that sealed up the wound."

"I did not see that," Tomasz says. "I was crawling into the car. I only saw it throw the thing through Seth and thought . . ." His face crinkles up. "I thought it had killed you. And I did not see Regine. And I thought . . ."

"I know," Seth says, putting an arm around Tomasz and letting him cry.

Regine shakes her head, before stopping at the pain it obviously causes. "That doesn't make any sense."

"No," Seth says. "No, it doesn't."

Regine puts a hand up to her cheek. "Jesus, my face hurts."

"And my whole body," Seth says.

"And my *hair*," Tomasz says, putting unhappy fingers on his new bald spot.

Seth's arm is still around Tomasz, who's resting part of his weight against Regine, who in turn nudges Seth with her outstretched leg. They just sit for a moment, together, injured, confused.

But alive.

82

Slowly, slowly, slowly, they gather themselves up, helping one another to their feet with a tenderness they don't need to discuss. Seth shows them the other scars the Driver left on him, still wondering at their very existence.

"How does it look?" Seth asks when Regine checks out his back.

"Like the one on your front," Regine says. "Except." She picks something off his skin and shows it to him. It's a piece of cloth, soaked with blood, the exact same shape as the tear on the front of his shirt.

"Looks like it cleaned out the wound, too," Regine says. "I don't get it. Why did it save you?"

"If it's a caretaker," Seth says, "maybe it's supposed to keep us alive."

"And throwing a metal javelin through you accomplishes this how?" Tomasz asks. "You could have died immediately."

"And it seemed pretty happy to try and kill me and Tommy," Regine says.

"I don't know," Seth says, but he says it quietly, still thinking about what happened, about why the Driver did what it did, about whether he *did* in fact die just now, right here on the pavement–

But what would *that* mean?

"Life does not have to go how you think it will," Tomasz says. "Not even when you are very sure what is going to happen."

Seth can tell he's thinking of his mother. Life *definitely* hadn't gone how they'd expected it to. Regine either, he thinks, as they start trudging toward Seth's house, each of them avoiding bits of the Driver, still burning in little puddles.

No, life didn't always go how you thought it might.

Sometimes it didn't make any sense at all.

You've just got to find a way to live there anyway, Seth thinks.

"I don't suppose you've got any painkillers in there," Regine asks as they walk up his front path.

"We can try the supermarket if there isn't," Seth says. "Rustle up some expired aspirin."

"Or expired morphine," Regine moans, holding her eye again.

"I could try to fix this," Tomasz says, holding up the baton. "Zap you with it. Might work."

Regine bops him on the back of the head.

"You are not feeling that bad then," Tomasz says.

They go inside. Nothing has changed. The front window is still broken, the kitchen and sitting room still piled with the furniture they hurled in the Driver's way.

"I can't believe it's gone," Regine says as Seth climbs over

466

the fallen-down fridge to get them some water. "How did it come back anyway? We saw it burn. Not even a machine should have survived that."

"And what will happen now?" Tomasz asks, flopping down on the settee. "Who will take care of all the sleepers?"

Seth doesn't answer because he doesn't know. He climbs back over the fridge with a bottle of water and three cups, and they all sit around the coffee table, drinking and resting.

They sit there for a good long time.

"*You* knew, though," Regine says, after a while, as if mid-conversation and snapping Seth out of an almost-doze he didn't even know he was having.

"Knew what?" he asks.

"You said the Driver was going to be there for one last attack, and it was."

Seth frowns. "I didn't think I was going to be right," he says, and it's mostly true.

Regine looks down into her cup. "Your idea of this all being a story in your head. Or that we're your–"

"Guardian angels," Tomasz says. "She is correct. Does this mean we *are* angels? Because I would be very cross that I was such a short one."

"It *was* there, wasn't it?" Seth says, feeling the scar on his ribs again. "Just like I said."

"Just like you said," Regine repeats.

They look at him as if he can provide some explanation they haven't thought of. He doesn't have one, though. The

Driver, who had previously shown no mercy, showed mercy. The Driver, who had killed him, also healed him. No single explanation–if everything was real, if everything was just in his head–covered everything.

Then again, maybe the point was that there *was* no point. Well, not *no* point, because looking at Regine and Tomasz, he can easily see two points without even trying.

So if this is all a story in my head, he thinks, *then maybe–*

"Oh, forget it," he says with feeling. "Nobody knows anything."

He looks up at the painting above the hearth, the terrified, screaming horse that has spent its life freaking him out, showing the pain he thought lay underneath the whole world.

But it's just a painting, isn't it?

He looks back at Regine and Tomasz.

"Shall we do what we came here for?" he says.

"Are you sure?" Regine asks him for the hundredth time since they came up to the attic.

"No," Seth says again, "but I'm going to try anyway."

"I think that is the last of it," Tomasz says, winding the metallic tape around Seth's bare stomach, taking care to avoid putting too much pressure on his scar.

It's taken them some time to get to this point. They cleaned themselves up with the block of dishwashing liquid and cold water, then they'd gone to the supermarket to get some expired painkillers, which they all took in rather too-large quantities. Next, they went by the outdoor store to pick up some boxes of the metallic tape Seth had seen there, and also some scissors, which Regine used to cut off the remaining bits of Tomasz's hair.

Seth had then started up his coffin. It didn't seem to be broken like Regine's. He powered it up and it came to life, asking questions on its screen, some of which even made sense. Seth programmed it in the very basic way he could guess, achieving–after some frustration and with help from Tomasz–a box that read Re-entry Process Ready.

He'd changed into shorts, and they'd put bandages around his legs and upper body, agreeing they would only try a test run, "for a count of no more than sixty," Tomasz had insisted, to see where Seth went in the other world. Brief enough so he wouldn't need tubes shoved into him and brief enough, too, for him to survive if the worst happened.

Seth doesn't feel like the worst *will* happen, though. For once.

"This may not even work, you know," Regine says, also for the hundredth time. "In fact, it probably won't."

"This is an encouraging sign," Seth says, tapping the light on his neck, which has been blinking a regular green ever since they started up the coffin. "But you're right, we don't know."

"There is only your head left, Mr. Seth," Tomasz says, holding up the bandages.

"I'll do it," Regine says, taking them. She starts to unroll them, then stops. "Seth–"

"Nothing might happen," he says. "I might never leave here."

469

"Or you could wake up at the bottom of the sea and die before we can save you."

"Or not."

"Or Tommy and I might not be able to get you back even if it goes all right."

"But you might."

"Or you could just want to stay there and forget all about us—"

"Regine," he says gently, touched beyond words by her concern, "I don't know what's going to happen. But I want to find out. And that's the first time that's been true in a really long time."

She looks as if she's going to keep challenging him.

But she doesn't.

"Mr. Seth," Tomasz says, solemnly taking his hand, "I am wishing you very, very good luck. But I am also wishing very, very much that you come back to us."

"So am I, Tommy," Seth says, then corrects it to, "Tomasz."

"Ah," Tomasz smiles, "this is where I am supposed to say that you can call me Tommy. Except I like the way you say Tomasz and want you to keep on saying it. For many, many years."

Seth nods at him, then he nods at Regine.

"You're sure?" she asks, for what he can tell is the final time.

"I am," he says.

She waits another moment, then she begins to wrap his head in the bandages, placing the first edge on his temple.

"See you soon," she says, and covers his eyes.

Here is the boy, the man, here is *Seth,* being laid back gently into his coffin, the hands of his friends guiding him into place.

He's uncertain what's going to happen next.

But he *is* certain that that's actually the point.

If this is all a story, then that's what the story means.

If it *isn't* a story, then the exact same is true.

But as his friends begin the final steps, pressing buttons, answering questions on a screen, he thinks that what is forever certain is that there's always more. Always.

Maybe Owen died, maybe he didn't, either way, it had affected his parents more than he ever considered, and maybe it was nothing to do with him.

And there's Gudmund, too, and H, and even Monica. They're weak and strong and they make mistakes, like anyone, like *he* has. And love and care have all kinds of different faces, and within them, there's room for understanding, and for forgiveness, and for more.

More and more and more.

Sometimes in the shape of other people, *surprising* people, with unexpected, unimaginable stories of their own.

People who looked at the world in a completely different way and by doing so, *made* it different.

People who could turn out to be friends.

And he doesn't know what will happen when those friends press the final sequence. He doesn't know where he'll wake up. Here. Or there. Or some third place, even more unexpected than this one. Because who can say in the end that any one of these places is more real than any other?

But whatever happens, whatever comes, he knows he can live with it.

And now it's time. There's a silence he can tell is expectation.

"Are you ready?" his friends ask him.

He thinks, *Yes*.

He thinks, *Go in swinging*.

And he says, "I'm ready."